THE
SONG
OF THE
MARKED

ALSO BY S. M. GAITHER

The Shadows & Crowns series:

A Twist of the Blade
The Call of the Void
A Crown of the Gods
The Queen of the Dawn

The Serpents & Kings series

The Shift Chronicles

The Drowning Empire series

SHADOWS & CROWNS

BOOK ONE

THE SONG OF THE MARKED

S. M. GAITHER

PENGUIN BOOKS

PENGUIN BOOKS

UK | USA | Canada | Ireland | Australia
India | New Zealand | South Africa

Penguin Books is part of the Penguin Random House group of companies
whose addresses can be found at global.penguinrandomhouse.com

Penguin
Random House
UK

First published by S. M. Gaither/Yellow Door Publishing, INC in 2020
Published in Penguin Books 2023
001

Printed and bound in Great Britain by Clays Ltd, Elcograf S.p.A.

The authorised representative in the EEA is Penguin Random House Ireland,
Morrison Chambers, 32 Nassau Street, Dublin D02 YH68

A CIP catalogue record for this book is available from the British Library

ISBN: 978–1–804–94580–3

www.greenpenguin.co.uk

This One's For Evie
(who isn't allowed to read it until she's older)

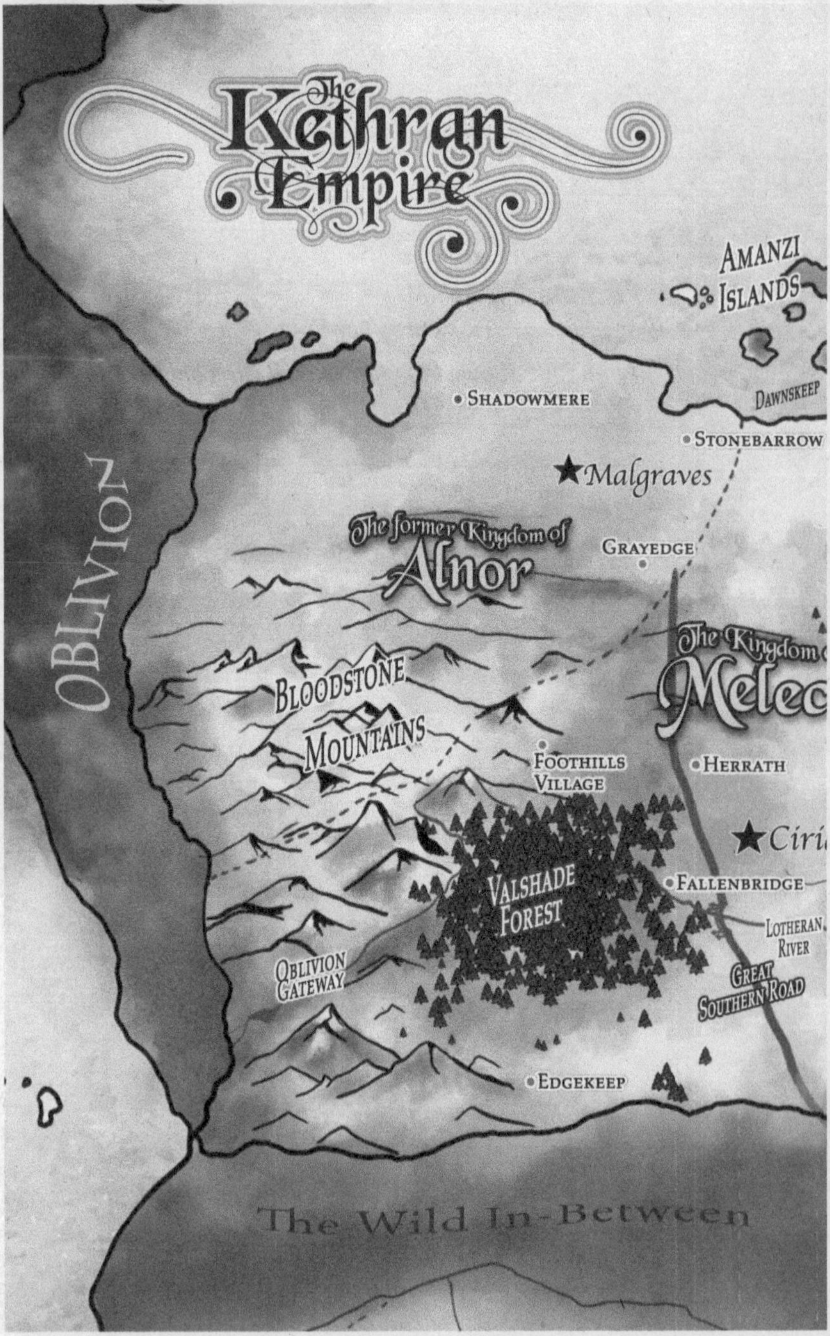
The Kethran Empire
Amanzi Islands
Dawnskeep
Shadowmere
Stonebarrow
Malgraves
Oblivion
The former Kingdom of
Alnor
Grayedge
The Kingdom of
Melec
Bloodstone Mountains
Foothills Village
Herrath
Ciri
Valshade Forest
Fallenbridge
Lotheran River
Great Southern Road
Oblivion Gateway
Edgekeep
The Wild In-Between

THE HIERARCHY OF GODS

Rook   Ice   Bone   Serpent   Fire

Sun   Star   Moon   Sky   Storm

Stone   Oak   Mtn.   Sand   Ocean

CHAPTER 1

CASIA HATED THUNDERSTORMS. THEY REMINDED HER OF THE night she had watched her mother kill her father.

A bone-rattling *BOOM* in the present, and suddenly Cas was unwillingly back in the past, nine years old and crouching behind a claw-footed chair, smelling the dust in the suede fabric, feeling the rough floor beneath her bare feet while her tiny body quivered from a mixture of fear and sickness.

Another clap of thunder. Back in the present, Cas shifted closer to the rocks lining the mountain path as the rain started to fall in earnest. She gave her head a little shake, trying to spill the remnants of memory from it. *Not tonight.*

Too many things were riding on tonight being a success.

Swiping the damp strands of hair from her eyes, Cas settled into a crouch, making herself as small as possible before creeping forward into the shadows cast by the rock ledges and the sparse bit of vegetation still growing this high up. She gripped the rough, knobby branch of a leafless and crooked tree, and then froze beneath it as she heard a low hissing sound. Her hand cautiously reached for the bow across her back.

The hissing soon grew louder, accompanied by the whisper of scales sliding against stone.

"Rock viper," she muttered to herself as she reached for an arrow, her eyes wide and scanning the nooks and crannies for its hiding spot...

There.

Yellow-slit eyes locked on her face. The viper flung itself from the ledge in the next instant, lunging toward her with its mouth open, its fangs flashing along with the lightning—

Her arrow released faster. It pierced the creature in mid-air, causing it to break into a violent, twisting dance as it fell. The viper landed belly-up and thrashed against the gritty ground for a few seconds—*thump, thump...thump...thump*—before the stillness of death overtook it.

Cas put a boot on its shovel-shaped head and yanked the arrow out, wiped the blackish blood off on a nearby cluster of weeds, and then continued on her way.

There were likely more of those serpents lingering nearby, so she kept her bow out, making sure to have an arrow nocked and ready every time she rounded a corner or crested a steep rise of the pebbly path—although the vipers were the least of her concerns, in spite of the venom they carried.

There were far worse creatures that haunted these paths.

Feral dogs, and the malevolent *kui* spirits, and countless other nasty things made of teeth and claws and ire... And most of those things would not be felled by a single arrow.

There were also soldiers allegedly waiting in the pass just ahead, and that was perhaps the most unnerving thing of all.

That skinny passage ahead was known as the Bone God's Pass—so called because of the white, crystalline structures that reached out from its rock walls like skeletal fingers. A half-mile of those clawing fingers awaited, according to the map Laurent had given Cas. After that, the pass would give way to a wider road, one that curved toward a gate made of metal, arched stones, and white trees that twisted together in a way that could only be described as *unnatural*.

That stone and metal gate was the ultimate point she and her team were attempting to reach. Beyond it, the domain that was known as *Oblivion*—at least in the common tongue—awaited anyone brave enough to keep going. This would be the first time Cas had seen it all in person. Her chest tightened a little more with every step she took. She rarely thought of herself as *brave*; she had simply become well-practiced at doing things in spite of her fear.

Investigate the Oblivion Gateway.

Bring me proof of whatever the King-Emperor is up to.

Those had been her lord patron's instructions. This was the reason she and her team were here in spite of the danger and the fear—because of those specialized soldiers from King-Emperor Varen's army, his so-called *Peace Keepers*, that were allegedly here as well. Her patron wanted to know *why* those Peace Keepers were here. Nobody frequented this dismal place without purpose. Most went out of their way to *avoid* it, believing that the Bloodstone Mountains were cursed.

And perhaps they were.

Or the domain of Oblivion was, at least. Nestled in the northernmost ridges of the Bloodstones, it was covered in silver-black clouds that frequently swallowed people up and never spat them back out.

Explanations for what lay beneath the clouds varied.

Some said the cover was a natural barrier created from the decay of strange flora and fauna underneath it. Others claimed that Kerse, the 'Bone God' who was other-wise known as the middle-god of Death and Destruction, had made a secret home there. That he still visited it whenever he grew tired of the various, far more divine places that he and his fellow deities more often frequented.

Still other stories said there was a monster hiding deep in the heart of that silvery darkness, and it stalked the edges of its territory without rest, breathing sickness and famine and disaster out into the empire whenever it grew angry or restless.

The truth was that nobody knew what happened in the shadows of Oblivion. And the not-knowing was enough to convince most that it had to have been something wicked and wild at work—something wicked and wild that the King-Emperor may or may not have been tangling himself up in.

Cas wasn't sure what she believed about this place. Not yet. But she tried not to think of the more terrifying stories she'd heard about it as she continued to wind her way through the uneven paths.

As she came closer to the Bone God's Pass, she returned her bow to the sheath slung across her back, and she reached instead for the small dart gun tucked inside her coat. The darts she carried tonight were tipped with a toxin derived from killsweed. Despite the plant's name, this particular toxin would do little more than put her target to sleep. She wasn't here to kill.

Not this time, at least.

Between the last king-emperor's rule and the Fading Sickness that had been ravaging the Kethran Empire for the past few decades, she couldn't help but feel there was enough death in the world without her gratuitously adding to it.

The path forked, and she took the route to the left. If she recalled that map she'd studied correctly, the Bone God's Pass was just around the corner ahead. She crept along until she reached the edge and paused for a moment to steady herself, pressing her back against the smooth bit of rock. Then, shielding her face from the driving rain with one hand, her dart gun raised in the other, she took a deep breath and rounded that corner—

Only to find the entrance to the pass unguarded.

Strange.

She had expected at least a few guards here, as the narrow way would have been an easy place to head off potential spies and intruders, such as herself, to keep them from creeping too close to the Oblivion Gate.

She might have thought it a stroke of good luck...*if* she actually believed in that sort of thing. But Asra, the woman who'd raised her, had taught her long ago that Luck was a lesser-spirit that only the lazy and the foolish prayed to.

Cas kept her guard up as she made her way down the hill. It was even darker here—almost like descending into a pit. She had a Fire-kind crystal in the small pouch on her belt, but she preferred not to use it; such crystals did not come cheap, for one thing, and she was also wary of attracting more attention to herself.

She carefully picked her way through the near darkness, sprinting short distances whenever a flash of lightning helped illuminate the way.

She made it to the pass, hesitated only a moment to study the cluster of elongated white stones glinting like fangs around its opening, and then stepped into that narrow mouth. The rain funneled down and the wind howled hauntingly loud in the more-enclosed space. She had only taken a few steps when she nearly tripped over... something. *A bit of fallen rock? A wayward root?*

She narrowed her eyes, let them adjust to the dark, and saw...

It was an *arm*.

Cas stumbled back, gripping her dart gun harder. Two men clad almost entirely in black lay on the ground before her. Silver brooches fastened their cloaks, engraved with the emblem of the King-Emperor's house—a tiger rearing on its hind legs with its jaws opened wide.

The men almost looked as if they were sleeping, so much so that Cas gathered a few shreds of courage and crouched beside them for a closer inspection.

Neither had a pulse. Their skin was rain-slicked and cold. One's eyes were still partially open, his hooded gaze staring up at the dark sky, unseeing. It was hard to tell in the blackness, but his irises looked grey...*unnaturally* grey, as if all of their true color had been leached out of them by the Fading Sickness.

They looked terribly similar to Cas's own eyes—albeit considerably more *dead*.

Heart pounding, she removed one of their brooches and dropped it into her pouch. She briefly wondered what had killed these men—had it been that Fading Sickness? —but then she pushed it all from her mind just as quickly; it wasn't her job to make sense of things. She was getting paid to collect proof, that was all, and here it was — hard evidence that some of the King-Emperor's men were at least in this area.

It was a start.

Hopefully her colleagues had found other things. They had split up to better search for these things—and to find the path of least resistance to the Oblivion Gate. A path that Cas seemed to have discovered; if two dead bodies and the occasional rock viper were the only things she had to face on this route...

She kept going.

Deeper and further through the pass of the Bone God she went. The stone walls squeezed more tightly around her. The air began to feel strange, to burn her lungs—almost as if it was woven through with invisible threads of poison. She grabbed for the mask that hung against her throat, buried under the cowl neck of her damp coat. It had allegedly been blessed by one of the Sky-kind—who were wielders of barrier magic—and Laurent had insisted they all wear them.

Cas wasn't convinced the mask would do much to protect against the evil airs of this place—or that she personally *needed* that protection, given her history—but she wasn't in the mood to hear another smug lecture from Laurent when he caught her not wearing it.

At the very least, the mask might help hide her identity from any of the King-Emperor's men waiting up ahead, so she pulled it up, secured its bands around the curves of her ears, and then picked up her pace once more.

The sound of boots thumping and chainmail rattling made her pause.

She twisted around, raising the dart gun to her lips, but cursed when she realized her mask was in the way and instead reached once more for her bow. She nocked and aimed an arrow into the darkness behind her.

Two men emerged from that darkness. They were dressed almost identically, save for their cloaks; the man in front no longer *had* a cloak—because Cas had stolen the brooch that once held it in place.

Impossible.

Despite their dead, vacant stares, now they moved as if they were alive. Alive and *fast*. The one in front rushed her before she could give so much as a startled yelp, whipping his short sword from its sheath with a fluidity that was otherworldly. The creaks and groans that tumbled from his mouth were equally unnatural.

A slew of terrified curses fell from Cas's own mouth as she loosed an arrow and then swiftly followed it with another. Both arrows hit their mark, and the first not-quite-dead man staggered back a few steps, the arrows jostling but not falling from his pale forehead.

The man regained his balance, and his hooded eyes darted upward, just briefly, as if the arrows were only a minor nuisance.

The second man drew closer, groans twisting into words, unfamiliar and terrifying. He seemed equally unconcerned about the arrows bouncing around in his companion's head—even as thick rivers of blood streamed from the puncture wounds.

The bleeding man responded to the second man in a tone that sounded almost...*amused*.

With a sick feeling wringing her gut, Cas realized what she was going to have to do to stop these two.

And she was going to need a sword for it.

The arrow-impaled man sliced at her arm. Cas ducked and darted around both men—a difficult maneuver in the tight space and treacherous mud—and then she planted a foot in the lower back of the second man, pushing him into the other. As the two became a briefly incapacitated, tangled-up heap, Cas aimed an arrow at the sword-wielding man's wrist.

It struck and pierced straight through. He didn't cry out—his dead body didn't seem to register any pain—but the strike jostled his grip enough that the sword fell from his hand. It clanged against the rocky ground and then skittered a short way down the path.

Cas tossed her bow aside, snatched up the fallen sword, and spun back around to face her enemies.

They finally untangled themselves and rose, swaying a bit as they did.

She managed to hook her boot around the ankle of the one closest to her, throwing him off balance, and kicked him away.

Quick as a shadow, the one she'd fired arrows into swept around behind her. A deathly cold washed over her as he neared, and suddenly the falling rain felt like needles of ice stabbing into her.

She spun around, gripping her new sword in both

hands. She hoisted the blade high, as if she planned on delivering a crushing overhead blow, and her target lifted his crossed arms so that his bracers would take the brunt of the attack, leaving his mid-section completely unguarded.

Cas shifted, pulling her blade down, and aimed a powerful kick into his stomach. As he doubled over and curled inward, exposing his neck, she swung her stolen sword in the arc she'd truly planned all along.

It lodged deeply into his neck. Cas twisted her torso, drawing strength from her core as she'd been taught to do, and swung again. The blade proved sharp enough to manage the rest of the job. The thunder and howls of rain and wind drowned out the gruesome noise of the man's head being severed from his neck.

The body crumpled, but then kept moving for a moment, writhing about, its hands beating along the ground and searching.

It might have been comical...if it hadn't been so horrifying.

Cas kept moving as well, afraid she might end up frozen in place if she didn't—either from fear, or from that strange cold that the undead men were still giving off. She found the severed head before its body could, and cringing, she drew back and kicked it as hard as possible, sending it hurtling back up the path she'd already traveled.

The headless body ceased its searching and went still.

The second undead man had stopped in his tracks,

watching her. His head lolled about on his shoulders, still attached but suddenly appearing too heavy for his neck— as if whatever puppet strings were controlling him had suddenly gone slack. His hooded grey eyes drifted over her, briefly locking on her face. On her eyes. Then his body slumped, dropping to his knees and falling forward onto the ground.

Cas heaved for breath as she stared at him.

What the hell?

CHAPTER 2

TREMBLING SLIGHTLY, CAS RETRIEVED HER BOW, RETURNING IT to its place on her back, and then stumbled away from the still bodies. She just wanted to keep going, to finish the job and get as far away from these strange mountains as she possibly could.

Still carrying her commandeered sword, she broke into a jog, slowing down only once she'd caught sight of what appeared to be an open trail on the other side of the Bone God's Pass.

She paused and took a diamond-shaped crystal from her coat pocket.

This particular crystal was embedded with Air-kind magic. The lesser-spirit of Air had once been a messenger to the upper and middle-gods, and for her services, she had been granted magic that made her capable of moving both herself and her messages more easily through space.

Now a tiny trace of that spirit's magic resided in the translucent green stone resting against Cas's palm.

A whisper of *I'm almost to the gate* against that crystal, a bit of concentration, and the spell activated and absorbed her words, her thoughts, her vision. Cas made sure to focus intently on all that she had seen and was seeing, so that the others might see it, too. She reluctantly pictured those undead monsters once more, so that her friends would be sufficiently warned about what they were walking into—though she also made a point to show them that the path to where she stood was more or less clear.

Even after her battle, she had managed to be the first of her team to arrive here, so she remained convinced she had chosen the right path—the one of least resistance— and that meant she'd won the bet she'd made with Zev. He owed her a drink, and she made sure to include *that* in the message she was sending, as well.

The thought of sharing a drink with her friends after this warmed her as she finished activating the Air-kind spell, even as the rain continued to soak her, chilling her to the bone.

The Air crystal crumbled to dust in her hand, and a spark of celadon-colored energy flickered before disappearing and carrying her message off to the others.

Then she waited, keeping watch. Five minutes passed. Ten minutes. Twenty minutes—

Where were they?

As the storm picked up its intensity, the adrenaline

surge from her fight continued to fade, allowing her memories to resurface. Memories of all she had lost on that stormy night just like this one, over thirteen years ago...

Suddenly restless, she decided to move through the remainder of the Bone God's Pass on her own, ducking and weaving through those strange, protruding white formations. In the darkness lit only by flares of lightning, it was even easier to believe that the crystal formations were skeletal hands grabbing at her hair, her coat, her weapons. Each flicker of light and peal of thunder made her heart slam a little harder against her chest.

Finally, after one last turn, she was back on a more open path, moving away from the skeleton fingers and away from the *actual* undead beings that she'd escaped in that pass. She was safe. She was okay. Her friends would be here soon, and she would be safe and okay—

She'd nearly convinced herself of this. But then...thunder, thunder, more thunder boomed through the sky, bouncing off the tall cliffs surrounding her, carving a vibrating, twisting path into her gut...

Cas leaned against the rock face on her right and slumped halfway down it. She could feel the anxiety clawing through her. Digging in. Threatening to become a full-blown attack.

Not here. Not now.

She tried to tell herself how ridiculous she was being. She had just fought off two undead monsters, and now she was letting a storm trigger her? Letting it steal her breath? Letting it tie its weights to her hands and feet and hold her in place this way?

But her anxiety was like that, unfortunately. It didn't always make sense, even to her, but that didn't make it any less real.

"Get it together, you fool," she chastised herself. And at least for a moment, both her body and the storm around her seemed to obey. The wind briefly calmed. The rain slowly transitioned to a mere misting, and Cas managed to anchor herself further by tapping her fingers against the stone behind her.

One, two, three...all the way to ten and then back down again. Her breathing settled. Her panic receded, somewhat, and the world momentarily turned oddly silent and still.

Footsteps echoed in the silence. She whipped toward the noise, lifting her new sword and pointing it at a target she couldn't see.

Something small and quick startled her as it brushed against her leg. She looked down, glimpsed a black-tipped fox tail bouncing away, and she realized what had just weaved its way past her. She lifted her eyes expectantly back to the path behind her. Lightning flashed a moment later, illuminating a dark face framed by darker curls and half-hidden by a mask just like Cas's.

Rhea.

Cas let out a small sigh of relief as she lowered her weapon. She peered around Rhea's shoulder, searching for Laurent and Zev. "Just you?"

16

"The guys are coming," Rhea assured her. "They were investigating something first—some more friends like the one you, um, relieved of his head back there."

"More dead bodies, you mean?"

"Mm-hm."

"Were they..."

"Alive? Yes. In a manner of speaking."

"I suspect there must be a Bone-kind around here somewhere, pulling the strings."

"Did you spot anyone of the sort?"

Unease prickled the hairs on the back of Cas's neck. "No. Which is what frightens me; how powerful would such a magic user have to be, to be able to control the dead so fully from a distance?"

Rhea frowned, but still managed to offer some reassurance after a moment of thought: "Maybe they're being helped by the odd energy of these mountains, and the collective residue of the strange magic that has gone on here for so long?"

"Maybe," mumbled Cas, unconvinced.

"All I know for certain is that this is an exceptionally neat place, and I'm really enjoying myself and all, but Casia?"

"Yes?"

"Next time I'm choosing the mission."

Cas huffed out a breath, too tense to manage the laugh she usually did at Rhea's dry and occasionally morbid sense of humor.

"...You okay, by the way?"

"Fine," Cas replied in a calm tone that likely would have convinced anyone but Rhea.

Rhea was almost completely blind—had been, for over a decade now—and she always said the loss of her sight had made her ears more attuned to bullshit.

Another crack of thunder and lightning made Cas shiver. She turned and started down the path before Rhea could question her further. Spying a shallow cave up ahead—an opportunity to get out of the rain for a moment—she hurried toward it with plans to wait there for the rest of their party.

Moments later, she heard Rhea catching up to her, feeling her way up the path with the use of a weathered grey staff. That unassuming staff, like the crystals Cas carried, was embedded with Marr magic—magic derived from the middle-god of Fire and Forging, specifically— and it doubled as a weapon as well as a guiding stick.

"Terrible storm tonight," Rhea commented innocently.

"This empire has seen worse," Cas said, squinting into the cave, studying it briefly before shuffling her way inside.

The storms that had roared through the former kingdom of Alnor thirteen years ago were unrivaled— they remained the stuff of legends to this day. The destruction had been catastrophic, with dozens of casualties and hundreds of homes flooded and otherwise destroyed.

The passing of the Lord and Lady of House Tessur, the

last members of the powerful house that had once ruled the largest of the Alnorian realms, had gone largely unnoticed in the aftermath—as had the disappearance of their adopted daughter, Silenna.

Silenna Tessur was dead, as far as anyone needed to know.

She had become dozens of other people since that death, but she was Casia Greythorne now, and she had worked hard to leave her other identities in the past where they belonged.

"Silverfoot's spotted some interesting things in this storm," Rhea said, climbing into the cave. She was slow, but surprisingly sure-footed, and Cas knew that she hated having people wait on her—so Cas hadn't waited.

"What kind of interesting things?" Cas asked as she subtly kicked aside a treacherously loose bit of shale in Rhea's path.

Rhea was quiet for a moment, concentrating. "I see metal stamped with the Bone god's symbol, and those twisted white trees that people talk about. The entrance to Oblivion...it's really as big and ominous as they say. And there are so many clouds beyond it. Looks like an ocean of grey waves and starlight; it's all got a weird glow to it."

Cas didn't doubt this vision, as Rhea's source—Silverfoot—was more sharp-eyed than either of them. This was the small fox that had brushed against Cas earlier, and he was one of the peculiar sort from the Twisted Wood of the Wild In-Between. Like most things that hailed from those wilds between their empire and the Sundolian Empire to the south, he carried a trace of divine magic—Air-kind, in this case. The creature's eyes were the same odd green shade as the crystal that Cas had used earlier.

His magic worked in a similar manner, too; he had bonded himself to Rhea after she'd found him, abandoned and hungry and hurt, as a kit. She had nursed him back to health, and now, perhaps as a way to thank her, he used his magic to pass messages—mostly images of whatever he was seeing—into Rhea's mind. He was the only way she clearly saw anything these days.

"The gate is less than a half mile ahead," Rhea continued. "Silver's spotted a small group of the King-Emperor's Peace Keepers hanging around it." She said *Peace Keepers* like it was a curse.

That wasn't too far from the truth.

"So Varen is certainly meddling in something up here," Cas said. "But *why?*"

"Doesn't matter, does it? We just need proof that it's happening," Rhea reminded her. "Let Lord Merric and his political allies confront Varen about it if they want to. That's nothing we need to get tangled up with." She wrinkled her nose, and muttered, "Least not beyond what we already are."

The King-Emperor needs to be investigated and held accountable, for the good of the empire, Lord Merric had claimed.

Cas was not a fool—Merric's motives were not entirely altruistic. The Stonefall Realm he oversaw was simply closer to these mountains than any other, and that meant his people would bear the brunt of whatever horrors the King-Emperor's meddling might awaken.

The Fading Sickness that had plagued their empire was already flaring in Stonewall as of late, and there were rumblings that Merric might soon be supplanted in favor of a new lord or lady who could better protect his people.

It seemed like almost *all* of the once-powerful houses of the Kethran Empire stood on unstable foundations now.

But if Lord Merric could blame at least some of his realm's troubles on the King-Emperor, he might be able to save face with some of his followers and shore up his house's rule once more.

He couldn't do that without *proof*, however.

Cas pulled the brooch she'd collected from her bag and twisted it around in her hands, thinking.

She knew Rhea had a point; they didn't need to get mixed up in the politics of this. And truthfully, she didn't *want* to get mixed up with anyone or anything beyond herself and the few people she cared about in this world. But still...

"You're sure it was actually Peace Keepers that Silver saw?" she asked, and then frowned as Rhea nodded.

The fox returned from his scouting of the gate a moment later, moving so silently that Cas didn't even notice him until he'd slinked up to his customary perch on Rhea's shoulder, wrapped his black-tipped tail around her neck, and settled there with a yawn.

"He took a high path to the gateway." Rhea was quiet for a moment, head bowed as she tried to see the full picture from Silverfoot's mental images. The fox's intelligent eyes shimmered with the glow of his magic. "The three of you should be able to take that same path. It looks narrow and steep as hell, but it appears as if it will take you to a good vantage point that overlooks that gate. Meanwhile, we'll stay here and keep an eye out for things." She gave the fox a little scratch under his chin and added, "And we'll keep *dry*, won't we, Silvie?"

"I'm jealous about that last part," Cas said, attempting a cheerful tone. She knew Rhea hated being relegated to the role of a mere scout.

Before she had come to live with Asra and the others —before she had lost her sight to a head injury she didn't like to talk about—Rhea had been a decorated soldier in one of the armies of the southern empire. She had lived and died by the sword. And she rarely complained about being forced to trade her sword in for a guiding staff, but Cas knew her well enough now to know that she would have been the first to rush that Oblivion Gate if she could have.

They sat in alert silence for a few more minutes, waiting for the others to catch up. Even though she was expecting footsteps, when they finally came, all Cas could think about were those undead monsters she'd left in the pass.

Every nerve in her body tingled to life, and her fingers wrapped more tightly around the stolen sword in her lap.

Silverfoot leapt from Rhea's shoulder and crept out of the cave.

"Zev and Laurent are almost here," Rhea said.

Cas crawled outside, stood, and wiped the gritty, damp dirt from her knees.

Zev came into sight first, wearing his usual grin. He was Rhea's younger brother, and he looked the part; he was just as absurdly tall as his sister, his skin the same warm-brown, his closely-cropped hair the same raven-wing black, and his eyes the same big, beautiful hazel-green that Cas imagined Rhea's had been before blindness had clouded them.

But unlike his sister, he had been born with the mark of one of the Marr on his palm—the middle-god of Fire and Forging. He'd fashioned the staff that Rhea carried himself, sacrificing his own blood in a ritual to enhance it with Fire-kind magic. But otherwise, he tended to keep his mark covered and rarely made use of the divine magic that coursed through his veins. He preferred his bow—it was the safer option in this empire, certainly. He was the one who had taught Cas to shoot well enough that she could spear a rock viper mid-strike.

"Were you napping on the job in there?" Zev asked, peering into the cave behind her.

"Hardly," she replied. "I was just waiting on your slow ass to finally catch up with me."

"Shall we get on with it?" The terse suggestion came from Laurent, who came up behind Zev. The half-elf walked past them both without waiting for their reply, his lithe body moving as silently as Silverfoot's. After bidding goodbye to Rhea, Cas and Zev fell into step behind him, making rude faces at his back—faces that Laurent likely wouldn't have cared about, even if he *had* bothered to turn around to see them.

Cas spotted the path that Silverfoot had found, and she took the lead, guiding the other two up the steep trail.

After a strenuous climb, the trio came to a section of stone that jutted out, overlooking the pass below. Loose rocks were piled along the edge, resembling the enclosing battlements of a castle. Cas made her way to one of the openings in this natural parapet and leaned forward. From there, she could see that the more-established path below came to its terminus some twenty feet in the distance.

She saw the Oblivion Gate that Rhea had described. Saw the emblem of the Death God glinting wickedly in its center. A strange rush of cold energy threatened to overtake her for the second time that night, but she gripped the stone beneath her more tightly and made herself focus and continue to observe.

She counted three soldiers in black. They walked a steady path back and forth in front of the wide gate, occasionally glancing into the mists on the other side.

They seemed...*expectant.*

But why?

Those mists were as Rhea and so many others had described them; like a rolling sea of darkness that occasionally pulsed with a silvery-blue light.

The rain had stopped, Cas realized suddenly; the wind had pushed the storm clouds away, revealing a nearly-full moon, allowing more and more light to pour down into those dark mists. But no matter how bright that light became, she couldn't clearly see the ground beneath the sea of fog. It was as if the energy of Oblivion was simply drinking up the moonlight as she watched. Or scattering it, perhaps...maybe *that* was where the pulses of silverly light were coming from?

Cas was starting to grow restless when she noticed something moving beneath that dark, moonlight-drinking sea—a shadow that looked vaguely human.

And then she saw another.

And another.

The figures swayed in a way that reminded her of the undead she had fought. She leaned forward, trying to get a closer look, but her hand slipped against the stone. She gasped as she tumbled forward, only to stop abruptly as Laurent grabbed the hood of her coat and jerked her back. He was always pulling her back before she went too far, it seemed like—usually after Zev had goaded her into going there in the first place.

"Did you see something?" Laurent asked, crouching beside her as she shrugged off his grip.

Zev joined them a moment later. The three of them stared together until Cas was certain enough of what she saw to whisper, "Is that...are there...*people* under those clouds?"

No sooner had she uttered the word *people* when

something decidedly inhuman-looking moved beneath the ominous canopy. Cas thought she caught a glimpse of a slender snout and two wickedly sharp, curved horns—or were they curved ears? It was hard to make out much more than a blurry outline.

"People or monsters," Zev said, voicing her own concerns.

"An army's worth of people or monsters," added Laurent, his usually placid voice betraying a rare bit of concern. "Look at the way the mist is moving in the distance there—I'm betting there are even more...*bodies* of some sort hiding further beyond the gate."

They studied it all in an awed, disturbed silence for several more minutes, until Zev said, "Well, it looks like proof that something weird is going on to me."

"Do one of you have another Air-kind crystal to capture that proof?" Laurent asked, his concerned tone giving way to his normal business-like one.

"We aren't going to be able to capture a particularly clear image unless one of us gets closer," Cas pointed out.

"Lord Merric seems like the type who would refuse to pay based on what he deems *blurry* proof, doesn't he?" muttered Zev. "So whoever is going to do it needs to get a clear look at things *and* they'll need to press these things into the crystal very quickly."

The older an image or memory was, the less clear it would be when pressed into a message. It was a limitation of the Air-kind crystals—most of these crystals had such limits; their abilities were generally weak compared to the powers possessed by innate users of divine magic.

There was a murmur of agreement after Zev's words, and then Laurent readjusted his mask and drew the hood of his coat more securely around the damp brown waves of his hair. "I'll go," he volunteered. "So long as one of you has a crystal we can use."

"Cas?" Zev glanced at her, one eyebrow raised expectantly.

She sighed.

Another expensive crystal, turned to dust.

It broke her heart a bit to hand it over to Laurent—at least until she reminded herself of how much money they would make if they successfully pulled this off. The Lord of Stonefall's pockets were deep indeed. And he was not a generous man, but he *was* a desperate one—and Cas had found that both sorts of people were equally as capable of filling her purse with silver.

"Try to do a decent job of covering me this time," Laurent drawled. "I don't need a new set of stab wounds to go with the ones I got the *last* time I relied on you two for cover fire."

Zev rolled his eyes. "Okay, firstly, it's not like you died from those wounds."

"Secondly," Cas put in, "the incident at Castle Grove was a one-time thing, and you know it."

"Let's hope so," Laurent said.

"It also wasn't really our fault," she added—but he

was already heading off, once again without looking back at them.

"Is it just me, or does it seem like he still thinks we're grossly incompetent?" Zev whispered.

Cas watched Laurent as he walked away, silently feeling his way along the rocks to find a section he could use to climb down. She shrugged. "Well, *one* of us is kind of grossly incompetent, in all fairness."

"Don't talk about yourself that way, Greythorne."

She cut him a sidelong glance as she pulled her bow out. "We both know you're the incompetent one."

"Well, that's bad news for you then," he chuckled, pulling out his own bow, "considering I taught you everything you know."

"*Everything?*"

"More than you could ever pay me back for, at least." He smirked at her as the two of them settled into a more covert position amongst the rocks.

Cas readied an arrow, though she hoped she wouldn't have to use it.

And there was a decent chance she wouldn't; Laurent had already made his way to within throwing distance of the gate, and *she* had barely noticed him doing it. Of the three of them, he was easily the most adept at stealth. He never talked much about the life he'd lived before joining up with her and her makeshift family, which had led to Zev concocting wild stories about the grumpy half-elf being a disgraced spymaster from some distant realm.

Ridiculous as those stories usually were, there was

certainly a clandestine sort of grace to the way Laurent moved; Cas kept losing him in the shadows as he weaved closer to the Oblivion mists.

The guards have no hope of noticing him, she told herself, trying to stave off the anxiety attempting to unfurl inside of her. She tucked her head to her chest for a moment and breathed in deeply.

"Look," Zev whispered, pointing.

Cas lifted her gaze...and saw something that made her stomach clench.

The mists were suddenly billowing more violently along the edges—building like a wave that pulled away from the shore, only to crash back against the gate.

And then parts of the wave spilled *over* that gate.

The soldiers started to yell to one another. Cas's gaze was momentarily drawn toward the noise, and when she glanced back to where she'd last seen Laurent, it was just in time to see one of those tendrils of mist swallowing him up. When the mist receded once more, he was nowhere in sight.

Her heartbeat pounded in her ears as she watched and waited for him to reappear.

He didn't.

CHAPTER 3

"WHERE IS HE?" CAS BREATHED. "*WHERE IS HE?*"

Zev was silent as he drew his bow, studying the wall. Fingers of mist were reaching out over it once again, as if feeling around for any other intruders that had gotten too close.

"I'm going down there," Cas said, pushing away from the rocks. Her breaths came rapidly, her anxiety building again, but she had to do *something*. "You stay here and get ready to provide that cover fire."

"Cas, wait—"

"You're a quicker shot than me," she said, "you could end all three of those soldiers on your own before I had properly aimed at *one*."

The flattery quieted him long enough for her to get away, just as she'd hoped.

She ran as fast as she could in the near-darkness, feeling her way around until she found the section

Laurent had used to climb down to the path below. She started down without hesitating, moving so quickly that she tripped towards the bottom, scraping her boot against a loose clutch of rocks. The soldier closest to her jerked his head toward the sound, so Cas leapt the remaining distance to the path below. She landed lightly, rebalanced the stolen sword in her grip, and lifted her gaze toward the soldier.

Their eyes met.

He drew his own weapon—a long spear with several wickedly sharp points.

"Who are you?" he demanded.

Cas straightened to her full height and took a step back into the shadows, hoping the man wouldn't follow her.

A fool's hope.

He stalked after her, jabbing his weapon as he came. "Either you start talking or I'll—" his threat was cut off as an arrow pierced his throat, courtesy of Zev

The other two rushed over to check on their fallen brother-in-arms, forgetting about Cas—if they'd seen her at all. She spotted a relatively low section of wall to the left of the gate, and she sprinted for it, vaulting over before the soldiers had a chance to stop her.

It was like jumping into deep, dark water. She seemed to fall forever before her feet finally hit ground made of smooth rock. Her eyes instantly teared up as the fog of Oblivion washed over her. She looked up and found that she could no longer see the moon—or even the sky that held it. Pressure pushed against her from all sides. Tendrils of pale fog and dark energy swirled about, making it impossible to see what lurked beyond a few feet. She was briefly paralyzed by the thought of running into whatever people or monsters had made the shadows they'd seen from above.

But standing still would not keep her safe, so she curled an arm over her masked mouth, squinted her eyes against the burning, and trudged forward.

She might not have believed in the lesser-spirit of *Luck*, but he was apparently on her side anyway— because she quickly found Laurent on his hands and knees just inside the miasma. The half-elf's hand was clutching his coat, pulling it over the mask that covered his face. The mists were obviously affecting him much faster than they were affecting her.

She reached him and dropped to her knees, but he only shook his head and pointed. It took her watering eyes a moment to focus on what he was pointing at—the Air-kind crystal. He must have dropped it when the mist pulled him in. It rested in a shallow depression in the ground, some ten feet away from them.

She tried to help him up first, but he shoved her off and waved her toward the crystal once more.

All business, as usual.

Gritting her teeth, she crawled toward the crystal. She snatched it up and turned back to help Laurent—only to smack into a hard body, sending her flailing backwards.

Her right shoulder slammed into the ground. Pain

fired down her back, but she kept her senses about her and managed not to drop the crystal or her sword as she rolled forward and fought her way up into a kneeling position.

A man loomed over her.

He was definitely not one of the soldiers from the other side of the gate; he was dressed differently than those soldiers, in black leather armor reinforced by metal bands across his broad chest. A black cloak fluttered like raven feathers around him. His head was wrapped in a thick scarf, and every other inch of his body was covered in some way, save for a strip that revealed a pair of blue eyes and beige skin. Those eyes were oddly bright—arresting, inhuman, and harsh, and yet...*beautiful*. If Oblivion was an ocean of nightmares, here was a reminder that morning still existed, even here, and that there was still a sky above it all. A cold, steely blue sky that she couldn't stop staring at—

At least until he attacked her.

He dove forward, drawing a broad sword from the sheath at his hip. And as Cas jumped up, barely tripping out of his reach, all she wanted to do was introduce her *fist* to those beautiful blue eyes.

She nearly managed it, too; one quick step and she was back in front of him, hurling a punch that missed his eyes but managed to catch his jaw as he twisted away.

"*You*—!"

She followed her punch with a kick into his side while he was busy trying to curse at her. He staggered away. She spun back out of his weapon's reach and fell into a more proper sword-fighting stance, setting her feet and lifting her blade as her gaze narrowed on him.

"Who *are* you?" His voice was too muffled by his face-covering to make out much of an accent, but her guess was one of the northernmost realms that had once made up the kingdom of Alnor. "And what the hell are you doing here?"

She didn't answer. Out of the corner of her eye, she saw Zev burst through the mists and hurry to Laurent's side. Laurent didn't seem to be moving; the airs of this place were clearly more poisonous—more potent—than they'd realized. Zev quickly lifted Laurent's lifeless body into his arms, and Cas forgot about trying to get back to Laurent herself; she just needed to distract the man in front of her so her friends could get away.

She charged, sword sweeping through the air.

Her target whipped his own blade up and parried hers at the last instant, knocking her away, and then he drew the sword up and sliced for her side. She was faster, bouncing away and then twirling back to swing—

Only for him to parry again.

Again and again, they danced away and then back together, while the sound of steel striking steel and the fluttering of his cloak echoed strangely in the foggy air. Soon, sweat dripped from Cas's forehead and down into her already-burning eyes, blinding her further. The man became little more than a blur of shadow and speed that she nearly lost track of several times.

She saw the silver streak of his sword breaking through the fog, hurtling toward her. She raised her sword into a guard position just in time, but the force of his blow threatened to buckle her knees. And he didn't stop once their weapons had locked onto each other; he kept shoving, kept trying to break her stance and push her to the ground.

Gods, he was strong.

He wasn't going to put her on the ground—she wouldn't allow it—but he *was* backing her deeper and deeper into the poisonous mists. And though she'd proven to be more resistant than her friends, she was still beginning to feel the effects; her arms shivered at the deep cold that coursed through her veins. It was traveling through her body and numbing her, slowly but surely, making her feel as though she'd sunk into the darkest, most frigid depths of the Glashtyn Sea.

Her wrists ached, threatening to cramp up on her. Her resistance was weakening, her knees slowly bending under the force of him. He had driven her onto a patch of slick mud—far away from the smooth stone she'd first touched down on. She tried to brace her boot against what looked like a more solid bit of ground, but it soon gave way. As she slipped, her enemy's sword slid a bit closer, giving her a glimpse of the hilt and something...odd.

A symbol of one of the Marr—of the wild middle-goddess of Ice and Winter—was engraved on the pommel.

No wonder she felt so desperately cold. This sword was a contraband weapon, infused with Ice-kind magic.

A strange weapon for him to be carrying, if he's in the service of the King-Emperor....

He yanked his blade away, scraping it over hers and causing a cringe-inducing metallic shriek. The cold swirling through her evaporated almost instantly.

"How are you still standing in the mist?" he demanded.

Seeing another opportunity to distract him, she grabbed the hood of her coat and yanked it down, letting the waves of her grey hair tumble free. Her hair had once been a beautiful shade of dark copper—like autumn leaves aglow in the late afternoon sun—but now just the sight of it, along with her equally colorless eyes, made the man before her stumble back in surprise.

"Fade-marked," he breathed. "You...*stay where you are!*"

She arched a brow. And then she grinned, even though she knew he couldn't see it beneath her mask. "Sorry, but I'm afraid I've got other places to be."

He lunged.

She sidestepped the attack and then swept a kick at his ankles, ripping him off his feet.

He landed in a crouch with catlike grace, but before he could spring back up, she pinned that fluttering cloak of his, driving her sword through it and deep into the muddy ground. The blade wasn't a particularly decent one; she didn't care about leaving it behind. And she could run faster without it.

She chuckled at the incredulity in the man's tone as he yelled after her to *stop*.

But as the silhouette of the Oblivion Gate materialized in the mists ahead, she realized...

She no longer held the crystal.

At some point during her battle, she had dropped it. She had no idea where it had ended up, and she wasn't hanging around to search for it. And her team...there was no sign of them anywhere. Were they okay? Had Zev managed to haul Laurent out of this hell and hoist him up over its walls by himself?

She prepared to vault herself over the low point in that stone wall once more.

As her hands pressed against the stone, she chanced one last glance behind her. As she leapt over the wall, she would have sworn she saw shadowy figures closing in, watching her go. Preparing to chase her out if need be...

She landed on the other side, and channeling Laurent's business-like demeanor, didn't look back.

Lord Merric had asked for proof of the King-Emperor's meddling, and all she had was the brooch in her bag, and enough mental images to haunt her for months—which might not have been enough for him.

But it was enough for *her*.

Enough for her to believe that something very disturbing was happening in these mountains, and she never wanted to set foot in them again.

CHAPTER 4

"CHEER UP, CAS." ZEV TIPPED HIS TANKARD OF ALE BACK WITH gusto, finishing it off in a single, long gulp before clanking it back down on the rough wooden table between them. "It could have gone worse."

"Laurent almost died."

"He would disagree with that assessment," Rhea said.

The half-elf in question had stayed at their hideaway to nurse his wounds—and also his pride, Cas suspected. Before they'd left him there, he'd insisted that he needed to do *neither* of those things and claimed that the alarming rattling of his breaths and the pallor of his skin were nothing that a bit of rest—and perhaps a touch of magic—couldn't fix.

Cas had her doubts, but she hadn't argued.

"Of course he would disagree," she said. "But it's the truth. And it shouldn't have happened; *I* should have gone over that wall instead of him in the first place. I don't know why I didn't."

"Maybe because nobody in their right mind readily volunteers to run into a terrifying abyss of darkness and death?" Zev suggested.

Cas shook her head. "I've already been touched by the Fading Sickness, and I survived it. And I've survived every ailment that I've come in contact with since. Remember the poisons they used on us at Castle Grove? And the monsters we exterminated at Westlore with their terrible breath?"

"I try not to remember either of those things in great detail," Rhea said with an exaggerated shudder.

"Neither of them gave *me* so much as a headache," Cas reminded them.

"No, but we still don't know the extent of your, ah..." Zev searched for a word, and with a slightly drunken grin he decided on: "*Weirdness.*"

"I never get sick," she insisted. She also rarely got hungry or tired like a normal person did. But she had suffered in other, stranger ways since the Fading Sickness had taken hold of her as a child, and she was still waiting for the day that it fully woke up and consumed her as it had so many others.

But for whatever reason...it still hadn't happened.

Yet.

"Why else would that be," she asked, "if not because of my being Fade-marked?"

Rhea patted Cas's hand but shushed her, simultaneously offering comfort and a warning. The warning was fair; Cas's voice had been loud, and Madam Rosa's tavern was more crowded than usual tonight. There were more than a few people close enough to overhear their conversation.

Of course, most of those people were likely too drunk to make sense of her words, and too far gone to suspect what she really was—especially since Cas had her hood drawn up, and she had disguised herself by way of a Mimic-kind crystal. Her normally grey hair was now a dark shade of brown, her disturbingly pale eyes, a much more pleasant shade of soft green. Another expensive crystal gone to dust—gods, she was really burning through them today, wasn't she?—but she was already in such a terrible humor after their failed mission...

She was certainly not in the mood to be gawked at while she sulked and drank away her frustrations. And that was precisely what would have happened had she walked into this tavern with her greyed-out hair and eyes on full display.

It had been years since Cas had seen another Fade-marked, aside from herself and Asra, so the rare sighting of either of them generally caused at least a minor uproar in most places. No one who caught the more recent form the Fading Sickness survived, and the ones who had made it through the earlier, weaker waves of the sickness had all been ruthlessly hunted down by the father of the current King-Emperor—allegedly because he'd hoped they might provide answers for a cure. The theory itself was not troublesome. What *was* troublesome was the fact that all of the Fade-marked he'd managed to collect had soon after simply...*disappeared*.

His hunting had been in vain, anyhow; three years ago, the tyrant King-Emperor Anric de Solasen had died a violent death of the very sickness he'd claimed to be trying to cure.

His wife had already died eighteen years before, which meant that his passing left his one and only child as the keeper of the high throne that ruled precariously over the twelve broken realms of the Kethran Empire—realms that had once been a part of four separate, proper kingdoms.

The current King-Emperor hadn't kept up his father's hunting practices as far as Cas knew, but that was likely only because Varen de Solasen believed that no more of the Fade-marked remained. And Cas had employed various tricks and disguises over the years—both magical and otherwise—to make sure that he and most of the empire *kept* believing this. It was a delicate balance, trying to build a reputation that could land her lucrative jobs, while also keeping any whispers of her true appearance and identity to a minimum.

And oh, how *stupid* she'd been to reveal her true appearance to that man in Oblivion. To just let him live after seeing her so clearly...

The mission was a failure in every sense of the word, she thought miserably, as she flagged down one of the servers and ordered a third drink.

"Marked or not, you aren't immortal, love," Rhea said, after the sound of the server's footsteps faded away. "And even with all the prepping we did, I *still* don't think we had a true understanding of what we were walking into. And no, we don't know everything there is to know about your *weirdness*, as Zev said. It could still catch up with you. Especially if you keep tempting fate by volunteering for the most reckless part of every mission we take on. Laurent would say the same thing. That's likely why he stepped up before you had a chance to."

Cas chewed on her bottom lip, thinking.

It could still catch up with you.

The mood turned noticeably more solemn at those words—because all of them knew the unspoken line that followed.

It could still catch up with you...just as it's catching up with Asra.

Cas tried to push away thoughts of the woman she had once seen as invincible. Asra had been asleep when they'd stopped by their hideaway before venturing out for a drink.

She was always asleep lately, it seemed like.

"Besides, we're a team, right?" Rhea continued, keeping her voice low. "If one of us is going to volunteer to run into a terrifying abyss of darkness and death, then it goes without saying that we *all* will do it, so it shouldn't matter which of us goes first."

Zev nodded and lifted his drink in a toast to the sentiment.

Cas felt marginally better as she clinked her glass against his. She drank in contemplative silence after that, letting their surroundings wash over her—feeling the vibrations of footsteps and laughter, inhaling the smoke and salty scent of roasting meat and wrinkling her nose at the occasional whiff of sweat that she caught instead...

It truly *was* more crowded in here than she'd ever seen it. She likely could have saved her Mimic-kind crystal; a hood would have sufficed. She simply wasn't worth gawking at compared to the abundance of rowdy singa-longs and heated games of dice and cards that were taking place all around her.

Which was why, when somebody *did* begin to stare at her, she felt it.

She tilted her head casually to the left and she spotted him quickly—a man seated by himself at a table in front of the largest of the tavern's multiple roaring fires.

His legs were too long to be easily contained beneath the small table; one was casually stretched out beside him, the other curled under that table. The shape he carved against the firelight made her think of a shadow cat resting in its claimed tree, looking perfectly noncha-lant and yet equally ready to pounce. He was observing her—and everything around her—with that same oddly powerful-looking passivity. None of the rude or rowdy patrons hovering around his table seemed to bother him.

His coat appeared cleaner and more finely made than most of the clothing worn by the tavern's regulars, with an equally expensive-looking silver cuff bracelet and set of boots to match. His hair, relatively long and loosely tied away from his face, was similar to the rich brown shade Cas had magicked hers into, though perhaps a touch darker.

Their eyes met suddenly, and he didn't look away.

Nor did she—though she did pull her hood down a bit further, and she subtly lifted one of the wavy stands of her hair to make certain it was still brown.

"He's handsome," Zev commented, nudging her with his elbow and making her jump.

She turned her gaze back to the chipped mug in her hands. "He's got a staring problem."

"I wouldn't complain if he was staring in *my* direction," said Zev with a shrug.

"Want to trade seats?"

Zev laughed. He rested an elbow on the table, his chin on his fist, and he squinted in the staring man's direction for a moment before cutting his eyes back to Cas with a sly grin. "A month's worth of cooking duties says you can't relieve him of that pretty bracelet he's wearing without him noticing it."

She chanced another glance at the man, considering.

Normally, she was above petty theft. But she wasn't above taking a dare. And it *was* a pretty trinket. It looked like Glashtyn silver, judging by the way it appeared to turn blue in the firelight—which meant that it would fetch a *very* pretty price.

It wouldn't fetch as much as their payment from Lord Merric, but that mission for the Lord of Stonefall looked as though it was going to take longer than she'd hoped—if they even managed to complete it at all.

She had to do something to hold her over in the meantime. She needed to buy medicine for Asra, and the only man capable of getting her that medicine was not known for his charity.

Also, she *hated* cooking duty.

But then, almost as if he sensed he'd become a topic of conversation, the man by the fire stood up. He dropped a few coins onto the table, smiled a handsome smile at the servant who was bowing and looking flustered over the generous tip, and then he disappeared up the stairs in the back of the room.

"Well, so much for that," Zev pouted.

Cas thought again of Asra; of the way she hadn't been able to get out of bed the morning before, and how she had started wasting away. Cas's last memories of her first adoptive parents were similar—the weakness, the protruding veins, the ashen color of their hair and eyes spreading over their entire body—except it had progressed much more quickly for them. The Fading Sickness almost always claimed its victims within a year. The rare, illegal, expensive medicine that Cas had discovered some time ago was the only thing keeping Asra with them.

Cas was not prepared to lose her simply because she couldn't afford that medicine.

Petty theft, here I come.

"You're on," she told Zev, getting to her feet.

"Really?" He leaned back in his chair, looking both amused and curious.

"Really."

"You have a plan?"

"Of course."

"Do tell."

She swallowed hard, and then proceeded to make one up. "They have certain kinds of...er...*room service* in this tavern, don't they? Shouldn't be too hard to get into his room under the guise of that, and then..."

"And then?" Zev prompted, grinning like a fool as the back of her neck burned hot.

"I...well, you know..."

"Do I? I'm not sure I do. Please explain in detail."

"Please bite me, asshole."

"Save that line for your target; he might like it."

"I'm pretty sure I can come up with at least a few lines that are better than that."

"I would love to hear them."

"Don't be an idiot, Cas," Rhea said with a sigh.

"She can't help it," Zev said. "She was born that way. Let's not be rude about it."

Cas flicked a crumpled-up napkin at his face, and Zev chuckled as he batted it away. "I do have to agree with my dear sister on this one, though," he said. "You're skilled in a lot of things, Cas, but flirtation and seduction are not among them. So while I don't doubt your thieving abilities, if that's *really* the method you're going to try and use...well...um..."

"Okay, so now you know I *have* to go to prove you wrong," Cas said.

He did know, judging by the way his grin widened even further. "Good luck."

Rhea sighed again. "This is almost *exactly* the sort of recklessness I mentioned earlier."

"Think of how many coins that silver bracelet might sell for," Cas implored.

"It might not even be *real* silver." Rhea pursed her lips and grumbled something about *children,* but after a moment she shook her head and relented. "Fine. I'll sign off on this *only* because I vastly prefer Zev's cooking to yours, and so I hope you win this bet."

"Take Silverfoot," Zev told Cas, "so that Rhea can see how horrendously this goes, and then she can describe it to me in all of its full, glorious detail."

The fox let out a squeaky yawn from his place beneath the table, sounding perfectly unenthusiastic about this plan, while Rhea massaged the space between her eyes and whispered what sounded like a prayer under her breath.

"Unnecessary," Cas muttered with one last cross look at Zev. "Because you'll see how *wonderfully* it's gone in just a few minutes, when I reemerge with that bracelet in my hand."

"I hope he lasts more than a few minutes for you, friend."

Neck flushing even hotter, she turned to Rhea. "I actually might need Silver's nose for a moment."

Rhea nodded, and at the click of her tongue, the fox rose, stretched, and leapt up into her lap. "Help Cas, please?" she asked, and with a nod toward her brother, added, "This idiot can be my sight in the meantime."

The fox yawned again, blinked the sleepiness from his big, bright eyes, and then obediently bounced down to wait at Cas's feet.

"Be careful," Rhea said.

Cas promised she would, and then she turned and strode purposefully toward the table where her target had been sitting, the tiny fox trotting at her heels.

"Just scream if it goes poorly," Zev called after them.

She wasn't worried about it going poorly; she could handle herself. Madam Rosa insisted on her bar patrons disarming at the door, so Cas no longer had her bow—they had left most of their larger weapons at their hide-out, anyway—but she still had a throwing knife hidden against her thigh, her dart gun tucked into the inner pocket of her coat, and Laurent had been giving her hand-to-hand combat lessons for so long that *she* was a weapon.

Let it go poorly.

It would give her a chance to work out her anxieties and frustrations.

She approached the table, pretended to be warming herself by the fire behind it for a moment, and then knelt down to stroke the fox's silky fur and whisper, "Can you pick up the scent of the man that was just sitting here?"

The creature went to work sniffing the chair and the

floor beneath it, helping himself to a few crumbs of fallen food as he did. After a moment, he lifted his head, snorted, and bounded off toward the stairs.

She followed him up the stairs, all the way down a narrow hallway and to the last room on the left. There, Silverfoot paused, stuck his snout beneath the door, inhaled deeply for a moment, and then settled back on his haunches while looking rather pleased with himself.

"Thank you. Now go on back to Rhea," Cas said, knocking lightly on the door. "I'll be fine."

The fox tilted his head. His tail thumped an uncertain rhythm against the floorboards.

"Go on—"

The door flung open.

49

CHAPTER 5

Silverfoot scampered away, and Cas turned to find herself staring into a pair of pale blue eyes. The fox's nose was accurate; this was definitely the same man that had been staring at her earlier. He seemed even more imposing up close. Cas was not particularly *small*, but the longer she stared at him, the more tiny and overshadowed she felt.

Was he part giant or something?

"Can I help you?" He had already started to undress after retiring to his room. That finely made coat was gone, revealing the shirt he wore beneath, untucked, but still clinging tightly enough to reveal well-defined muscles. He still wore that silver bracelet, too, as well as the fingerless gloves that were often used by those with divine magic. They hid his wrist and palm—and thus hid any sort of god or spirit symbol that might have been imprinted in either spot. Such symbols were present at birth, like a birthmark that glowed whenever their power was accessed, and they could not be removed.

She hadn't noticed those gloves earlier, and the sight unsettled her a bit.

It was unlikely that he would risk using magic on her in such a public place—there was a reason people like him hid their marks in this empire, after all—but the possibility that he even *had* it was still unnerving.

"Well?" he prompted.

Cas forced her eyes to trail away from his covered wrist. She twisted her mouth into a slight smile. "I...was told you might be in need of a little extra warmth on this frigid night? That you had requested some company?"

His gaze narrowed. "I didn't request anything of the sort."

She could practically hear Zev laughing at her, even all the way up here, but she steeled herself.

She was *not* losing this bet.

With what she hoped passed for a flirtatious batting of her eyelashes, she lowered her voice and said, "Well, perhaps you could at least honor me with a little...*chat*, so long as I'm here."

One eyebrow arched over those cold blue eyes. In the dim light of the hallway, it was difficult to tell whether he was intrigued, amused, or annoyed by her presence.

Probably some combination of all three.

She felt like a complete idiot, but she was too deep into her ruse to stop now. "I know you were watching me downstairs." Her tone had suddenly become less seductive and more accusatory.

Whoops.

It seemed to work in her favor, however, because he cleared his throat and said, "Right. That. My apologies if I made you feel uncomfortable. I was just...curious."

"Curious?"

For a moment, he looked as if he was still considering shutting the door in her face. But then a bit of the tension rolled from his shoulders, and he asked, "Are you from around here?"

She was from everywhere, and nowhere at all—that was usually the intentionally evasive response she gave to that question—but she could tell he was hoping for a *yes*, so she nodded and said, "I've lived in this town all of my life."

He considered this for a moment. "I wanted to talk to a local about a few things, and most of the others downstairs were a bit too..."

"Inebriated?"

"Precisely."

She was suddenly thankful for all the late nights she and Zev had spent in the countless other little taverns like this one; she could hold her liquor better than most. "I'm quite sober."

"It appeared that way."

"And yet you didn't approach me."

"I had second thoughts."

"Well, here's your second chance."

He regarded her with a dubious look before exhaling a little puff of air—not quite a laugh, not quite a dismissive snort, but something in-between. "Lucky me."

"I'm not *promising* you you'll get lucky," she retorted, "but we can at least start with that talk you wanted to have."

He stared at her.

Oh gods, why did I say that? He thinks I'm insane.

Her cheeks warmed, and she briefly hoped they might burn hot enough to simply melt her out of existence—but then a corner of his mouth inched upward.

He turned away before the smile fully took hold. "Come inside for a moment, then, and let's *chat.*"

She stepped into the room before he could change his mind. Her arm brushed his as she passed him, and she caught the scent of spice and earth beneath the fireplace smoke that had settled into his clothing and hair.

The door clicked softly shut behind her, the sound of it sending a hum of anxiety vibrating down her spine. She breathed in deep, tugged her hood more completely around her head, and sought out the exits, noting the way that part of the roof was visible through the large window to her right.

I can get away if I need to, she told herself, repeatedly, until she had forced down the lump trying to rise in her throat.

She looked away from the window and found her target at the dresser on the opposite side of the room, making use of the silver tray of bottles and glasses that rested on it. He turned back to her, two glasses in hand.

"So, I'm guessing one of my men paid you to do this as a joke." He casually leaned back against the dresser and took a sip of one of the drinks. Then another sip. Then he drained the rest of it in one go, momentarily wincing at what she assumed was the bite of alcohol before looking over at her with a droll expression. "This has Caden written all over it," he muttered, tilting his head toward the ceiling and frowning a bit.

One of his men?

She tried to mirror his casual appearance as she made her way around the room, studying it. He was very neat. All of his belongings were packed in an evenly spaced row of fastened bags against the back wall; nothing was scattered about on the floor, nothing tossed this way and that across the bed—which meant there was nothing to betray his true identity.

Her exploring was interrupted by motion; the man moved toward her with an unhurried, yet very deliberate, step. "They are constantly telling me I need to loosen up," he continued. "All of them, really; not just Caden."

She swallowed hard, forcing composure in spite of his abrupt closeness. She casually took a step back, but she couldn't go far—the wall was closer than she'd realized. The corner of a nightstand poked her hip as she tried again to shift away. "Then perhaps you do need to loosen up," she said. "If more than one person is saying the same thing, it's usually worth at least considering the advice."

"A fair point. Though sending a mistress to, err...*chat* with me seems a bit over-the-top as a first step toward loosening me up, wouldn't you agree?" He offered her the second glass he'd poured. His eyes sparkled with amusement, and it made them seem much less cold. Her fingertips accidentally brushed his as she reached for the glass, and he held that glass a little longer than was necessary, as if taking the time to memorize the feel of her touch.

She finally managed to pull the glass away, but she didn't drink from it.

She wasn't *that* foolish.

"Do you have a name?" he asked.

"Do you usually ask your *mistresses* personal questions?"

"I don't usually invite them into my room at all, so I'm going to say...no? But it's only a name. Not *that* personal, is it?"

She frowned, but ultimately conceded with a little shake of her head. "It's... Azalea."

"Like the flower?"

"No." She pretended to take a sip of her drink. "Like the elven warrior-queen that single-handedly slaughtered a legion of men at the Battle of Scatter Sun Ridge."

"Ah, of course." There it was again—that quirk of his lips that didn't quite make it into a full smile. It was undeniably attractive, which made her ruse easier to stick to, at least. "I'd forgotten about that legend," he said.

"It's one of my favorites."

"Rather violent, isn't it?"

"She was defending her realm from soldiers trying to overthrow it."

"By setting people on fire through a divine magic that was rare and unexpected for an elf to possess, as I recall."

Cas lifted her shoulder and let it drop. "If you don't want to be set on fire, don't invade people's homes."

"Solid advice. I'll keep it in mind." His brows knitted together with concern for the briefest of moments, and then he was back to looking amused. "And do you usually take that hood off, *Azalea*," he asked, "or is leaving it on part of your unique brand of...*service*?"

She couldn't help the heat that flushed over her entire body at the way he'd said *service*.

He closed a little more of the space between them. The movement brought him into a stream of moonlight from the nearby window, and the light caught on the silver of that cuff he still wore. The familiar rush of a goal in sight overtook Cas. She relaxed a little more fully into the role she was playing, lifted her gaze back to his, and smiled.

He was clearly growing increasingly amused and willing to go along with her game, and playing with this handsome man in front of her certainly wouldn't be the *worst* thing that had happened today...

Yes, she could work with this.

She reached up and pulled her hood away from her face, and then she tried to breathe normally as he studied her with the same powerful, yet relaxed, stare he'd fixed on her in the tavern below.

After a moment, his lips parted slowly in surprise, and she briefly lost that battle to breathe.

Could he see through her spell?

Could he tell a Fade-marked was standing in front of him?

She braced herself, but all he said was: "Interesting."

"I'm not the most interesting thing in this town, I promise you," she managed to say in a somewhat normal, if breathy, voice.

"Is that so?"

She froze as he reached a hand forward and traced a wayward strand of hair that had fallen over her collarbone. Hair that he apparently found *interesting*. Her heart hammered as his finger curled and uncurled the wave of that hair, and when she didn't pull away from his touch, he brought his other hand to her side, letting it trail down the curve of her waist and come to rest against her hip. His grip was as effortlessly powerful as his stare; just a casual hold on her, and yet for some reason, she felt as if walking away would prove incredibly difficult.

He tilted his mouth closer to hers, and her mind raced with thoughts of what kissing him would feel like—and then immediately with louder thoughts of how ridiculous she was being. She was no prude, but she also didn't personally make a habit of kissing strange men she'd just met. It *was* in the name of distraction and thievery, yes, but something told her that she would enjoy it for other reasons, too, if she—

No, it didn't matter.

Because he didn't kiss her. She was equal parts relieved and disappointed when he leaned in, but instead of pressing his mouth to hers, he moved it toward her ear.

"You're disguised with magic," he whispered.

She managed to shrug, though her heart felt as if it was attempting to claw its way into her throat. "So?"

"So that sort of magic is illegal."

"Are you going to report me?"

"Maybe." His lips brushed the sensitive skin beneath her earlobe with the word, and she shivered. He leaned back—though he didn't go particularly far. His hand still rested on her hip, his fingers tapping slowly, thoughtfully, against her as he considered the question. "Maybe not."

She exhaled a slow, slightly shaky, breath.

"Disguised with magic..." he chided, stilling his fingers against her. "And what's more? I don't believe you're from this little town at all."

"You don't have to believe a thing for it to be true," she countered.

He laughed—a quiet, but honest and deep laugh that shook his body and made his hand move against her. Just the slightest movement, but it sent another shiver tingling over her skin.

And gods, he was still so close.

"Your accent doesn't sound local," he informed her.

"No?"

"I'm not quite sure *what* it sounds like, or where you might be from, and I'm usually very good at picking up on those kinds of things. So that's..."

"Interesting?" she suggested. It made him laugh again, and the sound made her feel bolder. She promptly used the break in tension to draw him closer to her. Her hands moved to his arms. She traced the rise and fall of his muscles, pretending to be enamored with simply touching him as she felt her way toward the bracelet he wore.

Her fingers fell over the metal, and in the same instant, he leaned his mouth toward her ear once more. He didn't whisper anything this time. He just ran his lips over that same sensitive bit of skin beneath her earlobe— on purpose this time—and then swept a velvet-soft trail of kisses down along her throat. Her eyes nearly fluttered shut from the sensation of it.

Focus, she commanded herself. And she managed to. At first. At least until his hand slipped from its hold on her hip and traveled along the planes of her lower stomach, instead. His fingers inched underneath her tunic, the rough tips of them a far-too heavenly contrast against her smooth skin.

He went higher, found the curve of her breast, the thin undergarment cradling it, and his fingers slipped under the band—

She inhaled a little more sharply than she'd meant to in response.

He paused. "Something wrong?"

"No. I just..." She blinked and searched for something to ground herself with. Her gaze fell on a sheath propped between the bed and the nightstand. She hadn't noticed it before—which was surprising, given the elaborate gold designs it was painted with.

"You just...?"

"I just noticed that that's a fine-looking sword over there."

He looked confused for a fraction of a moment, and then a corner of his mouth lifted again. "Not the finest one I own."

He did not just say that.

But he had, and oh, he was clearly growing *very* amused with her now.

And she was suddenly too flustered to think of a clever response. Zev had a point about her inability to flirt under pressure. She held in a sigh at the thought; she *hated* it when he had a point about something.

She needed to finish this before she made an honest, irredeemable fool of herself.

"You should check the lock on the door," she purred.

He studied her for a moment, still looking amused—though there was also a hint of suspicion back in his gaze now. But despite that suspicion, he backed slowly away from her. He kept his eyes on her until he was halfway across the room, and then he turned around.

As soon as he turned, she reached into the inside pocket of her coat, feeling around for her dart gun. She pulled it out, loaded a dart with quick, expert fingers, and as she did, she found herself simultaneously moving closer to that sword she'd spotted. The gilded sheath truly was a thing to behold—perhaps more valuable than the bracelet she'd originally planned to steal—and the sword it contained, what she could see of its hilt was...

She gasped.

She heard her target locking the door. Heard his footsteps coming closer and closer. But she couldn't take her eyes off that sword, and the symbol on its handle...

The symbol of the middle-goddess of Ice and Winter.

It was the same blade she'd seen in Oblivion.

It couldn't be. He couldn't be.

But how many of these illegal, magical blades could possibly be floating around?

And his *eyes.*

She turned back to face him, and as she sought those cold blue eyes, she had a sudden urge to smack herself. How? *How* had she forgotten the way she'd felt when she'd stared at them in Oblivion?

But she didn't think beyond that; the dart gun was against her lips a second later.

"What the fuck are you—"

She fired. He twisted, but not quickly enough. The toxic barb sank deep into his throat.

"You will regret that," he growled, jerking it out and flinging it to the floor.

"Doubt it," she said, firing a second dart just as quickly as she'd fired the first.

He...caught it.

That was impressive.

And strange. And impossible. But it didn't matter, because his steps were already beginning to slow from the

61

first dart, and he stumbled as he lunged for her. She danced easily around his swaying body, and then she sent him the rest of the way to the floor with a well-placed elbow into his back. He reached for her leg, but she leapt over his hand and landed in a crouch, and while he fought to rise, she readied another dart and fired.

This one successfully struck him in the cheek.

Cas stumbled out of his reach again, moving so fast that she collided with a chair and knocked it to the floor. As she tried to avoid tripping over it, her ankle twisted awkwardly. She dropped to a crouch as a hiss of pain escaped her.

Thankfully, the man had slowed almost to a stop. His eyes were closing. He collapsed and rolled onto his side, cursing softly under his breath.

Then he was still.

She tucked her head against her chest, and braced her hands against the floor for a moment, composing herself. Her heartbeat settled—only to speed up again when she lifted her eyes to the man's now-peacefully sleeping face. A bit of lantern light flickered over his features, illuminating the sharp line of his jaw and the slight part of those lips that had been against her skin only minutes ago.

Impressive indeed.

He was painfully good-looking, really. It was a shame she couldn't stick around for that *chat* he'd seemingly been ready to have with her.

"Night night, beautiful," she said, crawling over and

slipping the bracelet from his wrist before rising gingerly to her feet. She briefly considered taking the Ice-kind sword as well. A weapon like that could potentially draw a disastrous amount of attention to her if she wasn't careful, but she could sell it off relatively quickly if she could just sneak it out of the inn...

She had nearly decided to risk taking it when someone knocked on the door.

With a curse, she forgot about the sword, darted for the window, and threw it open. She was out on the gently sloped roof without a second thought. She silently made her way across it, then down to the lower roof, and finally, she dropped to the cobblestone alleyway below.

Whistling to herself, she walked into the front door of the tavern, moving casually in spite of her still-pounding pulse and the occasional twinge of pain in her ankle

"This makes two bets you've lost tonight, if you're keeping count," she informed Zev as she approached their table.

He glanced up with a yawn. "Ah. So I see you survived, at least."

"After an impressive performance *and* a clean getaway." She gave a little bow, patting the leather pouch on her belt, where she'd safely hidden the bracelet.

He looked impressed for a fraction of moment before glancing behind her. "Not entirely clean," he mused, nodding over her shoulder.

She glanced back to see the man she'd robbed standing at the foot of the stairs, sword in hand.

He wasn't alone, either—two men brandishing swords flanked him on either side as he stepped into the room.

No way.

"He has two darts worth of killsweed flowing through him. There's no way he's still standing. He's some sort of...*monster*...or..."

Zev didn't argue for once; he simply rose calmly to his feet, and then ushered both her and Rhea toward the exit.

"What is going on?" Rhea demanded.

"It's time to go, that's what," her brother cheerfully informed her.

Silverfoot darted out from beneath the table and took his customary place around Rhea's neck. The four of them attempted to quietly and calmly head for the door—but their movement still gave them away.

Shouting at them to stop, the men gave chase, and Cas and her companions broke into a run.

"Madam Rosa!" Zev called as they sprinted past the tavern's proprietor. "Weapons!"

The sprightly old woman rounded in the direction he was pointing to. She caught sight of the three men and their swords, and she immediately summoned the attention of the security that she kept along the room's perimeters.

"*NO WEAPONS IN MY PEACEFUL ESTABLISHMENT!*" she roared, intercepting the sword-wielding men herself, viciously swatting her broom at the first one's head.

The proper security converged a moment later, and

then several of the tavern regulars joined into the fray, and the chaos was such that Cas and her partners in crime made it to the front door without being touched.

"May the fifteen greatest gods bless that cranky old woman," Zev laughed as they raced out into the cold night and scrambled down the tavern's steps.

"And may those same gods *curse* both of you," Rhea huffed. "All of your stupid betting and screwing around is going to get us killed one of these days."

"Not dead yet, are we?"

A violent crash sounded from the inn.

"But we should probably keep running," he added, still laughing as he linked his arm with his sister's and pulled her quickly over to their horses. He helped his sister into the saddle of the largest of the two, and then climbed up after her.

Cas mounted her own horse and followed a short distance behind them as they took off, inhaling deep lungfuls of the crisp air and feeling wild and alive and free...at least for the first surreal, half-mile stretch of road. But it wasn't long before her anxieties crept back in.

Her muscles started to tighten up, and she slowed to a stop. Zev and Rhea had already stopped at a bend in the road just ahead. The latter was still scolding her brother, who was—predictably—still laughing. Cas smiled wryly at the sight of them, but all of her humor faded as she glanced behind her.

There was no one there this time. But her memories of that man, of his touch and his scent and his strange, cold eyes...the memories were vibrant and confusing, and her mind raced with questions.

Who *was* he, precisely?

How had he overcome that poison so quickly?

And what the hell had he been doing in Oblivion?

CHAPTER 6

"Is that my Casia I hear?" Asra's frail voice drifted down the sunlit hallway, accompanied by the sound of wind-chimes and a whistling breeze.

It was late morning, but Cas still hadn't slept. Instead, she had tossed and turned the night away in her bed that was tucked in the hideaway's loft, staring out her diamond-shaped window and wrestling with all of the questions the previous day had left her with. When the first bit of sun had peeked over the distant hills, she had given up on sleep entirely and instead made a quick visit to the markets in Fallenbridge. She'd learned long ago that if she went to the markets early enough, most of the merchants were still too tired to haggle smartly—which meant she could walk away with twice as much for half the price.

Now she was carrying some of the spoils of her shrewd haggling—fresh sangos fruit and goat's milk—to the small room at the back of the house. There, Asra rested on a worn mattress, half-buried in every spare pillow and blanket the others had managed to collect for her. She had insisted on that old mattress of hers being dragged right up onto the raised platform beneath the room's only window, even after Cas had teased her and likened her to a fat cat spending its days sunning itself.

"Hey Mama," Cas greeted her, carefully settling herself onto the corner of the platform. She placed the freshly cut fruit and the milk on the tray resting beside Asra, and then she reached and pulled the curtains behind the bed aside, flooding the room with more light. The window was cracked open already; that explained why the sound of chimes and wind were so loud.

"Nessa left it open," Asra informed her with a shiver. "She insists I need the air, but—*bah*. Not going to make me feel better if I freeze to death from that unseasonably cold air, now, is it?"

Cas smiled, though her heart sank a bit with the words. The air wasn't cold at all. Quite the opposite, really —her chills were just another symptom of that damned Fading Sickness.

She moved to help Asra sit up, partly because she didn't want her hurting herself by trying to do it on her own, and partly because she hoped she might share some of her warmth. Asra's body felt so terribly *light* in Cas's arms—like picking up a baby bird that was all hollow bones, paper-thin skin, and limbs that didn't know which way to hold themselves.

"Would you like me to close the window?" Cas asked as she arranged the pillows behind Asra for better support.

Asra wrapped her thin arms around herself, considering, but then she waved a dismissive hand at the question. She turned to stare outside. Her colorless eyes got lost in the bright sun for a long moment before she blinked, tilted her head back to Cas, and said, "Let it be. Maybe we'll be okay now that the sun's chased away all of those storms from last night, eh? Should start to warm up soon."

Cas nodded, and the two of them sat in pleasant silence, nibbling at the tart fruit and listening to the wind stirring all the chimes hanging outside the window.

They made an awful racket, those chimes, and Laurent and Rhea had both petitioned Asra more than once to consider getting rid of them. Their hideaway was deep in the Valshade Forest, no less than five miles from the nearest house and protected by whatever various crystals they managed to procure on any given week. But when the wind blew hard enough, Rhea swore that the noise those instruments created could not have been contained by *any* spell, and that it could attract monsters dwelling in the deepest depths of Oblivion.

But Asra wouldn't listen to their complaints. The chimes reminded her of her childhood—of the bells they used to ring at one of the temples dedicated to Solatis, the upper-goddess of the Sun. That temple was almost certainly destroyed now, but Asra had once lived in sight of it, and she had fond memories of watching the Star-kind, servants of that Sun Goddess, perform their divination magic in the years before public displays of such magic were outlawed.

The closer I get to the end, she had told Cas once, *the more I find myself wanting to go back to the beginning.*

Cas had scolded her for talking about the end as if it was such a certain thing. But then she had promptly gone out to the market the next morning and bought another chime to hang outside the window, as if each one might turn the hands of Asra's life a little farther back toward those childhood days and somehow grant her more time.

After a few minutes of sitting together, Asra's eyes closed. She started to hum a soft, familiar song to go with the chiming. When she stopped, her body swayed a bit, and Cas was afraid she had fallen asleep sitting up again. Cas moved to catch her—but then Asra popped her eyes open and regarded her with a long, searching look. "You didn't sleep last night, did you?"

"I...um, no," said Cas, settling back against the sun-warmed wall.

"The storms?"

"Yes." There was more to it than that, of course, but Cas didn't want to give her anything else to worry about.

"Why are you in here, then, and not in your own bed?"

"I'm not tired."

"Hmph."

"It's the truth," Cas said with a shrug. "You know me."

Asra squinted at her, as if trying to make sure she was

looking at the real and true Casia, and then with a soft laugh, she said, "Yes, I suppose I do, don't I? My little restless heart."

Cas smiled a bit at the words; it was a term of endearment Asra had started using years ago.

What are you doing, my restless heart?

Where are you going, my restless heart?

You're safe here, my restless heart.

"But I still find it hard to believe, sometimes," Asra continued, her face scrunching up in concentration. "All these years we've been together, and I've *still* never heard of any other Fade-marked that got anything *good* out of surviving that nasty sickness."

"I just got lucky, I guess," Cas said dryly.

Lucky was not the right word. Not quite. Because while surviving that sickness seemed to have made Cas stronger in some ways, it had also left her with several unpleasant side-effects: strange, nightmarish visions when she *did* manage to sleep, another trigger for her occasionally paralyzing anxiety, and, of course, an appearance that made it impossible for her to blend in anywhere without using magic.

Still, it could have been worse.

For Asra, it had been.

It had been twelve years since Asra had caught the Fading Sickness, and during that time, she had also fared better than most—thanks to a bit of luck and a lot of illegal medicine.

But lately, every passing season brought more weakness with it. More pain. More instances where she seemed to slip away from this world entirely, only to return without any memories of leaving. And now it had progressed to the point that she could hardly crawl out of bed without help.

Every time Cas visited this sickbed, she was reminded of how it could all catch up with *her* in the same manner.

Her greatest fear was that it would catch up with her all at once, that it might strike her down in the middle of a job, and that she wouldn't be able to keep *doing* those jobs and earning enough coin to buy medicine and everything else.

And then who would keep Asra going?

She wasn't convinced that Zev and the others would go to the same lengths she did to keep her mentor alive and well. They never said it out loud, but Cas could tell what they were thinking—that it was only a matter of time before there would be nothing they could do for Asra, anyway. Before her mind would fade along with everything else, and then letting her go would be the kinder thing to do.

Deep down, Cas knew they were right.

But she still had no plans to stop fighting for Asra until her mentor took that inevitable last breath.

"Anyway, not sleeping is nothing new—but why spend so much on breakfast?" Asra asked. "What's the occasion?"

"No occasion, I just know sangos fruit is your favorite. And I assumed you were tired of porridge and bread."

"Nothing wrong with either of those things."

"Not the first one-thousand times you eat them, I suppose."

"I never spoiled you, so I don't know where you got the notion to do it from."

"I got a good deal." Cas reclined against the warm wall, grinning at Asra's stern expression before nibbling off another bite of the tangy fruit. "So, not really spoiling you at all."

Asra arched an eyebrow. "No illegal discounts, I hope?"

"Not this time."

"Good. You're above petty theft."

Cas nodded, though her grin did widen a bit. "Then again, petty theft is the reason we met," she pointed out.

Asra's look turned stern once more, but she soon yielded with a happy little sigh. "The only good thing to ever come from thievery."

"A very good thing," Cas agreed.

That meeting was both a bright and painful memory in Cas's mind. She had been a newly orphaned child wandering the streets of the city of Greyedge, half-dazed and stupid with a reckless kind of hunger that made her think it was a good idea to try and steal a bag that had been left unattended outside of a shop.

That bag, it had turned out, belonged to a guard who was accompanying King-Emperor Anric.

She'd been caught and beaten right there in the middle of the dusty street, whipped with metal-tipped weapons that bit like fire and drew so much blood she'd nearly fainted.

Then the King-Emperor himself had emerged from his carriage. He'd taken one look at Cas's appearance—at the tips of her clumsily dyed hair and her eyes that she hadn't yet known how to properly hide—and he had realized what she was.

Fade-marked.

He'd ordered her taken into custody. But Asra—with her own faded hair gleaming unapologetically in the sun along with her sword—had interfered. She and two of her cohorts had strode right into the middle of the chaos. Asra had ripped Cas from the grasp of the guards and raced away with Cas's bleeding body tucked against her chest.

She had brought Cas home with her, hiding her and doing what she could with all of the cuts and bruises, but the incident had left one particularly gruesome, crescent-moon shaped scar on Cas's jawline. Even all these years later, it still hadn't healed.

That day was not only the first time she had met Asra, but also the first and only time Cas had personally glimpsed Varen de Solasen, the current ruler of Kethra. He had been only a young prince at the time—a child, just like her—peering out of the carriage's window, his forehead lightly pressed against the glass, his breaths making little clouds against it.

He hadn't moved to help her.

He hadn't appeared distressed at all by what he was seeing, in fact. He had only watched her bleeding with a cruel, distant interest for a moment before disappearing back inside with a swish of the carriage's velvet curtains.

Out of all the horrors and changes that day had brought with it, that was somehow what Cas remembered most clearly: cruel, distant eyes that had so easily turned away from her suffering.

Which was one reason why, despite Rhea's insistence that they not concern themselves with politics, Cas could not stop wondering or worrying about why Varen was sending soldiers into Oblivion.

Was he searching for more power within that horrible place?

What cruel things did he plan to do with that power?

Almost as if she was reading Cas's mind, Asra suddenly asked: "How did the mission go last night?"

"Well enough. We nearly have all the proof we need for Lord Merric, and then the payout should be excellent." The half-lie tasted sour in Cas's mouth, but she managed to offer Asra a reassuring smile in spite of this.

"Good. Our stores are getting low, Nessa's told me."

"It's because of Zev. He eats like every meal is going to be his last."

Asra chuckled.

"But it's okay; soon we'll have enough coin for plenty of food *and* your medicine."

"Never mind that last part," Asra said, turning to stare out the window once more.

"I will mind it, thank you very much," Cas replied. "I have a plan to take care of it all, so don't worry."

"You and your *plans*," Asra tutted, fondly.

"Someone around here has to have them, don't they?"

"And here I thought Rhea had become the undisputed brains of our operations in my absence."

"She has brains, but she lacks the drive sometimes," said Cas with a shrug.

"You mean she lacks the *impulsiveness* that you have. And the *recklessness*, and the—"

"Okay, okay. I get it. You can stop." The two shared a quiet laugh. Asra went back to humming her song from before, and Cas stayed with her for a few minutes longer, helping brush the tangles from the wiry gray strands of her hair and then gently twisting them into the loose braid that had always been Asra's signature look.

As Cas worked, her thoughts strayed to her latest *impulsive* decision; the stolen bracelet currently hidden in her room. After she left Asra, she would be paying a visit to an incredibly dangerous man to sell off that jewelry— another decision that her mentor would no doubt label as *reckless.*

Cas could have sold the bracelet at the market this morning—a simple exchange of silver jewelry for golden coins. And then she could have used those coins to buy the next month's worth of their food and supplies; that was what Asra would have wanted her to do.

But the man Cas planned to sell it to would have something more valuable than coins—he had medicine that the legal markets in Fallenbridge didn't sell.

Her fingers stilled against Asra's hair. Cas could sense

anxiety—that old, familiar companion of hers—unfurling in her stomach, threatening to attack. Her thoughts began to pull away and scatter. It always upset Asra to see her like that, so Cas quickly started to work out an escape route.

"I wish I could spend the rest of the morning with you, but I've got a few errands to run, I'm afraid." She fumbled for a lie to chase away the curious look Asra sent her. "A... bit more research I need to do regarding the mission for Lord Merric. There's a lead in the Foothills Village that I need to find and talk to." She picked up a flower that had fallen from its planter onto the windowsill, threaded it into Asra's braid, and then rose to her feet. "Are you okay, in the meantime? I can send Nessa in to sit with you; I'm sure she's just daydreaming around here somewhere."

"Don't worry about me." Asra reached to pat her arm. "I always feel better after breakfast with you. Something about your presence makes me feel like I've grown stronger."

"You always say that."

"Because it's the truth."

Then why can't I make you strong enough to get out of bed anymore? Cas wanted to ask. But instead, she smiled brightly again and said, "I'll be back to bring you lunch, then."

"Good." Asra wrapped a leathery hand around Cas's and gave it a gentle squeeze. "Good," she repeated, and then—either because she had already forgotten what Cas had just said or because she missed the days when she was in charge of everyone and everything—she added, "Now get on with your morning elsewhere, and let me rest for a bit."

"Of course, Mama," Cas agreed.

AFTER LEAVING ASRA, Cas swiftly headed for her own room and retrieved that silver bracelet, along with a Fire crystal, her dart gun, and a belt and sheath that held her favorite dagger. She headed for the front door just as quickly—as if she could outrun that anxiety that had started to reach for her in Asra's room—but by the time she reached the first floor, her steps were starting to feel a bit unsteady. Her body was disconnecting from her movements as her mind panicked over what she was walking toward. She had to pause. Close her eyes. Lean against the wall and lightly rap her knuckles against it, counting.

All the way to ten and then back down again.
You're fine. You're fine...

She *wasn't* fine. But she was stubborn, and she would be fine in a few minutes, and then she would carry on. A deep breath in and out. Then another one, and the beginning of another...

It ended up taking less than a few minutes for her mind to settle, mostly thanks to a hand that suddenly touched her arm. From beneath that touch came a tingle of warm magic. The warmth flooded through Cas like the heat from a just-right cup of tea, spreading all the way to the tips of her fingers and toes. She opened her eyes. She was unsurprised to find a young woman gazing back at her.

"Hello, Nessa."

"Hi." Nessa smiled. Her eyes were wide, set deep in her narrow face, and they were a bright shade of brown flecked with lighter bits of gold that made them look like they were shimmering even in the softest of lights, as if she were constantly on the verge of crying on someone's behalf. Which was fitting, in a way, because Nessa was Feather-kind.

The Feather-kind owed their powers to a lesser-spirit, not one of the Marr, so their magic was not particularly strong. Nessa was not a true healer, but she was capable of creating small waves of comfort that could temporarily alter a person into *believing* they had been healed.

She was also naturally gifted at creating medicines from herbs and other things, and at reading emotions and empathizing with them—though those things may or may not have been related to the feather-shaped mark on her palm.

Nessa wasn't alone; Silverfoot was with her. She was usually the fox's second choice of companions, which meant that Rhea was probably still asleep. And Zev was *definitely* still asleep; Cas could hear his snores, even though his room was not particularly close.

"Thank you," Cas told Nessa, pushing away from the wall and shaking off more of the tension that had started to build in her shoulders and back.

"Welcome," Nessa replied in her honey-sweet voice. She reached out her arms, and Silverfoot leapt into them. He hooked himself to her as Nessa folded her arms in front of her, and he hung lazily from his perch; his tail was long enough that it nearly touched the floor as he swished it back and forth.

"You were visiting with Asra?"

"Yes," Cas replied, reaching to pat the fox's head as he lifted it insistently toward her.

"She always wakes for you, it seems."

"Not *just* for me."

Nessa frowned briefly, as if part of her regretted bringing it up. "I only meant...Well, I was in there earlier, while you were gone. I couldn't get her to wake up. And I couldn't get her to wake up and eat last night, either. So I...I'm glad she still seems to respond to you, at least."

Cas mirrored her frown. Her thoughts threatened to start spinning away from her again, to scatter in an attempt to avoid dwelling on the painful images of Asra, but she managed to turn the corners of her mouth up a bit. "I'm glad, too."

She turned away before the frown could overtake her features again, and she continued toward the front door.

Nessa followed her. Cas was getting used to it, the way this young woman always wanted to be in the company of *somebody*. Making up for several years of loneliness, perhaps.

She hadn't been with their group very long—a little less than a year now. Her parents had fled to the Sundolian Empire some time ago, searching for a tolerance of magic that didn't exist in Kethra, while Nessa had stayed behind because she was, to use her own words, *stupidly in love with a stupid boy*. A boy who had promptly deserted her just weeks after her parents left.

She had managed on her own for some years afterwards, before deciding to head for that southern empire herself—at which point she made it all the way to the border realm of Bywilds, only to get sidetracked by a village overrun by hundreds of cases of the Fading Sickness. Many travelers would have steered clear of the suffering; Nessa simply saw an entire village that was in need of the comfort that her particular magic provided.

Most of the locals had been grateful for her help.

But it had only taken one suspicious, ungrateful person to report her. She had stepped out of the village's sick house one morning to find herself surrounded by the King-Emperor's Peace Keepers.

Laurent had spotted her while in the middle of a separate, unrelated mission on the outskirts of that border realm. And, in a move that was rather uncharacteristic of his normally aloof self, he'd decided to help her.

Their meeting was not by chance, Nessa had insisted. Laurent had rolled his eyes at the notion. But he also hadn't objected to her coming home with him, nor to Asra's eventual insistence that she stay on as a permanent part of their team.

Cas was glad the young Feather-kind had decided to stay with them, but there was no doubt that Nessa would have been safer in the south. The southern empire practiced the sort of divine-derived magic Nessa and Zev carried with reckless abandon—so much so that an odd haze supposedly hung in the skies over Sundolia. The people of that empire were unaware of it, but it was said that a foreigner could see *and* feel the difference in the air as soon as they approached the border.

The Wild In-Between along that border had been established to stop the dangerous overflow of the haze. That magical residue rarely crossed into Kethra proper, but it settled into the flora and fauna of the In-Between—in creatures such as that fox Nessa now held. It was also where most of the crystals that Cas occasionally used were harvested from.

If any of the King-Emperor's men discovered what Silverfoot was—what he was capable of—the creature would likely be put to death. Likewise, Nessa and Zev and anyone else with a mark, as well as anyone who made use of those harvested crystals or other magic-infused things, were never truly *safe* in this empire. People, animals, objects...it made little difference to the King-Emperor and his Peace Keepers. If it contained any trace of divine-given magic, the ruler of this empire wanted it either confiscated, destroyed, or enslaved.

"Thank you for sitting with Asra last night, by the way," Cas said as Nessa caught up to her.

"I wish I could have helped her more."

"You did what you could."

Nessa hugged her arms tightly against herself, unconvinced. "I tried *everything* last night to get her to wake up. And what's more, I don't think my magic was reaching her as well as it usually does. No matter what I did, she seemed...agitated. Afraid. Like she was having a nightmare she couldn't wake from."

"I'm going to Darkhand's," Cas informed her. "I'll bring back more of the Prism-kind medicine, and that should help."

"Let me go with you."

Cas didn't reply right away. They stepped outside, and she spotted Laurent sitting on the steps of the porch that wrapped around the house. He looked considerably healthier than he had when she'd seen him last; that elvish part of his blood at work, she supposed. And Nessa had likely used her magic to help him calm down and heal faster, too.

He offered a nod in their direction, but otherwise didn't glance up from the sprawling parchment in his hands. It looked like the same map of Oblivion he'd given her to study a few days ago. Cas inwardly shuddered at the thought of having to go back to that place. It would almost certainly have to be done, but...

Well, she could only focus on so many dark things at a time.

"I'm tired of being left behind on all these missions," Nessa insisted, still following her.

Cas didn't look in her direction; she was busy fixing the belt around her waist and securing her dagger against her back. But she could feel Nessa's insistent glaring.

"It's safer for you here," Cas finally said. "Right, Laurent?"

Laurent glanced at her without lifting his head. He didn't look pleased about being drawn into the conversation.

"Right?" Cas pressed.

He inhaled deeply through his nose.

"Tell her she's safer staying here."

"You're safer staying here," Laurent recited in a droll, unconvincing—and completely unhelpful—voice.

"And what about Cas?" Nessa asked. "Don't you care if *she's* safe?"

"I..."

"And you can't expect me to learn to keep myself safe if you never let me help, right?"

Cas bristled. She had a feeling that pouting look Nessa was giving Laurent would be his undoing. It was one of the few things that *could* undo him, it seemed.

He hesitated only a moment more before he looked at Cas, shrugged, and said, "She has a point."

Cas shook her head, tilted her face so that only Laurent could see it, and silently mouthed, *You are so weak.*

He arched an eyebrow before folding up the map and reaching for the sword and sheath at his feet. A cloth and a bottle of oil rested beside it; he must have been cleaning that blade before taking up his map-studying. "So when do we leave?"

"Does this mean you're going too?" Nessa practically bounced with the words.

"Obviously."

"I'd rather go alone," Cas tried one last time.

"And I'd rather stay here and plan some more, or nap, or do anything else, really," said Laurent, "but if you two end up in trouble, then I'm going to have to come after you anyway. Might as well save myself that potential extra effort."

Cas bit her lip, thinking of Rhea's words from last night. *If one of us is going to volunteer to run into a terrifying abyss of darkness and death, then it goes without saying that we all will.*

"Fine," she told them. "But I'm leaving now. I told Asra I'd be back in time for lunch."

"After you," Laurent said, before glancing back to Nessa with a dubious look. The Feather-kind was still bouncing excitedly beside him, looking entirely too enthusiastic about paying a visit to one of the Bloodstone Realm's most notorious criminals.

Cas started into the woods without looking back. As she listened to Laurent's stern voice trying to persuade Nessa to take this little adventure more seriously, a slight smile tugged at her lips. Some secret part of her was pleased to not be going alone, maybe.

But after last night, she still couldn't help thinking about all the different ways this adventure might go wrong.

CHAPTER 7

THE SOUTHERN MARKET DISTRICT OF FALLENBRIDGE WAS BUSY and bright and filled with more people than Cas could count.

It was the exact opposite of the sort of place one might expect the likes of Savian "Darkhand" to set up shop. And Cas suspected that this was *why* Darkhand had done as much—just to prove that he could. That he was untouchable, unafraid of the King-Emperor's Peace Keepers or anyone else who might want to drop in and pay him an unannounced visit.

His actual dwelling was on the other side of the Market Road, situated on the banks of the Lotheran River. The river flooded often—and violently—but Darkhand didn't seem to care about that either. He had enough illegal magic at his disposal to protect himself, after all.

Cas and Laurent walked side-by-side with Nessa trailing a short distance behind them, taking in the sights of the marketplace with the same boundless enthusiasm she'd displayed back at their house. She stopped often to talk to the more friendly merchants, and though she didn't actually *pay* for anything, by the time they were halfway through the marketplace, she had collected several beautiful flowers and an armful of fruit samples that she kept trying to entice Cas and Laurent into taking.

After her third attempt, Laurent finally gave in and accepted an offering of a handful of cova berries and a single, long-stemmed flower with swirled pink petals. Nessa drifted away again a moment later, heading down to walk closer to the river and wave to the occasional person on the opposite bank.

Laurent looked to Cas, and in a mildly exasperated tone, he asked, "Why does she act as if we've kept her locked in our house for the past year? She's been to a marketplace before."

"I think she's genuinely just enjoying herself. It's a nice day, a nice walk, and some people are just naturally...happy."

"How strange," he deadpanned, scattering the cova berries into a bush while Nessa wasn't looking.

"Is it?"

"Very."

"Oh, loosen up," Cas laughed. He smirked, and then proceeded to tuck the flower into the breast pocket of his coat, letting its pink petals stick out on full display— while looking properly grumpy about it, of course.

Cas rolled her eyes, still laughing softly to herself. But

her own words had triggered an avalanche of anxious thoughts.

Loosen up.

The man she had robbed last night had claimed his friends often told him to do the same thing, hadn't he?

That man...She had managed not to think about him since her breakfast with Asra, but now the images fired through her mind, one after another: The fog of Oblivion; the ice of his eyes; the strange sword he carried; her darts, clearly piercing his skin; his body, unconscious, until suddenly it wasn't...and on and on the memories and the questions went.

Her hand strayed to the pouch at her belt. Tracing the solid outline of the bracelet within it grounded her somewhat. Noticing the movement, Laurent tilted his head toward her once more.

"Are you all right?" he asked.

"Perfect." She thought of how pale and lifeless he had looked when she'd found him in Oblivion, and she couldn't help but wonder if the airs of that place were going to leave lasting effects. "Are you?" she asked.

He turned his eyes straight ahead once more. "Always."

"Good. It's all settled, then."

She saw a wry smile briefly pass over his face, but he left it at that. Cas liked that about their relationship— how uncomplicated it was. He kept his distance. He never pried. He would follow her into the dark, he would pull her back from the edge, but he wouldn't insist on having deep, prolonged conversations about any of it—not the way Rhea and Asra often did. And he didn't relentlessly tease her about it the way Zev did, either.

She loved all of her friends for different reasons, but the two beside her now were the two she most *needed* today. And she could finally admit to herself that she was glad they had come along. The one to her left kept her steady. The one trailing behind them had an optimism that was contagious, not to mention that calming magic she possessed...

A magic that Cas needed even more a moment later, when her eyes fell upon a house that had draped black cloth over its windows.

"Another dead," Laurent muttered.

The three of them slowed to a stop and watched for a moment. Two royal soldiers had just arrived in the house's yard. They were dismounting and striding toward the front door, while around the side of the house, a young boy was gathering up what looked like small stones and piling them into the upturned bottom of his too-long shirt. Those stones were likely painted, hastily scattered offerings to the Bone God—desperate attempts to appeal to that middle-god of Death and Destruction, to bargain for a comfortable afterlife for whatever soul had been lost. Such relics would not be looked upon kindly by those soldiers at the door.

As the boy pressed close to the house, hiding, a loud

sniffle escaped him. One of the soldiers craned his head toward the noise.

Cas held her breath.

But the front door opened a moment later, and the boy, and any sound he'd made, was quickly forgotten.

Cas wondered who he had lost—*a parent? a sibling?*—and her heart ached for him. He looked no older than she had been when her parents died.

Nessa was moving, suddenly, her steps determined and her hand clenching and unclenching while her lips moved with a silent spell. The air became unnaturally warm, just as it had when she'd interrupted Cas's panicky thoughts earlier.

But Laurent swiftly caught her arm and held her in place. "You can't," he said, his eyes still watching the soldiers as they disappeared into the house. "Not with the King-Emperor's men so close. That would only be asking for trouble."

"That little boy—"

"He'll be fine."

Nessa picked at the glove she'd put on to cover her mark. A rare flicker of irritation crossed her face, but she didn't disagree with Laurent and she didn't move from his side when he finally let go of her.

The boy felt their staring, and he froze, eyes wide with the fear of being caught. Then he sprinted out of sight, spilling stones and nearly tripping over them as he went.

"I wonder who died? And how many that makes for

this city as of late?" Nessa's voice was soft, but still strong with indignant fire. "Rhea mentioned that she overheard some travelers talking in Madam Rosa's place last night. They said the number lost to the spread of the Fade up in Stonefall was approaching a hundred just for this week... which means they've totaled nearly a thousand dead since Feast Day. Is that outbreak spreading south?"

Laurent shook his head. Between the king-emperor's meddling and the realms' increasing hostilities towards one another—and decreasing desire to work together on solving the empire's problems—there was no way of telling the truth of any of it.

Cas didn't even want to think about Nessa's questions. All she could think about was Asra adding another tally to it. "Let's just keep moving," she said, pulling her eyes away from the house and its black windows.

A SHORT TIME LATER, they reached the top of a steep, twisting path, one that led down to the point where the River Lotheran bent and started to weave its way away from the city.

On the banks of that rain-swollen river stood a small, unassuming house with a curling flame carved into its front door. Darkhand, like Zev, was one of the Fire-kind. That symbol on the door was the same one that they both carried on their palms—and it was yet another blatant disregard for the King-Emperor and his laws.

A man—a guard—milled about casually in the house's yard. Cas and her friends kept walking until they were out of the man's sight, coming to a stop behind a row of tall trees with tufts of red flowers on their tops.

"Wait here," Laurent told Nessa. The trees were thick enough to conceal her while still allowing a view of the house. A perfect hiding place, really. But the purse of Nessa's lips suggested she disagreed with the idea of *hiding*.

"For cover fire," Cas added with an encouraging smile, cutting off the protest she could tell was rising. She took the dart gun from her coat, along with a case of darts, and offered it to Nessa. "You've been practicing with Zev, right? He told me you were getting to be an even better shot than he is."

"You know he exaggerates," Nessa replied, though it was clear she was trying to hide her pleasure at the compliment. She took the pipe and loaded one of the feather-tipped darts, looking only briefly and mildly disgruntled about it before her usual calm expression returned.

They parted ways.

Nessa moved more fully into the trees, quietly weaving her way to a point that would allow her to both see and shoot if need be.

Cas and Laurent did not look back as they started down the steep path, for fear of giving Nessa away. As they approached the man in the yard, a glint of sun against steel revealed a small knife in his hand. He tossed it casually back and forth as they approached him.

"I have an appointment with Darkhand," Cas informed him.

She had no such thing, of course, but a large part of surviving and thriving in her line of work was acting as though she belonged in places that she most definitely did *not*.

The man eyed her up and down, still tossing that knife for a long moment before he finally said: "Very well, then."

They cautiously started forward, but stopped as the man snatched the knife in mid-toss and lifted it toward Laurent.

"But only one customer at a time, I'm afraid. The lady can go first, since she has an... *appointment*." He eyed her up and down once more, only with far less discretion this time. His mouth parted, his tongue slipping out and running along his bottom lip.

Gross.

She had to try very hard to resist the urge to stomp her boot into whatever sorry-looking bits he carried between his legs.

"We're a package deal," Laurent told the man as he stepped between him and Cas, blocking the cretin's view of her.

The man opened his mouth to reply, but Laurent unsheathed the sword at his hip and pressed it to the guard's throat.

"I don't make the rules." The man kept his tone casual, but his eyes no longer drifted anywhere near Cas, and they widened a little more every time they lowered toward the sword at his throat. "Master Darkhand makes 'em."

Two more men appeared from the side yard, followed by two women. They all had weapons—an assortment of blades and bows—lifted, aimed, and ready to strike.

Laurent did not flinch, nor did he lower his own sword from the man's neck.

Cas reached for his arm and lowered it herself. "It's fine," she told him.

"She'll be fine," the man agreed, his words edging toward mocking now that he had numbers in his favor. "Master Darkhand knows how to treat pretty ladies."

A muscle worked in Laurent's jaw. But he pulled his sword away from the man, inch by ever slowing inch, and sheathed it.

And then he slammed his fist into the man's stomach.

The man doubled over and hit his knees, wheezing for breath. The two women laughed, as did one of the men who had appeared with them. The other man looked as if he was considering retaliating, but a closer look at Laurent—at his pointed ears, his fair skin, and oddly-shining, silver-green colored eyes—made the man hesitate.

Cas knew that Laurent's mother had been human. But he looked more elvish—and like one of the elves of the Moreth Realm, at that. And judging by the hesitating man's expression, he had heard plenty of the stories about the sort of elven warriors that came from the harsh, desert parts of that realm.

Laurent walked over and leaned against a nearby tree. Nobody followed him.

"Hurry up," he told Cas.

Cas took a deep breath, trying to dredge up something like bravery from deep in her chest. She had gotten used to the idea of her friends coming along with her, and now she was not looking forward to meeting with Darkhand alone—particularly since their last private meeting had ended rather...well, *violently*.

Darkhand had been born from violence, in a way; his nickname referred to his right hand, which had been disfigured and permanently charred black by divine Fire magic. There were several legends swirling around regarding where those burns had come from, but the most common one began with a freak accident—a newly constructed bridge had collapsed into a canyon, dragging dozens of people down with it. His brother and sister had both perished in that accident. Days later, his parents had ended themselves in a blaze of their magic's own making. The flames that had engulfed them and their home *should* have engulfed their only remaining child as well.

But they hadn't.

Because Darkhand's own magical abilities, many of the stories claimed, had chosen that moment to emerge like never before; with only a flick of his wrist he had parted the fires closing in on him, allowing him to escape with nothing more than a few severe burns.

His history twisted a little too closely to Cas's for her liking—parents mad with sickness and grief, turning to violence to try and prematurely end their suffering. She had escaped her house's volatile end, but not without gaining a few scars in the process, same as Darkhand had. So she knew better than most what it was like to carry the weight of such things around.

But his tragic backstory did not excuse the fact that he was a complete and utter bastard.

Her skin began to crawl the second she stepped into the house. It always did, no matter how hard she tried to steel herself against this place.

Darkhand was bent over a table in one corner of the front room, in the middle of a conversation with a stringy-haired woman with nervous eyes. As soon as he caught sight of Cas, he held up a finger to silence the nervous woman.

"Casia." Even from the other side of the dimly lit room, she could see the flash of his crooked smile. "To what do I owe the pleasure?"

He stepped closer, moving into a brighter patch of the fireplace's light. The same divine flames that had once wrapped his hand and left it blackened had also kissed his face, leaving a less gruesome, but still obvious, path of destruction over the right side of it. It didn't completely ruin the skin; it simply made parts of it shine in an odd way when the light hit them just so.

Cas wasted no time with pleasantries. "I've brought you something I think you might like."

"Is that so?"

She threw a wary glance around the room.

"Well don't be shy about it," drawled Darkhand. "I have other things to do, you know."

She took the bracelet from the pouch on her belt and held it out to him.

He plucked it quickly yet gingerly from her grasp, in a way that made her think of a rook bird that had just spotted something shiny. He eyed her with interest for a moment, and then carried the shiny thing closer to the fireplace to better study it. The flames in that fireplace grew bigger and brighter with only a casual wave of his hand.

Cas tensed, sensing movement at the edges of the room. Too much movement. Even with the more-brightly blazing fire it was still too dark to see clearly, but she counted at least five other people lurking in the shadows.

She clenched her fingers into fists, trying to keep them still. They wanted to tap in the familiar rhythm that she often used to soothe herself, but she wouldn't allow it just then, wouldn't let anyone in this room see the evidence of the anxiety tearing its way through her insides.

She could—she *would*—be fearless for Asra's sake.

"It's a nice piece," Darkhand eventually concluded, beckoning one of the figures from the shadows and tossing him the bracelet. Cas nearly allowed herself to exhale her relief, until he added, "But you still owe from last month, don't forget. So this hardly makes us all squared up, does it?"

"I know it doesn't cover everything, but—"

"But you're here to ask for more." He settled into one of the chairs in front of the fireplace, balanced an ankle across his knee, leaned back, and rested his chin on his hand. He motioned for her to sit in the chair opposite him.

She did, stiffly, on the very edge of the chair's cushion, and while making certain she was well-aware of the exact location of the dagger against her back and the Fire crystal in her pocket.

"Because that *is* why you're here, is it not?" Darkhand asked. "I'm guessing it's not because you missed my handsome face."

"I..."

"Let's hear your sob story."

She cleared her throat. "You already know the story, Savian. Asra needs more of the Prism-kind flowers that only exist deep in the In-Between, and you know I don't have the means to go there and harvest them myself. It's suicide for someone like me—or even *you*—to try and brave the deeper parts of those lands."

The only people who *could* spend the prolonged amount of time it took to harvest magic-infused plants, or crystals—or anything else from the In-Between—were the ones who had made a profession out of doing that sort of thing. People who had the proper, expensive equipment, and who had been training for years to deal with the various unstable energies of that area.

"But you have contacts who frequently bring you spoils from that place," Cas continued. "I know you do."

"Yes. But it would be bad business for me to keep *giving* you any of those spoils for next to nothing, considering I also have to pay those expensive suppliers of mine."

"I have more payment coming, a lot more, I—"

"That's what you said last month." He sighed, accepted a steaming mug of something from the woman he'd been speaking with earlier, and took a long sip before turning his attention back to Cas. "Not landing many lucrative jobs as of late, I'm guessing? The infamous *Greythorne* is losing her touch."

"No, I'm not," she snapped.

"But speaking of touch..." He placed the mug on the table beside him and leaned forward a bit, putting both of his boots squarely back on the floor and resting his elbows on his knees. His shadow stretched long and tall against the back wall while his eyes roved over her. "...I am, of course, always open to *alternative* methods of payment."

She scowled. "That would be overpaying what I owe, and I'm afraid I don't do that. *Bad business*, you know."

"You honestly think you're worth more than the enormous sum you owe me?"

"Yes. And I assure you that you can't afford what I'm actually *worth*."

"Perhaps not." He chuckled darkly, settling back in the chair once more. "But I bet we could make a deal of some sort if we really tried."

"Or perhaps we could skip all this foreplay and I'll just go straight to slitting your throat," she said with a saccharine smile. "Since we both know that's eventually how it's going to end between us, right?"

He laughed. "Not likely, my love. At least, not without getting a few cuts of your own in return."

She didn't take her eyes off Darkhand, but she could see movement in the corner of her vision again. Several more people seemed to have joined the original five she'd counted.

She had been a fool to agree to come in here alone.

"And my men are known for cutting deeply. Without restraint." Darkhand was no longer laughing. His lips were drawn in a tight line, making the waxy, disfigured skin along them shine all the more prominently in the firelight.

"Give me one more week to settle these debts, and it will be worth your while." She tried to make her voice sound more like a command and less like a plea. Judging by the smirk that twisted that scarred corner of his mouth, she didn't quite manage it.

He rose to his feet.

Her hand slid to the dagger at her back.

"I wouldn't touch that if I were you."

She froze.

He withdrew his own weapon, a short sword with a

blade that pulsed to a fiery red when he gripped the hilt, and he fixed her with a threatening look. "So," he mused, "what am I going to do with you, Greythorne?"

Her hand inched again toward her knife.

His blade moved faster. The tip of it pressed into her chest, just above her heart. "Behave," he ordered. "Let's not have a repeat of the last time you came here."

Last time she had carved a new wound on the left side of his face to match the scars on the right. It looked to have mostly healed already. It wasn't that deep, but she had paid for it dearly all the same, as he had cut her off completely—refused to even *see* her for months, much less do business with her.

He had only recently offered her a chance at a truce; a calling card of his had found its way into her room while she slept last week. She had been disturbed by it at first —*how had it been delivered without her noticing?*—but by the time the Fire magic that laced that calling card had caused it to incinerate itself in her hands, she had already made up her mind to pay this bastard another visit.

Because the months that had passed between that last scuffle of theirs had been brutal for Asra; without the medicine to abate her sickness, she had declined more steeply and swiftly than ever before. Cas felt responsible for that. If she hadn't lost her temper with Darkhand the last time she'd dealt with him, if she had just—

No.

She wouldn't think about that now.

She just desperately needed *this* visit to go productively.

So for the moment, she stood perfectly still. Weighed her options. Darkhand's blade tapped and moved across her chest, lazily snagging and pulling at the cloth of her tunic but not quite tearing it. Sweat beaded her skin. She wasn't sure if it was the blade's Fire magic or her own anxiety causing the sweaty flush.

Finally, he stilled the blade and lifted his eyes to someone who stood behind her. Cas didn't dare look away to see who it was. She just watched as he gave that person a curt nod.

Then came the sound of boots walking away, and a minute later, a man came to Darkhand's side with a small leather bag in his hand. Cas knew what it was the second Darkhand took it and undid the twine securing it; she could smell the bitter, cloying scent of the Prism flowers from a mile away.

"You have some," she said, breathlessly.

"Of course I have some. Because I'm good at my job— unlike you, apparently."

Cas scowled but held her tongue.

"Anyway, that *was* a pretty little bracelet you brought. And I'm feeling rather generous today, so I'd be willing to give you this entire bag..."

She narrowed her eyes suspiciously.

"All you have to do is beg a little."

"I am not *begging* you for anything."

He shrugged. "Have it your way then. I don't actually

have a *need* for these flowers, personally. So perhaps I could take a loss, just this once..." He lifted his hand and twisted his fingers. A whisper of Fire-kind language passed through his lips, and the flames in the hearth jumped even higher at his command. They burned so bright that Cas's eyes watered.

Darkhand took a few steps toward the fire, tossing the bag of those precious flowers up and down as he went.

"Wait." Cas was on her feet, suddenly, and across the room in the next instant. "Don't...don't destroy them. Please."

"You finally said *please*. Good job." He turned back to her, cocked his head to the side and pointed to the rough wooden floor. "But now I want you to practice those manners while on your knees."

She bristled. She would never beg for *herself*. Not even for her own life.

But it wasn't her own life she was worried about.

And the man standing before her knew it.

With a mocking flourish of her arms, she dropped into a little bow, and then fell to one knee. Then to both knees. Her hands balled into fists that shook from the effort of not slamming a punch into Darkhand's stomach, but she managed to brace them against the floor.

"You look beautiful from this angle." He knelt and cupped her cheek for a moment before grabbing a fistful of her hair and jerking her face up to look at him.

"And you still look like a bastard from my angle." Her smile was more of a baring of teeth.

He let go of her and straightened to his full height once more. The room went very still for a short moment.

Then came a flash of movement, and his blade was against her bottom lip. It edged higher, the tip of it wedging between her teeth, parting that vicious smile she'd been giving him. The scrape of its edges and the cold, metallic taste of it on her tongue made her shudder.

"That mouth of yours is sorely testing my patience today," he muttered. "It seems it needs something to *occupy* it with."

A dark chorus of snickers and whispers sounded from all around the room.

She couldn't respond, as he pressed the sword deeper into her mouth. It would take nothing at all for that blade to burn and cut a path down her throat. But he wouldn't do that.

Would he?

Their history was messy, but long, and their few physical scuffles had never resulted in anything more than minor burns and scrapes. But still—

The sound of the back door creaking open caused Darkhand to whip the sword toward the noise, cutting a path out of Cas's mouth and across her cheek as it went. The blade flared red, and a singeing pain quickly overtook the sting of the cuts the blade had left behind. She bit down a cry and swallowed the bile that rose up as the scent of her own burning flesh filled the air.

Darkhand kept his sword angled at Cas's face as he glared in the direction of the door—and the woman who had just entered through it. The woman said something in what sounded like Fire-kind language. Darkhand responded with a short, clipped sentence in the same language, and the woman hurriedly closed the door, locked it, and disappeared down a hallway to the right.

Darkhand then turned back to the man that had brought him the Prism flowers.

This man, Cas noticed, had a mark on his wrist.

After a hastily whispered spell, that mark began to glow, and its shape became more obvious: *Air*. The strongest of those marked by the lesser-spirit of Air could transport more than just images and messages—they could create portals that could physically transport entire objects, even *people*, to distant destinations.

And this man was apparently among those strongest, because within moments he and his spells had conjured up one of those portals—it rose up from the worn, wooden floors like a geyser of pale green steam and smoke, eventually solidifying into a glowing, vaguely door-shaped gateway.

Blood dripped from Cas's mouth and from the crooked, burned path that had been cut along her cheek. She couldn't stop the pained, shuddering whimper that escaped her when she attempted to open her mouth wider, to work the tightness from her jaw.

Darkhand looked back at her. His distracted expression turned briefly smug. "Well, at least we're somewhat even after that nasty little cut you left me with last time, hm?"

She pushed back onto the balls of her feet. Her eyes fell on the small bag still clenched in his hand. Then they lifted slowly to his face, to his eyes that were already back to darting around the room, and to his brow that was creased with a concern she had rarely seen from him.

He was distracted again.

She was outnumbered.

But Darkhand was *distracted,* and she wasn't going to let him disappear through that portal with the bag of valuable flowers in his hand.

As soon as he moved away from her to start giving more orders, Cas reached for her dagger and leapt to her feet. The motion was fluid and lightning quick. She came within *inches* of introducing that trusty knife of hers to his throat—

Darkhand twisted out of the knife's path at the last second and slammed a knee toward her stomach. Cas spun away, and he struck the bone of her hip instead, causing a jarring pain that slowed her down, but it didn't stop her. She could sense others coming to Darkhand's aid; she knew she likely only had one more shot at hitting him before they reached her.

She flung herself at his throat once more. The recklessness of the assault seemed to catch him off guard. He knocked her swiping attack away with a well-timed punch to her forearm, but it left him unable to side-step her other swinging fist. She slammed it in just beneath his ribcage. He doubled over, and she threw her weight against him, sending him toppling backwards. They crashed against the wall, and she braced her boot against it, giving her the strength she needed to pin him beneath her.

He still held tightly to the bag of precious flowers, but his arm was outstretched and vulnerable beside him.

Her dagger came down hard and fast, stabbing into his wrist.

His arm spasmed with pain, blood spraying them both as he jerked his wrist away from her.

The bag dropped.

She snatched it and rolled away from him. She shoved the bag into the pouch on her belt and managed to secure it just before two of Darkhand's minions got their hands on her and twisted her arms painfully behind her back.

Darkhand rose to his feet, clutching his bleeding wrist.

He stepped slowly toward her in spite of the frantic pace of the rest of the room. Two people had already disappeared through the Air-kind portal, and others were bracing themselves to follow. Darkhand appeared to have forgotten that portal existed at all. He had eyes only for Cas. He stopped directly in front of her, and once again he cupped her chin and lifted her gaze to his. The blood from his wrist dripped down, mixing with hers.

"You will pay very dearly for this," he said, his voice low.

She fought the urge to close her eyes as he gripped her more tightly, his just barely contained aggression making his fingers shake against her skin.

A chorus of voices floated in from the yard.

His hand drifted back down to his side. "Let her go... for now." He didn't take his murderous gaze away from her as he spoke. "I don't want to rush her punishment. I want to make sure I can take the time to enjoy it."

The ones holding her arms obeyed, and then they swiftly joined the others in escaping. One after the other, they disappeared through the portal, until for a brief, terrifying moment she was alone with Darkhand. The fireplace behind him blazed brighter once more, and Cas felt a brief tinge of panic as she remembered the stories of his childhood home going up in flames.

He lifted a few fingers. Pressed the tips of them together. Whispered something...

And the fire went out.

Shades covered the windows, and so the only light in the room now came from the portal that awaited him.

"Until next time," he told her.

He was gone in an instant, and the portal collapsed seconds afterward, leaving her in darkness.

Cas wiped the blood from her lips. After several attempts, she managed a deep, somewhat normal breath. She almost smiled. There would be painful consequences for this later. But for now she was still alive, *and* she had the bag of magic-laced flowers.

And yet her elated feelings of victory were short-lived as the strangeness of their meeting settled over her.

Why had he run away?

It wasn't like him to run. *At all*. She was still trying to make sense of his actions, when all of a sudden someone started pounding on the front door. The thunderous voice that accompanied that pounding didn't sound familiar. Fear raked an icy hand down Cas's back and froze the air in her lungs.

Because in the end, she could think of only one thing that could make monsters like Darkhand run away.

Bigger monsters.

CHAPTER 8

CAS CREPT INTO THE DARKEST PART OF THE ROOM JUST AS THE front door flung open and two men entered, speaking the language of the King-Emperor. *Peace Keepers.*

Then came a third man.

One she *recognized*.

The man she had robbed last night stood in the doorway, silhouetted against the sunlight and looking every bit as large and intimidating as he had the evening prior.

She almost would have preferred dealing with Darkhand—at least he was an enemy she *knew*, an enemy she could make some sense of.

Cursing under her breath, she silently made her way along the edges of the room, feeling her way through the blackness until her fingers landed on a metal doorknob. The door creaked entirely too loudly as she opened it, but she slipped out and dashed away without looking back to see if anyone had heard her.

The sight that greeted her was somehow worse than the one she'd escaped; a dozen soldiers had overtaken the front yard. Two of them held Nessa captive, and the rest were standing between Nessa and a furious-looking Laurent. More soldiers were making their way down the hill. Too many more. The standoff was not going to end in Laurent's favor, regardless of how angry or powerful he might have been.

Cas hesitated, still out of sight of most of those soldiers.

She heard footsteps behind her, and then the voice of that man from the inn, sounding a bit too self-congratulatory for her liking. "Miss Azalea, wasn't it? And these, I'm assuming, are some of your partners-in-crime?"

She spun around, molding her face into an expressionless mask as she did. "I actually don't know these people at all."

"No? So you won't care if we bring them with us for a bit of questioning?"

"Not at all."

"Fair enough." He walked to her side, his movements unhurried. "But...just so you're aware, I would happily order them to be let go in exchange for *you* peacefully cooperating with your arrest."

Her heart fluttered, skipped several beats, and then crashed back into a steady but quick rhythm, all in the span of only seconds. "And what, precisely, am I being arrested for?"

"For theft against the crown, of course."

"Theft against... the crown?"

He briefly cut his eyes toward her, but otherwise kept his appraising gaze on the scene before them. Without another word or glance at her, he casually removed the glove covering his wrist, revealing the mark she hadn't been able to see last night. It was dark, the color of a fresh bruise, and it resembled a skull with shadows woven through it.

She had to hold in her gasp, and to dig her feet more firmly into the grass in order to keep herself from swaying on the spot. Because now she realized who he must be—and he was not just some random soldier she had flirted with in Madam Rosa's Tavern.

He was the *Death Speaker*. The right hand of the King-Emperor. And he was also something of a legend—one of the few Marr-kind that the former King-Emperor had not outright slaughtered, but only because the magic he commanded was so powerful. It was Bone-kind magic, a power gifted to a chosen few by the middle-god of Death and Destruction, Kerse.

"Damn it," she breathed, more realizations washing over her—including the understanding that the *questioning* her friends would be subjected to was very likely going to be with the King-Emperor himself.

She thought of the feather-shaped mark on Nessa's hand.

Nessa's magic was weak; it was unlikely that the King-Emperor would deem her life worth sparing. She would be considered just another blight that needed erasing, as her innate, supposedly *bad* magic outweighed any good she might bring to the empire and its ruler.

"My name is Elander Revenmar," said that man Cas had foolishly, regrettably robbed. "First Speaker for King-Emperor Varen de Solasen, and captain of the Peace Keeping regiment of his Grand Army."

"Pleasure to meet you."

In no way did he acknowledge her sarcastic tone. "And now that we've been properly introduced," he continued, "let's start again, shall we? We can even be civil about it, if you'd like. We only came here in search of you; your friends, as I said, are welcome to leave as long as you comply."

She no longer bothered with pretending she didn't know them. She even acted as though she was considering his offer for a moment. Then her eyes found Laurent's, and he gave the slightest of nods.

She understood the look on his face perfectly.

We go down fighting, no matter what.

"Well?" Elander pressed.

"I've given it a lot of careful thought," she replied.

"And?"

"And I've elected not to take you up on that offer, generous as it is."

That handsomely smug smile of his wilted a bit in the corners. "I had a feeling you would make this more difficult than it needed to be."

"You know me so well after such a short amount of time. I'm oddly flattered by that."

"Don't be." He sighed, removing the glove on his other hand and tucking both into a pocket of his coat. "Arrest them all," he ordered.

The men on either side of him rushed her. Cas dove underneath their reaching arms and sprinted toward Nessa, spinning to avoid a third man that attempted to grab her. She drew her dagger and went for the biggest of the two men holding Nessa. Her stabbing blade missed its mark, but it still came close enough that the man was forced to twist away, loosening his hold enough that Nessa was able to wrench one arm free.

With that free arm, Nessa slammed her elbow into the face of the bigger captor. The second man holding her tried to readjust his grip to make up for the loss, but Nessa was quicker; she twisted and slammed an upturned palm into his nose.

The man stumbled back, clutching his bleeding nose. Cas swiftly put a boot in his stomach and knocked him further off balance. As his back thumped against the ground, she grabbed the sword still sheathed at his hip and yanked it free, handing it to Nessa.

Nessa hated battles of any sort, physical or otherwise —but she was also naturally good with a blade. *Terrifyingly* good. The surprise on people's faces when they realized they were being outmatched by such a dainty-looking little thing was always entertaining to Cas, and this time was no different; she paused just long enough to listen for, and laugh at, the shocked curses of the two men Nessa turned on first.

And then Cas was spinning away again, seeking a new target for her own, smaller blade. She continued to duck and cut her way through the crowd that had converged on them. Her dagger slashed and stabbed without ceasing, and soon, it all turned into a blur of bodies and blood amongst the growing heat of the early afternoon sun.

Suddenly, Laurent called out a warning, and Cas turned to spot a woman braced against the hillside, drawing an arrow and pointing it at her.

The *twang* of the released arrow sounded surprisingly loud amongst the chaos. Cas hit the ground just as it soared past. A soldier moved to take advantage of her awkward landing against the dirt, but she rolled, rose into a crouch, and sank her blade deep into his calf. His yowls of pain were deafening. Cas made quick work of yanking the dagger free and half-stumbling, half-crawling away from the terrible noise.

As she fought her way back upright and regained her balance, she caught sight of Laurent again. Two men lay unconscious at his feet, and he held two swords in his hand. One was his own. The second was stolen. Their eyes briefly met, and he offered that stolen one to Cas. She sprinted to his side and took it, while Nessa danced away from the latest soldier she'd put on the ground and joined them as well.

The three of them stood, back-to-back, as the remaining Peace Keepers closed in around them.

But none of those approaching soldiers attacked,

because in the next moment, the Death Speaker himself stepped forward, parting the flock of them.

His eyes narrowed on Cas.

"Enough of this." His tone was no longer the casual, darkly amused one that she had started to expect from him.

She let her gaze sweep quickly over the number of soldiers who stood behind and on either side of him, their bodies tense and ready to converge at the most subtle order. It felt like they had multiplied—three more of them arriving for every one that she and her friends had disarmed and knocked to the ground.

Cas found herself actually considering the Speaker's offer from earlier.

As if she could sense this, Nessa darted in front of Cas before she could agree to anything. Her sword lifted, only shaking slightly, toward that speaker for the King-Emperor. Sunlight bounced off the blade, illuminating drops of blood that had congealed on the metal.

The Speaker calmly reached a hand toward Nessa. The mark on it glowed faintly.

Nessa's body went instantly rigid. The air shivered. The sky seemed to darken, and Nessa dropped to her knees, clutching her head. A terrible, guttural sound forced its way through her lips.

"What are you doing to her?" Cas demanded as both she and Laurent rushed to her side. Laurent lifted Nessa's suddenly limp body, cradling her lolling head against his chest, while Cas's livid gaze lifted toward the Speaker.

His eyes were strange-looking; they seemed to have darkened from blue to grey along with the sky. She shouted her question again—louder this time—and he blinked and slid that odd gaze in her direction once more.

He didn't answer her.

Cas leapt to her feet and charged him, blade drawn. He leapt back and away as she swung forward. He almost floated, with a grace that seemed inhuman. He kept his glare locked on her. He still didn't answer her question— but an instant later, his magic rushed over her instead of Nessa. The power of it shattered through Cas and gripped at her insides, making her feel as if she was freezing to death from the inside out.

That brutal chill soon washed through her entire body. She looked for that Ice-kind sword he'd used against her the other night. But though he had a blade against his hip, it didn't appear to be the same one.

This magic washing over her was a different sort of power, she realized.

It was Death magic.

His *innate* magic.

And soon it was not simply *cold* that she felt. It was...it was the absence of all the heat she had ever known. Seconds passed in that deathly cold, and she became convinced that she would never feel warmth again. That her lungs were filling with ice, and then with fire and ash, as the sky turned an even darker shade than before.

She couldn't *breathe.*

But she could still move.

So she stubbornly charged for him again.

Her hand swiped for his face, for those strange, magic-darkened eyes; she wanted to claw them out. To dig in and twist and do whatever was necessary to throw off his concentration and break his spell.

Her fingertips found skin, and she sank them in. Seconds later, a strange sound—like a bowstring snapping—vibrated through her, and then a current of energy and light exploded between them.

She stumbled back, still wheezing for breath. The cold gripping her began to thaw. The sky lightened. The sun returned, seemingly brighter than before.

And the Death Speaker was staring at Cas, shocked, as if she herself were the sun and he had never laid eyes on it until that very moment. "How did you do that?" His voice was a whisper that only the two of them could hear.

"What *was* that?" Nessa's shaking voice was much louder, but it sounded distant and faraway.

Cas didn't reply to either of them, because she didn't know the answer to either question.

The Speaker was still staring at her, still looking just as shocked as she felt. The mark on his hand was still glowing.

Finally, he drew his hand back and cleared his throat. He appeared to be searching for words, for the composure and commanding voice that her touch had apparently stolen from him. In the end, he simply glared at her.

She felt as if she could still sense the fingers of his magic hovering over her, like a light but potentially deadly frost in late spring. She was terrified of that power fully overtaking her again. She wanted to run. But she didn't. She kept herself positioned between him and Nessa, and she glared right back at him.

"Let them go," Cas said, quietly, "and I'll go with you. That was the deal, wasn't it?"

"They attacked my men. That deal is void, I'm afraid,"

"We *defended* ourselves!" snapped Nessa, her voice still trembling a bit with terror.

"And we didn't *kill* any of those men," Laurent added, giving one of the bodies on the ground a swift kick that elicited a painful moan.

"They're right," Cas insisted. "Your soldiers started it, not us."

He absently ran a hand over the strong line of his jaw, fingers tracing the place where her hand had touched his skin. Dark curiosity burned in his eyes, mingling with the beginnings of what might have been resolve.

"Give me one last minute to talk to them," Cas implored, "and then I'll go with you. No more fighting. No more tricks—I swear it." As a show of good faith, she tossed her stolen sword to the ground at his feet.

He stared at it, a muscle working in that strong jaw of his. "One minute," he finally said. "If you try anything foolish, I swear to the fifteen middle-gods and goddesses that it will not end well for you."

Cas swiftly turned, grabbed Nessa's sleeve, and pulled her as far away from their enemies as she dared.

"We're not leaving without you," Nessa said, almost immediately.

"Yes, you are," Cas hissed back.

"Casia—" Laurent began, but she stopped him with a look. A look that reminded him that they were vastly outnumbered, and that there was no telling what other terrifying kinds of magic the right-hand man to the King-Emperor might possess. It was clear now: This was not a fight they could win. If two out of three of them could get away—and take that medicine to Asra as they went—then this would be, by most accounts, a victory.

"You need to go before these bastards change their mind," she told Laurent, and then took a deep breath and smiled before turning to meet Nessa's eyes, which shimmered with unshed tears. "Don't worry about me," she insisted. "But don't wait up for me tonight, either. Just focus on getting *this* back to our place." She deftly pulled the bag of flower petals from her pouch and shoved it into Nessa's grasp. "And work your magic with these ingredients, okay? Asra needs you more than I do right now."

She sensed movement behind her. Cas quickly dropped to one knee and pretended to adjust the sheath at her boot, taking the opportunity to slip the second object she'd taken out of her bag—a Fire crystal—into a new hiding place inside of her boot.

I'll get away, she mouthed to her friends as she stood and took a step back from them.

Laurent's reply was equally silent—*we're coming after you if you don't.*

With that, he took Nessa's arm and pulled her towards safety.

Cas watched them disappear into the distance, finally exhaling a slow breath once she felt they were out of harm's way. A moment later, a hand closed on the sleeve of her coat and spun her around. She found herself in the grip of a burly man with a shallow, bleeding cut across his stubbled chin. Was that blood the work of her own blade? She'd lost track of who she'd struck, but this man was certainly squeezing her arm as if he had a personal vendetta against her.

"Shall we get the shackles, Captain?" asked a second soldier to her right—a pretty, red-haired woman who couldn't have been much older than Cas herself.

Captain Elander considered it for a moment, his head tilting toward Cas. "Do I need to restrain you further, or are you going to come along with us now?"

"I told you I would go peacefully, didn't I?" She shrugged out of the bleeding soldier's grip with more force than she'd meant to, and then automatically braced herself for the captain's retaliation.

But he just arched an eyebrow at her violent motion. Then he breathed in a deep, resolved breath, and gave her a little shove. "Walk," he ordered.

She walked. Begrudgingly, but without stopping, while her mind raced with questions.

Once they reached the top of the hill that overlooked the Market Road, she couldn't help but blurt one of those questions out. "What exactly is the punishment for *theft against the crown?*"

"You'll find out soon enough, won't you?"

She rolled her eyes at this non-answer—and the assumption it made.

He really thinks he's powerful enough to keep me from getting away.

Then again, maybe he was.

Her gaze drifted toward his hand before she could help herself. Gloves covered his mark once more. He apparently noticed her staring, because a slight smirk twisted his lips.

She scowled and fixed her eyes straight ahead.

They had walked less than a half-mile when the sound of shouting reached them. It was a group of towns-folk closing in behind them, yelling protests and wielding an assortment of objects—from shovels to sticks—as makeshift weapons. A few of them also had *real* weapons.

Cas thought of that crying boy they'd seen on their way to Darkhand's house. Was this group related to them?

How had the Peace Keepers treated that family and the deceased?

"Deal with them," the captain ordered.

Fear for the townspeople skipped through Cas at the cold command, but she couldn't focus on it for very long —not once she realized that the majority of the soldiers surrounding her had moved away to follow their captain's command.

The odds of her being able to escape were suddenly much greater, and far too tempting to resist.

"Keep moving," the captain growled at her.

She did. For the moment, at least. She waited until most of the soldiers were properly tangled up in their quarrel with the townspeople, while she covertly searched for something she could use. She spotted a tree with a thick, supple looking branch hanging at precisely the right height...

As they passed, she veered sharply toward it.

Captain Elander followed immediately, right on her heels.

Perfect.

She slammed her hands into the tree branch as she ran through it, and then she let it go and ducked out of the way. It snapped back with violent force. With a hasty glance over her shoulder, she saw the captain avoid the strike—but he stumbled in his attempt to do so, which gave her enough for a head start.

And that was all she needed.

She ran for the river. She was a strong swimmer, and most of the soldiers still close by wore far more armor than she did. They would sink like rocks in the muddy, swift-flowing waters of the Lotheran. The captain was as lightly dressed as herself, but he hesitated behind her, still looking slightly off-balance and torn between chasing her down and dealing with the townsfolk situation that sounded as if it was escalating.

She was actually going to get away.

Just as the thought crossed her mind, she caught sight of him breaking into a run.

A run toward *her*, who he had apparently deemed a greater threat than the civil unrest behind him. And within seconds, he was somehow closing in on her, growing closer, *closer*...and then he dove. His arm caught her around the waist and knocked her off her feet. They fell together and rolled down a short but steep hill, and as they tumbled to a stop, he managed to grab her arms and twist them behind her back while he straddled her, using his weight to keep her pinned on her stomach.

He wasn't using magic.

He wasn't drawing any weapons.

He was just...sitting on her.

Well, this is embarrassing.

"*Really* now," she muttered, after spitting out a mouthful of dust and grass, "is this position befitting of a supposed *captain* of the King-Emperor's army?"

He ignored her question, reaching for the pair of shackles that one of his men jogged down to give him. "I didn't particularly want to use these, for the record."

With a quick snap of his hand, a shackle closed around one of her wrists, and then he wrestled the other wrist close enough to allow the second cuff to snap on just as effortlessly. She struggled against their impossibly quick and secure hold, but that only made the cuffs tighten on her. They were clearly enhanced by some sort of magic.

"Because they hurt like hell, don't they?" he continued. "They're Mountain-kind blessed, and that divine strength of the Mountain-kind is unmatched. Trying to break free is pointless."

She didn't reply, focused as she was on not giving him the satisfaction of hearing her cry out in pain as the cuffs tightened again.

"So yes, *sorry*," he continued, not sounding particularly sorry at all, "but no one escapes me a second time, I'm afraid. Most don't escape the first time, so give yourself some credit for that stunt you pulled last night."

I've gotten away from you twice, already, she thought, smugly. But he apparently didn't realize that she was the same woman he had faced off with in Oblivion—thanks to the magic of the Mimic crystal that was still disguising her Fade-marked qualities—and she wasn't stupid enough to reveal her true identity to him a second time, however badly she wanted to rub that first escape in his face.

"I give myself credit for a lot more than that." She twisted her head as far toward him as she could manage and gave him a nasty smile.

He responded by tapping one of the cuffs, making it tighten and send another bout of pain jolting up her forearm. The pain made her arm spasm, and the movement caused *more* pain as it just made the cuffs tighten all over again. A vicious cycle, really.

"It would hurt less if you'd be still," he informed her.

She hissed out a mostly unintelligible string of curses.

He laughed.

"Take these *off*, or else I swear I will—"

"You'll do what?" Those bright blue eyes danced with dark amusement once more as he got to his feet. "You'll try seducing me again? Please don't; it was painful enough the first time around."

"You didn't seem like you were in pain when you were kissing me last night. In fact, I'm quite sure you were enjoying yourself."

"Well, I was slightly intoxicated and acting generous, now, wasn't I?"

"I am going to *stab* you," she huffed.

"And now I'm going to add *threats against the crown* to your arrest documents."

"Go ahead and add *assault against the crown*, too, as long as you're adding things." She rocked up into an awkward sitting position and aimed a swift kick at his shins.

"*Attempted* assault," he countered, leaping over the kick and then calmly reaching down to grab her arm and pull her up.

They glared at each other for a long moment after she made it to her feet and found her balance, the cuffs sending a fresh pulse of pain through her with every breath she took.

Finally, Cas exhaled a long, careful, slow huff of air, and she averted her eyes toward the ground. "Just...can you loosen them a bit? Make them stop doing the tightening thing? It kind of hurts."

He was still watching her closely, his expression now

caught somewhere between suspicion and that amusement from before. It was the exact same way he'd looked at her last night—right before she'd shot him.

And he hadn't learned his lesson last night, apparently.

"Are you done making my job difficult?" he asked.

Another flash of pain burned up her arms. She twisted her grimace into another clenched-teeth smile. "For now."

"And you're going to cooperate?"

"I'm all yours. You win. Just lead the way."

He moved cautiously behind her, reaching for the cuffs. She couldn't see what he was doing, but she could tell when he was done—the cuffs remained wrapped securely around her wrists, but the magic in them seemed to have been deactivated somehow. They tightened much less viciously with her movements, now.

"There's a caravan waiting for us just up the road," he told her. "Come on."

He started to walk. He didn't look back to see if she followed, but several of his soldiers had drifted closer, drawn in by the spectacle the two of them had made, and they all wore a similar expression. One that said *don't try anything funny.*

With a resolved sigh, Cas trudged her way back up the hill.

Elander was telling the truth about the group that was waiting for them, at least. They only had to walk for a few more minutes before they reached the edge of town, where the road curved sharply to the north. And just beyond that curve, dozens of soldiers were standing by. A carriage stood amongst them, drawn by two stunningly white horses. The carriage's sides were painted with golden designs that gleamed in the afternoon sun, and its swooping curtains were drawn back to reveal the plush benches inside. Elander walked to it and indicated for her to climb in.

Cas's eyebrows lifted. "You're letting me ride inside this thing?"

"Would you rather I made you walk? Or maybe you're going to insist on us tying you to the back of it and dragging you along like a true criminal?"

"If you don't believe I'm a true criminal, then why are you arresting me?"

His eyes narrowed.

She shrugged. "It's a good question, you have to admit."

"Because perhaps I still want to have that *chat* you owe me, and I am personally not in the mood to walk while we have it."

She swallowed hard. A quick count of the soldiers surrounding them told her that trying to run again would be suicide; she would have to come up with a better escape plan than that.

In the meantime, she was resolved not to show fear or hesitation.

She climbed into the carriage, steady even without the use of her hands, and she plopped down onto one of the benches. After a brief conversation with one of those other soldiers, Elander followed her in. He situated himself onto the bench opposite her. His long legs reached all the way across the aisle between them, occasionally brushing against her own several times after the carriage jerked into motion. Not on purpose, she didn't believe; there was simply no other place for them to go.

He was quiet for the first few minutes that they rolled and bumped along, his gaze staring out at the vast fields dotted with white and yellow flowers. Eventually, that gaze drifted to her. He studied her with the same powerful, curious look he'd fixed on her last night.

"What are you staring at now?" she demanded. "Are you still trying to figure out if I'm a local?"

"No. I told you last night that I knew you were lying about that."

The memory of how close he'd been when he'd called her out on that lie made her shiver all over again. She tried to suppress it. She dug her fingers into the velvety cushion beneath her. Squeezed. Forced herself to think about more important things than his voice so close to her ear, his lips against her neck...There were a *thousand* more important things she could have been thinking of just then. *At least.*

So why did her mind keep tracking back to the way his whispering had felt against her skin?

She continued to glare at him, as if he were somehow purposely, magically inserting these unwelcome thoughts into her mind.

He parted his lips several times to speak. But every time, he softly shook his head and thought better of whatever he'd been about to say.

Finally, he asked, "How did you stop my magic earlier?"

"I don't know."

"Don't lie to me."

"I didn't *do* anything," she said—and for once, it was the truth. She had only been trying to distract him. To knock him off course. She hadn't expected the explosion of energy between them. She hadn't anticipated his powerful magic just...*dissipating*. And she certainly hadn't done any of it on purpose.

He went back to staring out the window, but after a moment, he offered an offhanded comment: "Brave of you to let your friends go in exchange for your capture."

"Yes, well, bravery and desperation look very similar sometimes, don't they?"

"I suppose they do." His gaze slid back to her, unabashedly curious once more. "Your face is bleeding, by the way."

"I'm aware."

"And it looks as if it's been burned as well."

"That would be because it was burned, Captain Observation."

He pressed his lips together, and for a moment she thought he might give up on the conversation and turn back to staring at the outside world. But then he asked, "Why were you in that house by the river?"

130

She winced slightly at the memory of Darkhand's knife against her skin, her teeth, her lips, and that sweltering sting of his magic eating at her flesh. "Is this part of my official trial? Because if so, I want a few more witnesses." Her eyes darted through a small opening in the drawn curtains, to the men and women moving alongside the carriage. "And I want them to look less...*surly* than the group currently escorting us."

One of those men snorted—presumably at her droll comment, although he didn't look her direction.

Elander seemed less amused. "The man that fled from that house is wanted for a host of...*unsavory* things..." He trailed off, perhaps inviting her to tell him what she knew about those unsavory things.

She said nothing. She knew what sort of crimes Darkhand had committed. The trail of burned-out and otherwise defiled bodies and lives he'd left in his wake. She couldn't blame this *Captain Elander* for being curious about how she had gotten mixed up with a man like that, but it would be a bright day in all three of their world's shadowy hells before she gave him any more information about herself and her relationships than she had to.

"Well?"

"I have a better question," she countered. "If you know about his crimes, then why haven't you and the King-Emperor's so-called *Peace Keepers* done anything about him before now? Too busy rounding up all the petty thieves in the empire, eh?"

This shut him up rather quickly. He stared at her, his

brow furrowing in a way that made him appear down-right dangerous. The air felt colder, suddenly. She convinced herself that it was her imagination and not his magic. That it was only the sudden wind that had picked up in intensity outside, funneling in through the narrow opening in the curtains...

But perhaps she needed to shut up too—just in case that magic of his was close to making another appearance.

They sat in prickly silence for several minutes.

"It was hardly *petty* theft," he finally replied. "That bracelet you stole has a very specific, royal purpose. Whoever holds it holds the full authority of the King-Emperor himself while outside the palace. And it's embedded with Serpent-kind magic that can help persuade anyone who might disagree with that authority into behaving otherwise."

She made a face. "What a disgusting tool. Very befit-ting of a disgusting ruler and his royal soldiers—who I find myself having less respect for with every moment that passes."

"It isn't a power I use lightly," he said flatly, but other-wise ignored the blasphemous statement. "It is an extremely *dangerous* object, and now it is in the hands of one of the empire's most notorious criminals. So I will let you use your imagination about all the ways that could end poorly."

She wasn't thinking about that, yet. Later, maybe. But

right now all she could think was—*did Darkhand know how valuable that bracelet was?*

Most likely. Which meant that he *also* knew that it was worth more than enough to pay off a substantial amount of the debt she owed him. And that tiny bag of Prism-kind flowers... He'd clearly underpaid her. And he'd made her beg for it, no less.

That son of a bitch.

Elander lifted his boot and gave her knee a kick. Just a light one, but it startled her. She forgot her hands were bound, and she nearly lost her balance and toppled out of the seat. "Was that necessary?" she hissed, twisting her way back upright and leaning against the rough backing that separated her from the driver's quarters.

"You looked like you were plotting something."

"I usually am."

He huffed out an almost laugh at this, and that was the end of their conversation until they reached the royal city of Ciridan nearly an hour later. The carriage rocked to a brief stop outside the city gates, and while his soldiers spoke to the guards, Elander stretched and said, "The magistrate will decide what your punishment for the theft will be. But either way, I plan on keeping you in the holds until I figure out just precisely what sort of magic you used against *my* magic earlier."

"You best be quick with your research. I'll be gone before sunrise tomorrow."

"We'll see."

She smirked, but her insides were already twisting and sharpening to glass shards that made each breath more painful than the last. Because Asra would be expecting her for lunch *today*. And despite her bravado, there was one very large problem with Cas's plan to be gone by this time tomorrow: That Mimic-kind spell she'd used yesterday wasn't indefinite. In her experience, they lasted three days...at most.

Usually, they lasted a lot less.

Any moment now, it could dissipate. Elander would know she was the woman from Oblivion. He would know she was Fade-marked. The King-Emperor would find out, and the consequences of *that* would be far greater than any punishment for theft.

Somehow, she was going to have to find a way out of this mess before that happened.

CHAPTER 9

THE MIMIC SPELL HELD THROUGH THE NIGHT.

Cas hadn't slept, again. Instead, she had stayed up and continuously checked the strands of her hair to make certain they were still brown. She had counted the hours as best as she could guess them, marking each one by scratching a fingernail against the relatively soft stone walls, keeping track of the guard rotation outside of her prison as well.

Every four hours, it seemed, they switched off.

As another of those rotations approached, she pretended to be asleep. She listened for the new footsteps approaching, waited until she heard the old ones walk away, and then she cracked one eye open.

There was only one new guard for the moment.

Another was likely on the way—there had always been two, thus far—but in the meantime, she knew she could handle getting past a single, already-bored-looking sentinel. And Captain Elander hadn't been back to question her for several hours, so hopefully she wouldn't have to worry about that awful magic of his on her way out. The path she'd taken down to this dingy cell had been winding, and she might not be able to—

No. It didn't matter.

She had no choice but to try; she had been here long enough already. She couldn't wait around to find out what would happen once her disguise wore off.

She would escape this palace, however she had to do it, and then she would get as far away from it as possible. There would be an impressive bounty on her head afterwards, no doubt—but she could change her name. *Again.* She could talk the others into moving their hideout. *Again.* Asra might be too frail to move at this point, but Cas would carry her across the twelve realms herself if she had to. Her *and* her silly, noisy wind chimes.

But first...escape.

Cas kept her cheek pressed to the gritty ground and her body curled up in a sleeping position as she peeked at the guard's station once more. Still just one of them standing there. She studied him a bit closer. A loose belt hung around his waist, and thanks to a flicker of torchlight bouncing off metal, she could tell there were keys hanging from it. There was also a sword on his belt, a knife sheathed at his ankle, and the black gloves he wore had metal studs over the knuckles. Those studs looked like they would sink very painfully into her skin if he managed to strike her.

Meanwhile, Cas herself was...considerably less armed. Nessa had kept her dart gun. And the royal soldiers had stripped her of most of what she carried before tossing her into this prison. They had searched her with rough hands, ripped away her weapons, and attempted to take her dignity along with them.

But they hadn't taken her boots.

Which meant they hadn't taken the Fire-kind crystal, either.

Her gaze moved to the barred door of her cell. The spaces between those bars were exceptionally narrow. She could get a hand through—enough to grab the guard's arm or his belt, perhaps—but she wouldn't be able to twist her own arm to reach the lock on the cell door, even if she could manage to steal the guard's keys.

That settled it—she would have to pry the bars of her cell apart, somehow.

Her eyes lifted to the flickering torch above the guard's head. And as she stared into the flames, a plan started to unfold in her mind, twisting in between the anxious thoughts that were trying to overwhelm her.

She breathed in several deep lungfuls of musty, earthy air. Tapped her fingers against the cold floor to the count of ten, and back down to one, and she grounded herself in the feel of that solid floor.

Then she pushed up to her feet and went to work.

"Hey!" she called.

The guard cut his eyes toward her but didn't move.

She whistled for his attention.

He made an irritable noise deep in his throat, darted a quick glance around—perhaps hoping to spot some incoming backup—and then finally turned and clomped over to her, the keys on his belt jingling and his hand resting lightly on the pommel of his sword.

"What do you want, thief?"

"You all forgot to take this from me." She held up the Fire crystal.

He squinted at it in the low lighting, and then his eyes widened as he clearly realized what it was. "That's...you shouldn't have that. Hand it over. *Immediately.*"

"I will." She closed it back into her fist. "I told the captain I was complying now, didn't I? I *want* to hand it over. I didn't want anyone to find it on me, because I don't want any more trouble, believe me. I'll give it to you..."

The guard furrowed his brow, clearly not believing her at all.

"...In exchange for an easier sentence, of course," she added, causing those furrows in his forehead to smooth a bit. "So let's make a deal? I'll give you this, and you inform the magistrate that I've been a good little prisoner, so he'll go easy on me."

"We'll see. Hand it over first."

She hesitated—mostly for the sake of making her performance more believable—swallowed hard, and then she unclenched her hand. Pinching the crystal delicately between her fingertips, she pushed it through the bars.

As soon as the guard reached for it, she deftly twisted

her hand back and flattened her palm. The crystal rolled back onto it as Fire-kind words flew from her mouth.

The words came quickly, smoothly, easily—so much so that the spell still caught him off guard, even as suspicious as he'd been of her. Cas had gone over this particular spell with Zev several times, enough times that she could have recited it in her sleep. It was a spell meant to entangle its target within flames. She couldn't amplify or fully control its power the way Zev and his innate Fire magic could, but she could still do enough to accomplish what she needed.

The crystal dissipated with a *crack* and a burst of red smoke. That smoke roiled and writhed through the air, igniting into ropes of flame that quickly wrapped around the closest solid target—the guard. The guard spun around, smacking wildly at the parts of his uniform that had been swiftly set ablaze.

But this was no ordinary fire.

It would not be extinguished so easily.

It continued to burn while he twisted and yelled. Yells that, thank the gods, went unanswered for the moment. Cas doubted that would last, however, so she hurriedly gave another simple command in Fire-kind language: *Vendit.*

Move.

The rope of flames moved. It left the groaning guard —who was now rolling on the ground, delirious from pain—and it found another solid thing it could properly wrap around: The bars of Cas's prison. Within seconds, parts of those bars had turned red and pliable from the divine magic's heat.

She heard shouting in the distance. Footsteps pounding against stone stairs. The scrape of swords being unsheathed.

She bounced from one foot to the other, hardly breathing as she waited for that rope of fire to twist higher and leave her with a section of heated bars that she could work with. After what felt like an eternity, it finally happened: A section nearly as tall as herself had burned brightly and then cooled to a soft shade of orange. The bulk of the flame rope was now entangled around the cell door, weaving itself toward an upper corner—a safe distance away from her.

Cas placed the bottom of her boot against those glowing orange bars. They were no longer hot enough to eat through her boot, but still hot enough to be somewhat flexible. She carefully pushed them, first this way and then the other, until there was an opening large enough for her to slip through. Her arm brushed one of the hot bars, singeing her, and bits of melted steel clung to the soles of her boot, making her step awkward, but it didn't matter.

Because she was *free*.

She wiped her boot as best she could on the floor, and then she dropped to the guard as he continued to groan and curse her name. She took the keys and sword from his belt and then leapt back to her feet—

Just as three more guards thundered down the steps in the corner of the room.

"Vendit!" she shouted.

The rope of fire unraveled from the cell door and shot like a burning hawk across the room. It circled first around the guard it had already attacked, and then, as if sentient and able to deem him an already-incapacitated target, it flew instead to the next-closest guard. He stumbled and slammed against the wall as the flames wrapped around him.

The second guard reflexively moved to help him, and Cas saw her chance for a one-on-one battle she knew she could win. She darted for the helpful guard, sword at the ready.

He deflected her swing with a powerful one of his own, knocking her back with a strength that was somewhat surprising, given his lean frame.

She regained her footing. Gripping the slightly too-heavy-for-her sword in both hands, she stepped into a second swing—only to be forced to duck and spin awkwardly away as the guard jabbed wildly for her. She found her balance more quickly than he did and eyed the back of his knee—unpadded compared to the rest of his armored body.

He twisted around to face her. Lifted his sword into an on-guard position and stalked forward...

She waited until he was only a few feet away, and then she swung in a wide arc, purposely keeping the edge of her blade just beyond his reach. His automatic response was to parry, but as her sword was not actually close enough to strike, he hit nothing but air. He stumbled. Quick as lightning, she moved behind him, her blade slicing deep into the back of his knee.

It was a cheap move.

Zev would be proud to hear about how well she had pulled it off.

Blood sprayed the floor, and he buckled and fell with an agonized cry.

Meanwhile, her Fire spell had rendered its second victim immobile; the first backup guard was now slumped awkwardly against the wall, heaving for breath.

Cas thought of finishing those guards off, but ultimately kept her sword lowered at her side. These fools were only following orders. Maybe they deserved to die for that. Maybe they didn't. She didn't have time to properly debate the matter; all the noise they were making had to have caught more attention from the ones up above, and she needed to get out of here while she still could.

Without another second of hesitation, she turned and raced for the stairs. She shouted out another simple command to the summoned fire as she went: "Bindem!"

Follow.

She took the stairs in leaps and bounds, that twisting cord of flame trailing close behind. Once at the top, she immediately broke into another sprint. She was still winded from her battles below—her lungs felt as if the cord of fire had wrapped around them and started to squeeze—but she would have to catch her breath later; in her limited experience, Fire-kind spells were short-lived. The man she'd purchased this particular spell from had assured her over and over of its high quality, but one could never be certain of their true potency and purity.

None of the magic tricks protecting her were indefinite, so the exit...*where in the three hells was the closest exit?*

The floor directly above the dungeons seemed to have been made to purposely confuse any prisoner that might ascend from the dungeon depths. Hallways led in every direction. The lights were dimmed. There were no windows to help orient herself to where she stood in relation to outside.

But she could hear one of the guards clambering up the stairs after her, so she just picked the brightest-looking hallway and started to run.

She made several servants scream as she passed. But none were armed. No one made a move to stop her, so she kept commanding that Fire spell to follow her closely, and she kept running.

As she reached what she believed to be the main floor of the palace, that rope of fire spinning after her suddenly returned to smoke. And then to *nothing*. She whispered a quiet curse as it faded, but there was nothing to do except keep moving. She still had that guard's sword, at least.

She rounded a corner and spotted two tall windows that flanked a large, burgundy door. Through those expansive windows, she spied a courtyard overflowing with flowers, and what appeared to be the tops of houses in the distance. She started immediately toward that door

—but stopped short as she spotted a line of soldiers filing in from the right of it.

She quickly ducked into a small recess off the hall-way. There was nothing in this alcove except a table that displayed a marble bust of the former King-Emperor. Not the best of hiding places, but the walls of it were angled in such a way that she could press against them, out of sight, and still have a relatively clear view of the door.

She saw him as soon as he approached: *Captain Elander*. The Death Speaker moved toward the burgundy door, crossly shouting orders at the guards that had gathered in front of it. Orders to secure all of the exits at any cost.

"*Damn it*," she breathed, pressing lower to the floor and crawling as far back as she could. She briefly closed her eyes and pressed her hands against the floor, same as she'd done in her prison cell, trying to ground herself before her anxious thoughts could carry her away.

She opened her eyes just in time to see a flash of grey and black moving across the mouth of her hiding spot.

Her breath caught in her chest as she realized what it was. *Who* it was.

Silverfoot.

She remembered the last words Laurent had said to her before they'd parted yesterday.

We're coming after you if you don't.

She should have known he would make good on that promise. He was certainly here—and if Silverfoot was here, then it meant Rhea was, too…and *that* meant that Zev likely was as well.

Cas pursed her lips as the fox darted into her hiding place and leapt into her arms with a tiny, happy little squeak.

"Shh," she ordered, holding in a sigh.

Those idiots should have known better than to come here.

It was too risky for *all* of them to be gathered in a place like this at once. If they were discovered…

She clutched the tiny fox to her chest. She was tempted to cover his eyes, to keep him from passing any information about her whereabouts to the others. Maybe they would leave if they couldn't find her.

Or maybe they'll just storm in blindly and try to rescue me anyway.

Frowning at the thought, she quickly decided that she might as well try to help them. While pressing as far back into the shadowy alcove as she could, her eyes lifted to the high window on the opposite side of the hallway.

It featured a dazzling array of colors and symbols. Along the top curve of the glass were symbols of the three upper-gods that had created their world, the Moraki, while etched beneath them were the symbols of the twelve middle-gods, the Marr, that had served those upper-gods most faithfully.

It was strange to see such a design here, considering the hostile feelings the keepers of this palace held for that ancient, divine magic. Cas suspected that the window itself was very old, and left over from a time when perhaps those feelings had not burned quite so bitterly. Either way, she doubted there were many other windows like it elsewhere in the palace.

Which meant it was a distinct landmark to share with Rhea.

She pointed to it, and Silverfoot followed her gaze. He understood what she was doing; his eyes shimmered as he studied those strange, out-of-place symbols on the glass. Next, he crept to the edge of their dwelling, and he cocked his head to the side and took in the sights of the hallway, lingering the longest on the burgundy door and the windows beside it. With all these windows and the door as markers, hopefully the others could pinpoint her general location and meet her once she managed to slip outside.

The fox's job finished, the two of them sank back into their hiding place. Silverfoot crawled into her lap and nuzzled his head up underneath her hand, demanding pats.

"Do you know another way out besides that door?" Cas asked as she ran her fingers through his silky fur. "A less...*populated* route, maybe?"

He leapt from her lap in an instant. His tail twitched excitedly.

"Good," she whispered. "But let's wait just a minute." She pressed a hand between his shoulder blades and held him still. She wasn't entirely sure what she was waiting for, but she had a feeling it wouldn't take long for the others to find their way to her and create a distraction.

Several minutes passed.

And then that *feeling* was proven correct by a sudden shout from one of the soldiers standing guard at the door. "Fire!" he cried. "There's a fire in the courtyard!"

The door was flung open, wind howling in with it. Nearly half of the guards ran outside, with several more following after the first group shouted for assistance.

If nothing else, my friends are exceptionally good at creating chaos, Cas thought with a rueful grin.

Only three guards remained by the door, and their eyes were on the chaos.

"Okay," she told Silverfoot. "Lead me out. *Carefully.* And remember that it's not as easy for me as it is for you to move about unnoticed."

He briefly tilted his head to the side again, as if considering her size and her ability to hide. He turned and bounded into the hall, heading in the opposite direction of the door and the fires outside of it.

Cas took a deep breath. Then, keeping as close to the walls and shadows as she could, she followed him.

The hallway they were traveling made her nervous. It seemed to stretch on forever. There were too many doors, too many rooms; any second now, she was certain one of those doors would fling open, and guards—or perhaps the King-Emperor himself—would come thundering out to block her path. The sounds of footsteps and voices floated toward her from all directions, and it was difficult to tell whether they were getting closer or farther away.

It wasn't long before Silverfoot darted through a door

that was slightly ajar. Cas slowed her step, worried about *why* the door to the room was ajar, and who might be inside, but ultimately she decided to trust her guide. She rushed in after him.

It was as quiet as a fresh snowfall inside—and almost as cold. It also appeared, after a quick once-over, to be empty. Cas carefully leaned back against the door until she heard the latch *click*. She locked it and stepped further inside.

They were in a library, she realized.

A small library that appeared to have been abandoned years ago.

Cas loved books, but they were rare and expensive in this empire. She had only a tiny collection of them back at their hideout, most of which Asra had obtained for her in one way or another. She had read all of them several times over, everything from fairytales, and the riveting, mostly-true story of the elven warrior-queen whose name she'd borrowed the night before, to the sleep-inducing history of the three Marrland empires and their relationships over the centuries. She fretted every time one of her tome's pages accidentally creased, or their bindings loosened, or when any part of them suffered even the tiniest of tears or stains.

So it made her die a little inside to see all of the neglected books gathering dust on the shelves around her now. And she hated King-Emperor Varen a little more for it, because it was not how a royal library should look—there were no caretakers fluttering about, no scholars lovingly poring over pages, no lamps to read by, even. The only light came from a few evenly spaced skylights along the roof, but even that was dimmed by the thin coating of dust and spiderwebs across the panes of glass.

The one place that looked as if it had been recently visited was a small desk against the back wall. And it had been a *very* recent visit, judging by the lingering smoke and wax scent of a newly extinguished candle. Two candles, in fact; they were situated in holders that flanked either side of a large piece of yellowed parchment.

Cas took a few steps toward that desk, her curiosity getting the better of her.

She drew close enough to read the parchment. She didn't recognize the language written on it, but there were a few, bolded names that *were* familiar—the names of the fifteen most powerful gods and goddesses of their world. Those names were the same in every mortal tongue, at least as far as she knew. And their symbols were here as well, arranged in their hierarchy, just as they had been etched in the window earlier.

Her eyes fixated on the symbol of the Sun on the top row, and the name *Solatis* beneath it. And to the left and right were the symbols of Anga and Belegor, the Rook and Stone upper-gods, respectively. These three were the most powerful of all the deities—the ones who had created the world itself. Cas took a few more steps forward. She felt a desperate need for a closer look, all of a sudden.

Why was this here?

Who had been studying it?

What did those foreign words scribbled on the sides of the parchment say?

A sharp bark from Silverfoot caught her attention. Seconds later, she heard someone rattling the door she'd locked. Heart pounding in her throat, she turned and continued her escape, sprinting after the fox as he rocketed across the room and underneath an arch inscribed with words that Cas didn't take the time to read. That arch marked the entrance to a short passage with a weathered door at the end of it.

The walls of this passage were made of glass. Planters lined the bottom, but there was nothing growing in them; the soil was dry and hard. When they reached the door at the end of the glass tunnel, Silverfoot wedged himself behind one of the planters that had fallen away from the wall, and then he promptly popped back up on the other side of the glass. A closer inspection revealed a crack in the lower corner of the pane; a small, barely noticeable crack, but Silverfoot could press himself into impressively tiny places, and it looked like he had done some work digging up the ground underneath it, as well.

That must have been how he got in.

Cas opted for the door. After a brief struggle with the ancient, rusty handle, she shoved it open and rushed out into the cool morning air. This part of the palace yard looked as ill-tended as that library, with dying plants and scattered, dead leaves covering most of it. There was a rock wall surrounding the space—too high to vault over, but it was bordered by several sprawling trees with thick branches that looked like they would support her weight. She watched as Silverfoot bounced through a maze of those branches and then sprung over the wall.

There was a fountain near one of these trees. A moss-coated, tiger-like beast made of stone overlooked a pool of dirty water, its mouth open in a roar. At one point, water had likely poured from those open jaws, but now it was dry, which meant it wouldn't be slick to climb.

After tossing her stolen sword over the wall in order to free up her hands, Cas quickly made it to the tiger's shoulder, high enough to reach a sturdy tree branch. She was preparing to grab it and swing herself up into the tree when she heard a familiar voice.

"Stop!"

She glanced behind her and scowled as she saw the captain of the Peace Keepers striding into the yard.

Him again.

"I said *stop!*"

The space around her began to chill, and the world took on the same muted and grey quality that it had outside of Darkhand's house.

Cas hesitated, just for a moment. But it was enough, and she lost her footing on the curves of the tiger's body. She flailed and stomped her feet down, trying to find purchase, but the movement only ended up chipping away at the weathered stone—until suddenly there was nothing but air beneath her right foot. She slipped, and she was forced to jump to avoid falling. She landed awkwardly in the waist-deep water, painfully jarring her knee in the process.

The cold and shadows went away. Captain Elander reached her in the next instant, grabbed her arm, and wrenched her to the edge of the fountain. He froze abruptly as their gazes met. His eyes widened.

As she struggled to free herself, she caught a brief glimpse of her reflection in the dark and dirty water...

And she realized *why* he was looking at her like that.

Because her reflection was back to normal. Her *appearance* was back to normal—or *her* normal, at least—with her greyed-out eyes and her colorless hair.

"You..."

"Let me *go*," she snarled.

"You're the woman from Oblivion."

"And you're the *man* from Oblivion—and I have a lot of questions about just what the hell you were doing in that place, but at the moment I don't care about the answers to them. I just need to get away from here."

She tried again to jerk free, her breaths starting to come faster as she felt the world closing in around her.

He held tight.

"Let me go." Her voice had grown softer without her say-so. Detached, really—the way it often became when she felt the panic reaching for her. It was an automatic defense; sometimes she could stave that anxiety off, at least temporarily, if she refused to give it or anything else her full attention.

Elander's brow creased, studying her.

She gritted her teeth and braced herself for the deathly cold magic she knew was coming.

But he didn't summon any magic.

He let go of her arm.

And then he said something she did not expect: "We need to get you out of this palace. Now."

CHAPTER 10

CAS STARED AT HIM. "WHAT?"

"Walk with me. Act natural."

"*What*?!"

"Okay, just so you're aware," he said in a harsh whisper, "screeching *what* at me over and over doesn't come across as particularly *natural*."

"I was not *screeching*."

His reply to this was cut off by the sound of paws skittering along the top of the stone wall that Cas had failed to climb. Cas looked up and caught a flash of grey as Silverfoot barreled closer and closer—and then launched himself, claws outstretched, toward the captain's face.

Elander moved just as quickly, catching the fox by the scruff of his neck. "Is this yours?" he asked, holding Silverfoot at a distance to avoid the tiny black claws that were furiously swiping at him.

"Let him go!" Cas snapped, starting forward.

Elander swiftly stepped out of her reach. He hesitated with the fox still dangling from his grip. He *looked* as if he was actually considering letting him go...

And then Silverfoot made the decision for him—by twisting his little body viciously back and forth until he managed to slip free. He landed on Elander's chest. His claws sank into the light leather armor there, and his tiny jaws snapped for the captain's throat. Elander swiped and swatted until he'd managed to detach those claws, and finally knocked the fox from his chest.

Silverfoot hit the ground with an indignant yelp. His fur bristled, and a growl rose in his throat—but that growl was drowned out seconds later by the sound of people approaching from their right.

Elander cursed before glancing back at Cas. "Call off your little beast, and *come on already.*"

That beast was already stalking back toward the captain, his hackles raised and his tail erect, puffed up to twice its normal size. Cas knelt quickly beside him, and with her suspicious gaze still fixed on Elander, she offered her arm to the fox and ordered him to come to her. The fox obeyed. Reluctantly. He hopped from the ground, to her outstretched arm, and finally to a precarious perch on her shoulder.

She stood, and Elander gave her an impatient, expectant look as the sounds from the right grew louder.

She didn't believe for a second that the man next to her really wanted to get her out of this place, but the alternative was turning to face who knew how many other soldiers—all of whom certainly didn't want her to escape either.

So when Elander started to move, Cas followed cautiously behind him.

They walked swiftly, but as naturally as possible.

As if anything about this could be called natural.

They rounded a corner and came to a small iron gate guarded by two men. Cas's body threatened to seize up with panic. Elander grabbed her arm and marched her forward. The guards stood up a little straighter as they approached. They exchanged a look with one another, and then both pairs of their eyes darted from Cas's Fade-marked appearance to that hold Elander had on her arm.

"Open this gate," Elander commanded them.

After a long pause, one of them found the courage to talk. "This woman is—"

"The business I have with this woman doesn't concern you."

And that was that.

The guard opened the gate and sank back with it against the wall. It was as though he'd been physically struck down by Elander's words.

"I get the impression people don't often disagree with you around here," Cas mumbled once they were out of sight of that guard and his partner.

Elander didn't reply. His gaze, his grip, his silence—it was all relentlessly focused on whatever his goal was, on wherever he was dragging her.

They swept a wide route out away from the palace

proper. But that side trail they were on soon led to a wide path lined with white stones, and this path stretched between the largest and grandest gate on the grounds...and the main door of that palace.

"We're walking straight out the front gate," Cas breathed in realization.

"It's called hiding in plain sight."

"In my experience, that literally *never* works."

"You don't have the benefit of authority or magic the way I do."

"You think very highly of yourself, don't you?"

"I do. And I exceed those high standards time and time again."

Cas rolled her eyes, but she picked up her pace until she was side by side with him. Some deeply buried part of her was a bit jealous of—and impressed by—that unrelenting confidence he seemed to carry with him wherever he went.

Some *very* deeply buried part of her.

"Are you going to explain to me *why* you're escorting me out of this place when you're the one who dragged me into it?"

"Now isn't the time," he muttered.

She had to admit he had a point; there were a score of people in this section of the palace grounds. Several servants tended to the flowers, while others greeted visitors that had just been granted passage through the main gate. A handful of guards were stationed in various places, as well—at that gate and otherwise—and all of these guards appeared tightly wound, just barely suppressed coils ready to spring into action at any sudden movement; they whispered together, their eyes occasionally glancing into the distance, toward the smoke that could be seen snaking up toward the periwinkle sky.

Cas wondered how many fires Zev and his magic had set. It wasn't like him to rely on that magic at all; it was too risky. And to use it *here*, of all places...

Had they all safely gotten away after creating that distraction for her?

Or were they waiting around to see what they needed to do next? Communicating via Silverfoot and his magic had its limitations; Rhea could *see* what was happening, but the sounds—the spoken words—didn't always translate as clearly. Nor did the fox's thoughts. Rhea could occasionally manage to read the lips Silver saw...but what would she make of the things Elander had said, even if she *had* managed to read his lips?

Her concerns continued to rattle around in her mind, even as Cas turned her attention back to more immediate problems. Stares followed their every movement. But over and over again, people shied away from Elander after he spoke only a few calm words that bristled with power and purpose. Cas thought that perhaps she sensed the pulse of his magic rising more than once, though it wasn't as terrifyingly cold as before. But maybe she imagined it. Or perhaps she was already getting more used to it, somehow.

They were nearly to that front gate when Elander suddenly slowed and spit out a curse.

"What is it?"

He sighed, taking her arm once more and pulling her to a stop. And then he finally answered one of her earlier questions: "There's at least one person in this palace who disagrees with me on a fairly regular basis."

Before she could ask who this person was, he motioned slightly to their left.

Cas looked and saw a man emerging from a rose bush-lined path. Dread crept over her skin at the sight of him, raising bumps as it went.

"Run back to Rhea," she whispered to the fox on her shoulder, who nuzzled his cheek against hers for a quick moment before hopping down and darting away. He was smarter than most creatures. Hell, he was smarter than most *people* Cas knew.

And any smart person would have known to run away from the man approaching her now.

It had been thirteen years since Casia had seen him in person, but she didn't need anyone to tell her who he was. He still had that same proud, haughty way of holding his head, and the same cool and distant, earth-colored eyes. He wore a simple yet elegant silk shirt over finely tailored pants, and he parted the crowd of soldiers and servants without so much as a word or harsh look. The silver and black circlet resting on his pale, red-tinged hair curled to sharp points at its center; those points were fashioned out of obsidian and meant to resemble black tiger claws.

King-Emperor Varen de Solasen—arguably the most powerful man throughout all the broken realms and fallen kingdoms of Kethra—was staring at Cas as if he'd forgotten that anybody else existed.

"Don't tell him how you escaped," Elander whispered.

"I'm not an idiot. Obviously I'm not going to tell him about the *illegal* crystal I was carrying."

"Actually," he continued, as if she hadn't spoken, "it's probably best if you just keep your mouth shut in general."

Cas started to tell him to keep his own mouth shut, but Varen reached them before she could.

"I hope you don't mind my interfering, Captain," he said, "but I heard the commotion, and I couldn't help myself."

"You shouldn't have concerned yourself with it, Your Highness," said Elander. "This criminal has proven dangerous; I was bringing her to the Truth Taker on the city's edge in hopes that he might be able to draw a full confession from her, so that we might punish her to the fullest extent of our laws."

The young ruler held up a hand without taking his eyes off Cas. "On the contrary, it seems maybe I should have concerned myself with it much earlier."

"But the Truth—"

"We don't need to concern the Taker and his barbaric magic with this."

Elander bristled—it seemed the word *barbaric* had irked him—but he otherwise didn't reply.

"I don't believe this woman is a criminal, at all," continued the king. "In fact, she looks like an honored guest to me."

Cas was surprised by his words and his tone, both of which sounded unexpectedly kind. But she *shouldn't* have been surprised, she supposed.

Because it was, of course, a trap.

Of course he wanted her as a guest. Just as his father had collected other Fade-marked as *guests*...only for them to disappear weeks later. She hadn't missed the way Varen's eyes had traveled over her grey hair and eyes before he registered anything else about her. And she'd worked with enough unsavory clients to know when she was being appraised as a potential tool.

"Assuming she'd like to grace me with her company, that is," he added.

"I can't stay." The boldness in her tone surprised even her.

"Is that so?" His interest seemed oddly, unexpectedly genuine once again, so Cas continued blurting words out in spite of the fear trying to squeeze the breath from her lungs—and in spite of the warning look that she could feel Elander watching her with.

He had apparently not yet realized that she wasn't the type to *keep her mouth shut*.

"Yes," she said, her gaze purposely fixed on only the King-Emperor's. "I...I have to get back to my friends. One of them is very sick, and I promised her I would be back soon to help take care of her."

He considered this for a moment. "I'm sorry your friend is sick." He looked toward those spirals of smoke rising in the distance. "Perhaps they could join us as well? Also as my guests, of course."

"Her *friends* are the ones who started those fires in the south gardens," Elander interjected. "I told you, sir, both she and the rest of her group are dangerous. You need to allow me to deal with them properly."

Cas clenched her fist and willed herself not to look at the captain. Did that bastard *really* have to tell on them like that?

But Varen only chuckled. "Setting fires to try and save her? We should all be so lucky to have such good friends, eh?"

"Your Majesty, that is madness—"

"Haven't you heard the rumors of my *madness*? They're rampant, as of late. And who am I to make liars out of the ones who seem to get so much joy out of spreading those rumors?"

Elander didn't seem to have a reply to that.

"Either way, those fires didn't cause much damage. No worse than any of the raids we've been dealing with. Or...well, any of the other issues we've been facing as of late. It's not worth your attention, Captain. And certainly not worth getting the Taker involved."

"I—"

"Stand down, Captain."

For a moment, Cas was afraid Elander was going to ignore his order. She was almost certain of it; the unnatural chill that came from his magic use was seeping into the air, making the flowers and trees and all the other living things in the yard—herself included—shiver.

But then he gave the tiniest of bows. "As you wish."

The sun's warmth once again reached her skin, and Cas opened her mouth only to close it again, unsure of what to say.

"We can discuss the details of your friends joining us later, if you like," said the King-Emperor, turning back to her with a smile. "But for the moment, I hope *you* will at least consent to joining me for a quick brunch?"

He truly seemed to be asking for her consent.

She wondered what would happen if she said no again.

And then it occurred to her: It would be foolish to deny a personal audience with him. If nothing else, this was a golden opportunity to get answers about what was happening in Oblivion. Answers that could lead to that handsome payout she still intended to collect.

Lord Merric would be beside himself if he learned that she had *dined* with the man he had so many questions about. The lord would fill her bags with so many coins she wouldn't be able to carry them, and with that much money, surely Cas could find someone willing to deal in the medicine she needed.

Someone who *wasn't* Darkhand.

"I could stay for brunch, I suppose," she agreed.

Varen's face brightened, though his eyes still seemed oddly distant, as if he was thinking of a dozen faraway things in addition to that promised brunch. "Wonderful."

She felt Elander's grip tense, and she realized he still held her arm. For whatever reason, he honestly seemed to want to protect her from the King-Emperor.

But *why*?

The questions surrounding him were too many—and too messy. She couldn't get her anxious thoughts to slow enough to even *start* to formulate possible explanations. Not at the moment, anyway.

But a brunch with the King-Emperor...that could just be part of the mission she needed to accomplish. And she had always found it easier to deal with missions. To make lists in her head, steps that she could fixate on, points to anchor herself to whenever the waves of anxiety came.

Varen reached out his arm to her.

Step one.

She willingly locked her arm with his and let him steer her away from the captain of his Peace Keepers.

Step two.

"I need you to go focus on putting out all of the aforementioned fires," the King-Emperor told Elander. "And deal with any other fires that you might come across after the bit of chaos we've had this morning—whether physical or otherwise. Do you understand?"

Elander gave only a curt nod in response. It was borderline rude—particularly given who he was responding to—but Varen didn't seem bothered by it. He and Cas strolled into the palace without another word to any of the people staring at them.

Every instinct Cas possessed still bristled, warning her that this could be a trap.

But at least she was no longer running for her life, nor being roughly pulled along by obnoxious guards. And with that in mind, she took the time to cautiously examine her surroundings a bit more.

She'd pictured the memory of Varen's cold expression so many times over the years that she had already formed an image of his palace in her mind—an equally empty and unwelcoming void that should have been made of marble and other cold, uninviting stone.

But as they wandered deeper into the palace, she couldn't help but think it seemed oddly, well, *cozy.*

The predominant materials were warm, natural wood, and there were fireplaces blazing in almost every room she peeked into. A host of colorful artwork—most of it featuring smooth edges and bright colors—lined the walls. The tiled floor soon gave way to halls lined with plush, thick carpet. Cas longed to take her boots off just so she could sink her toes into the plum-colored waves of it.

And the light...there was light everywhere, it seemed. From countless crystal-adorned chandeliers, to large windows that often stretched all the way from the floor to the ceiling, to a number of sapphire-flecked statues that looked as if they had been placed in certain areas solely for the purpose of catching sunlight in their gemstones. It was all undeniably bright and warm and sparkling, and it was beginning to feel like something from a dream rather than a nightmare.

She nearly woke from that dream as they turned into a long, narrow hallway, and she felt an odd tugging in her chest that she couldn't explain.

To her right was a door with a silver-black sash tied around its handle. A woman was making her way through this door, nudging it open with her hip while she balanced a full tray in her hands. Cas slowed as she watched her disappear into the room, and the pressure against her chest grew heavier.

But it was only a brief flicker. The door closed just as quickly, the pressure faded, and Cas hurried to catch up with the King-Emperor once more.

The room they finally stopped in was the brightest and most inviting of them all—a space lined with nothing except more of those floor-to-ceiling windows, and filled with plants that grew every which way to embrace sunlight that seemed to be coming from all directions.

A grey cast over the windows kept that light from being too bright or too hot. It was warm, but pleasantly so, and there was an ethereal quality to it all that made Cas feel as if she was floating—at least until her stomach twisted as she thought of Asra, of how her mentor had insisted on dragging that bed of hers right up to that rickety window seat at their hideout.

She would love this room.

Several servants flitted about. Most of them greeted

their King-Emperor with polite smiles and bows. He responded to them all with equally polite smiles and, occasionally, even a bit of friendly small talk.

Cas watched him interacting with these people, the same curiosity that had overtaken her outside flooding back. Because it was obvious enough to anyone paying attention: Those servants *liked* this man. And this didn't fit the tyrannical picture she had drawn of him in her mind. At all.

She gave her head a little shake. So what if he was friendly to his help? This was the man who had, by almost all accounts, inherited his father's bloodthirsty nature. Who was loyal to the cause of ensuring the unmarked continued their rule of this broken empire. Who had *proven* that loyalty, the stories said, by personally slaughtering dozens of divinely-marked prisoners while his dying father looked on and nodded his approval. There was even a name for that horrifying slaughter-fest—the Blood Rising, the history books called it. It was the night that King-Emperor Anric had officially ceded his rule to his son.

His son, who had bathed in enough blood to be considered worthy of that clawed crown he wore.

His son, who had looked the other way when Cas was being beaten to death in the middle of the street.

Cas absently started to reach for that moon-shaped scar on her jawline, but she stopped herself, clenching her fingers into a fist that she lowered to her side.

"I apologize if Captain Elander treated you roughly."

The King-Emperor motioned for her to sit at a small table in the corner of the space. "He's an ass at times, but he's damn good at his job, so I can't bring myself to get rid of him. My soldiers listen to him better than they listen to *me* most of the time. That's rather sad, isn't it? But they fear him in a way that I can't seem to replicate. My advisors say I'm too soft—it drives them mad." His lips quirked a bit in one corner, as if part of him enjoyed frustrating those advisors.

Soft did not fit that narrative of him in her head either, but she kept that to herself.

"He said you were the only one who ever disagreed with him," she recalled.

"Did he?" He settled down in the chair directly beside her and thoughtfully twisted one of his many rings for a moment. "Well that's true enough, I suppose. I don't fear him the way so many of those soldiers and servants of mine seem to."

"Maybe he respects you because of that."

"A clever thought," Varen said, summoning a servant with a wave of his hand. After a brief conversation, the servant left with a bow. She returned a few minutes later carrying a pitcher in one hand, while the other held a tray with two goblets, a loaf of fresh bread, and several plates full of fruits and cheeses and nuts.

The two of them ate in silence. Or *Varen* ate, at least. Cas's stomach was twisting so horribly at this point that she wasn't sure she would ever eat again, and the cut Darkhand had left made opening her mouth painful, anyway. She did sip from the goblet she'd been given, but only in an effort to be polite and thus keep her target friendly and forthcoming with his words. The drink the servant had poured them was a wine of some sort. Bitter, but she assumed it was safe, since the King-Emperor was drinking from the same pitcher.

Finally, Varen leaned back in his chair, crossed his arms over his chest, and spoke. "Casia Greythorne."

She flinched.

Then it got worse.

"Sonja Ritter. Pyer Elasidir. Mari Blackburn."

"You've been doing some research." She kept her eyes on the other side of the glass windows, watching a red bird hopping along the branches of a tree.

"We arrested one of Darkhand's men along with you, if you didn't notice. He was very quick to divulge everything he knew about you—and once I had the name of that current alias you've been going by, I did a little digging of my own to unearth some of the previous ones you've used."

The red bird hopped from the branch and soared away, and she briefly envied its wings.

"You're a fascinating subject, you know."

"Fascinating is what I aim for."

"You've achieved it."

"And that's why you wished to have brunch with me? Because you discovered some more *fascinating* facts about me, I presume?" She tilted her head back toward him, and she found him smiling in a way that she could not decipher. It was part friendly, part amused, and part...something else. Something darker, perhaps.

"I didn't discover as much about you as I wanted to, unfortunately," he said. "There's still much I haven't figured out. I'm wondering, for example, how it is that our paths haven't properly crossed before now."

The memory of that day in the street flashed in her mind. She could feel blood trickling down her jaw, sliding down to the tip of her chin, dripping down into the dry dirt road in little deafening plops.

Plop.

Plop.

Plop...

She gripped the edges of her chair to keep herself from squirming in her seat.

"Because there are records of your crimes, *Casia Greythorne*," the King-Emperor continued, "and there is a fascinating collection of notes that the magistrate's assistants put together regarding your criminal history. The collective criminal histories of *all* of your many identities, that is."

"I doubt you've found them *all*," she couldn't help but quietly, smugly interject.

"No, I would say not." He chuckled softly, ruefully, before continuing, "But within the notes we *have* collected, none of them mention you—or any of your aliases— being Fade-marked. So imagine my excitement when one of my guards came rushing in to tell me that he'd seen the truth of your identity. Which is why I had to intervene and make sure you didn't get away. I usually let Captain Elander and Magistrate Tarik deal with criminals; I don't have much of an appetite for justice...again, much to the chagrin of my advisors."

"So if you don't plan on handing down justice, then what do you want with me, precisely?"

"Can you not guess?"

She *could*. But she was not going to be the forthcoming one; she was here to pry information from him, not the other way around.

"I need your help."

"My help," she repeated, dubious.

"You survived that sickness that's killed so many of our empire's people."

She almost snapped at his use of the words *our empire* —as if they were really equals that lived in the same world—but she managed to bite her tongue once more.

"I am looking for a cure."

"Like your father supposedly was?" she asked, flatly.

"Yes." He didn't sound ashamed of this at all.

Cas couldn't manage to keep her face impassive this time. She narrowed her eyes at him, which made his expression sour a bit for the first time since they'd started talking.

"I know the horrific stories that have been told about him." The King-Emperor rose to his feet and paced in front of the window for a moment. The sunlight made him look even younger than he was, somehow—the way it ignited the shadows on his face and softened his eyes to the color of gold. "But most of them get it wrong," he insisted. "They paint it all with such broad strokes, and they only focus on the gruesome bits. They never talk about how much good he did, or how close he came to curing that sickness that has devastated so many."

"Perhaps not," said Cas, flatly. "Likely because of the way the ones with that sickness mysteriously disappeared after he took them in."

"There was nothing *mysterious* about it. They died of a sickness that was *known* to kill almost all of its victims, and then their bodies were carefully disposed of, for obvious reasons."

Cas shifted uncomfortably in her seat, realizing that she didn't have a quick rebuttal for that.

"His many enemies created that foolish narrative and fed it to people hungry for a target to attack." He frowned, and almost more to himself than her he said, "How disappointing that you seem to have eaten it up as well."

"But he had those enemies for a reason," she insisted, stubbornly. "What about the wars he raged against anyone carrying a divine mark? What difference does it make that he did any good, when he and his armies slaughtered thousands of people simply because they were born with a mark?"

"What do you know about those *wars*?" It was phrased as a question, but it sounded like a dismissal.

"I know enough," she snapped back.

His eyes widened a bit, as if he wasn't used to his dismissals being ignored.

Cas attempted to rein in her temper before it fully erupted and ruined any chance she had of prying information from him.

He was quiet for a long moment, studying her. "So you know, of course, that those marked believed they were chosen by the gods to rule over the *unchosen*. That they were on the verge of rising up and crushing people like me and you before my father stepped in.

"And he stepped in because he was a scholar of history and worldly affairs—so he had studied how this *exact* thing happened in the Sundolian Empire to our south. Years and years ago, the wars those divinely-marked southerners waged destabilized their empire's three kingdoms almost beyond repair."

Cas wanted to argue this point, but she couldn't.

She was no scholar, but she knew that each of the three kingdoms of that southern empire were ruled by one of three 'clans'. Those clans were determined by the marks they'd been born with—the symbols of the three upper-gods, in this case. The ones marked by the middle-gods, and some of the lesser-spirits, enjoyed status and power as well. But there was always a contest, and occasionally a war, over which of these divinely-powerful clans was the *most* powerful. And those with no marks at all rarely led happy, or long, lives.

It was the opposite of what Kethra had become. Here, it was mostly the *unmarked* who were the oppressors and destroyers. So Cas almost had to admit that Varen had a point about one thing: If his ancestors had not crushed those marked ones, then perhaps history *would* have seen the magic-users rise to a destructive power.

Perhaps this was simply how the world was, no matter what? An endless trading of places between the oppressors and the oppressed? The same song on repeat, with continuously rewritten lyrics...

She wanted to wither up and escape the depressing thought, but she couldn't get it out of her head.

"The marked are dangerous," the King-Emperor concluded, his tone not inviting an argument.

"Several of my best friends have divine magic," she said, defiantly, "and they don't deserve to suffer because of something they were born with. They should be judged by what they do, not what they are."

"I'm assuming they all also have criminal records as long and as colorful as yours?" he asked, drily.

She let out an irritable snort. "Would it matter if they *didn't?*"

He didn't reply.

"You have no idea what it's like for them thanks to those barbaric laws your father and grandfather enacted."

His smile was thin. "You don't think I have any personal compassion for the marked?"

"Why would you?"

He considered the question for a long moment, as if trying to decide whether or not he trusted her with the answer. "Because I have at least one divine magic user within my own family. Or I *did*, anyway. An older sister."

She stared at him, uncertain if she should believe him. It seemed like a strange thing to lie about.

"She was a year older than me," he said, "and by rights *she* should have been the heir to the throne, not me."

"I've never heard of her."

"Not many people have. My parents kept her a secret because of her magic."

"What happened to her?"

"She's gone."

"Gone?"

"My father got rid of her after my mother died."

"Got *rid* of her?"

"His words, not mine. That was his reply when I became old enough, and intelligent enough, to start asking questions."

Cas was speechless for a moment. She was equal parts disgusted at the former King-Emperor, and distraught for the current one before her, whose eyes had taken on a sort of glazed, distant look. "I...I'm sorry."

He waved her words aside. "I hardly remember her."

"Nothing at all?"

He hesitated, looking somewhat flustered—or perhaps surprised—by her apparent concern on the matter. Cas briefly wondered how often he had managed to find somebody to talk to about these traumatic things. Likely not often; she had always imagined the role of a ruler to be a lonely, solitary thing.

"Sometimes I think I remember the feel of her magic,"

Varen said after a pause. "But it isn't clear, just a hazy light and a memory of warmth. It probably means nothing; I often picture the same thing whenever I try to remember my mother. The mind and the memory are strange beasts, aren't they?"

Cas nodded.

"Anyway—apologies." He sighed. "We've gotten off track, I'm afraid. Though my father insisted I continue his crusades, I actually care far less about carrying on that war against the marked than he did. It's a pressing concern that I have to stay on top of, of course, but the Fading Sickness is first on my priority list, personally— and that brings us back to *you*, doesn't it? A far more interesting subject than my family history, to be sure."

"Am I, though?"

"Yes." He lifted his eyes to the ceiling, looking lost in thought. "I never thought I'd see a true, long-term survivor of the Fade."

"Well, it doesn't matter that you have," she muttered. "Because I don't *know* how I survived. I don't know how Asra survived, either, or—"

"Asra?"

Shit.

Cas pressed her lips together and went back to staring through the grey glass, searching for the bright red bird from before. It hadn't returned.

Varen let her sit and stew in her foolish mistake for several minutes, strolling through the room and checking the soil of several of the potted plants, before he casually asked, "Is Asra one of the friends you mentioned earlier? You said you needed to get back, as she was sick, correct?"

She said nothing, which made him sigh again.

"Do pardon my outburst a moment ago." He walked back over to his chair, and drew it a bit closer to her before lowering himself into it once more. "I want us to be friends, Casia."

She took a long sip from the goblet still clutched in her hand. And then another. And another.

This time, he took her silence in stride. "I still need to earn your trust, I see. That's fair." His brown eyes seemed to sparkle at the challenge. "And I shall do it, whatever it takes."

We'll see. Cas pretended to take another sip of her drink, despite the fact that her goblet was empty.

"I stand by what I offered earlier, by the way. Your friends are welcome to join us here. My servants— including my personal doctor— could help tend to the ill one. And the divinely-marked you mentioned would be safe as well."

"Despite their long, colorful criminal histories?"

"You realize I have the power to expunge those histories—yes?"

Cas stared at him, speechless for what felt like the tenth time that morning.

He took the pitcher the servant had left, and he refilled her goblet himself. "You don't have to trust me about this, either, of course. But do think about it."

She was thinking about it.

She couldn't *help* but think about it.

But she also couldn't help remembering his face, staring at her from his gilded carriage, looking so unmoved by her suffering.

She hardly realized what she was doing—where her hand had strayed to—until the King-Emperor said, "That's an odd scar on your jaw there. How did you manage to acquire such a thing?"

"I don't remember." She twisted her lips into something like a smile. "I believe it happened during one of those more *colorful* criminal escapades of mine."

"I see." He returned the smile she'd given him— though his was, once again, more genuine. "Well, the doctor I mentioned before? He's Oak-kind. And a damned talented healer, as such. He might be able to take care of it, if you like—that one, and the fresher ones you have along your mouth. Those look rather painful."

"I'm fine, thank you." Some part of her felt oddly protective of all her scars, suddenly. As if she needed to keep them to make certain she didn't forget where she'd come from—or that moment when she'd first met the King-Emperor.

Her oddly quick, aggressive reply had caused his smile to droop a bit at the corners. They sat in an uncomfortable silence for several minutes after that. Not entirely enemies, but certainly not allies...

This was already messier than she'd hoped it would be.

"What have you managed to discover about that

Fading Sickness?" she asked, determined to steer the conversation back into useful territory.

If he truly *was* most concerned about the sickness as he claimed, then perhaps it was his research regarding it that had led to him meddling in Oblivion.

He didn't reply immediately. She wasn't sure he was going to reply at all, until he finally cleared his throat to speak—

Only to have a scream cut him off.

CHAPTER 11

WITHOUT A WORD, VAREN ROSE TO HIS FEET AND RUSHED
toward the sound of the scream.

Cas stared after him for a moment, dumbfounded.
She was surprised he hadn't run in the *opposite* direction.
Yet another thing that didn't fit the selfish, cowardly
narrative that she had written about him in her head.

She shook out of her stupor and pushed away from
the table. It briefly occurred to her that she could try to
escape again while everyone was distracted, but the
curiosity she had about this palace and its ruler were far
too great now—and the potential rewards for sticking
around could be far greater. So instead of running away,
she quickly surveyed the room, searching for some sort of
weapon. She settled for the dull knife resting on the tray
between the bread and a dish of butter. Grabbing it, she
raced after the King-Emperor.

It wasn't difficult to find him. There was a small group

of people gathering just down the hall, crowding around the door with the silver-black cloth tied around its handle. It was the same one they had passed on their way to the sun parlor earlier—the same room that had caused that brief, unsettling feeling to tug at her chest.

She slowly made her way toward it, and as she reached it, she noticed a familiar face approaching the crowd from the opposite side of the hallway—Captain Elander.

Why was he here?

"Weren't you supposed to be dealing with the chaos on the *other* side of the palace?" she asked.

He gave her a quick, uninterested glance. "Mm-hm. And yesterday you told me you were going to be *gone* from the palace by this time—and yet, here you stand. So it looks like neither of us are where we're supposed to be."

She scowled, but he didn't see it because he was already walking into that dark room.

People parted to let him through. Cas stepped after him before the crowd could converge once more and block the path. In the darkness, and in her haste not to be shoved out again, she accidentally stepped on the back of his boot. She tripped as she tried to separate herself from him as quickly as possible.

He caught her by the arm and steadied her just before her knee hit the ground. "If you need another fake alias— you know, for your next late night *chat* at a shady inn— then I think you should go with *Grace*." It was too dark to see his smirk, but she could hear it in his voice.

She jerked out of his grip.

People were staring at them, so Cas didn't respond to Elander's comment. She put several feet between them, smoothed the sleeve he'd rumpled up when he grabbed her, then lifted her chin and walked deeper into the room with as much dignity as she could muster.

The room was somber. The King-Emperor was surrounded by servants with their heads hung low, and they were all gathered around a bed against the back wall. A few were whispering, but most were quiet. One held a young woman who appeared to have fainted—the source of the scream, perhaps. All of their faces were stricken with exhaustion and grief.

Varen glanced up briefly at Elander as they approached, but he didn't seem to register that Cas was there as well.

"Another dead. And she went violently. Quickly." His words came out on shuddering breaths. All of the color had drained from his face, making his already fair skin appear perfectly ghost-like in the darkness. He looked... terrible. Like a completely different man than the one she had just been sipping wine with.

But his complexion was nothing compared to the woman he was standing over.

The dead woman looked as if she had been pulled up from a grave—one that had been dug at least six months prior. Her skin had all but wasted away. Her hair, what few patches of it remained, was the same colorless shade as Cas's, as were her eyes. Those eyes were open and staring at the ceiling. Their wide-open horror, paired with the twisted shape of her peeling lips, made it look as though she had seen the middle-god of Death himself just as she took her final breaths.

The air smelled of earthy spices and lavender. One of the servants was rubbing oils on the woman's shriveled up arms; that seemed to be where the smell was coming from, and the scent made Cas feel as if she might vomit. She felt oddly small, and she swore the room was growing darker—like she was standing at the bottom of a well that someone was pulling a cover over. And when she managed to climb out of that darkness, the only thing there to greet her was that dead, unseeing woman on the bed before her. But it wasn't simply some unknown woman.

It was the mother she'd lost.

It was Asra.

It was *herself*.

Heart thundering, her eyes darted around in search of something to ground herself with. She was determined not to lose her balance again while Elander was near—to not reveal her anxiety to him or anyone else. She took a small step back and braced her hand against the wall. Tapped her fingers against it. Focused her thoughts on that rhythmic sound. *Only* on that rhythmic sound, until it had successfully driven most of her racing thoughts away.

She kept her eyes open and looked on as the king-emperor dismissed most of those servants hovering around the dead woman. After they were gone, he turned to Elander. "You know what I have to ask of you."

Elander nodded.

Cas wanted to ask what he was talking about, but she was still too close to panicking to trust herself to speak.

Perhaps Varen could sense this, because he finally lifted his head in her direction. "Come with me, Casia dear. The captain doesn't need us distracting him." He offered his arm, and she found herself accepting it as willingly as she had when they were in the courtyard earlier. They walked in silence toward the hallway.

He didn't look back at the dead, and she certainly didn't either.

The crowd in that hallway seemed to have doubled in size. When they spotted their ruler walking toward them, a few members peeled away and went back to whatever it was they should have been doing just then, but several lingered.

"Disperse, if you please," the King-Emperor said tiredly. "What's happened in this room doesn't concern any of you for the moment."

There were a few hasty bows, a few disappointed whispers, but no one disobeyed, and soon, Cas stood alone with Varen in a hallway that suddenly stretched longer and darker than she remembered.

"Are you all right?" he asked her.

She nodded. She was better, now that she didn't have to look at that woman anymore. She leaned back against the wall. Folded her arms across her stomach. Took several deep breaths and watched her arms rise and fall with each one. "Who was she?"

"One of the kitchen servants," he replied distractedly. "She first took ill twelve days ago."

"Twelve *days*? It progressed that quickly?"

He gave the barest of nods.

Ice slid through Cas's veins. From a normal, healthy person to that...*corpse* in the room, all in twelve days. Her adoptive parents had lasted nearly a year, at least. They had...

No.

She hugged her arms more tightly against herself, refusing to think of that grim part of her past again. Swallowing hard, she asked, "And what is Elander doing in there?"

The King-Emperor took a long moment to answer this time. "You've heard the moniker people have given him, I'm assuming? The *Death Speaker*, some of the empire calls him."

"I've heard that before, yes."

"Well, it's a very literal nickname, in this case."

"You mean he's...?"

"The dead usually do not keep secrets very well. Particularly when they first pass from this world into whatever awaits them next. Elander first served my father in this capacity several years ago, using his magic to collect information that was invaluable to King-Emperor Anric and his conquests. That magic allows Elander to see the lives of the deceased pass before his eyes—which comes in very handy when you've killed an enemy target who has valuable secrets, for example. It's also an excellent magical skill to assist healers in bettering their craft, because it allows them to see the details regarding what killed a person. Usually."

"Usually?"

"For those who have passed from the Fade, when they depart to the afterlife, there's..." He trailed off, looking frustrated.

"Nothing but silence," Elander finished as he stepped out of the room. "Silence and a bright light that won't let me read anything about their life, including how it was prematurely ended."

"This time as well?" Varen asked, softly.

"I'm afraid so."

The King-Emperor herded them into a more private room across the hall. It was a sitting room, cozy and dark, with two chairs facing a small fireplace. The mantle of that fireplace featured a carving of two tigers, their long tails curling lazily down on either side. He stared up into the stone face of one of these tigers, his eyes distant and lost in thought. "It's as if their very souls have been leached away, along with their lives," he finally said, more to the tigers than to the two people standing behind him.

Cas fought off a shudder at the words. "Earlier...you said this was *another* dead," she recalled. "How many have come before her? Just in this palace, I mean."

"Ten—no, eleven?"

"Fourteen," Elander supplied, tonelessly. "Just in this past month."

Varen blanched at the words. "And the prior moon cycle was not much better."

"Ten dead during that one," said Elander. "And silence and bright lights accompanied all of them out as well."

The back of Cas's neck grew hot as a gross thought overtook her. "So is *this* why you're most concerned with the Fading Sickness, and not waging war? Because that sickness is sweeping through the halls of this palace, and you're afraid you're going to be next?"

Elander raised an eyebrow at her harsh accusation, but he said nothing in defense of his employer. He only rested one shoulder against the doorframe, made himself comfortable there, and watched as Varen spun around to face her.

"Of course I'm afraid." Varen's tone was calm, but she could sense the frustration seething just underneath the surface of his words. "What sort of ruler wouldn't be concerned about this wretched sickness? But I'm not only afraid for *myself*, thank you kindly, and I would appreciate it if you would keep such blatant assassinations of my character to yourself, *Casia Greythorne*. Or whatever your real name is."

Elander snorted at this last comment, but he still offered no other input into the conversation.

"You don't know the half of what me and my family have done for this empire," added Varen.

"I know enough," Cas growled.

"You keep saying that. But I don't believe you know very much at all."

She clenched her fist—the one not holding the knife she'd carried away from the sun parlor. Her nails bit so sharply into her skin that she was certain they were leaving more crescent-shaped scars to go with that one on her jaw.

But Varen was suddenly too distracted to continue their argument, as someone outside called for him. "Wait here, please," he said, frowning, "I need to see to a few things."

Cas glared after him as he left, a very large part of her considering chasing him down and showing him at least a few of the things she *knew*. Things like how to use that knife in her hand, or how to break a nose with a single thrust of her palm.

Elander's voice pulled her away from her fantasy. "Do you have to start some sort of argument with everyone you meet?"

"Yes," she snapped, purely for the sake of being argumentative.

"You shouldn't push him like that. Especially not after you maimed several of his guards today."

"You should mind your own business."

"I am the right hand of the King-Emperor, his highest ranked soldier, and one of his closest confidantes. So this is all very much my business."

If you're so close to him, she wanted to ask, *then why were you trying to sneak me away from him earlier?*

But she didn't ask, because she was afraid Varen was still near enough to overhear. So instead, she simply put as much space between her and Elander as she could, settled herself down into one of the chairs in front of the fireplace, and waited.

After a moment she asked, "Speaking of your *business*, did you tend to that business in the south gardens? Those fires, and the people who set them...."

"Your friends fled the scene of their crime, if that's what you're asking. We didn't arrest any of them."

She inhaled and exhaled a deep, relieved breath.

Part of her wondered if they'd truly escaped, or if he'd let them go—just as he'd apparently been planning to let *her* go until the King-Emperor had interrupted them.

Questions swirled in her mind as the minutes passed. Elander eventually pushed away from the door and came to sit in the chair beside her. He plopped down in a perfectly undignified manner, letting his long legs hang over one of the high armrests, then wiggling down into the supple leather cushions. She was more aware of him than she wanted to be; in the intimate space, she couldn't help but notice every movement he made. Every breath he took. If she listened closely enough, she could hear what sounded like his heartbeat—or perhaps it was the pulse of his magic.

It was unnaturally loud, but not frantic. Unlike her, he didn't seem uncomfortable at all. On the contrary, his eyes were peacefully fluttering shut. She thought he might have been going to sleep.

Then he popped one eye open, and he caught sight of the dull bread knife still clenched in her fist. "What is that for?"

"Nothing."

"Nothing?"

"I just...I heard that scream earlier, and I thought..."

"That it might have been an assassin or something?"

"Perhaps."

"And what were you going to do? Use that to butter them to death?"

"I'm going to use it to poke out your eyes if you don't stop talking to me."

He grinned at this—the first true, *full* grin she'd seen from him. It stayed on his lips even when he closed his eyes and settled back down into the chair. The roguish smile made for an interesting contrast against his otherwise peaceful, handsome face. It intrigued her.

He intrigued her.

Which for some reason only made her want to stab him *more*.

The King-Emperor walked back in before she could, accompanied by a pretty young woman with silvery blonde hair. "Casia, this is Anneka. She will take you to one of the guest rooms and get you settled in while I continue to tend to a few matters. I'm sorry to leave you, but I hope we can continue our talk later. This evening, perhaps?"

She bit her lip, but nodded. As much as she hated to admit that Elander had a point, she had likely already caused enough trouble today. Irritating the King-Emperor any further wouldn't lead to her gaining anything useful.

After bidding farewell to him, she followed the servant woman out of the room to a winding staircase that brought them to what was either the fifth or sixth floor—Cas lost count as they climbed, distracted by the wall of windows that followed that staircase up. Beyond the glass lay a sweeping view of the foothills, the Lotheran River that cut through them, and—further in the distance—the coppery red silhouettes of the Blood-stone Mountains.

Anneka kept glancing at Cas as they walked, offering a friendly grin every time. Her eyes were kind, even when they took in the sight of Cas's own strange eyes and hair, and that smile of hers was disarming, making the long walk to this latest new, strange place feel slightly less intimidating at least.

"His Majesty insisted on putting you in the grandest of our guest rooms," Anneka informed her. Her expression remained friendly enough, but her tone—her true thoughts on the matter—were both impossible to read. "He's really taken a liking to you, it seems."

Cas said nothing, but her cheeks warmed a bit, suddenly embarrassed about her earlier outburst.

On the other hand, her anger toward Varen still felt justified, as she couldn't help the suspicions about *why* he had supposedly taken a liking to her. He'd said he understood why she didn't trust him, that he was going to *earn* that trust, but...

We'll see, Cas thought again as she and Anneka reached the last door at the end of a wide hallway. Anneka slipped a silver key from her pocket and used it to open the ornate door, before stepping back and gesturing for Cas to enter first.

The room that greeted Cas on the other side was the largest she had visited in the palace thus far. It was essentially its own miniature palace, with a separate sitting area as large as some entire houses in the city of Ciridan, a private bathing chamber, and a private balcony. The room held more drawers and trunks and wardrobes than could possibly be necessary, while the bed in the corner was more like a shrine —gauzy curtains cascaded down from above, the sheer fabric catching sunlight and making it appear to shimmer with fairy lights. That bed reminded Cas of a picture in one of the books Asra had given her. In the book, a princess had slept in a similar place, and when Cas was a child, her heart had ached with desire over how beautiful it all was.

As an adult, she couldn't help thinking that *this* was beautiful. Pristine. But it was...

It was entirely too much, and she was suddenly homesick for her cramped loft back home. She would have taken that loft's little window and its too-low beams over the massive glass panes and the swooping, stamped tin ceiling above her now, no questions asked.

Anneka was rattling through a drawer next to a

folding privacy screen in the corner of the room. After a moment, she straightened up and turned back to Cas, her arms full of pins and fabric swatches and measuring tapes. "Now," she began, "we can get you into some better clothes if we could just get your—"

"I like my clothes."

Anneka's smile never slipped, though it did tighten a bit in the corners. "Well, perhaps I could find you a spare change of things to wear while I clean yours?"

It still unnerved Cas, the thought of accepting even spare, secondhand things from the King-Emperor. She didn't want to be any further in debt to someone she didn't trust; if they were going to collaborate in any way, it seemed smart to keep the playing field as level as possible.

But she also didn't want to take her suspicions out on this friendly woman.

So she nodded. "Fine. Yes, of course—thank you."

Anneka looked relieved. With a little bow, she left the room and returned a short time later with the promised clothing. It was a simple dressing gown made of fabric so soft that Cas half wondered if it might have been enchanted with something.

"I'll find more that fits you," Anneka promised, "but I thought you might want something comfortable to sleep in for now. You look exhausted, if you don't mind me saying so, my lady."

"I'm fine."

"Then perhaps I could draw a bath? Or bring you something to eat?"

"I...actually, I suppose I am tired," Cas lied, because it seemed like the quickest way to get rid of this woman.

And it was.

Anneka clearly felt as if she had done her due diligence, because she stopped her questioning, and she gave a little bow. "You can leave your dirty things by the door; I'll be back to collect them." With that, she left.

Cas heard the latch *click*. She watched the door for several moments, making sure no one else was going to barge in and assault her with offers of comforts and fineries, before she moved again.

She changed into the gown that was not only sinfully soft, but also *not* covered in dungeon dust and spotted with flecks of blood. She left her dirty clothes by the door as she had been instructed, and then she went to the small pedestal sink next to the vanity against the far wall to wash the grime of the past days from her skin.

It had been a lie when she'd told Anneka she was tired, but when she sprawled out across the bed fit for royalty, it wasn't long before her eyes closed, and she fell asleep for the first time in days.

And she dreamed.

She always dreamed when she finally gave into sleep, and it was usually the same dream: A winged woman bathed in golden-white light watched her. This woman didn't speak. She didn't move. She didn't *help*, even as darkness wove into the dream and pulled it into the realm of nightmares instead.

Always, Cas found herself standing alone on the edge of a cliff at the beginning of the nightmare, watching the darkness roiling in from the distance.

Always, that darkness twisted and took the form of a great black wolf with shadow-wrapped teeth that opened wider and wider, until its jaws were unhinged enough to swallow the cliff, Cas, and everything else in its path.

Always, the golden-white woman's face would contort with fear and regret as she watched it all happening—her agony so great that Cas could *feel* it like a physical thing wrapping around her. But always, always, *always*...

Always, this woman only looked on as the wolf swallowed everything whole.

When Cas woke, covered in sweat and shaking from the memory of shadowy teeth, it was dark outside.

She grabbed a dressing robe that had been left by her bed, and she wrapped it around herself before stepping out onto the balcony.

There were two small, trickling fountains on either side of this balcony, and a bench situated between the two of them. She settled onto the bench and stared into one of those fountains, watching the rippling reflection of the three-quarter moon.

The moon had always given Cas an immense feeling of peace when she looked at it. In the first house she'd lived in with Asra, her room had had a window that opened out onto the roof. As her Fading Sickness took a deeper hold over her—and sleep grew increasingly harder to come by, and less necessary—Cas had passed countless nights on that roof, staring up at that heavenly body and losing herself in her thoughts.

Asra had found her up there one night, gazing into a moon the color of rust. And instead of scolding her for being out of bed yet again, she had told Cas a story of the Moon-kind people, whose magic took on as many different forms as the moon itself had phases. Most of their magic revolved around discovery—the ability to find paths and unlock things, to show people and things for what they truly were.

Nothing, Asra told her, *is ever truly lost or hidden to the Moon-kind.*

She had joked that Cas never slept because she was secretly one of the followers of Inya, the middle-goddess of the Moon, and thus too enamored with that main symbol of her.

Cas had taken her seriously—as seriously as a ten-year old could take things—because it meant she could pretend that the crescent-shaped scar on her jawline was a mark of magic, and not a reminder of those horrible whips cutting into her skin. And she liked the idea of never being lost, too, of always being able to find the truth and reflect it back for people to see.

Her gaze lifted away from the water and looked toward the city of Ciridan.

Had her friends stayed in that city, or did they go back to their hideaway?

She would have liked to have gone and found them now—and she was surprised that the royal army *hadn't* found them and dragged them back. Assuming Elander had told her the truth, anyway. For all she knew, they could have been in the palace dungeons at that very moment.

Even if they *had* been let go this time, it was only a matter of time before they came back for her.

And then what?

If she stayed, they would no doubt end up here as well. As prisoners... Or as *guests*, maybe—if she could trust the King-Emperor's word on that.

She lifted her eyes to the true moon, not its reflection, and she sighed.

If only I really did have the Moon Goddess's power to see the truth.

An uncomfortable thought occurred to her: Perhaps she was not seeing *some* truths because she was willfully refusing to consider anything other than the ones she had always believed.

She could not get that memory of being beaten in the street from her mind. The feel of the whips. The blood. The heat of the sun. The sting of the dust stirring up and assaulting her vision...

And Varen watching her.

But he had only been a child when it happened. A

prince under the control of his father, with nowhere to run. *She* had escaped that day, but he'd had to go back to this very palace. Back to his role as a prince—whether he'd wanted to or not. A child, but also a royal sworn to duty...

They should be judged by what they do, not what they are.

Her own words haunted her.

She looked down at her reflection in the fountain, and she frowned.

"Hypocrite," she muttered.

And then she went back into her bedroom in search of more substantial clothing to wear to a meeting with a King-Emperor.

Her own clothes had not reappeared—she strongly suspected Anneka might have 'accidentally' lost them— but there were several items neatly folded on the bench next to the embroidered folding screen. They were more simple but soft garments, likely borrowed from a servant similar to her size, but they were clean and perfectly comfortable.

She dressed quickly. When she stepped outside, a guard greeted her with a slight bow of his head. He was well-armed. She immediately noted a sword and three knives—and that was just what she could *see*.

Not exactly free to roam as a guest, am I?

But then, having an escort in this sprawling palace might not be the worst thing.

"Do you know where the King-Emperor is?" she asked.

The guard thought for a moment before nodding.

"Likely in the eastern library, given the hour. I can take you there if you'd like?"

"Please do."

He led the way, and Cas followed closely behind.

The palace at night seemed far less warm and inviting. The halls were mostly empty, so their footsteps echoed, harsh and hollow-sounding, off the walls. The massive windows that had offered such a spectacular view earlier were now eerie, distorting the wind-swept trees and clouds on the other side, and letting in odd patches of moonlight and shadows that played tricks on Cas's eyes and nearly made her stumble more than once.

They made it back to the main floor, and after a bit more weaving through the seemingly countless hallways, they finally came upon a pair of doors that each featured a carving of the Solasen family coat of arms. Two more guards stood on either side of this door.

"She needs to speak with His Majesty," her escort informed them. "Is he inside?"

The guards nodded and pulled open the doors. Cas steeled herself and stepped into the library.

CHAPTER 12

Cas's gaze was immediately drawn upwards as she took in the endless shelves of books lining the walls. She looked up and up and up...but no matter how far back she tilted her head, she couldn't seem to see where those books ended.

Finally, she stopped searching for that end, lowered her eyes, and instead examined the rest of the room that stretched before her. Strings of lights hung everywhere; the lights themselves were tiny spheres that looked to have been enchanted by magic that caused them to glow.

Directly ahead of her, and the most arresting feature of the room, was a spiraling staircase winding its way up to the higher levels. It was made up of polished, gleaming red wood and black iron posts that were twisted into elaborate designs, and the whole thing wrapped its way around a marble statue of a woman holding a book in one hand and a raised sword in the other.

Just to the right of that staircase was a series of comfortable looking chairs. The King-Emperor sat in one of them, reading.

Her guard escort gestured for her to keep moving. She thanked him for leading her and made her way over to Varen.

"Hello, Casia dear," he said without looking up.

On the way to this room, she had rehearsed precisely what she was going to say and how she would steer their conversation.

But before she could get any words out, she was distracted—as she so often was—by a book. The book resting open in Varen's lap had a striking illustration of a beautiful man dressed in black, holding a sword that he was using to drive away a horde of demonic-looking creatures. A woman stood back-to-back with the man, her hands lifted toward another swarm of demons on the other side.

Cas studied the drawing over Varen's shoulder for much longer than she meant to, until he finally pulled his gaze up to hers.

She swallowed to clear the sudden dryness in her throat. "I'm here to finish that talk we were having."

"Of course," he said, marking his page by turning down the corner of it, which made Cas cringe.

It doesn't matter to him if he destroys expensive books, she thought with a touch of resentment, *because he can just buy more.*

She forced her eyes away from the blasphemous sight.

"Did you accomplish those tasks you needed to see to?"

"Enough of them."

"That woman who died..."

"Will have a proper sending and burial. A cleansing in rose water, a marking in oils and then a burning, as is custom in the Windhaven Realm she hails from."

Cas nodded, grateful to hear it. She didn't know what had become of her adoptive parents' bodies after they'd died; she had fled too quickly from the scene. But she had often wondered if she should have gone back and taken care of them, or found someone to help her do so. Maybe the ghosts that haunted her would ultimately have been quieter ones, if only she had found a way to properly lay their bodies to rest.

The King-Emperor closed the book and placed it on the table beside his chair. "And just so you're aware, one of the other tasks I was tending to was preparing a formal summons for your friends, inviting them to come stay in my palace." He paused, reading her reaction before continuing. "I didn't send it yet, however; I wanted to wait for you to agree to our working together before I followed through on that particular task."

He stood, and Cas couldn't help looking him over once more as he did. It was still strange to be so close to him; she felt as if she had to recommit his appearance to her mind, to study some new part of him and convince herself of its realness, every time they were together like this.

He was only slightly taller than she was, she noticed

this time—not as tall or imposing as the captain of his Peace Keepers. She believed him when he said that captain commanded more fear and respect than he himself did, and yet this wasn't necessarily a slight against Varen. The King-Emperor still moved with an understated, graceful sort of authority that was befitting of the crown he wore. His power was simply...quieter. And she assumed *most* men paled in comparison to his captain. To that power that Elander seemed to emanate with every word he spoke and every move he—

Elander isn't even in here.

Why was she thinking about him?

She forced her attention back to the man in front of her. To those bright brown eyes that were watching her with the same intense curiosity he had been studying his book with.

"So, have you given any more thought to what I asked you earlier?" Varen asked. "About staying here and helping me?"

"Yes." She wandered along one of the bookshelves, occasionally pausing to investigate a spine more closely as she spoke. "And I've thought about how that servant woman caught the Fade only twelve days ago, correct? And now she's already gone. Which doesn't give me much confidence regarding your earlier offer to take care of my sick friend."

He frowned. "That's a reasonable conclusion, I suppose."

"But still, I was thinking that there might be a way

you actually *could* help me."

"And what might that be?"

She hesitated, tapping her fingers against a book with a spine as thick as her fist.

There was a decent chance her next suggestion was going to get her thrown back into the dungeons.

She forced herself to keep talking all the same. "Well, I've been taking care of that friend of mine for years now, and I've managed to find one particular remedy that staves off the effects of the Fading Sickness. Not indefinitely, but..."

"For years? Really?"

"Yes."

"Fascinating..." He braced a hand against the side of that chair he'd been sitting in and stared at her, his lips slightly parted and his brow furrowed, as if he couldn't bring himself to fully believe this claim.

She fought the urge to reach for the scar on her jawline.

He'd *seen* her and her Fade-marked self—and had glimpsed Asra as well, possibly—thirteen years ago, whether he remembered it or not.

"Well then," he began after a moment, "do tell about this remedy you've discovered."

"The problem is that this, um, remedy, is rather hard to come by. As in, it's only available through means that aren't entirely... legal."

He arched an eyebrow.

"*Fractal*, some people call it. It's a name people have

204

given to a plant that has absorbed the by-product of Prism-kind magic. There's a particular kind of flower that seems to absorb and hold the Prism-kind energy best, and this flower is usually harvested from the In-Between, and it—"

"I know what Fractal is."

"Oh. Well, that's...good?"

"I may be a young and inexperienced ruler," he said drily, "but I am not entirely naive. Though I've only ever heard of Fractal being used in...*recreational* ways." He was quiet for a minute, and then he added, "My father outlawed *all* magic-tainted items and substances, regardless of their purpose—and that law remains to this day. You're aware of this?"

"Yes."

"Yet you're willingly admitting to me that you've been illegally buying and trading for one of these substances for years."

"I...Yes. I guess I am."

"And you're wide awake at this time? You do realize who you're talking to?"

A warning tingled over her scalp. For a brief moment, she thought she might have overestimated his true desire to ignore her questionable history and to work alongside her. She regretted not hiding any sort of weapon on herself. Surely she could have found something worth using in that massive room they'd stuck her in. A sewing needle, a bit of pottery she could have broken into sharp shards, or—yes—even just a butter knife.

But then Varen's expression relaxed, and a small smile broke through. "It seems I've earned a bit of your trust, then."

She slowly released her breath. "A very tiny bit."

"It's a start, isn't it?" He chuckled softly. "Prism-kind flowers. Hm. Yet another clever thought," he said, striding over to a nearby table that was stacked high with books and scattered with paper and quills. "You're full of those, aren't you?"

She blushed. She couldn't help it. She wasn't generally one to be won over by flattery, but he had a way of delivering it—with that genuine smile and the easy tone of his voice—that made it difficult not to believe what he was saying.

"So anyway," she stammered, "I was wondering if maybe you had the resources to, um, help me procure some more of those plants. And perhaps those servants and doctors you mentioned might even be able to create a more efficient medicine using them."

"In exchange for?"

"For me helping you find more answers about the Fade, whatever that may entail."

His eyes flashed with excitement as he stepped closer to her once more. "Excellent. It seems we *do* have an understanding, then." He offered his hand.

She hesitated only a moment before shaking it.

He gave an extra little squeeze before letting go. Warmth flooded through her, despite her best efforts to guard herself against it.

So very *strange*, being here with him this way.

But perhaps...

Perhaps she'd been wrong about him. Perhaps they *could* successfully work together for the good of the empire—or for the good of her friends, at least. It wasn't as if she had a plethora of other options available to her, especially after that disastrous meeting with Darkhand. That Fire-kind bastard would likely be cutting off her supply of those life-sustaining plants indefinitely now, regardless of how much money she threw at him.

But surely the man beside her had more power and useful connections than even Darkhand did.

"Well, now that that's all settled," Varen went on, "I suppose I should tell you what I've been doing in here this evening. Since we're now proper partners in this, and you've revealed some things to me tonight..." He beckoned for her to follow him as he walked back to the table, and she did. Once there, he shifted some of the mess aside until he found a rolled piece of parchment, sealed by wax that was stamped with three separate symbols.

She stared at that seal, as transfixed as she'd been when she'd seen those symbols on the window during her failed escape attempt.

"You know what these are, yes?" he asked.

"They're...they're the symbols of the three upper-gods."

"Precisely. And I assume you know the stories surrounding those gods?"

Cas nodded, hesitantly. "Some of them."

"Of course you do. Because despite my ancestors' attempts to erase divine magic, and the stories surrounding those gods, both things persist. Stories in particular have a way of enduring in spite of everything, I've noticed. I'm sure you've heard the stories about the beginning of our world, for example."

She had, but she was curious to hear his version of things, so she feigned ignorance for the moment.

"As I've heard it told," he went on, "in the beginning there were, as you said, three upper-gods—the Stone, Sun, and Rook. The *Moraki* deities. The Stone God gave the world its form. The Sun Goddess brought light and life into that world. And the clever Rook God filled that created life with knowledge, with an awareness of right and wrong and what it *meant* to be alive. This trio departed soon after their work was finished, but each of the three upper-gods had four main servants that continued to roam these mortal lands for a long time afterwards."

"The Marr," Cas recalled. "The middle-gods."

"Correct. And that brings us to this..." he carefully broke the seal of that parchment, unfurled it, and spread it on the table between them. "A map of all three empires in our known world. Isn't it lovely? Have you ever seen one so detailed?" He seemed to lose himself for a moment, admiring the craftsmanship of it. "I had one of the master scholars up at the institute in Bellmere put it together for me. It shows the locations of what most of those researchers *believe* to be the twelve godhavens."

"The twelve what?"

"The sacred places where the middle-gods made their homes when they dwelled among us." He weighted the corners of the map down with an odd assortment of objects from the messy table, and then he started to tap his way across the mapped empires, pointing out places as he went.

Cas followed his pointing, counting along in her head. Twelve locations. Twelve identical triangles next to twelve different divine symbols.

The triangle closest to the palace she now stood in was located in Oblivion, and the symbol beside it was the same one that Captain Elander had on his wrist.

She stared at it, at the name of the God of Death swirling beside it in elegant letters, while Varen continued to speak.

"Although it was the Moraki who created our world," he went on, "it was their powerful servants who have truly shaped this world's history; this is why you will hear most scholars referring to our empires collectively as the *Marrlands*. And some of these godhavens where the middle-gods once took up residence are now sacred shrines or landmarks that locals regularly pray to, while others are completely inaccessible to us due to powerful magic or other oddities surrounding them."

Cas thought of the silvery clouds that surrounded Oblivion. "This one...this *godhaven*...is very close." She let her finger tap against that triangle over Oblivion's dark-ness, trying to sound only casually interested. Like an

209

outside observer who had never witnessed that darkness firsthand.

"Yes." Varen ran a hand along the curve of his jaw, his eyes distant with thought once more. "I recently sent Captain Elander to pay that place a visit."

Cas inhaled and exhaled slowly, forcing her excited pulse to slow and her burning curiosity not to show.

"As he's one that carries the mark of the God of Death," he explained, "the deadly airs of that place don't seem to bother Elander as much as others, so he was the perfect candidate to go explore it for me."

They didn't seem to bother me either, and I have no such mark, Cas thought—and she had to bite her tongue to keep herself from saying it out loud.

He obviously didn't know that she had been in Oblivion, or that she already knew Elander had been there. Which meant that the captain of his Peace Keepers had said nothing of the matter.

She would also be keeping her mouth shut about it. She might have decided to cautiously trust Varen, but that didn't mean she needed to spill every secret she kept.

"And did he find anything interesting?" she asked.

"Unfortunately, no. Not really."

Nothing aside from me, she thought. 'Interesting' was precisely the word he'd used in the room at the inn, wasn't it?

"But what exactly was he looking for?" she asked.

"Anything useful to my research. Some sign that the middle-god had been there within the past few decades,

210

or that his magic might still persist in that place—enough magic to adversely affect my empire. Or something that proved the opposite."

Cas considered his words for a minute. "So...you believe the Fading Sickness may have originated in Oblivion—from the God of Death himself? That it's trickling out from that place he used to inhabit, somehow?"

"I can't say for sure. But I *do* believe it is divine in origin. As did my father. It's too powerful, too unpredictable and strange, to be anything else. Also? I can't think of a single instance of the Fading Sickness that has taken the life of one of the divinely marked. Can you?"

When she stopped to think about it, she realized he had a point: Every victim she had personally witnessed had been unmarked.

"Kerse is the most obvious divine culprit," Varen continued, "given the things he and his magic reign over, but it could have been any one of the twelve more powerful deities, I suppose. Or even one of the three upper-gods who lord over them."

"A divine sickness..."

"And if that remedy you've been using on your friend is having an effect, then that lends some more support to that theory."

"How so?"

"The Prism flowers are stained by divine magic." His words were coming out in a rush, suddenly, as if he was on the verge of discovery and his mouth couldn't move quickly enough to keep up with his thoughts. "But the

Prism-kind's power is only from the lesser-spirit Charu, so even a large, concentrated amount of this power wouldn't be enough to cure or fully counter magic from one of the gods above it—thus it hasn't cured your friend. It's only kept her alive. Do that make sense?"

Cas had to turn this theory over in her mind several times, but then she nodded. Because even here—where this sort of magic was outlawed—people still knew of that hierarchy of the gods and their magic.

That lesser-spirit Charu served the middle-goddess of the Moon, who in turn served Solatis, the upper-goddess of the Sun. This meant that the magic used by the Prism-kind ultimately derived their power from Solatis—but it was a watered-down magic. It could never be as powerful as magic wielded by the Moon-kind. And Solatis herself was the only one who could wield Sun magic; there were people who carried her mark, but Cas had never heard of any of those people being capable of using Sun magic without killing themselves in the process. The same was true of those marked by the other two upper-gods.

"So if the Fading *is* divine in origin," she thought aloud, "it was likely a middle-god—or one of the upper-gods— who created it. Because otherwise, the flowers laced with Prism-kind magic would probably be enough to cure it."

"My thoughts exactly," said the King-Emperor, looking pleased. "You seem rather well-educated about the hierarchy of magic."

"I have a few books on the subject."

212

She had *one* book, precisely.

And she was briefly embarrassed, thinking of her dilapidated bookshelf shoved into the corner of her room back home, and how tiny and insignificant it seemed compared to the vast amount of knowledge that this room—and the King-Emperor himself—held.

"Well, there are plenty more here, and you're welcome to them anytime," he said, almost as an afterthought as he started to pace between those plentiful shelves.

She mumbled a *thank you*, and then she quickly continued to add to their theory, trying to prove that she *was* as knowledgable as he seemed to think she was. "Everything I've ever read on the subject suggests that no middle-god or lesser-spirit has fully descended into this world for at least a century, and neither has their magic. That magic exists only in diluted form, in the blood of the ones marked at birth by those deities." *In the people that your father slaughtered without restraint,* she wanted to add.

But she pressed her lips tightly together and kept those words inside of her for the moment.

"But the first case of the Fading Sickness was only, what, just over twenty years ago?"

"That's true." He hesitated, as if they had reached the edge of his personal understanding on the subject, and he wasn't certain he wanted to jump off into the unknown. "But more powerful *shades* of these gods have still paid us visits, even in more recent history," he eventually said.

"Shades?"

"Supernatural beings that originated from the more

powerful gods and goddesses. More so than just those who are born with a mark, a blessing, of one of those deities; these shades could be considered actual *pieces* of those gods that broke off from the ascended and returned to our world as full beings."

Cas stared at the map, at those twelve scattered symbols, as she tried to picture what one of those gods or goddesses might look like strolling through the streets of Ciridan, or Fallenbridge....

"The current High Queen of the Sundolian Empire is the daughter of such a shade—of a shade and a human," Varen said. "Her magic, the rumors say, is terribly powerful, but also unstable, because of it."

Cas was aware of this woman. The *Dragon Queen*, people called her. But she knew little about her beyond that—and beyond the fact that she and that powerful, unstable magic of hers had helped the current High King of Sundolia overthrow his father's rule.

"The divine are fluid, complicated, and unpredictable." Varen massaged the spot between his eyes, the weight of his crown and the obligations it carried on obvious display to Cas for perhaps the first time. "Could you imagine if we truly *are* dealing with one of them? This is yet another reason my predecessors wanted to stamp out all of our empire's ties to those dangerous gods and their magic."

"But you said you weren't interested in waging wars against divine magic, right?" she reminded him.

"I'm not as obsessed with it as my father was," he

replied, somewhat stiffly. "But it may all be related. And I am only trying to point out that when the gods begin to meddle, even the tiniest bit, it does not end well for us mortals."

"We still have no real proof that anything divine is at work when it comes to the Fade, correct? Nothing beyond theories, I mean."

He stopped pinching the bridge of his nose and looked up. His eyes narrowed, and for the second time that evening, she feared she might have overstepped her bounds.

"Not yet," he said. "But that is what I aim to find. *Proof*." His voice was calm and cordial enough, though any trace of that warmth she'd felt from him earlier was gone.

She didn't reply right away.

She could understand why he was concerned. The possibility that they might be up against the gods themselves was terrifying.

But more immediately terrifying—at least to her—were the potential side-effects of a crusade against those gods.

The divinely-marked like Nessa and Zev were already treated poorly enough in this empire—what would happen if it turned out that the Fading Sickness really *was* derived from something divine, just as their magic was?

Varen no doubt considered those marks her friends carried to be part of the gods' *meddling*. He could use all of this to reignite that war against the marked. He claimed that he had no interest in that war, but it would be all too easy...

She absently clenched and unclenched her hand, part of her already wishing she had never used it to shake his.

Or perhaps I'm just assuming the worst again.

"If you do find proof, then what?" She tried to keep her voice as even as he had. "You said yourself that it would likely take divine magic to cure this sickness. And your own Captain Elander uses magic given to him by the gods—so you can't believe that *all* divine meddling is bad."

He watched her for another moment, his eyes still narrowed and dark, and she held her breath.

Then a slight smile played at the corners of his lips.

"Clever again." He slowly pulled his gaze away from her, walked to the end of the table, picked up a decanter of wine, and poured himself a glass. "I don't need you to point out my hypocrisy, however; I am well aware of it. But Elander's magic is a necessary evil, I've come to accept. And as for a divine cure...Well, we've tried that kind of magic on a smaller-scale, of course. I mentioned my personal doctor was one of the Oak-kind, didn't I?"

She nodded.

"He carries more power of the Goddess of Healing than any other person I know. And yet, he couldn't alleviate that kitchen servant's suffering—or the suffering of any others that came before her."

Cas fought off a shudder at the memory of that dead woman's face.

"I suspect that any cure will be more complicated than the basic magic carried by one of those average, marked magic users like my doctor. It's something we can further explore if we find the proof that this sickness really *is* caused by something divine." He paused. Gave his head a little shake, and then continued in a determined voice. "But collecting that proof comes first, and that is where *you* come in, of course."

"Is it?"

"Yes. Because of two reasons: One, because as the cases in this palace have increased, fewer and fewer of my soldiers are willing to go investigate any *new* cases. They believe that sickness might be contagious. I don't think it is, for the record, but on the off chance that it could be…"

"…I can't catch something I already have."

"Exactly." He poured a second glass of wine and carried it over to her. "And secondly, I wonder if there's something I've missed while studying those cases; something that somebody touched by this same sickness might be able to see if they were to witness it happening in someone else."

She thought of that strange pull she'd felt when she'd walked by that death room earlier. Maybe she should have mentioned it to him.

But she still did not fully trust the man standing in front of her, so she kept quiet. She swirled the wine around in her glass. It smelled of oak and bitterness, and it tasted even worse, but she managed not to grimace as she swallowed it down.

The King-Emperor lifted his eyes toward the upper levels of the library, staring into the strings of lights woven through the railings for a moment before he spoke again. "And I hope you realize that you will be doing a great service to me—and this entire empire—by taking on this task. You could be the savior we've been waiting for, you know."

Savior.

The word settled oddly over her. She shifted where she stood, as if she could redistribute its weight and make it more comfortable somehow.

She had only been trying to save Asra; she wasn't entirely sure when that had changed, but now it seemed there was no way of turning back—so she stopped her shuffling just as quickly, and stood calmly in spite of the vicious anxieties unfurling inside of her.

She didn't intend to show Varen her doubts.

Because she had already decided she would see this through in spite of her fears, as she had done with so many other missions before it. So as far as anybody else in this palace would know, she was fearless, with a heart made of steel and a resolve that would not wither, even if she had to face the gods themselves.

With a smile, she raised that glass full of bitter wine. "To saving the empire, then," she said.

CHAPTER 13

An hour later, Cas left the King-Emperor to his research and musings and headed back to her guest room. Her escort had not waited for her. She'd insisted that she could find her way back to her room on her own, and, perhaps as a show of trust between them, Varen hadn't insisted on summoning another guard to make sure she didn't stray from that path.

She found her way easily enough, and when she arrived, there were no longer guards outside of her room. The inside of it was free of servants as well—though some had clearly visited while she was away; there were new clothes laid across the massive bed, along with a silver tray full of fruits and cheeses, flaky pastries, and delicate chocolates.

Cas changed into a clean nightgown that she plucked from amongst the newly delivered clothes, then she sat at the edge of the bed, absently nibbling on the food that had been left for her. She lost track of time while her thoughts tumbled restlessly. She *let* those thoughts race this time, because the only thing worse than her anxiety taking her into its full grip was the threat of loneliness doing the same thing.

Here in the quiet, sitting only with the impossible tasks that loomed in her future, she couldn't deny it any longer: She missed her friends.

Nessa would be beside herself at the sight of this room. Rhea would pretend to be unimpressed by whatever images Silverfoot sent her of it, but secretly, she would be in awe too. Zev would be mostly concerned about the food being served, and Cas already felt sorry for the kitchen servants who would be tasked with attending to him. Laurent would likely grow bored of it all very quickly—*if* he agreed to grace the palace with his presence at all.

And Asra...Asra would be truly safe and comfortable in this palace full of bright windows and warm fireplaces, and maybe that comfort meant she would respond better to whatever medicine Cas and the king could give her.

Cas ached to have them here. Now. To have *anybody* here in this room that somehow felt like an expansive, barren cavern despite all the sparkling, expensive things it was overflowing with.

Then came a knock at the door. And as soon as she walked over and cautiously pulled it open, she instantly regretted ever thinking just *anybody* would do for company—because Captain Elander stood on the other side.

"*Why?*" she asked, her eyes lifting toward the ceiling, demanding answers from whatever god was apparently amusing themselves by finding new ways to torment her.

"Why what?"

She lowered her eyes back to the man before her. "Why do you keep showing up everywhere I go in this place?"

"Because I live here?"

"It's a giant palace. Surely you could find somewhere else to be, rather than where *I* happen to be at any given moment."

"I absolutely could. But I am also at the mercy of the King-Emperor's orders—and he sent me to see you. It's all very unfortunate, I agree."

Before she could think of a properly venomous response to this, she caught sight of a pair of women watching them from the end of the hall. She pressed her lips together, trying to remain civil. She *liked* not having guards standing outside her door and escorting her everywhere. Shouting at the highly-ranked man standing in front of her would likely put that bit of trust she'd earned in jeopardy.

Elander apparently noticed the people watching them, too, because he lowered his voice and added, "Could we talk somewhere a bit more private, perhaps?"

Her body reacted strangely to this suggestion. Strangely and *traitorously*. She should have closed the door in his face. Should have insisted he write his message to her down on a scrap of parchment and slide it under the door.

She didn't.

Her hand stayed braced against the doorframe, just for a moment, while her heart skipped a few too many beats at the thought of being someplace *private* with him. She turned around and walked back inside without a word.

But she left the door open.

After a moment, he followed her in, softly shutting that door behind him. She thought of the latch clicking shut in his room back at Madam Rosa's, and an involuntary—and not entirely unpleasant—shiver coursed through her. She forced herself to turn and face him.

His gaze slid briefly up and down her body before determinedly fixing back on her eyes.

And Cas suddenly remembered that she was wearing only a thin night gown, and equally thin undergarments beneath it.

Heat flooded over her. She could have crossed the room and grabbed the robe that hung from the hook by the washroom door, but that would have made it seem entirely too much like she was reacting to his gaze. So instead, she just tried harder to seem indifferent, and to suppress that shiver that was now threatening to rattle her very bones.

His appearance made suppressing this...difficult.

Much like he'd been when he'd flung open the door to

his room at Madam Rosa's, he looked as if he'd been on his way to bed. He was wearing a thin shirt draped loosely over his broad chest, and she couldn't help but think of how easily she had been able to feel his well-defined muscles when he had been so close to her on that night they'd met. Her fingers itched to feel them again. To run their way through his hair, which was completely loose—the first time she had ever seen it like that. The dark waves of it framed his face in a way that again made her notice the contrasts. Soft elegance against the sharp, powerful lines of his jaw...it didn't make sense. It was beautiful. *He* was beautiful—but in a disorienting way that she couldn't neatly explain or understand, and she *hated* not being able to explain people.

Her lip curled in annoyance. Not only had he shown up here and insisted on barging into her room, but he had also decided to look even better than usual while he did it.

The audacity.

"I take it you're still upset with me for some reason," he said, "even though—as I already told you before—I let your friends go."

"Only *after* you tried to get them thrown into a prison cell! Did you think I would forget that you blatantly told the King-Emperor that they started those fires?"

"I told him that because I was trying to persuade him to let me deal with the whole lot of you myself." That powerful jaw tightened. "And only so that I could *save* you."

"Well, thanks so much for thinking of me. I mean, if

only you could have saved me from this horrible prison."
She gestured to the bed, and to the tray of sweets and the
piles of clothes that had been left for her.

"Don't be stupid."

"Excuse me?"

"Is that all it takes to convince you that a place is safe?
Some fluffy pillows and silk sheets?"

"And don't forget the fancy, delicious chocolates," she
added, plucking one of the raspberry-powder dusted deli-
cacies from the tray and offering it to him.

He looked as if he was considering smacking that
chocolate from her hand, but he refrained. "Congratula-
tions," he said. "You are the world's most oblivious
prisoner."

"I'm not a prisoner. I could leave if I wanted to."

"Sure you could."

"Even if the King-Emperor tried to keep me here
against my will—which he isn't doing—I'm exceptionally
good at getting away, if you haven't noticed."

"Not good enough, apparently."

"I escaped *you* twice already," she reminded him.
"And I would have done it a third time this morning, if
things had gone a bit differently. I *could* have done it a
third time. But I decided to trust you to get me out
instead. Which, oh, by the way, means that *you* are actually the reason I ended up in this so-called prison. So if it
turns out that that's what this really is, then it's your fault
I'm here."

"Yes, of course—your thieving, lawless lifestyle had nothing to do with your ending up here."

She irritably popped the chocolate into her mouth, chewed it, and swallowed it.

He was still standing there when she finished.

"Will you please just go away?"

"Nope."

"*Nope?*"

"Nope, because I was sent to talk to you, as I said—and I want to know what you met with Varen about, first. He didn't give me any details when he sent me after you. He only said that you had agreed to do whatever was necessary to aid him."

"Perhaps he didn't give you the details because it's none of your business."

"Again, I am trying to *help* you."

Cas chewed on her lip, suddenly remembering the way he had held so tightly to her when they had encountered Varen in the shadow of the palace gates. That hold had felt so powerful and, yes, *protective*. But she wasn't convinced she needed protecting from Varen—and if she did, she was positive she didn't want it from the annoying, confusing soldier currently standing in front of her.

She left him and walked out to the balcony, hoping the moonlight and fresh air might help her keep her thoughts calm and her words clear.

He followed her.

Of course.

She'd expected he would, but she ignored him anyway.

He didn't seem to be in a hurry to make her speak or otherwise acknowledge him. He folded his arms across his chest and leaned back against the palace wall. His eyes fixed on the city in the distance, on the faintly glowing lanterns lining the great Circle Road that enclosed that city. Her own eyes fixed on the stars above for several minutes, until finally, she cut her gaze back toward him. "What is it with you and the king-emperor, anyway?"

"I don't trust him." His reply was sharp and unapologetic.

"You *serve* him. How can you serve someone you don't trust?"

"For someone with a mark and magic like mine, the alternative would be death."

Cas's mouth was already open, a retort ready to fly—but something stopped her. She turned away from him again, this time fixing her eyes on one of the balcony's fountains, on the tallest of the white lilies that were planted in a trough running along its edge. "I think I would choose death."

He laughed softly.

"What are you laughing at? I'm serious."

"All I know is a lot of people say they don't fear death —that they would face it boldly, if need be—and yet they all run screaming away from my magic, which is only a shadow of it." As he talked, he stepped closer, and he lazily waved his hand toward one of those white flowers.

Out of the corner of her eye, Cas saw his mark glow a soft shade of whiteish-blue. The edges of the flower's petals shriveled, and the vibrant green stem darkened, starting to collapse under the weight of its bloom.

"It's not the same," she insisted.

"No?"

"No." She moved closer to that flower, shooing her hand at him until he stopped casting his magic.

He curled his hand back to his chest. He looked mostly amused by her gesturing, but his mark had stopped glowing.

Cas gently reached for the flower. It seemed to perk up a bit at her touch, its stem standing straighter and straighter with her continued coaxing. "And besides, *I* am not afraid of you or your magic. And no—not of death, either."

That was partly a lie, of course, but he didn't need to know that, just as Varen didn't need to know that she was afraid.

They were silent. Elander stared at that flower cupped in her hand, his eyes iced over in thought. He stood so very close; he hadn't stepped back when she'd waved at him to stop his magic a moment ago, and now he was close enough to her that she could smell his earthy scent, and she could almost feel the space around them rippling with his restrained power every time he took a breath. That power seemed to have stilled the breeze and sucked all the sounds from the air, leaving the two of them enclosed in a silent, intimate darkness.

It was quiet enough that his next words needed to be no more than a whisper. "Please. Just... tell me you don't fully trust him."

She was startled by his use of the word *please*. "Of course I don't *fully* trust him." She let go of the flower and turned to face him. "But he and I have the same goals, so I..."

"Debatable."

"We may have different reasons for wanting to meet those goals, I'll admit. But he'll see things the way I do eventually, if we just work together at this for long enough."

"Ah. I see."

"You see what?"

"That you're delusional."

"No, I'm an optimist."

"That's essentially the same thing," he countered. But there was less bite behind his words, suddenly. He seemed to have abruptly resigned himself to the fact that she fully intended to ignore his warnings about the King-Emperor.

Good for him.

It was a waste of time to keep arguing with her. She would decide for herself whether Varen was ultimately worth trusting.

Their conversation obviously at an impasse, Elander sighed and walked to the outermost point of the curved balcony's railing and leaned over it.

She stared at him, wondering what she was supposed

to say next.

Was he just planning to stay here and irritate her all night?

"*Azalea*," he laughed suddenly.

"What's so funny about that?"

"That wasn't your real name, I know. And I'm guessing Casia Greythorne isn't either, is it? How many other aliases do you have, precisely?"

"They're just names." She shrugged. "They all suit me well enough."

He turned around and leaned casually back against the railing. "The *Thorn* part of that last one does, at least. Because the old saying *a thorn in my side* comes so very vividly to mind whenever I think of you."

"It's long been an aspiration of mine to be a thorn in the side of Peace Keepers everywhere." She gave a little bow. "So thank you for that compliment."

"You're welcome."

She bit her bottom lip, and she almost laughed in spite of her determination to *not* enjoy this frustrating man's company. "You were actually the first person I've ever used the Azalea alias on."

"So, I was her first client."

"And *only* client."

"How special."

She rolled her eyes.

"Though I can't say I would have recommended her services to anyone—even if Miss *Azalea* had intended to keep soliciting more clients. Because personally, I was left very unsatisfied."

"Sorry to hear that."

He pushed away from the railing and sauntered closer to her. "Of course, if she ever wanted to try and win my business back, well, you know where to find me."

"Indeed I do. I can't seem to get rid of you." She put a hand on his chest to hold him at an arm's length. He once more seemed amused by the gesture, but again, he didn't fight her unspoken command to stop. "Although I wouldn't get my hopes up if I were you," she told him. "Something tells me Miss Azalea isn't—nor will she ever be—interested in *servicing* you again."

The smile slowly spreading across his face was devastating enough on its own; the low, dulcet tones he next spoke in were simply...*unfair*. "I'll stick with Thorn then, I suppose."

She swallowed. Hard. And with a coolness she did not in any way feel, she lowered her hand back to her side and said, "Works for me."

He tilted his head a bit to the side, studying her again, a ghost of that arrogant smile still on his face.

She fought the urge to fold her arms across her chest, to help the thin nightgown shield more of her body from view. The air, her skin, her blood—it was all humming with an odd electricity. It was distracting. Annoying. And she didn't know how to make it stop.

Finally, he spoke again, his suddenly casual voice

disrupting that current of electricity. "I hope you were serious about not being afraid of me, Thorn."

"Why's that?"

"Because the reason I came up here was to tell you that the King-Emperor is concerned about a string of deaths in Belwind, the infamous city on the Point. And you and I are going to be working together on investigating it."

She barely suppressed a groan. "Together?"

"We head for the Great Southern Road at sunrise."

"Do you think Varen would consider returning me to that dungeon I escaped from instead?"

"Probably," he replied, matching her dry tone. "But something tells me you're too soft to survive another night in that dungeon, so why would you insist on such a thing?"

"The last person who assumed that I was too *soft* to survive is dead now."

"Is that a threat?"

"It absolutely is."

"Well, I'll be sure to sleep with one eye open, then."

"I hate you. So much."

"Fantastic." He yawned. "Anyway, you should probably get some sleep. If you aren't awake when my company and I head out, I won't think twice about leaving you behind."

"Maybe I *want* to be left behind."

"That will certainly win you Varen's favor. I'm sure

nothing bad will come of disobeying his commands. Because you aren't his prisoner—like you said."

She glowered at him.

"Goodnight, Thorn."

"Goodnight, Ass."

He smiled that devious smile again, and she turned away before he could see the way it made her face flush to what she imagined was an embarrassingly bright shade of red.

She kept her eyes on the sky while she listened to him walk away. The moonlight seemed brighter than earlier—or perhaps that was just wishful thinking. Because she wanted that moon to illuminate everything within and around her, and she wanted its goddess's magical ability to see the truth even more desperately than before.

Because which was she, really?

A prisoner or a savior?

CHAPTER 14

THE FOLLOWING MORNING, CAS WAS NOT LATE—BECAUSE SHE had not gone back to sleep. She had dressed for a day of riding and packed a bag with Anneka's help, and just before sunrise she'd descended the stairs into the main entrance hall, where she found Varen surrounded by a circle of servants and advisors. They were all discussing last minute details of that mission she was to go on with the captain—a mission that she had spent the night mentally coming to terms with.

She would just do her best to ignore Elander and keep her focus on more important things.

As soon as Varen caught sight of Cas, he excused himself from his conversation and walked over to her. He looked happy to see her—or at least thrilled for an excuse to escape those stern-faced advisors.

"Good morning, Casia dear," he said. "You slept well, I hope?"

"Yes," she lied.

"And I trust that Captain Elander found you last night, and that he explained the assignment I have for you two?"

"We talked. Briefly."

"Good, good..." The King-Emperor started toward the door, motioning for her to follow him. He led her outside, and then along a path that eventually wound its way down toward a stable, stopping several times to chat with both nobles and servants who were strolling along the same path. Cas took in the scenery as she walked, doing her best to avoid eye contact with people unless Varen insisted on introducing her to them.

They reached the stable's entrance before Varen spoke directly to her once more. "I also wanted to let you know before you headed out..." he began, after nodding hello to a man Cas assumed to be the stable master, "...that I have officially sent word to your friends, and, should they agree to come to the palace, I will send escorts to make certain they get here safely. So I imagine they will be here waiting for you when you return from this little mission."

The thought of coming back to such a reunion made Cas's heart feel lighter—even as she heard Captain Elander's annoying voice thundering orders somewhere in the distance. A moment later, she spotted that captain emerging from the stable.

"Thank you," she told Varen, turning her gaze back to him and keeping it there for as long as she could, even as Elander approached them.

"Take care of one another, you two," the King-Emperor said. "I am expecting great things from this partnership."

And I'm just hoping I can get through this without stabbing him, Cas thought. But she followed Elander's lead and gave a small bow to the King-Emperor's request. Varen smiled at them both before leaving to speak further with the stable master.

Elander looked her over, his lip curling a bit in distaste, as if he was annoyed by her very presence. No doubt he'd been hoping she would oversleep.

Too bad, asshole. You're stuck with me.

He averted his eyes and beckoned a servant who was holding the reins of a dappled grey horse. "You ride, I hope?"

"Well enough," Cas replied, snatching those reins from him. She swung into the saddle and trotted away without looking back.

She was, in fact, an excellent rider. They'd had those two horses—Rose and Faus—at their hideaway back in the forest for quite some time. Both were rescues. As in, her team had *rescued* them from a client who hadn't paid Cas the agreed-upon sum for the job he'd hired her to do. She had spent a week clearing his land of dozens of tullies, nasty little monsters with teeth made for stripping flesh from bones. The reward was supposed to have been a hundred gold coins; the client had coughed up only half of that when the time came. And no horse deserved to live with, to quote Zev, *a greedy son of a bitch who doesn't keep his word.*

So, two days later, those horses had found a new home in the Valshade Forest.

Problem solved.

Cas's mind was flooded, suddenly, with memories of long trail rides with Laurent, and early mornings spent tending to those horses alongside Nessa. But she quickly shook her head free of those things. She couldn't think of home. Last night had been brutal after Elander had left; as much as his company had grated on her, she had been right to think that being alone would be worse. And she needed to be alert today. She couldn't afford to let her mind wander back toward those lonely thoughts.

A group had gathered at the crest of a nearby hill, their horses fully packed and their bodies tense with nerves over their impending mission. She walked her horse closer to this group. Close enough to not feel alone, to blend in and let them know that she was ready to leave with them, but far enough away that hopefully they wouldn't actually *speak* to her. At the moment, she was more interested in getting acquainted with her horse.

"Lily," she read, running her fingers along the name stitched into the leather reins. Cas patted the horse's neck. "Nice to meet you."

Lily gave a whinny and tossed her head happily at Cas's touch. She especially seemed to like it when Cas leaned up and scratched her between the ears.

"I see you've made fast friends with your mount,"

came an airy, cheerful voice. Cas turned to see a woman stepping her jet-black horse closer to Lily. The bright red hair of the woman was vaguely familiar, and it took Cas only a moment to place her pretty, impish face; she was one of the soldiers who had helped arrest her at Darkhand's.

A man followed closely behind her, his gigantic horse moving with slow, plodding steps. He looked as if he might have been related to Varen; he had the same fair skin, the same sharp nose, and sparkling brown eyes that seemed to be trying to draw a confession—or at least information—out of everything he glanced at.

And following closely behind *him* was the captain and current bane of Cas's existence.

"This is Tara Graylock," Elander told Cas, nodding toward the red-haired woman, who gave a theatrical bow. He looked to the man and added, "And this is Caden Fellmirr. Both of them are experienced in what we will be doing over these next days; they know what I expect of them, and I expect *you* to listen to any commands they give. Do not make me regret agreeing to let you work with me on this. Understood?"

Cas fought the urge to give him a mocking salute. "Yes," she replied.

He looked briefly surprised—perhaps at her decision to not fight this particular battle with him—but then he left without another word. He mounted a silver-grey stallion and cantered to the head of their gathered group, calling for that group to move out as he went.

They were a company of thirty at most. The King-Emperor had said that some were flat out refusing to go on this sort of mission...how many had refused to go along because they were afraid?

Tara misinterpreted the frown etching itself deep onto Cas's face. "Don't worry," she said with a wink, "we aren't too harsh on the new recruits."

"Just don't do anything stupid," Caden added in a bored tone, "and I'm going to do my best to ignore you. Which will be easier, by the way, if you do something about your appearance." He dug into one of his saddlebags for a moment, and then his hand reemerged holding a Mimic-kind crystal. The attention her features would draw outweighed the contempt Varen and his followers felt toward using divine magic, apparently. That Mimic crystal was just another...what had he called it?

A necessary evil.

With a slightly disgusted look at her pale hair and eyes, Caden tossed the crystal to her. As he did, she noted the special gloves that covered his wrists—and any divine mark that might have been on his skin.

A quick, curious glance at Tara's hands revealed the same.

So many of these necessary evils.

Before she could inquire about either of their marks or the magic they signified, Caden turned away and led his horse after the others with a quick snapping of reins.

The morning was not getting off to a promising start. Cas tried—and failed—to hold in a sigh at the thought.

"It won't be that bad," Tara insisted in a laughing voice. "The ride to Belwind is actually quite scenic, for what it's worth." She kicked her horse into a quick trot to catch up with their dispersing party, but not before calling back over her shoulder, "You might even enjoy it if you try!"

AFTER A HALF-DAY OF RIDING, Cas had to admit that Tara was right. She was enjoying herself. A *bit*. It wasn't the same rush she felt when she took on a challenging job with her friends, and she still *missed* those friends terribly, but this was better than being alone in her room at the palace.

Caden had done nothing except ignore her—as he'd said he would.

Tara had talked non-stop for the first several hours, supplying her life story, the *very* occasional useful piece of information about the group they were traveling with, and brief recaps of previous, similar missions that group had been on.

But for the past few miles, even she had been silent, trotting just ahead of Cas. Resting her voice, maybe. Or perhaps she had simply gotten tired of being the one carrying the conversation while Cas only nodded along.

Cas didn't make much of an effort to pick up that dropped conversation; she preferred observing, especially when she was surrounded by people she didn't know. She could learn more that way.

Lily was a steady, well-trained horse; she followed the others without much need for input, so Cas let her own gaze wander over the scenery as they went. They had passed out of the Bloodstone Realm some time ago, and now they were cantering through the realm of Prymarsh... an area lorded over by the House of Brightwood, if she remembered correctly.

There was water *everywhere* here—a hundred tiny little lakes and a thousand streams feeding and taking away from them. There were still some pockets of mist rising off the waters, despite it being late in the day; early mornings often produced so much fog that it was nearly impossible to navigate even the well-kept roads in this area, which was why people often referred to it as *The Veil.*

Cas was staring at the edge of one of those many lakes, watching a herd of deer move tentatively in for a drink, when a shout rang out and made those deer scatter.

She jerked her head to the front of their company.

One of their scouts raced to Captain Elander's side. After a brief conversation between them, a call to *halt* rang out. There was a bit of nervous shuffling and conversation as everyone complied with this order. Elander moved calmly to the rear of their group, where Cas had been riding, but his eyes skipped over her and found

Caden, and then Tara as she turned and walked her horse back to them.

"There's a blockade on the road ahead, just before it forks at the Kirith Woods," Elander explained.

"A blockade?" Cas repeated.

Caden's gaze drifted over to her. He looked slightly less disgusted now that her hair was disguised to a soft shade of reddish-blonde and her eyes were pale green— but his tone still sounded like that same mixture of boredom and soft exasperation over having to explain further. "The House of Brightwood that rules the realm we're currently standing in has strong ties to the former royal family of the kingdom of Alnor. Even after the Alnorian king and queen went into exile, the Brightwoods refused to acknowledge the emperor that took their place. And their feelings toward his son are no better. So they— along with many of the people they lord over—tend to be rather hostile to anyone carrying the Solasen banner."

"Even when he's sending people to help their sickened cities?"

"They see that sort of thing as nothing more than a hollow gesture. Too many of them believe the rumors that he and his family are in some way *responsible* for the sickness."

Cas had heard these rumors. Not that she had really been listening for them—it was just more of that political noise that she had, until these past days, done her best to tune out.

The idea had seemed preposterous to her, anyway. As much as she'd disliked the King-Emperor, to say his family was responsible for something as severe and far-reaching as the Fading Sickness just seemed like people desperately looking for a scapegoat. And now, after seeing Varen's reaction to his dead servant and how passionate he'd been about finding a cure, she believed those rumors even less.

"So what do we do?" she asked. "Fight our way through? Turn around?"

"Neither," said Elander, leading his suddenly anxious horse in a circle and trying to calm it.

"Neither?"

"The new plan is to take a different route—through the Kirith Woods themselves. We'll head to the north side of the woods, and then we can cross the Aldwater Bridge into Belwind. Nobody uses that route anymore, so I doubt anyone will be setting up a troublesome blockade on it."

Tara visibly shuddered.

Caden's lips twitched, just the tiniest bit, as if he was considering objecting to this plan. But he didn't.

"Why does nobody use that route?" Cas asked.

Elander finally let his gaze settle on her. "Because people believe the Kirith Woods are haunted. Or, more specifically, that its namesake—the lesser-spirit Kiri—still walks the overgrown paths in that wood."

"Kiri?" The name didn't sound familiar to Cas.

But Elander had already turned back around and moved to give the rest of the nervous crowd their new orders, so it was Tara who responded.

"Kiri is the patron deity of the Mist-kind," she said. "And the magic that this deity and his marked ones possess supposedly allows for walking through walls and things, and sometimes dissolving those things altogether to reveal new paths. So there are a lot of stories of people going into those woods and seeing entire sections of the trees disappear. They choose the suddenly more open path, thinking it's a blessed shortcut, when really it's just the lesser-spirit leading them deeper and deeper into his domain and getting them hopelessly lost. Kiri allegedly enjoys a good prank, and sometimes he takes things too far and it...well, it ends in tragedy."

"There are marked paths, overgrown or not," Caden added, his voice even more prickly than usual. "We'll follow the paths, we won't take any tempting, magical *shortcuts*, and we'll come out on the other side. It's simple."

Cas bit her lip, casting an uncertain look toward the distant trees.

"He's right." Tara's friendly smile suddenly seemed forced. "Kiri isn't truly malicious in most stories...just playful. We'll be fine."

"We won't be able to make it through to the other side before nightfall," Elander said, trotting back to them. "So we'll make camp on the edge of the woods and continue on in the morning."

Cas's heart sank at the thought of extending their campaign by another day. How long would it be before she saw her friends again?

But there was no arguing the matter. People were already riding closer to the edge of the woods and dismounting, and soon the area was a bustling hub of activity as tents were pitched, rations were distributed, and fires were built.

She tended to Lily's needs first, and after the horse was brushed and tied, and her hooves properly cleaned, Cas helped collect firewood, which she brought to the fire closest to the forest's edge. She settled down on the outskirts of the fire and quietly sipped from her canteen, listening to the soldiers swapping both stories and insults in equal measure.

While those conversations rose and fell around her, her gaze kept drifting toward the woods. A warm wind began to blow from the south, carrying the scent of rain with it. The trees swayed and danced in the breeze, and a strange prickling sensation started crawling along the back of her neck. Cas tried to focus her attention on the people sitting around her. She tried, and tried, and tried harder.

But she was almost certain she could feel something watching her from the forest.

Several minutes passed, and she still felt it staring.

Finally, she clutched her canteen more tightly and tilted her face to look at the treeline, at the dark space between two of the largest pines.

She saw a pair of glowing white orbs staring back at her.

They blinked.

She froze.

She was imagining things. Those were not eyes. Fireflies, perhaps. It was getting close to early evening, and that, along with the threat of storms, always brought those bugs out in full force. Except...

The orbs blinked together. They moved together. And soon they moved far enough from the shadows of the forest that she saw, without a doubt, that they were part of a face. A long, narrow face that made her think of a deer; it even had barbs along the curve of its skull that could have been the beginnings of antlers.

Cas inhaled sharply.

What *was* that?

She couldn't take her eyes off it. She searched desperately for a sign that it was only a trick of the light. But then it bowed in a very obvious, very solid sort of way, and it swept what looked like long, elegant fingers toward the trees behind it, as if welcoming her into them.

An elbow jabbed into her side. Cas turned to find the soldier to her right leering at her, clenching a flask in his meaty hand. His nose and cheeks were tinged with red, and she could smell the faint hint of alcohol on his breath.

"Curious, are you?" he chuckled. "Want to go play with the Mist spirit—or maybe the fairies that lives in them woods, eh?"

"S'no such thing as *fairies,* wise ass," said the sleepy-eyed soldier across from him.

This drew an incredulous huff from a third soldier—Killian, she remembered Tara calling him.

Tara herself arrived at their circle a moment later, settling down across from Cas and listening intently to the argument that had started.

"There *is* such a thing as fairies," Killian said. "And they're trouble, seeing as how they answer to no one 'cept the very Sun Goddess that created them, and according to some stories they don't even do *that*. But they exist, sure as all three hells. Just not in these parts—and that's lucky for us."

There was a rumble of agreement and acceptance.

Cas went back to staring at the woods.

"My cousin was duped by a fairy," insisted Red-Face. "The damn thing led him out into the middle of a field—had him believing he was in the company of a pretty lady that was about to show him a good time. Next thing he knows, he's waking up butt-naked for an audience of very unlucky field hands."

"If he's as stupid as you are, then it was probably just a big butterfly that tricked 'em into taking off his clothes."

Laughter roared through the circle, followed by what sounded like a metal cup being thrown and missing its target. The stories continued for a long time after that; everyone, it seemed, had had a strange moment they believed could be blamed on these mischievous fairies.

Cas listened absently to the crude conversation while she watched the edge of those woods, still searching.

Where had that creature gone?

CHAPTER 15

No matter how long she stared into the darkness between the trees, the creature didn't come back.

"Our Fade-marked friend's got a look on her face like she's been duped herself," said Red-Face suddenly. He started to jab her in the side again, but Cas was faster. She caught his wrist and twisted it away from her.

"Most likely a bird or something," said Killian, now sounding bored of the conversation.

"Bet she's not brave enough to go find out, one way or the other," snorted Red-Face, jerking his wrist from her grip.

Cas glared at him.

And then she rose to her feet.

"The captain ordered us to stay out of those woods until morning," Tara reminded her. "Don't listen to these brutes, Casia. Just ignore them."

Cas would have had no problem doing so—but this

247

wasn't just about proving to the king's soldiers that she wasn't afraid.

She had seen something in the woods. Something that had *wanted* her to see it. Something that had wanted her to follow it, as foolish as that seemed.

"I'll be right back," she said, earning herself a chorus of uncertain laughter from the soldiers surrounding her.

Tara wasn't laughing. "If the captain asks, I told you not to do this."

"Agreed," Cas said, giving her one last distracted look before resuming her decisive march into the woods.

"Should we stop her?" she heard someone ask.

"Leave her be."

"But the Mist spirit's magic..."

"She wants to make a fool of herself, let her."

"Could be dangerous."

"Who cares? Don't know why Varen's expectin' us to work alongside her anyway, after what she did in the dungeons the other day. Let her get herself killed—it'd serve her right."

Cas walked on, their words making her more determined than ever to prove that she wasn't crazy.

Once she crossed the threshold of the forest, the world seemed to quiet to nothing except the sound of her breaths and the occasional rustling breeze that smelled of pine and honeysuckle and mud. Sunbeams streamed through breaks in the canopy above her. These patches of light glittered with falling, fluttering leaves and small insects, but they grew less and less frequent as she moved into deeper, thicker clutches of leaves and tangles of branches.

The forest was clearly very old. The air felt heavy, as though it had been collecting dust and memories for centuries. Her attempts to see the tops of the centuries-old trees left her dizzy and spinning circles. It was disorienting, but she couldn't help looking up toward those mesmerizing heights. She moved in a sort of trance with her eyes straining upward.

When she finally lowered her gaze and looked at the world closer to the ground once more, she realized she didn't recognize her surroundings. She couldn't tell which direction she was walking, nor could she remember which direction she had walked *from*. And no matter where she looked, there was no sign of flickering fires or smoke from their camp.

Lost.

She was lost.

"You invited me in," she called into the heavy silence. "Now show yourself!"

She didn't expect a reply. And she didn't get one. With a sigh, she pulled the knife from her boot and started to mark the trees she was passing as she searched for a path that looked familiar to her.

Then she heard the softest of footsteps, a rattling whisper of branches and leaves being shoved aside...

She turned around, only to find the trees she'd marked had disappeared, leaving nothing but an open, leaf-littered trail where they had once stood—a bright, inviting path with what appeared to be the camp at the end of it.

"Oh, that's very clever," she muttered. "But I'm afraid I'm not foolish enough to follow that path."

A swift breeze shook the leaves, carrying a twinkling, high-pitched sound with it.

It sounded like laughter.

It should have frightened her, perhaps. And yet there was something almost...*familiar* about it. Something that made her feel as if she had been here before, and as if she had heard that laughter—in a dream, perhaps. That dreamy feeling dulled all her usual anxiety in a way she couldn't explain.

"Come out," she called, softer this time.

And this time, her command did not go unanswered; the same creature she'd seen on the edge of the camp slinked out from behind a gnarled grey trunk. It stepped into a patch of dappled sunlight, tilting its head curiously.

It had made her think of a shadow when she'd first spotted it—the way its body moved and seemed to shift and spread out as it fell over trees and rocks—but in the splash of sunlight, it was not as dark. It was more soft blue than shadowy black, and yet it still moved more like a shadow than a solid body. Or more like...mist.

As she watched, it turned entirely to mist, and it twisted through the air for several seconds before wrapping around a thick tree branch and reforming itself into a deer-headed, but otherwise human-like, body.

Oh.

"You really are Kiri, aren't you?" The realization left her in a breathless whisper. It seemed impossible, even now, but she couldn't deny the evidence right in front of her.

Those burning orbs disappeared for a moment, as if the lesser-spirit was closing his eyes and considering his next move. He disappeared again—only to reappear on the forest floor and rush toward her, propelling himself with the use of both his lanky arms and legs. He slammed to a stop almost directly in front of Cas and arched back to his full height, towering several feet above her.

She stood her ground, though her heart beat wildly in her chest.

This close, the swirling mist that made up his body seemed more solid. The spirit smelled of rain and rotting wood. The air around him quickly grew even heavier, damper, and it rumbled softly with the possibility of magic.

Cas took a deep breath. "No more tricks. Just tell me the truth: You *are* Kiri, aren't you?"

The creature took a step back and bowed its head.

In the distance, she heard what sounded like Tara calling for her.

"I...I have to go back," she told the spirit before turning toward Tara's shout. But since that spirit seemed to be listening to her, for whatever reason, she added, "Do me a favor and let us pass tomorrow morning, won't you? No tricks. No slowing us down." She glanced over her shoulder, determined to fix a commanding look on those odd glowing eyes of his.

The lesser-spirit was gone again.

There was only a bit of mist swirling in the sunlight, and a moment later, that was gone as well.

But then the trees she'd marked with her knife reappeared. And as she stepped toward them, a feeling of peace overwhelmed her, and she realized...the camp was to the right. It was just ahead. She was certain of it; she was no longer lost.

In fact, she felt as if she had never been lost at all.

Her step was lighter walking out than it had been walking in. Much lighter. She moved toward that group by the fire, and several heads turned in her direction, their expressions a mixture of astonishment and confusion.

Elander was among the group now. And she thought she saw something like relief flicker across his face as he turned and caught sight of her—though it was quickly replaced by fury as he walked over to meet her.

"What were you doing in there?" he demanded.

She rolled the gathering tension from her shoulders and tried to keep her voice calm. "I saw something, and I—"

"You *saw* something? And you thought it would be a good idea to follow it into that forest where all manner of monsters and bandits are likely hiding?"

"I didn't encounter either of those things, so—"

"I thought I made it clear that you were to listen to the orders given to you. Didn't I?"

She chewed on her bottom lip. "Yes."

"And those orders included staying *out* of that forest until morning, didn't they?"

"*Yes.*"

His voice lowered to a soft, dangerous tone. "I swore to Varen that nothing would happen to you on this excursion. That I would bring you back in one piece."

She looked down at herself, and then brought her defiant gaze back up to his. "Well, you're in luck. Because it looks like I'm still in one piece."

They glared at each other.

He snapped first, and in a seething voice he said, "Disobey me again, and you will regret it. Do I make myself clear?" He looked like he was waiting for her to cower under his threat.

He would be waiting for a long time, if that were the case.

She didn't answer him. She didn't wilt beneath his stare. She just kept glaring back at him until he turned and started to storm away.

She wanted to let him leave. But irritation forced more words out of her in a tight, clenched voice, "I saw the lesser-spirit of Mist."

Elander stopped walking.

A few people snickered.

Tara was staring at her with a mixture of pity and bewilderment.

But Cas ignored them all and took several steps toward Elander. Why she cared so much about making *him* believe her, she wasn't sure. She didn't want to think about it.

"I saw him, and he saw me," she insisted. "And that's why I went into the woods; I asked his blessing, so that we might pass through his woods tomorrow with no more delays."

Elander turned back to face her. "The stories of that lesser-spirit walking in those woods are just that —stories."

"I am not a liar!"

A muscle worked in his jaw. He seemed acutely aware of the audience that was growing around them. His steely gaze flashed over that audience, commanding their attention before he took a step back to Cas, making certain they were all listening. "Even if the Mist spirit *did* still dwell in those woods, I sincerely doubt he would show himself to the likes of you."

"Well he *did*."

His smile was almost cruel. "Was he alone? Or perhaps there was an entire host of gods and spirits accompanying him? Perhaps you alone were chosen to be the sole witness of this random, divine party in the woods?"

The snickering around her grew louder.

Her words failed her, but she kept her chin lifted in that same defiant way, refusing to respond to his cruel teasing.

Because she knew she was right—whether he believed her or not.

"Nothing else to report, I see," Elander said.

Cas still didn't reply. She knew she was right, but she *also* knew that she was only going to make herself look more foolish if she kept arguing with the group's captain. No one here was on her side.

"I'm telling the truth," she snarled, low enough for only Elander to hear.

And then she stomped off in the direction of her tied horse, expecting Lily to be far better company than any of the soldiers surrounding her.

In what felt like no time at all, hours had passed since her incident in the woods. Most of their group had retired to their bedrolls. Aside from their assigned lookouts, only a few others were still wandering the camp and holding hushed conversations. Nobody else seemed to want to sit at the fire that Cas had made herself comfortable at. She told herself that it was because it would have meant being close to the woods, and that it had nothing to do with them not wanting to be close to *her*.

Not that she particularly cared whether they wanted to be close to her or not.

But it was going to be a lonely next few days, it seemed. She had already been the outsider that nobody trusted, and her odd antics in the woods clearly had not earned her any affection.

She hadn't even attempted sleep. How could she

when she couldn't stop thinking about those strange woods, or about the Mist spirit within them?

Had she imagined the conversation with him?

What about the way he had seemed to listen to her commands?

Even more sleep-deterring than these confusing thoughts was the storm that had been on the air earlier. It was rolling toward them in earnest now, lighting the sky with wickedly bright bolts. Its rumbles of thunder grew louder and louder, and Cas felt as if she was absorbing the sound, the vibrations, until an entire piece of that storm raged and rattled around inside of her. She tucked her head to her chest and strangled down the panic trying to rise up.

She just wanted it all to go away.

She wanted Rhea and Laurent and Asra and their steady, no-nonsense advice. Nessa's calming magic. Zev's laughter.

But then again, it was probably better that she was alone, really. Because she could already feel that panic overcoming her attempts to strike it down, and she didn't want an audience for *that*.

It occurred to her that she should seek better shelter from the incoming rain, but she couldn't seem to make herself stand. Only her hand obeyed her commands to move. She had just started to tap out ten identical, evenly-spaced holes in the dirt when she heard foot-steps. With some effort, she managed to still her hand. To brake her runaway thoughts long enough to stop obsessively counting the dimples in the dirt and look up.

The steps belonged to Elander. She assumed he was here to further irritate and interrogate her—perhaps about her walk in the woods, or that conversation she'd had with Varen last night.

She wanted to talk about neither of these things, so she spoke before he could. "I'm not in the mood."

"Not in the mood for what?"

She gestured vaguely at his entire being.

He snorted at that, but didn't pressure her into speaking right away. He only set about gathering up a few stray sticks and other bits of kindling. He added them to the fire and steadily stoked the dying flames back to life. It seemed like a pointless endeavor, given the approaching rain. Was he simply looking for an excuse to stay close to her?

She watched him out of the corner of her eye for as long as she could, until her thoughts became too distracting—racing so quickly that her breaths quickened and her vision blurred. She closed her eyes.

"I'm sorry about earlier," he said suddenly.

Sorry?

That was not what she had expected to hear.

"But I can't let you ignore my orders. The King-Emperor may be showing you preferential treatment, but I can't. Actually, it's better for you if I *don't*. You may have noticed that a few of the soldiers we're traveling with are rather...rough around the edges. They aren't going to take

257

kindly to anybody I play favorites with. Especially since many of them are already questioning why Varen allowed you to go on this mission, given your record."

She was too absorbed in her panic to properly form words. So she just nodded and went back to tapping her fingers against the dirt.

A few more minutes, a few more rumbles of thunder and cracks of lightning, and then he asked, "Are you okay?"

Gods, why is he still here?

"Thorn?"

"I'm fine."

It should have been the end of it. He should have gotten the message that she really was not in the mood to chat. Instead, he crouched beside her. "Can you talk to me, please?"

No.

She wasn't trying to be rude. Not this time, at least. It was simply too hard to focus on words at the moment— so hard that she felt almost physically *unable* to talk to him.

"I said I was sorry."

"It isn't *you*." She hated how breathy her voice sounded.

"It isn't?"

Her entire body itched, suddenly. It needed to move. Fighting with him hadn't worked, and he wasn't *leaving*. She needed to escape. Him, the storm—the entire situation.

Run, run, run.

But something held her in place. Something made her fingers still once more in the dirt beneath them, and she mumbled out a few more words: "I just...I struggle with anxiety, sometimes. With these...*attacks.*"

He was quiet for a long moment.

"Define *struggle.*" He genuinely sounded like he was asking; for once, his tone was more curious than condescending.

But oh, how to put it into *words.*

He watched her, patiently, while she breathed in and out, in and out, until she finally found the strength to speak again. "You honestly want me to explain how this feels?"

"Yes. I do."

In and out.

In and out.

"Can you explain it?"

She didn't know—she had never tried. No one had ever asked her to.

But then she felt it: A single calm breath rising up, briefly abating that storm raging through her. As welcome as it was, such breaks never lasted long, so she blurted out the words while she still could: "Okay. Well, I guess it's like...everything feels so weighted, suddenly. It feels like every breath, every inch I try to move might end in disaster and so I just...I can hardly breathe. I can hardly move. And I can't make it go away. I can't turn it off, can't lift that weight from my chest, my lungs...my entire body is encased in that heaviness."

He had gone back to stoking the flames, but the furrow of his brow told her he was listening intently.

"Look, I just need to sit for a minute, and I'll be fine. When this happens, I, um...I like to imagine a rock in the middle of the sea. In a storm. The waves crash over it, higher and higher, but the rock doesn't move. It's still there once the waves are calm again."

He nodded slowly, seeming to understand. "You're the rock."

"I'm the rock."

Silence for a moment, and then, "Can I sit with you?"

Her chest tightened. The storm still swirled on inside of her. The waves were lifting, threatening, and she could feel them...but they didn't crash back over her. Not yet. It was as if something small, something as faint as fluttering bird wings, was trying to hold them at bay. It wouldn't last, of course; such things never did. It wasn't that simple. But that small fluttering kept the darkness at bay long enough for her to reply, at least—

"If you want to, I guess."

So he did. He sat in the waves with her. He didn't speak. He didn't do anything to fight them off. He just waited, and after several minutes Cas finally wiped away the holes she'd dug in the dirt with her fingers, and she felt calm enough to talk again.

"Sometimes," she began, slowly, "it happens for what feels like no reason at all. Other times, the triggers are obvious." Her eyes lifted toward the distant sky, and at that exact moment a bolt of lightning violently forked its way down to the earth. She closed her eyes until her involuntary shuddering had subsided, and then she opened them again and added, "Storms aren't the only trigger, but they're one of the worst."

He fixed her with a curious look...and she found herself oddly compelled to keep talking.

"It was storming the night my parents died."

"Fading Sickness?" he guessed.

"Not exactly. They both *had* that sickness, but that isn't what killed them."

"What did, then?"

"My mother. She killed my father. She tried to kill me, too. And then she took her own life. You probably already know this, but oftentimes at the end of the sickness, the mind breaks down. The hallucinations can be terrible. Mother knew that end was coming, and she didn't want us to suffer that terribleness, I guess. So she tried to perform a mercy killing for all three of us."

"But you escaped her."

"I...I wanted to live. Even if it was only for a little while longer. Even if I went mad at the end of it all."

"But you *didn't* go mad."

"Debatable," Cas said with a small, crooked grin.

He laughed softly. "You seem relatively sane to me," he insisted. "Just with occasional severe lapses in judgment."

"Thanks, I guess?"

"And you lived for more than a little while too," he added, sounding almost as if he was thinking out loud now.

"It's been thirteen years."

His eyes widened slightly at the number, which didn't surprise her. Nobody lived that long after being touched by the Fade. Nobody except for her and Asra.

"Sometimes I wonder if they might have lived, too, somehow," she said, softer. "If only my mother hadn't acted so rashly. I used to get so *angry* about it all."

"It sounds like you had a right to be angry."

It warmed her to hear him say that, but she still shook her head. "I don't know. Looking back, I suppose I never felt like I could get angry with them for long, because they weren't even my real parents."

"They weren't?"

Her body threatened to seize up, suddenly. Why was she telling him all of this?

She didn't know, but she couldn't seem to get herself to stop talking.

"They took me in when I was four years old. And for five, almost six years after that, they gave me everything they could. They *felt* like my real parents. So how angry am I allowed to be at them, really?"

He didn't seem to have a response for this.

"They were the first family I really remember. Everything before that is a blur."

"Everything?"

"Well, not *everything*. I remember an orphanage, and I

remember it being some place very, very cold. Then they plucked me from that cold, and I just...I wish I could have saved them the way they saved me."

"How old were you when they died? Nine?"

"That's not the point."

His eyes narrowed toward the fire as the first few drops of rain fell, making it hiss. "You were too young to be worried about saving anybody."

"Maybe." She shrugged. "Anyway, I was lucky enough to be saved *again* after I lost them, when Asra took me in. But now..."

"She's the one you mentioned to Varen?" he guessed. "The one that's sick."

"Yes. And I can't lose her too. Which is why I will do everything I can to keep getting her the medicine she needs until I can figure out a better way to cure her."

He was quiet for a beat, staring into the hissing and crackling fire. "...That's why you were at Darkhand's."

She nodded. "And it's why I agreed to help Varen—so that he can help me, hopefully."

Elander frowned at this, clearly still unconvinced that the King-Emperor's offers of help were worth trusting.

"If there's even a *chance* we could help—or even cure —Asra by working together, then I would do almost anything Varen asks me to do."

Elander looked like he was holding in a sigh. But then one side of his mouth inched up. "Even if it involves working with me?"

"Even if it involves working with you."

He laughed softly, and they fell silent again.

That silence lasted several minutes, until Cas said, "I'm sorry about this, by the way."

"Sorry?"

"For keeping you up."

"I was already up."

"I just meant that you don't have to worry about me distracting you or slowing you down because of all of that anxiety stuff. I'll be fine by morning, even if it's still storming. I...I promise I'll find a way. It's a weakness, but I'll deal with it."

He kept his eyes on the fire as he replied, "It's hardly a sign of weakness to be able to keep going in spite of the weight of everything you just told me." He got to his feet. "You should get some sleep. But I'll be in the tent at the bottom of that hill over there, if you need me."

Her lips formed the word *okay,* but that word didn't make it out. She just stared after him, dumbfounded by those last four words.

If you need me.

He made it halfway to his tent only to turn around and walk back to her. "One last thing."

She cleared her throat. "Yes?"

"Whatever you saw in the woods earlier... just, if you see anything strange tomorrow morning when we pass through those woods, keep it to yourself this time, please."

It took the meaning behind his request a moment to sink in.

"Wait. Are you saying you actually *do* believe that I saw something?"

He frowned and stepped closer, as if he didn't want anyone else to overhear. "All I know is that we don't need any distractions from what we've been assigned to do. Let's stay focused, shall we?"

She nodded slowly, but she couldn't fully settle the odd excitement now flickering through her.

He *believed* her.

"It was the strangest thing," she whispered, that excitement building. "I swear Kiri was trying to lure me into those woods. And not just to play tricks—because he *listened* to me when I told him to stop. I think...I think if I hadn't heard Tara calling, if I'd had more time with him, we might have actually found a way to communicate."

Elander's frown only deepened. "If the lesser-spirits really *are* trying to communicate with you, nothing good will come from it, I promise. They can't be commanded. Or trusted."

She wasn't sure she agreed, but she couldn't really explain *why,* so she said nothing.

"Ignore them. All of us—including you—will be much better off if you do."

She nodded again, reluctantly.

His blue eyes turned distant. Lost in thought. "Good-night, Thorn."

"...Good-night."

She watched him go.

She had felt something different building between

them earlier, she was certain. Something like trust. Something almost warm and familiar and...comforting.

But as he disappeared into his tent, she couldn't help feeling her usual frustration and contempt toward him once more.

What wasn't he telling her?

CHAPTER 16

THE NEXT MORNING, WHETHER DUE TO LUCK OR BECAUSE OF THE command Cas had given the Mist spirit, she and her party passed through the Kirith Forest without incident.

They found the road on the other side as empty as they'd hoped they would. It was steep and poorly maintained, but it soon brought them near enough to the city of Belwind that the walls of that city became clearly visible, cutting a crumbling shape against the hazy blue sky.

As they approached the outermost gate, their party began to splinter into several smaller groups. After the blockade incident of the day before, the consensus was that they would be better off not attempting to use the King-Emperor's authority to get what they needed out of this city; an undercover operation would better serve their purpose.

So Cas joined Elander, Tara, and Caden in shedding any and all regalia that marked them as servants—or saviors—who were working in the name of that King-Emperor. Once they looked like civilians, and their horses like common beasts, the four of them covered the last miles into Belwind alone.

Or they *appeared* to be alone, at least. In truth, several more groups of royal soldiers were trailing at a distance, better armed and prepared to intervene if it became necessary.

But her group carried only the simplest of weapons themselves. Cas had a well-balanced short sword that Varen had insisted on sending along for her use, and a simple weapon was not a strange thing to see in this city. Belwind was a bustling trading hub, given its location where the three realms of Bloodstone, Prymarsh, and Bywilds came to a gathered point. They were also not far from the In-Between, which meant that Belwind also hosted an elaborate underground market that dealt in the illegal trade of crystals and other magic-infused objects. All of these things led to streets that were not safe to walk after sundown—particularly if you were unarmed—as well as a native population that knew better than to interrogate strangers about whatever they might be carrying.

This *mind your own business* mantra was evident as soon as Cas and the others stepped onto the main street that divided the city into its northern and southern sections. No one made eye contact with Cas. Even the few street vendors they encountered kept their gazes fixed on something in the distance as they shouted out their deals and the endless merits of their products.

"We're heading for the Misthill district, on the north side," Caden informed them. "According to my informant, that's where the majority of the cases have been quarantined to."

He led them down that main street at a casual pace. Since people didn't seem interested in staring at *her*, Cas was free to observe everyone they passed. After several minutes, she still hadn't made proper eye contact with anybody. There was an odd energy in the air that she couldn't quite decipher; it was almost as if the entire city was *braced* for something. Their steps were hurried more often than not, their bodies rigid and prepared to scamper into their houses and slam the door at the first ill gust of wind. And it felt like there was more to their nervousness than the general wariness that came from living in a crime-filled city.

Was it that sickness that had them all on edge?

Or perhaps they all knew by this point that the King-Emperor had sent a company of soldiers into their midst?

Most conversations they passed were hushed, so when the sound of unrestrained laughter and chatter reached her, Cas's eyes were immediately drawn to the establishment that it was coming from—to a tavern with a porch that looked like it was dangerously close to collapsing under the weight of its patrons.

The Horny Dragon, read the banner above that rickety porch, and the name was accompanied by an image of a red dragon and a princess posing in a very...*suggestive* manner.

Elander caught her staring at that bawdy sign, and he chuckled. "If you need to go meet with some clients in that questionable-looking inn over there, we'll wait for you, Azalea."

She drew Lily right up next to his horse and punched him as hard as she could in the arm.

It only made him laugh harder.

Tara raised an eyebrow, but otherwise trotted on without comment. Cas followed this example—putting as much space as she could between herself and Elander.

As they wove deeper into the city, she continued to observe everything in silence. They soon came upon a square edged with flowering white trees. In the center of this square was a gleaming marble likeness of Varen's father, Anric. The former King-Emperor had seen better days; his raised arm—which had likely held a sword to go with the shield in the opposite hand—had been broken off at the wrist, and his face was stained with red paint that oozed out from underneath his crown in a way that was clearly meant to resemble blood.

They turned right at the square, but Cas's eyes stayed on the statue for a moment—watching it over her shoulder, even as Lily dutifully followed the other three horses.

"Well, this is not an encouraging sign," Caden muttered, suddenly.

Cas didn't have to ask what he meant. As soon as she shifted her gaze to study the latest street they'd just turned onto, it was nearly impossible to notice anything except black curtains fluttering in the breeze.

They had reached the Misthill district.

"So many..." Tara whispered.

"It's more or less what we expected," Elander insisted —though there was an unusual edge to his voice that sounded suspiciously like nervousness.

Cas rubbed the chill bumps from her arm and commanded Lily to walk on.

After a mile or so of black curtains and solemn, wary gazes following their every step, the four of them came upon a large house surrounded by a black iron gate. This house had no black curtains covering its windows.

Not yet.

But there was a large group of people gathered around its front steps, and they held little stone bowls that burned with bright blue flames.

"*Sonas* flames," Tara informed Cas in a quiet voice. "The paths to the upper heavens are said to glow with blue lights in some stories, and so the people around here have a tradition of lighting these colored flames around death beds. The idea is that the departing soul will see them, and then the soul will continue to look for similar lights as it leaves this mortal realm—thus finding their way more easily to those highest heavens."

"Which means that someone in this house is about to depart for those heavenly realms," Cas guessed. "And presumably because of the Fading Sickness?"

"That would be my guess as well," said Elander, guiding his horse through the creaking iron gate. He seemed unconcerned about the people around the house's steps—oblivious to the less-than-friendly looks those people gave him as he approached.

While Cas and the others stood back, he dismounted and marched straight up the crowd, finally coming to a stop with his foot balanced on the bottom step.

"Someone in this house is close to passing into the Afterlands." It was not a question, but a statement—one that rang with the sort of effortless power Cas had come to expect from him; he didn't need any of the King-Emperor's regalia to project authority.

After a bit of nervous shuffling, an elderly man stepped forward to meet Elander, parting the crowd as he came. A stone vessel trembled in his hand, making the blue flame in it dance in a slow, shaky rhythm.

"My daughter is perilously close, now." The old man's voice trembled right along with his hands, but it was clear he was trying to steel both of these things as he added, "But what business do *you* have inquiring about such things?"

"We are traveling healers," Elander lied. "We come from the blessed forest cities of Calah, from the temple built within the sacred space where the Oak Goddess herself once dwelled." He gestured back to Cas and the others. "Each of us has spent years studying that middle-goddess's words and wisdom, and we are here in hopes that we might be permitted to try a healing spell we've developed to offer relief from the Fade."

Cas nudged Lily forward, following Tara and Caden as they dismounted and tied their horses near the front gate.

Cas rubbed Lily's neck while she strained to hear what was being said at the porch.

"We have already been visited by other Oak-kind who have made similar claims," the old man was informing Elander. "Their magic has had no impact."

There was a murmur of agreement from the crowd on the porch. A few members of the group moved restlessly, and Cas instinctively reached for the handle of her sword.

"He's lying," muttered Caden.

"Why would he lie?" Cas whispered back.

"To get us to go away."

Cas frowned, but she couldn't really argue. Earlier, she had finally learned what kind of divine magic Caden possessed: A Blood-kind mark graced his hand. Which meant that he, like the lesser-spirit that this mark symbolized, could read minds.

It was a disturbing type of magic—to be sure—even though Elander had assured her that Caden's power was limited. He could divine *all* of a person's secrets and history by way of their spilled blood, but without the use of blood, he could only read occasional snippets from minds that were weak or under some sort of distress—such as the mind of a clearly distressed old man about to lose his daughter.

"He probably thinks we're only trying to trick a few coins out of him, doesn't he?" Tara asked, speaking even more quietly. "I'm sure such scams are growing common around here."

Before Caden could reply, Elander threw them a cross

look. The three of them ceased their whispering. After forcing her hand away from her sword, Cas took a few cautious steps closer to the porch.

"No person gifted with divine magic is entirely like another," Elander said, turning back to the old man. "You are aware of this, I'm sure."

The man gave a slow, stiff nod.

"We are more gifted than most. I assure you that you haven't yet seen any magic like ours."

The old man considered this for a moment, the faintest glimmer of hope appearing in his eyes. It made Cas's stomach flip uncomfortably to see it.

"Rather heavily armed for healers, aren't you?" he finally asked.

"The roads in this empire are particularly hostile as of late," said Tara, in her friendly voice. She stepped even closer than Cas had, and Cas and Caden both followed her lead a moment later.

The old man sized them up as they came, his gaze running along the assortment of blades and bows they carried. "Be that as it may, *this house* is not hostile. I see no reason for you to come inside with so many weapons."

After a tense pause, Elander acquiesced with a smile. It was a sharp, rather unfriendly smile, but the man didn't seem to notice; he only watched them all for a minute longer, his eyes glazing over, as they started to remove their weapons and lean them beside the door.

Cas reached for the belt that held her sword at her hip, but she hesitated to remove it.

The old man didn't notice this, either. His gaze had dropped to Elander's hand, to the one branded by a divine mark that had been covered by a glove once more. The same was true of Tara and Caden's marks, but Cas had now seen all of them at some point during their travels together, and she knew that *none* of them were marks that signified healing magic.

She held her breath, waiting for the other, more unsettling magic to be unleashed.

It happened quickly: The old man's eyes glassed over, and then they appeared to sink deeper into his skull as he swayed and pressed a hand to his head, mumbling to himself. Or to someone else within his mind—someone that only he could see.

Cas didn't look at Tara, or at the glove over her mark, but she had a feeling that if she'd stared closely enough, she would have seen the Shadow-kind mark on Tara's wrist glowing faintly.

The lesser-spirit symbolized by that curved cross mark was one of the few that Cas had some familiarity with; the dark spirit had once been a servant of the Death God, Kerse, and the middle-god had given her his ability to weave shadows and create hallucinations—and now some carriers of the Shadow mark could do the same thing.

Tara was exceptionally skilled at this. Skilled enough that whatever false images she was planting in the old man's mind were enough to convince him that the people standing in front of him were trustworthy. After his balance returned, he seemed entirely at peace with the situation. He had no further questions for them; he simply turned and indicated for them to follow him inside.

"My name is Amon," he told them once they had stepped into a small atrium and closed themselves off from the crowd outside. "And my daughter is Brynna. She took ill approximately a week ago, and as of this morning we haven't been able to wake her, or to get her to respond to us in any way."

A week ago.

It was progressing even more rapidly than the latest case back at the palace.

"Her symptoms were mild at first," Amon continued, "but last night she became delirious with visions."

"Visions?"

"Yes. She was mostly incoherent, but within the babbling, we managed to decipher a few words—a few sentences. She was rambling on and on about shadows and gods and monsters. The upper-god, Anga the Rook... she mentioned him at least three times. Him, and the God of Death that serves him."

Caden and Elander exchanged a concerned look as Amon led them into a long hallway.

They came to an abrupt stop at the end, and Cas stiffened again as the man turned and gave them another glance-over. He seemed to have forgotten about the covered marks of her companions—he didn't give their gloved hands a second look. But what he *did* notice was

Cas's own hand, which was grasping the pommel of that sword she had never removed. His sunken eyes settled on it, and an uneasiness crawled through her. She couldn't explain it; this man before her *looked* harmless enough.

But a small, quiet voice inside of her begged her not to step forward unarmed, so she quickly came up with a lie of her own.

"Forgive me. I didn't leave my blade by the door because it has been forged with the Healing Goddess's magic, its edge eternally sterilized by her divine, cleansing power—and thus it plays an important part in these healing spells we've developed."

Amon pursed his lips. Cas's stomach twisted uncomfortably again. Lying was often a part of her jobs—one that she didn't think twice about. But this man looked so...worn down. Too tired to properly argue. Too desperate to listen to whatever warnings might have been firing through his mind—a mind that Tara's magic had likely left feeling hollow and senseless.

She felt Tara tense beside her, perhaps readying another wave of that magic. She spoke before the Shadow-kind could unleash anything else.

"We can help you," Cas said to Amon, surprised by how sincere her lie sounded. "I promise we can, if you'll just let us in to see her. We mean you no harm."

The old man shifted those hooded eyes to the door at the end of the hallway. Nodded, and then slowly kept walking.

"A smooth lie," Caden whispered. He sounded

begrudgingly impressed, which was an improvement over *condescending* at least. "But you shouldn't have *promised* we could help," he added. "You're just getting the poor man's hopes up."

That man stopped at the door. His fingers fumbled with the handle, and another wave of pity washed through Cas. "If you can just wait here a moment..." he said as they caught up with him. "I should speak with Brynna's nurses before I show you in."

"We need a moment to prepare ourselves for our healing ritual anyhow," Elander assured him.

The man finally managed to open the door, and he disappeared inside.

"This isn't about *helping*," Elander reminded them in a low voice. "Not directly, at least. It's about gathering information that we'll hopefully be able to use to help the entire empire." His gaze shifted to Cas, and he added, "Varen seems to think that you might be able to connect with the infected in some way that we haven't been able to thus far. Your job is to focus on that."

She nodded.

A moment later, Amon returned and showed them inside.

The room on the other side was not so much a bedroom as a greenhouse. Plants and sunlight filled the space. Every level surface—the window sills, the dresser, the shelves on the walls—hosted some sort of flowering greenery. The shelves above the bed held two large planters, and vines twisted out from them, draping low enough that they skimmed the bed's headboard. A statue of a squat little deity sat in between the planters. Cas did not know this deity's name, but she assumed it was another one of the lesser-spirits—one whose magic granted vitality and growth, if that jungle of bright plants around it was any indication.

Cas kept her eyes on that statue for as long as she could, but soon she had no choice but to lower her gaze to the bed.

The girl resting there was so pale that she was nearly lost amongst the drifts of white quilts and blankets. Her cheeks were sunken in, as was the hollow of her throat. She was little more than a skeleton with an afterthought of thin, mottled skin stretched over it, bones protruding like wires bent at odd angles. Her hair was the same shade that Cas's would return to after her latest crystal wore off. A sprig of white lilies rested on the girl's chest, tucked beneath her folded hands; the white lily was a flower commonly used in rituals meant to honor the God of Death.

The girl's hands looked so terribly small over top of the withered stem.

They hadn't asked Amon how old his daughter was, Cas realized.

She didn't want to know. If she had been forced to guess, she would have said that this girl, Brynna, was around the same age that she herself had been when the Fade had touched her. And the familiar question nagged at her mind—

Why did I live, when so many others have died?

This girl was not dead yet, no. But the rise and fall of her chest was so subtle that Cas second-guessed this assessment several times as she stood there, taking in her surroundings.

Amon was speaking in a soft voice to the three women serving as Brynna's nurses. Caden and Elander both stood a short distance away from the bed, pretending to prepare for the *ritual* they'd claimed they were here to perform. After a moment, Amon left the nurses and went to stand by his daughter's bedside.

While Elander and Caden moved closer to the bed as well, Tara walked over and stood with the nurses, grasping their hands and praying in what sounded like it might have actually *been* the Oak-kind's language.

They're very committed to this ruse.

Newly determined to fulfill her own part of the mission, Cas's eyes drifted once more around the room, studying things more closely. There had to be an answer here. A sign. Something that she could bring back to Varen that could aid them in finding a cure.

When she focused, *truly* focused, she thought she felt the same odd, pulling energy that she'd sensed outside that dying servant's room back at the palace.

Was that what she had felt just a few minutes ago too? That twisting in her gut that she'd taken as a warning, as a plea not to enter this house unarmed...

What did it *mean*?

Caden lifted a hand over the girl, keeping all the eyes

in the room on him while Cas continued her investigation. He spoke in the same language that Tara had prayed in while Brynna's father and all her nurses watched and held their breath, hoping.

But nothing happened, of course.

Because Caden had no true healing magic.

And even if he did, it wouldn't be enough on its own.

There was no simple magic spell that could save this dying girl, just as there was no simple spell that could have saved Cas's parents, and no simple spell that would save Asra. Everyone present knew this, and the hopelessness in the room soon turned palpable. Raw. Familiar. *Overwhelming*. Cas desperately wanted to do something to alleviate it, even though she knew there was nothing to be done about it all at this moment. And yet...

She stepped forward, suddenly overcome with a desire to do something to help these poor people right *now*.

Her hand grabbed the girl's much smaller, much colder one. An odd spasm twitched across her palm as she intertwined her fingers with the girl's, and then a flash of light briefly obscured her vision, like sunlight glinting off a sword and blinding her.

She convinced herself she had imagined it.

Until one of those plants on the shelf over the bed wilted, impossibly quick, to a dead shade of brown.

One by one, its leaves broke off and fluttered down onto the white quilt.

Cas felt another spasm building in her hand.

Spreading up her arm. Tightening her muscles. She exhaled slowly, and she forgot to inhale again for a long, dizzying moment. Another shimmer of light crossed over her vision. Another plant died.

Three more times this happened—her muscles tightening, her eyes briefly blinded by strange light, another plant dying.

The room went completely still.

And then the girl on the bed opened her eyes.

CHAPTER 17

Tʜᴇʀᴇ ᴡᴇʀᴇ sᴇᴠᴇʀᴀʟ ᴀᴜᴅɪʙʟᴇ ɢᴀsᴘs.

Elander breathed out a soft curse.

Two of the women who had been tending to the girl dropped to their knees. The third woman clutched the beads around her thick neck, lifted her eyes to the ceiling, and began to fervently pray.

Cas let go of the girl and took a step back as Amon fell against the bed and clutched his daughter's pale hand, his expression a wildly shifting mixture of horror and elation and disbelief.

Silence fell over them.

Caden and Tara were staring at Cas, brows furrowed and mouths slightly parted in almost identical fashion.

The women on their knees rose to their feet, and then all three of those nurses hurriedly left the room together.

Elander's hand was against the small of Cas's back a moment later, his touch firm and unyielding. "Stay with your daughter," he told Amon, calmly. "We need to take a moment to...*pray* to our generous Goddess of Healing."

Amon was too overcome to reply.

Elander ordered Tara to stay with Amon, and then he and Caden headed toward the door. Cas moved slowly with them. If it hadn't been for Elander's insistent, guiding touch, she might not have moved at all. She felt oddly dazed. Oddly separate from the world and...*drained.*

Once they were back in the hallway, Elander grabbed her by the arm and dragged her more quickly, more roughly away from the sick room, weaving wildly through the house and stopping only once they reached the kitchen, which was separated from the rest of that house by a heavy wooden door. Caden followed close behind, closing the door and swiftly grabbing a chair to wedge underneath its handle.

Once this makeshift barricade was in place, Elander immediately turned on Cas. "*Why would you not tell me you could do that?*"

"I...I didn't know I could!"

He opened his mouth to shout something in response, but then stopped and made a visible, obvious effort to calm himself before he spoke to her again. "How could you *not know* that you have such powerful magic?"

"Magic?" She nearly choked on the word. "I don't understand. I don't have magic...I've *never* had magic." She held up her hands, turning them over and around for him to see. "I have no mark! I don't even know what sort of mark would allow me to do...whatever it was that just happened in there!"

The look he fixed her with was so fierce that she almost drew away from him. But she held her ground, and after a moment he rolled some of the tension from his shoulders and turned away from her, shaking his head.

"I don't understand, either." He raked a hand through his long hair, leaving the dark waves disheveled and wild. "But whatever this is—whatever just happened—you have to keep this to yourself. You cannot tell Varen about this. *He cannot know that you have this kind of magic.*"

"Someone else is going to tell him, Captain," Caden pointed out. "Did you see how terrified those women were when they left? They were running to tell someone what they'd seen. And our own backup soldiers are nearby by now. I'm sure they've already heard the commotion and started asking questions. Those women... we should have stopped them."

Elander hung his head in exasperation. "Damn it. *Damn it.* How many people already know what she did?" He tossed Cas an irritable look—as if he still believed she had done all of this on purpose—but then moved away from her and started for the door, reaching his hand toward it only to clench it back into a fist. "It's too late to keep this entirely to ourselves."

"Yes," Caden agreed.

Elander's hand remained clenched in a tight fist, and his eyes darted around the room as if he were searching for the most satisfying thing to hit.

Cas had never seen him look so flustered.

She hadn't thought he was *capable* of looking flustered.

"Our soldiers..." he began, finally unclenching his fist. "I'm going to have to threaten every single one of them within an inch of their lives. If any of them even *think* about going to the King-Emperor with this information, then I swear..."

"Which ones do we need to deal with first?" Caden's question was chillingly calm.

"Deal with?" Cas spun toward him, incredulous. "What do you mean, *deal with*?"

"What do you think I mean?" His tone remained so calm—so *blasé*—that Cas had to resist the urge to slap him. Even Laurent displayed an occasional flicker of empathy underneath his outer shell of cold indifference. But Caden...

"Are you two honestly thinking about killing people over this?" she demanded, her gaze shifting to Elander's.

He didn't reply right away, but to her horror, he looked as if he was mulling the question over.

"No one is going to die because of this," she snapped. "Are you *insane*? It was just a fluke! I don't have magic! If I did, I would have started using it to save people a long time ago. Whatever happened in that room, it isn't worth making a big deal over. And it certainly isn't worth *killing* people over."

Elander met her frantic gaze—truly met it—and for a

brief moment she thought he might have been considering her words.

But he only looked back to Caden and growled out a command. "Get back outside and figure out who knows what. Spill their blood and use your full magic on them if you have to. And stop the ones you need to stop, by whatever means necessary."

Caden gave a slight bow of his head, and an instant later he was gone, leaving her alone with Elander.

She stared at the door in stunned silence. The space seemed to shrink around them, the world shriveling into something entirely too small to contain everything that had happened in the past few minutes. She wanted to run, but Elander walked over to that door and leaned against it, blocking her path. His gaze lifted to the ceiling.

"Tell me the truth, Thorn," he said, very quietly. "Have you ever done anything like that before?"

"No," she whispered. "I already told you no."

He slowly lowered his eyes back to her. "You're really not lying, are you?"

She could tell by the tone of his voice that he already knew the answer to his own question, but she still shook her head, just to confirm it.

"But it's strange, isn't it?" he said after a pause. "The airs of Oblivion didn't bother you as they should have. And then you attacked my magic, somehow, outside of Darkhand's—"

"I didn't *attack* it."

"—and now this. And not to mention that odd bit of... whatever it was that happened in the Kirith Forest."

Her breaths shuddered out of her. She didn't trust herself to speak.

"What *are* you, Thorn?" He asked the question more to himself than her, but the way he stared at her made her feel as if he were trying to unravel her, piece by piece. It was uncomfortable—and yet, she didn't want him to look away. She didn't want him to leave, either. Because she had the exact same questions he did. The same doubts, the same fears...

And she didn't want to be alone with all of those things.

He was infuriating. Annoying. But at the moment, he was also the closest thing she had to a partner in all of this madness.

"Okay," he sighed.

"...Okay?"

"Okay, we'll figure this out. Let's just calm down and think this through."

Before she could respond, a low roar sounded from somewhere outside—and the screams that followed an instant later were decidedly *not* calm.

"What now?" he groaned.

Cas raced toward the window and peered out. "Something is happening near the center square." Houses blocked most of her view, but she could clearly see a crowd of people running away from it.

A strange shadow overtook several of the houses in

the next instant; at first, she thought it might have been a low cloud passing over. But the shape of it was odd, as was the way it moved—and the sky was currently a perfectly clear blue. There *were* no clouds.

Elander moved in behind her. The window was narrow but tall, and his height allowed him to see over her without her moving. She pressed closer to the glass, he pressed closer to her, and together they stared at the scene unfolding outside.

Dozens of people flew down the street toward them, like rabbits fleeing their destroyed burrow. The shadow didn't fall over anything else, not that Cas could see, but a second roar confirmed her fear: *something* was out there. Something that sounded nasty. And big.

"I think we should get you out of this city," Elander said, stepping away from the window. "Now."

"What about Tara?"

"She'll be fine. She knows how to make a quick exit without our help—as does Caden."

Another roar sounded from outside, and Cas felt inclined to agree.

They made their way to the front yard and untied their horses; the other two horses were already gone— taken by their rightful owners, hopefully.

The porch crowd from earlier had mostly dispersed, and the few who remained were too focused on whatever was happening in the square to ask Cas or Elander about what had happened with Amon and his daughter. Elander was able to retrieve his weapon without interruption, and the two of them swiftly led their horses across the street, to a small path between two houses that kept them out of sight while they readied those horses for riding.

Another roar sounded from the direction of the square.

Cas wanted to see what was making such a terrible noise, but she gave her head a little shake and kept fiddling with Lily's bridle instead.

Then came the sound of something...*breaking*. Glass shattering. Bricks crumbling and clattering. And more screams.

"Focus," Elander insisted.

Cas nodded, even as a steady stream of people ran past their hiding place, casting terrified looks over their shoulder as they went by. Lily's eyes were wide and white as she pranced nervously. Cas put a hand on her flank and tried to soothe her. The horse shuddered under her touch and stamped a hoof.

Another roar.

It sounded as if it might have been moving away from them, and Cas could no longer contain her curiosity. She looped Lily's reins over her neck and darted out of their hiding place before Elander could stop her.

She saw it as soon as she crept out into the street: A *monster*.

It stood on a distant stretch of that same street, entirely blocking her view of the center square. It was nearly as tall as the houses hedging it in—taller, if the curled and wickedly pointed horns on its head counted. Its face was long—not unlike a horse's—but the flesh on its face appeared to have melted away, leaving only a narrow skull with deep sockets that glowed with a strange red light. It loped along on four tall, muscular legs that made Cas think of tree trunks, splintering at the bottom like roots with sharp ends, digging into the ground and pulling it up with every step. Its hunched back featured even more sharp points—an entire cloak of spines that waved with its movement like a field of spiny, petrified grass rolling as the earth quaked beneath it.

She stared, frozen in place, as it reared onto its back legs and swiped toward the nearest house. Those sharply-tipped roots at the end of its right front leg sank in, puncturing the bricks as if they were mere paper, and with a slight flex of its leg, it ripped the house's face off.

It fell back to all fours. Crouched. Its mouth dropped open. Cas was too far away from it to get a good look at its teeth, but she could see a strange cloud of blackness rolling out. That cloud engulfed the street, moving like...

Like that shadow from before.

She watched as it swept over a small crowd of people. It dissipated a moment later, but not before several of the people dropped to motionless heaps on the road.

"Oh gods," Cas whispered, stumbling back a few steps. "What in the three hells *is* that thing?"

Elander grabbed her and pulled her against his chest, rolling them both back behind the house and out of sight once more. She was pinned between him and the warm brick of the house for a moment, unable to move against his strength. He held her in place even as he leaned out and studied the creature for himself.

He stared far longer than she had—so long that he seemed to forget he was holding her. His hand pressed hard against her hip, his earthy scent enveloping her— and for an instant she somehow found herself distracted from the monstrosity just around the corner.

"Why is that monster here?" he finally muttered, more to himself than her.

"Um, is the *why* really important right now?"

He slowly tilted his gaze to her. "That beast is the garmora—one of the ancient creatures that used to accompany the Rook God, Anga. It has been dormant for centuries, chained up in the lowest hell at the behest of the other two upper-gods because of its uncontrollably vicious nature."

He stepped away, and she immediately put several feet between her and his distracting touch and scent.

"So yes, the *why* is important," he insisted. "Because this is not a normal monster sighting....That thing shouldn't be here in the mortal world. And do you remember what Amon said? About his daughter mumbling the Rook God's name during her delusions?"

Icy heat crawled down her neck as she realized what he was suggesting. "You think that god is somehow involved in all of this?" Her recent conversation with the King-Emperor fired rapidly through her mind.

The Fade could be divine in origin...

"I don't know," Elander said. "But that beast showing up now? After what you did in that house...it seems like a strange coincidence, doesn't it?"

She bristled. "I had nothing to do with this."

"I didn't say you did." He frowned. "Not necessarily."

She could read the rest of his thoughts easily enough, even if he didn't say them out loud—*and yet here is another weird thing that's happened around you...*

"Then why are you looking at me like that?" she demanded.

He didn't reply right away, turning his attention back to his horse and finishing adjusting the straps on its saddle with a few quick jerks.

"You did something in that house," he finally said. "Something *strange*. I've never seen anything like it. And I just wonder..."

She glared at him, daring him to finish his sentence. Part of her wanted to know *exactly* what he was wondering—even though she was terrified of what it might be.

But he said nothing else. He walked over to her horse, grabbed its reins, and then walked that horse to her and shoved those reins into her hands.

She swallowed to clear the sudden thickness in her throat. "So what is our plan here?"

"The plan is that you stay very close to me," he said, his eyes darting toward the street at the sound of another roar, "and you hope that your horse is fast enough to get away. And you try not to die."

"That's a pretty vague plan."

"If you have a better one, I am very much open to hearing it."

She opened her mouth. Clamped it shut. Scowled.

"Well? Do you?"

She did not.

"That's what I thought." He winced slightly at the sound of more clattering bricks and shattering glass, but he didn't stray from his plan of leading her in the opposite direction of that chaos. "Now, *quickly* follow me."

"We're just...sneaking away from it?"

"Again, if you have a better—"

"We're sneaking away, *while it just destroys this city*?"

"Yes."

She palmed the grip of her sword, squeezing it a little more tightly with every step he and his horse took away from her. "But what if you're right and it's all related? Shouldn't we investigate it more closely? That seems like part of our original task, doesn't it?"

"I didn't say we were running away from it indefinitely," he said without looking back.

"But what if what I did *is* responsible for drawing that monster into this world?"

"Then just be glad it got distracted before finding you, how about? Unless you actually *wanted* to try and die today?"

She didn't reply.

She might have, if not for that chorus of screams growing louder and louder in the distance. She was no stranger to death—no one in this empire was—but she wasn't comfortable with people dying because of *her*. If that monster was here for her, running away might make it even angrier. Even more destructive.

And running away was not going to get her any answers about anything, besides.

Elander finally paused and glanced back. He caught the look on her face and immediately started toward her. "Don't you dare," he warned. "Thorn, listen to me, you cannot *possibly* be thinking of—"

He made it halfway to her before she turned and started sprinting for the square.

She passed dozens of people on the road—all of them running the opposite way. She questioned her sanity more than once. A few well-meaning villagers tried to grab her and redirect her, as if she somehow hadn't seen that monster she was racing toward.

She saw it perfectly well; both it *and* the latest mass of shadows it had expelled. But she had never been susceptible to such things. Oblivion's poisonous clouds had not brought her to her knees. The Fading Sickness had not taken her. She was not invincible, but she was better equipped to deal with nasty, toxic monsters than the villagers running and screaming around her. And she'd had plenty of experience dealing with such things.

Or at least, that's what she kept telling herself.

Elander and his magic would have been helpful, too. But a few quick glances over her shoulder revealed that he was not following her.

Partners or not, he apparently wasn't prepared to die with her.

Not that she blamed him. Or even cared what he was prepared to do or not do, one way or the other. She could take care of this on her own.

She set her eyes on more important things, such as finding a more covert path as she approached the square. The garmora's size was terrifying, but it actually gave her an advantage within the cramped city streets; that monster had to knock things over to get to where it was going. She could slip in and out of the main road, dart up and down skinny alleyways, leap from the cover of one street vendor's stall to the next—and that was precisely what she did.

She stole her way around the square, stopping once the monster's back was to her. Directly above her spot was a wall with a walkable path on top—a guard post that the city officials used to keep an eye on the bustling marketplace below. This post looked as though it had been abandoned...likely because a second, similar post across the square had already been reduced to a pile of dust and rubble.

It was risky, but it would be a good vantage point.

Cas found the ladder that led to the top of the wall, and she shimmied up.

Bodies dotted the streets below. She counted ten people not moving before she willed herself to stop focusing on the lost and redirect her energy on those she could still save.

The garmora was moving down a street adjacent to the square, its long, powerful strides shaking the ground and knocking over vendor carts and people alike. It never strayed far from that square; it would make it a hundred feet or so before stopping, twisting around, and loping powerfully back toward her, then retracing its steps while its gaunt face lifted into the air and appeared to sniff.

It was clearly hunting for something.

Was it hunting *her*?

A few brave souls had taken up weapons and started attacking the beast. Cas watched from her perch for a moment, trying to see if they had managed to expose any weaknesses. They were attempting to corner it, jabbing its massive body with everything from proper swords to farm tools. It swung back at every jab, often catching several people at once and lifting them off their feet. Bodies flew through the air like clods of dirt, breaking against houses and shops before tumbling limply to the ground below.

Cas winced with every collision. Her mind attempted to fog over, but she swiftly brought a hand down onto the stone beneath her and anchored herself with several quick taps of her fingers.

Tap tap tap.

Focus.

What would Varen think if she brought back parts of that monster? If what Elander said about this creature was true, then it was proof that at least one of the gods was meddling directly in their empire's affairs....

Surely that would be worth at least several months of care for Asra.

Her hand gripped the sword sheathed at her hip with new determination. She had never faced off with this particular beast—and never a beast so large—but she had completed her share of monster-hunting jobs. This was just another one of those jobs.

She had her target.

Now she just had to figure out the best way to take it out.

She watched it for another moment, and she noted how it swayed whenever it tried to make quick movements. It wasn't built for agility, clearly, and if she could get under its belly, those awkwardly long legs would make it difficult for it to twist and aim any sort of attack at her. And she *could* get under that belly, so long as the bravery of the people distracting it held up.

She flew down the ladder before she could talk herself out of it.

CHAPTER 18

THE CITY SHOOK AND SCREAMED AND SPUN AROUND HER, BUT Cas kept running—hesitating only long enough to pick the safest path around the garmora's stomping, swiping feet.

One of those feet slammed down directly beside her. Its root-like claws sank deep into the road, and a massive crack split across the cobblestones. Cas leapt toward more solid ground, steadied herself, and withdrew her blade. She rolled around the tree-trunk leg closest to her—

And the sunlight disappeared.

She was fully underneath the monster, and it was so large that it blotted out the sun.

It smelled like an odd mixture of dirt, blood, and sweat. She brought an arm up over her mouth and nose, trying to keep the scent from overwhelming her and leaving her too dizzy to focus. She had to *focus*. The ground they stood on sloped upward a bit, and the monster's front legs were bent slightly for balance—allowing her to reach parts of its stomach even with her relatively short blade.

She ran forward and stabbed upward. The creature's underbelly proved mercifully soft. It didn't take much to pierce it—or to swipe her blade through a long swath of that fleshy stomach. It was a messy strike that promptly spewed hot, dark blood across Cas's shoulders and back, which might have made her vomit if she'd had even a second to focus on it.

The garmora bellowed and buckled, and Cas twisted wildly, narrowly avoiding being crushed by a crumpling leg.

As the creature continued to thrash about, Cas continued to duck and weave through its legs. While it was distracted by pain, she scurried out from underneath it, slashing her blade into the back of one of those legs as she went. Once she broke back out into the sunlight, she sought higher ground once more. The wounds in the monster's stomach and leg had slowed and destabilized its movements, but she needed to get high enough to strike at a more vital area.

She planned to target its throat. There were no spikes there—unlike the coat of them that ran across the back of its neck. She could clearly see its pulse throbbing with every furious roar it bellowed out. A bow would have been more useful for hitting this particular target...but she didn't have a bow.

So, she was going to have to make do with what she

did have.

Her eyes found the destroyed guard post next, along with what was left of the patrolling walls that stretched away from it. She scaled a section of a wall with the help of a broken ladder, and then she ran along the top, heading back toward the monster. She moved as quickly as she could—which was not particularly quick, given the massive cracks splitting the stone rampart, and the entire pieces of that stone that the monster had already knocked away.

But she kept going, and after a moment the garmora lifted its head to follow the sounds of her thundering footsteps, just as she'd hoped it would.

The movement stretched its neck up and made her target all the more visible.

She was questioning her sanity yet again as she rocketed toward what appeared to be the end of the wall. The edge was close enough to where the monster stood that she should be able to leap off and strike it if she moved quickly enough—

But was she honestly going to jump?

An instant later, the decision was made for her—the garmora reared back and rammed its narrow skull into the wall, and that wall rumbled and started to shift and give way under Cas's feet.

It was either leap, or crash down and be buried under the rubble.

She leapt.

With the wall falling away beneath her, it wasn't a

clean jump. And the monster snapped its glowing red eyes toward her at the last moment, further ruining any chance of a proper strike to its throat. She stabbed forward anyway. The tip of her sword pierced its right eye. But before it could sink all the way in, that monster managed an impressive bit of coordination; it leapt back, dislodging her sword and sending her into a complete free fall.

She was an instant from the ground when the garmora swiped her with its claws and sent her flying.

She slammed against what was left of the patrolling wall and flopped down to the broken, stone-scattered earth with a gasp. Another hunk of stone fell off from somewhere above and came perilously close to landing on top of her. She clenched her eyes shut—it was impossible not to, with the amount of pain radiating through her body—but only for a moment. Only until she felt the ground beneath her shaking with heavy steps that were stalking closer and closer.

Her eyes fluttered open, accompanied by a groan. Every ounce of strength she could muster was focused on not dropping her sword. It was a miracle she still had it after falling. Not that it mattered at the moment; her arm was still throbbing from its impact against the wall, and she didn't think she could bring herself to swing that sword again just yet.

She fought to push herself up and turned to face the approaching monster as best she could.

Its mouth opened, revealing multiple rows of serrated

teeth. The air around that mouth darkened as Cas struggled into a crouched position. As she watched, the darkness twisted into a more solid-looking, shadowy mass. It was the same kind of shadow that had felled so many already, dotting the square around her with limp bodies. It roiled between her and the monster, billowing bigger and bigger.

Sunlight glinted off Cas's blade. She suddenly remembered the way her vision had flickered at the girl's bedside, right before she had somehow opened her eyes. The plants had died. The girl had lived. Almost as if Cas had...*redirected* the sickness from that girl into something else.

Maybe she could redirect this monster's sickness, too? Send that shadow it was creating somewhere far away from this city, away from the people here?

Desperately, Cas lifted her hand, reaching out toward that dark mist descending toward her. *Please. Please let me be able to do something useful here...* She wasn't even sure which deity she was begging for help, or what kind of divine magic she might summon that actually *could* help her—if it even *was* divine magic that she'd used earlier.

She kept her hand stubbornly lifted all the same.

But nothing happened.

There was no twitching in her muscles, no flash of light, no transfer of life, no redirecting of darkness.

The cloud sank over her, leaving her momentarily blinded. Coughing violently, Cas rolled as far and as fast as she could. She struck the stone steps of a shop and instantly reached toward the top, scrambling to pull herself up them with one hand while the other still clung desperately to her sword.

She made it out of the cloud of darkness and kept climbing, finally managing to stagger to her feet by the time she reached the top of the stairs.

She looked back and found the monster searching for her. The eye she'd stabbed was bleeding freely, flecks of blood flying with every twist of its neck. It had to turn its head at an awkward angle so it could fix its one remaining eye on her. It seemed furious about this—and confused that its breath hadn't dropped her like all of its other victims.

Confused and furious.

She could use both to her advantage.

She ached in so many places that she couldn't even pinpoint the worst of her injuries. But they didn't matter at the moment; she still had to *move*. So she heaved in several deep breaths. And then, while the flustered monster continued to toss its head angrily about, she bounded down the steps and rushed forward again, holding her sword as high and steady as she could, despite her pain.

She swept to the outside of its left legs, slashing one, then the other, and then she kept running until she felt far enough away that she could safely turn back.

As she turned, it rose up onto its two uninjured legs, trying to take the pressure off the bleeding ones. It teetered on those legs for several seconds, hopping awkwardly before tripping over the cracked, debris-littered ground. Then, with a pained roar, it began to fall, its injured legs crumpling beneath it despite its swaying efforts to stay upright.

Cas felt a brief spark of hope—she'd at least done some significant damage to the beast—but then she caught sight of what that beast was toppling toward: The same stairs that she had climbed a moment ago...

And a young woman who was pinned to the side of those stairs by a broken slab of stone.

The woman let out a scream as the monster staggered closer to her. If it didn't kill her by crushing her, it's shadow breath would certainly finish the job.

Cas turned and raced back, and though the world seemed to slow and stretch the way it did during such horrifying moments, she knew her sprinting was pointless.

She wasn't going to make it in time.

The pinned woman screamed again. She twisted away, covering her face with her hands. The first tendrils of shadow washed over her, and her body slumped, either from inhaling poison or from shock. Cas could not bring herself to look away—so she saw the second person sprinting toward the woman from the other side.

Apparently, Elander had decided to follow her into battle after all.

It's about damn time.

Just before the full weight of the garmora's body crashed to the ground, Elander shoved aside the stone that was pinning the woman down. Quickly, he turned and lifted a hand toward the beast as it flailed about. Cold shot through the air, waves of it rippling outward, momentarily stealing Cas's breath and making her stumble to a stop.

The air warmed again as the monster *thumped* to the ground and went completely still amongst the rubble. The black clouds it had already breathed out were still drifting dangerously around, but no more joined them.

Elander snatched the woman up in his arms and bounded away, carrying her out of reach of the rolling shadows as easily as if she were made of nothing but shadows herself. He didn't stop—didn't even *slow down* —until he reached the edge of the city, where the cobblestone street gave way to a dirt road that stretched toward the distant woods. There was a group of trees along this road, and both of their horses were already tied there, waiting.

He carefully leaned the woman back against one of the trees. She appeared to be unconscious. Meanwhile, Elander didn't even seem to be breathing hard.

How is he so strong? The question was a dull pulsing in the back of Cas's mind as she raced toward him. One that she didn't get the chance to ask, because as soon as she reached him, he spun around and grabbed her roughly by the shoulders. "You stupid, *stupid* woman. What the fuck were you *thinking?*"

"I'm fine," she lied, forcing herself not to wince from the fiery ache twisting through her entire body.

He looked as if he was torn between wanting to shake her and embrace her. In the end, he did neither; he only slid his grip down to her arms and held them so tightly that it was almost painful.

"You could have been *killed*," he growled.

Before she could reply, a roar startled her. Cas watched in stunned silence as the garmora emerged from the city's edge, bursting violently through a high wooden fence and leaving it in splinters before limping off toward the edge of the distant forest.

"It's...not dead," she breathed.

"Oh, brilliant observation," Elander snapped, finally letting go of her.

"Well, it's *retreating*, at least," she shot back.

"Yes, but I have a very strong feeling that it's going to return. And it's going to be very pissed off when it gets back."

"Can't you just go after it and...wave your hand harder and magically make it, you know...die *completely* this time?"

"My magic doesn't really work like that."

Cas pursed her lips.

"I can't just kill everything and anything in existence by pointing a finger at it as hard as I can."

"That's unfortunate. At least for this particular situation."

"Tell me about it," he muttered.

She had a sneaking suspicion that part of him was currently wishing he could wave his hand and make *her*

307

drop—if not dead, than at least as unconscious as that woman against the tree.

The horses stamped their hooves and tossed their heads, whinnying nervously.

A moment later, a flock of birds exploded out of the woods that the garmora had disappeared into.

Cas took a few steps toward those woods, frustration bubbling inside of her and momentarily pushing aside her pain and fear. "If I'd had arrows, I could have finished the damn thing off."

Elander shot her an exasperated look. "Were you even listening earlier when I told you that this beast was a servant of the Rook God himself? No mortal-made sword *or* arrow is going to end that creature. *I* couldn't even drain its entire life force."

"But it's going to come back, so we need to do *something*—"

"If you charge recklessly after it again, I swear to every god and lesser-spirit in existence that I'm not coming after you this time."

She crossed her arms and fixed him with an impatient look. "So what do we do?"

He glanced at that woman he'd saved, still slumped and unconscious against the tree. "Stay here and protect her," he said, before walking over and untying his horse.

"Wait, weren't you *just* furious with me over this exact thing? About me running off by myself to fight that thing?"

"Yes. But the difference between you and me is that I

have magic that I know how to use—and so the chances of me getting myself ripped in half are significantly lower."

"You said your magic couldn't kill it either!"

"No, but I might be able to make it go fully dormant again. Either way, I'm more capable than *you*."

"We could debate that."

"There's no time for a debate."

"You're going to get yourself killed."

A corner of his lips quirked. "You don't have to worry about me, you know. I'll be fine."

Her face burned. She wanted to tell him she didn't care one way or the other, but instead, she stared at those distant woods as she said, "You'd better come back in one piece. That's all I'm saying."

"Or else?"

Or else I'm coming after you, because...

No.

No, it wasn't that. She *refused* to believe it was that. She wouldn't even think it. Because she *didn't* actually care what happened to him—at least not because of her own personal feelings toward him.

It was business, nothing else.

"Or else Varen will be disappointed in me," she told Elander, "because he was so excited about the two of us working together, remember?"

"And we can't disappoint the King-Emperor." She could hear the eye roll in his voice.

"Not if I want him to reward me as handsomely as

he's promised."

He shook his head, exasperated again. "Take care of that poor woman, and stay here until I come back. Don't do anything stupid. Stay *safe*. Can you manage that?"

She gave him a mocking little salute. He swung up into the saddle and galloped off without another word, and Cas reluctantly went to the unconscious woman and plopped down beside her. She checked to make sure the woman was still breathing relatively normally, and then she trained her eyes in the direction Elander had disappeared in.

Several minutes passed.

The breeze swirled dust and scattered leaves around them, and Cas held her breath, waiting for the sight of Elander reemerging, triumphantly, from those distant trees.

A sudden groan sounded from beside her. The woman's body slumped against her a moment later, and when Cas looked down, that woman's eyes fluttered open.

"You're awake," said Cas, relieved.

"Who are you? Where am I?" The woman leaned away, her body wobbling dangerously. She pressed one hand against the ground and the other to her bloody forehead. Her fingers shook as she pulled them away from that bloodiness, and she stared at the red staining their tips for a long, dazed moment before shrieking, "*What happened?*"

Cas patted her gingerly on the arm as her eyes turned

back to those woods. "You're...um...you're going to be fine."

"*Fine*? I'm covered in blood!"

"It's not as bad as it looks. Head wounds bleed a lot," Cas informed her, distractedly. She rose to her feet. She hadn't heard one of the garmora's roars for several minutes now, and it had been far too long since she'd seen any birds or other wildlife fleeing that forest in the distance. It was all too quiet. Too still.

The woman was moaning something incoherent beside her.

"Can you walk?" Cas asked her, eyes still on the distance.

"I..."

"You need to get up. Go back to your home, or some other, safer place. I have to..."

"Where are you going?" the woman called after her.

But Cas still didn't look back; she had made up her mind. She felt oddly energetic, suddenly. It didn't make any more sense than the strange moment of magic in Amon's house. But for whatever reason, she wasn't in pain anymore, despite the way that monster had knocked her around.

And so, stupid or not, she was already jogging toward her horse.

"I hope you're feeling brave today, Lily," she said as she untied her. She gave the mare a quick rub on the nose before climbing into the saddle and kicking her into a gallop.

They sped toward the trees. The sun burned hot against her back, and reaching the shade of those trees was a small mercy—though the darkness it brought with it was swift and disorienting.

Lily slowed to a canter, and then to a trot, tossing her head anxiously. Cas rubbed soothing circles against the horse's neck while her eyes adjusted to the lower light and she took in their surroundings. She spotted the trail the garmora had torn through the trees easily enough, and she guided Lily toward the path of broken trees and upturned earth.

Sounds drifted toward them as they walked—mostly the creaking of trees and the snapping of branches. All far in the distance, and only soft and occasional at first. But soon the sounds grew louder, building into such a cacophony of noise that Cas was certain that, somewhere, entire sections of the forest were being razed to the ground.

A pair of deer hurtled out of the brush directly in front of them, and Lily reared, nearly throwing Cas from her back. Cas leapt from the saddle and took a more commanding hold on the reins, planting her feet firmly on the forest floor and pulling the horse to a full stop.

But she couldn't bring herself to force the terrified creature forward. So once she managed to calm Lily, she encouraged her back toward the city with a swift swat against her backside.

With her hand on the pommel of her sword, Cas continued deeper into the forest on her own.

After only a few minutes of walking, the sounds in the distance abruptly stopped. Nothing creaked. Nothing snapped. Nothing roared. She was reminded of the strange, otherworldly silence in those woods kept by the spirit, Kiri—except that the silence here seemed much more...*ominous*.

Then she heard a soft growl.

The hairs on the back of her neck stood on end. She withdrew her sword and walked slowly in the direction of the echoing growl, tapping her thumb against that sword's handle and willing herself not to panic.

She was starting to fear she might lose that battle against her anxiety, when all of a sudden, she heard a new, terrible sound—the guttural, pained cry of a man.

"No, no, no," she muttered, pushing herself into a quick jog, and then a sprint.

What had that idiot gotten himself into? Why had she let him run off on his own? Where *was* he?

Wherever he was, she never made it to him.

A monster stepped into her path before she could.

It was not the garmora. It was a different monster entirely—although it was just as large. A large, black wolf with eyes like collapsing stars and teeth wrapped in swirling shadows.

And she *knew* those eyes.

She knew those teeth.

Because this was the same wolf that had haunted her nightmares for years.

CHAPTER 19

"YOU AREN'T SUPPOSED TO BE REAL," SHE BREATHED.

It lunged.

She stumbled away, tripping over a root and landing hard on her bottom, before scrambling back to her feet.

The wolf padded to a stop several dozen feet away, its jaws working with furious motions. Like it was preparing to unhinge them and swallow her up.

Just as it did in her nightmares.

Maybe *this* was a nightmare. Or maybe she had stepped into some web of dark magic—into another trick, like the ones in the Kirith Forest? Maybe she could wake up? She tried clenching her hand into a fist, digging her nails into her palm until it hurt. She tried biting her tongue, pulling at her hair. But it was all solid, all painful; nothing she did made her wake up. Nothing made the scene before her flicker or fade in any way.

The wolf started to circle her, eyes burning into hers.

It was so large that she had to look up to meet those eyes, its legs so long that it could have been on top of her with only a couple of quick strides.

She lifted her sword.

The wolf bared its teeth.

Over the growl rumbling in its throat, Cas thought she heard another pained cry in the distance. That cry flooded through her mind until it was all she could think about. She wasn't going to collapse under the fears and anxieties trying to press in; she *couldn't*. Elander needed her.

She stepped forward, holding her sword more tightly.

The wolf let out another growl and lowered its head. Its burning-star eyes flashed. The shadows around its mouth swirled more viciously. The forest grew darker. Colder. Smaller.

It was going to swallow her up.

The beast closed its eyes, and without those stars to follow, she lost sight of it in the darkness. *Everything* was darkness and coldness, and Cas felt as if she was shrinking in the center of it all. There was no way out. *There was no way out.*

But she kept her eyes open. And then, far, far above her, she thought she caught a glimpse of sunlight through the trees.

She felt a twitch of pain across her palm—

No, not pain.

Power.

She shoved her hand toward the last place she'd seen

that wolf's eyes, and the twitch in her palm became a throbbing in the muscles of her forearm.

Light exploded around her.

A pure, golden-white light that embraced the shadows and then chased them away—shooting through the forest and growing brighter and brighter until Cas could no longer make out even an outline of the trees amongst the vividness.

When it finally faded, Cas found herself kneeling in the forest, alone. The wolf was gone, the shadows were gone, the golden light was gone—it was *all* gone so quickly.

Maybe it *had* been a dream.

Trembling, she rose to her feet. Dusted leaves and dirt from her pants, and then lifted her hands in front of her, turning them over and over. She didn't know what she was looking for. Another flash of light? Had she *really* caused that explosion of light a moment ago?

What in the world is going on with me?

She heard a weak cough, and she suddenly remembered why she had raced into these woods in the first place. She ran toward the sound, and she finally spotted Elander in a small clearing just ahead. He was lying on his back, one arm over his face. She hurried over and dropped down to his side.

His shirt was in tatters, and the skin beneath it didn't look much better; his chest had clearly not fared well against whatever monster claws or spikes had ripped through him. There was an alarming amount of blood, and he was entirely too still. Cas momentarily froze, wondering what she should do.

She had almost made up her mind to try and hide him, and then run to find help, when he finally moved. He lifted his arm from his face and lowered it stiffly to his side. After a bit of straining and blinking, his eyes found hers. His chest rose and fell with a deep, somewhat normal breath.

Cas breathed a sigh as the world slowed and steadied a little. "You're alive."

He winced as he pressed a hand to his bloody chest. "Of course I'm alive," he muttered, slowly trying to sit up.

She barely suppressed a snort. *His arrogance really knows no bounds.*

She offered him a hand, and she was surprised when he actually took it and let her help him into a sitting position. She kept a hand braced against his back while he regained his balance and inspected his wounds more closely.

As she held him up, her eyes nervously scanned the woods around them, her body tense and already prepared for whatever disaster might befall them next. "The garmora..." she began after a moment. "Where did it go?"

He paused his inspection of a bloody slash mark on his leg, and he lifted his gaze to follow hers. "I'm guessing you saw that wolf stalking around in here."

She nodded, her stomach sinking horribly. She had still been trying to convince herself that it had all just been a strange—perhaps magic-induced—nightmare or hallucination. But if he'd seen it too...

"Well, I think that wolf chased the garmora away," Elander said.

She hugged her arms against her chest. "And then *something* chased that wolf away."

"Yes. Which...what was that strange light a moment ago?"

It took her a minute to answer him. To find her voice and meet his eyes, to make herself believe her own thoughts enough to whisper them out loud.

"I think it was me."

HOURS LATER, Cas and Tara were reclining next to a table in the shabby sitting room of a tiny inn.

They had fled Belwind and found a smaller, more secluded village to the north. Most of their party was camping in the valley on the outskirts of the village, but Tara had insisted on procuring an actual bed for Elander to recover in. He hadn't argued. Despite all of his arrogance and feigned indifference, it was clear that the wounds he'd sustained actually *had* taken a toll on him... even if he wouldn't admit to it out loud.

And it was no wonder that they had taken a toll; once they had cleaned away all the blood, Cas had been able to see how truly deep the wounds on his chest were—and they were far worse than she'd first thought. So much

worse that she wasn't entirely sure how he wasn't *dead*.
And she still thought there was a decent chance that he
could die from those wounds, which was why she could
not stop turning her head in the direction his room was
in, even as she tried to carry on a conversation with Tara.

"Just go check on him," Tara finally said. "And see if
you can get the stubborn bastard to eat while you're at it."

Cas agreed to try. Tara retrieved a canteen of water
and a plate of breads and fruits from the inn master
himself, and Cas took it from her and headed for
Elander's room.

The door to it was unlocked, thankfully, so she quietly
stepped inside. Elander's head was tilted toward the
window, and he was so still that she thought he was
asleep at first. But as she came closer, she realized that his
eyes—though heavy with exhaustion—were still open.
The moonlight streaming in through a break in the
curtains made their pale blue color shimmer in a way that
sent an odd shiver down her spine.

He'd managed to clean himself up without help, and
he now wore a loose, unbuttoned shirt that revealed the
many bandages that had been wrapped around his chest.
He acknowledged her with only a slight nod, and then he
pulled himself upright and leaned back against the
wooden headboard, drawing one of his legs toward him,
and draping an arm over his bent knee. The movements
were fluid enough, but they still made him wince slightly.

He refused both the food and drink she'd brought. Cas
pursed her lips at that, but she decided not to fight about

it for the moment. Instead, she focused on assessing his wounds.

She was no nurse, but she could tell that he had been messing with the bandage around his left bicep, and it looked like the wound underneath it might have still been bleeding slightly. She reached for his arm and pulled it closer to inspect it. She didn't ask permission. She knew he wouldn't give it, anyway.

He let out a small grunt in protest, but otherwise didn't object as she started to unravel the ruined bandage. He lifted his gaze to the window once more, and it stayed there even when he spoke again a moment later.

"Why did you run after me earlier, when I told you not to?"

She kept untwisting that bandage, frowning as she saw precisely what she'd been afraid of—fresh blood. "For the same reason I stupidly ran straight at that monster to protect those villagers back in Belwind," she told him.

He cut his eyes toward her, his mouth drawn in a tight line, apparently not following her reasoning.

"Because I don't enjoy letting innocent people die if I can help them."

"I'm not like those villagers, though."

"What do you mean?" she asked, distractedly, as she went to fetch a damp cloth from the adjoining washroom.

"I'm not helpless. Or innocent, for that matter. I'm the farthest thing from it. If you knew..." He trailed off, shaking his head.

"If I knew what?"

He didn't reply.

For a moment, she stood with that damp cloth in her hand and simply studied him, all of the many questions she had about this man surfacing all at once.

Who was he, that he stayed in the service of the King-Emperor—even when he didn't trust him? Did Varen really trust *him*, or was there something else that kept the two of them working together?

And how had his magic been powerful enough to stop that garmora beast—a servant of the Rook God himself—in its tracks?

And how had he been strong enough to carry that woman to safety? To then run off to fight those monsters in the woods *and* survive it all?

He was watching her closely, questions shimmering in his own eyes.

They were an interesting pair, weren't they? Nothing but questions and doubts between them. It would have been smarter to keep her distance, she knew.

And yet she hadn't been able to fight off her need to come check on him.

She cleared her throat. "Well, I'm sure plenty of those villagers weren't actually innocent either," she said. "Nobody really is, in my experience. But nobody deserves to die by being ripped apart by monsters. Now, hold still so I can clean this up and redo the bandage you've ruined."

He continued to watch her, silently, as she worked.

Minutes passed. The questions about him did not quiet in her mind; she had to say something.

But where to start?

She tried to begin the complicated conversation with a lighthearted comment. "So...does that divine mark on your hand make you immune to death or something? Because this wound over your heart here *really* looks like it should have killed you."

He was quiet for another moment. Then a trace of a smug smile fluttered over his lips. "No, Thorn. I am not immune to death. I am just very good at negotiating with him."

"Well, I hope you'll negotiate on my behalf if the need ever arises."

"I'll do what I can."

Her cheeks warmed at the oddly soft tone his voice had suddenly taken on. She inhaled and exhaled a deep, slow breath. Questions. Answers. *That* was what she was supposed to be focusing on.

"Your magic today, it was...impressive," she said. "The way you dropped that garmora beast, even if it *did* get back up again...I've never seen anything like it."

"It wasn't that impressive."

"It was more than I managed."

"And yet it was *you* who drove away that wolf in the woods, as I recall."

"Another fluke," she insisted.

"I'm not so sure about that."

She wasn't either, but she didn't say so. Instead, she

said, "You know, if we were having a competition between us, a contest to decide which of us was the most mysterious...I'm not sure who would win."

"I'm not mysterious."

"You're a bit of a mystery to *me*."

"What do you want to know about me, precisely?"

She considered all of her many, many questions, and she decided to start with an easy one, in hopes of getting him to relax and divulge the more complicated things.

"Where are you from?" she asked, settling down on the edge of the bed.

"The royal city of Ciridan itself. My parents worked for the former King-Emperor—they worked for him even before he took the title of *emperor*, back when the four kingdoms still existed with their four separate kings and queens."

"And your parents were divinely marked, like you?"

"No. They were both unmarked, and so my magic came as a surprise. One that probably would have seen me killed if my father hadn't been on such good terms with that former king. Instead of death, I was given an opportunity to go to the southern empire, where I received training from others who carried the same mark I do."

"So you didn't grow up in the palace?"

"Afraid not. I lived a far less extravagant life until I was eighteen and completely in control of my magic. I stayed at a monastery in that southern empire, alongside servants of the Death God, who trained me. Five years ago, I came back, along with Caden and Tara. I came to serve King-Emperor Anric as my parents had agreed upon before sending me away."

"By helping steal secrets from his freshly-killed enemies," she recalled. "And leading some of his soldiers, and...?"

"And helping him convene with the kings and queens of Kethra's past, so that he could glean whatever sort of advice they were able to give."

It took her a moment to properly wrap her mind around what he was saying. "You mean you can summon the dead?"

"In a manner of speaking," he said, almost casually—as if this sort of power was commonplace. And again, she found herself marveling and wondering at the depths of his magic.

She had never encountered anyone with such power, and something told her that she had only just scratched the surface of what he was capable of.

No wonder the royal family decided to keep him around.

"And now I serve his son in the same ways," Elander added, his jaw tightening a bit with the words. He suddenly looked dangerously close to being done with the conversation, so Cas circled back to easier inquiries once more.

"Okay, next question. Favorite color?"

His gaze briefly locked on hers. "Green," he said, sounding as if he'd just decided on it at that exact moment.

She fought the urge to check her reflection in the window—to look and see what color her eyes were. Had that Mimic-kind crystal worn off completely yet?

It doesn't matter one way or the other.

She swallowed and went on. "Favorite...kind of weather?"

"I prefer rainy days."

"Favorite place?"

"The mountains."

"Favorite animal?"

"Bunny rabbits."

She made a face. "You aren't taking this seriously, are you?"

"Excuse you, I am *very* serious about my love of bunnies."

"Idiot."

"Be nice. I'm gravely injured over here."

"Speaking of which," she said, suddenly remembering that damp cloth in her hands, "let me see your arm again. I need to finish what I was doing."

He held it out to her without comment, and she finished wiping away the dry bits of blood before reaching for the roll of fresh bandages on the bedside table.

"No messing with the bandage this time," she scolded as she started to rewrap his arm.

He didn't reply, too busy biting his lip against the pain. Knowing how powerful he was made it strange to see him showing any physical signs of discomfort; so very odd to see him wincing slightly underneath even the lightest of her touches...

"Just close your eyes and try to relax," she encouraged. "I'll be done in a second."

He didn't close them. "That wolf," he said, "and that light from the forest—*your* light—I keep seeing it every time I shut my eyes."

He was watching her again, she realized. Watching and wondering.

What are you, Thorn?

He didn't ask it out loud this time. But she felt compelled to answer all the same; maybe they could make sense of her together. "Before that light came..." she began, still a bit uncertainly, "I felt the same odd spasm in my hand that I felt back at that house."

"An odd spasm?"

"Right before those plants withered and died and... and right before that girl opened her eyes."

He was quiet for a minute, mulling this over, and then he said, "Something protected you from the Fade all those years ago. *Something* you did protected that girl from the same thing. And now, it seems, it's also protecting you from monsters."

It had also protected her and Nessa from *his* magic that day outside of Darkhand's. She thought about pointing that out, but decided against it.

"There's something else that's strange."

A corner of his lips quirked. "There's simply no end to your strangeness, is there?"

326

She frowned, shaking her head.

"Well? What is it this time?"

"That wolf..." She took a deep breath. "I've seen it before. I've had nightmares about it. Lots of them."

He stared at her for a long moment—as if this was the strangest, most disturbing thing she had said yet. Finally, he averted his eyes and went back to staring at the moon. "That wolf is another servant of the Rook God," he said.

She thought for a minute. "The shadows around its teeth were similar to the ones the garmora breathed out. Similar to the ones in Oblivion too."

"Yes."

She waited for him to elaborate.

He didn't.

His forehead was creased in thought, and he didn't look her way no matter how long she stared at him.

"I...I'll leave you to get some sleep, I guess," she said after a few more moments of that uncomfortable silence.

He still didn't look at her at first, not until she stood up, and then he said, "I'd rather you stayed close." It still sounded like a command—as his words so often did—even in his weaker-than-normal voice.

"Close?"

He nodded toward the empty spot on the bed beside him.

"I'm not sure what you have in mind here." She bit her lip, shifting her weight from one foot to the other. "But I told you, my alter ego is not interested in providing any more *services* for you."

327

He rolled his eyes. "I meant I wanted you close in case that wolf monster comes back. Or some other new, equally terrifying or weird monster...You seem to be a magnet for terrifying and weird things, as I believe we've established."

"Oh," she said, rather stupidly. Her face burned for a moment, but she quickly recovered and gave him a little smirk. "You're right... I suppose we should stay close to each other so I can protect you."

He snorted. "Other way around."

"Oh yes, because I feel incredibly safe next to you and your half-dead self."

"Body's a bit weak at the moment, I'll give you that. But my magic is still perfectly capable of protecting you."

"So what do I do if that wolf comes back? Just pick up your weak, corpse-like body and fling it at the thing's feet so you can use your magic on it?"

"That could work."

"I'm not sure I can carry you very far," she pointed out.

"You've proven resourceful in the past. I'm sure you'll come up with some sort of plan."

She pretended to give it deep thought. "I think I saw a wheelbarrow in the yard outside; I could load you into it and roll you into battle."

"Brilliant," he deadpanned.

"Varen was right—I think we'll make a good team, after all, one way or another."

"If we're all done making jokes, I think I'm going to sleep."

"I'm done for now."

"Good-night, Thorn."

"Good-night, my wheelbarrow warrior."

He breathed out a sigh and then closed his eyes. She lowered herself onto the bed once more, tentatively reaching for a pillow. Hugging the pillow, she curled onto her side, and again watched Elander's chest rising and falling, making certain that his breathing stayed normal. After a moment, it occurred to her that she still had approximately a thousand unanswered questions.

She had gotten distracted from her interrogation plans.

Damn it.

He must have felt her staring at him because he cracked an eye open. "Feel free to build yourself a wall of blankets and pillows between us, or sleep on the floor if it makes you feel better. I won't be offended."

She lowered her gaze to the pillow clenched in her hands. "It's a big bed. I don't think that will be necessary."

It *was* a large bed—at least as large as that ridiculous bed back in her guest room at the palace. And as she settled down into it, she couldn't help feeling like it was *too* large. There was too much space between them. Too much emptiness. So she tucked the pillow under her head instead of against her chest, and she inched a bit closer to him—close enough that she could have reached out and touched his arm.

And after a few minutes, she did.

Her fingers reached and tapped a steady rhythm against the corded muscle of his forearm. Not on purpose. She didn't even realize she was doing it until several moments later—not until his eyes fluttered open again and he gave her a curious look.

"Sorry." She thought of their conversation from the night before, of how he'd sat with her, and she suddenly felt brave enough to add, "It's another anxiety thing. Touching things, tapping things...it helps me feel anchored. Keeps my thoughts from flying and carrying me away with them."

He closed his eyes once more. "You don't have to stop. I kind of like the feel of your fingers against me—it tells me that you're still here."

Her breath hitched. Audibly.

He smiled without opening his eyes. "Sorry. Did that make you more anxious?"

"No," she lied.

Well, not in a bad way, at least.

She kept her hand against his arm, but she tried to keep it still. She managed it for perhaps half of the next hour, but then her fingers were moving again of their own accord, not tapping this time but circling against his skin in an absent-minded pattern.

"You're still not asleep," Elander mumbled.

"No."

"Why not?"

"Because I don't sleep very often. More of my weirdness. And I can't stop thinking..."

He sighed. But then, with a soft grunt of pain, he rolled onto his side so they were facing each other. "About?"

"What you said earlier—about how I protected that girl."

"And?"

"Why did she live? Why did I live all those years ago, when so many others have died?"

He didn't seem to have an answer for her. Then again, she hadn't really expected him to.

"I just...I guess I haven't thought about it as much as I should have, maybe."

"What do you mean?"

"The question surfaces in my mind every now and then. But maybe I should have been spending more time figuring things out? What if I could have used my weirdness to help people before now? You mentioned that I protected that girl, but if that's the case, then why haven't I been protecting other people? Like my parents, and..."

"I don't know." His tone was blunt, though not unkind. "But obsessing over it won't bring back the dead. And it's a terrible way to spend the extra time that you *were* given, for whatever reason you were given it."

"I suppose."

"I told you the other night—you aren't the reason your parents died. You were a child; it wasn't up to you to save them, whatever magic you may or may not have possessed at the time."

She wanted to nod. She wanted to believe what he was saying, but her thoughts refused to cooperate.

"You have to let some things go, Thorn," he said, gentler. "Not everything—just whatever things you can. Or else it's all going to get too exhausting to carry one of these days."

She sank back into the pillow and stared at the ceiling. They were quiet for a long time. She moved her hand to the bed between them and tapped it instead of him, while he appeared to be drifting back to sleep.

But then he grabbed her tapping fingers and stilled them within a cage of his own, holding them tightly as he spoke again, in a sleepy little voice that still sounded unusually gentle for him. "I was thinking, too, actually."

"You were?" The words almost stuck in her throat as his thumb started to trail a path over her palm.

"Yes. I was thinking...and trying to figure you out."

"Let me know if you manage to do that. I'm still trying myself, most days."

He chuckled softly. "It's just interesting to me that the same woman who can't sleep because of anxiety was *also* able to run straight at the Rook God's monsters. You're a rather...captivating combination of fearless and faint-hearted."

She slowly pulled her hand from his. She wasn't sure she could speak clearly with him running his fingers over her skin.

And had he just used the word *captivating* to describe her?

She kept her eyes on the ceiling as she said, "I was terrified the entire time. I'm always terrified. The fear never entirely goes away—but I've just learned to do things while I'm afraid. I can't always pull it off, obviously. You saw that the other night by the fire. But when I think of my friends or...or even other people that need my help, it kind of overrides whatever fear I'm *personally* fighting with. I can't be fearless for myself. But for other people...it's different."

"Admirable," he commented, and there was no hint of sarcasm in his voice. "And as long as we're being honest, I have to admit that what you did was impressive. If you're going to run recklessly into battle the way you did, at least you're clearly a capable fighter."

She tilted her head toward him, momentarily speechless.

He had called her interesting, captivating... and now he honestly sounded as if he was trying to compliment her—and she wasn't sure how she felt about any of those things.

She went back to staring at the ceiling. "You're much nicer after you've had a near-death experience. You should almost die more often."

"Just to clarify," he said, drily, "I still think it was incredibly *stupid*, what you did, whether admirable or not. Honestly, sometimes I think there's something wrong with your brain."

"And *there's* the Elander I know."

They shared a small smile that felt entirely too familiar, and a blush warmed her cheeks.

"Fighting in spite of fear isn't all that admirable," she said, after a moment of thought. "That fear does give me a bit of an advantage in those battles, though."

"How so?"

"I see things coming, because I'm used to walking into a room and immediately noticing everything that could kill me or dismember me. Everything that could go wrong...my mind is constantly turning the possibilities over and over, so..." She trailed off with a shrug.

"That sounds exhausting," he said, yawning.

"It is." Her smile was a bit sad, her voice a bit more vulnerable than she intended. "And yet, I still can't sleep most nights."

They fell silent. Her gaze soon fell away from the ceiling, and she found him staring at her again, a curious gleam in his eyes.

"Come here," he said.

She hesitated.

"I'm not going to bite you." A corner of his mouth hitched. "Not unless you want me to."

Her eyes narrowed.

His laughter was soft and sleepy. "It was a joke."

"I know that." She hesitated a moment more. Then, perhaps against her better judgement, she scooted closer to him, and she let him wrap his arm around her and pull her against his chest.

"Doesn't that hurt?" she asked.

"I'm fine." He sounded like he was losing his battle to stay awake. "Just go to sleep," he added, yawning again. "You're safe here."

Safe.

She had always had a difficult time believing in that word. His embrace did not magically fix that. But with his fingers trailing a mesmerizing path up and down her back, she decided she could at least try to close her eyes and focus on his touch instead of her own tapping fingers.

And at some point, with her head against him and his heartbeat in her ear, she did something very strange: She slept.

CAS SLEPT through the rest of the night—and she didn't dream. So when the morning came and she opened her eyes to bright, warm sunlight, it was disorienting for a moment. She wasn't used to waking up slowly like this. Or in someone else's bed. In the past, whenever she had shared a bed with a man, she had always made a point to be gone well before morning.

This time, she was the one who woke up alone.

The bed still smelled of him—of earth and spice with a hint of the alcohol used to treat his wounds—and the sheets beside her were still wrinkled up in the shape of his tall body, but he was gone.

She sat up and quickly ran her fingers through her tangled hair—it was grey again, she noticed with a frown.

She twisted it into a messy braid before jumping to her feet and padding out into the hallway. She didn't look back into the room.

She still couldn't believe she had *slept* in that room, in his arms...

What had she been *thinking*?

"You weren't thinking," she muttered in response to her own thoughts.

She moved slowly, wanting to find Elander, but also *dreading* finding him. How strange would things be after last night?

Voices floated toward her—Tara, Elander, and Caden. It sounded like they were all breakfasting in the same sitting room she and Tara had chatted in during that previous night. Cas steeled herself and walked toward them.

"I'm concerned about her," Caden was saying, quietly. "I can't seem to read her mind, even during the times she's seemed upset, and I don't like it."

Elander's reply was quieter still, and dark and bristling with barely suppressed irritation. "I thought I told you not to even *try* to use your magic to read her."

"Sorry," Caden said, sounding anything but apologetic. "But I don't trust her."

Cas slowed to a stop and pressed closer to the wall, just out of sight of that sitting room's cracked door.

"She's harmless," Elander insisted.

"I think you're growing too attached, either way."

"I'm not attached."

"You *slept* with her last night."

"It wasn't what it looked like." Elander's voice had turned sharp.

Caden continued as if he didn't hear the threat in it. "She isn't a part of our plan."

"I know that. But Varen asked me to take care of her. What else do you propose I do? I won't jeopardize my standing with him by ignoring that request. I have to follow at least *some* of his orders if we're going to keep him from suspecting us—she's just an extra factor that we're going to have to put up with for now."

Cas braced a hand against the wall and took a deep breath. So him running after her yesterday, and his comforting her last night... it was all just a part of him trying to stay on Varen's good side.

Of course it was.

But more importantly, what was this *plan* they were talking about?

"What about the magic she apparently has?" Tara asked. Her voice was much softer than Caden's had been, but somehow it stung more. Cas had been starting to form a friendship with her. Or so she'd thought.

"I'll figure that out," Elander growled.

"Whatever happened in the woods..."

"She seems genuinely clueless about it all, so I don't think we need to worry about it yet—or ever. Harmless, as I said."

Cas clenched her hands into tight fists, suddenly more determined to find out what was going on with her and her apparent magic—and how she could properly use it all.

Harmless.

They'd see about that.

"We're very close now," said Tara. "Let's just stay focused."

"Close?" Cas heard herself whisper.

Close to *what*?

She strained to hear more details, but all three of their voices abruptly dropped to even quieter whispers. And a short time later, the sound of chairs pushing away from the table sent Cas's pulse skipping. She hurried back to the room she'd slept in, only to reemerge a moment later, acting as though she'd just woken up. Her gaze immediately met Elander's as he made his way down the hall.

"Good morning," he greeted her.

She offered him a small smile. "Good morning."

"You slept well, it seemed like."

She managed a stiff nod. It wasn't a lie, unfortunately. She *had* slept well. She had felt as safe as she ever did in his arms—which only made that secretive conversation she'd overheard all the more painful.

"So did I. I wish we had time for another nap like that, personally." His gaze felt almost like a physical touch as it looked her up and down, moving over her body as intimately as his fingers had just hours ago.

It was unapologetic, and tempting, and she had to remind herself not to fall for it. To make herself *stop* thinking about crawling back into bed with him, and to ignore the flush of heat that those thoughts caused. She didn't fully understand what he had been talking about in the sitting room, but gods, he was...not safe.

She'd been wrong to think he was anything of the sort.

And she needed to get out of this place before she said or did something else she'd end up regretting.

"Shouldn't we be preparing to leave?" she said, pointedly. She didn't wait for him to reply. She walked past him, heading to collect her things from the room that she *should* have slept in last night. She could feel him staring after her.

But, somehow, she willed herself to not look back.

CHAPTER 20

The ride back to Ciridan was uncomfortable and awkward, as Cas had predicted it would be.

She refused to travel any closer to Elander than she had to, to keep up the friendly banter that had become their norm, or to acknowledge anything that had happened between them in that bed they'd shared. She could tell he was curious about—or at least, confused by—her sudden coldness. But he didn't seem eager to confront her about it in front of his soldiers, so she managed to keep this silent treatment going for the entirety of their first day of riding.

On the second day, Elander did not even look in her direction.

Caden—and even Tara—followed his example and didn't confront her about her aloofness. It made for a lonely ride, but it was better this way. The less they interacted, the less temptation she would feel to trust them.

340

She had started to let her guard down before—that was a mistake.

A mistake she didn't plan to repeat.

When they arrived back at the palace after that second morning of traveling, she was overjoyed to immediately spot people with whom she *could* let her guard down—Nessa, Laurent, and Zev greeted her with a wave from one of the balconies above the front courtyard. They disappeared into the palace and reemerged through the main door a minute later. Cas left the rest of her traveling party at the gate and hurried forward. She almost cried with relief as Nessa rushed to meet her and swept her into a tight embrace.

"You kept us waiting long enough," Nessa scolded, while simultaneously squeezing the life out of her.

"So rude," Zev added, coming up beside them.

"As if you've really been suffering while we waited," Laurent said, cutting his eyes toward Zev.

"I actually *have*, thank you very much. It's been a very difficult moral dilemma for me, trying to decide whether or not I should accept the hospitality thrust upon me by this regime that I don't particularly care for."

Laurent scoffed. "Don't you need an actual, functioning conscience to be capable of having a moral dilemma?"

They continued their debate on the matter, while Nessa hooked her arm through Cas's and pulled her toward the palace, practically skipping as they went.

Cas couldn't help but glance back one last time as

they walked. Elander was still at the gate, still giving final orders to their traveling group before they dispersed. His gaze briefly snagged on hers, and she immediately turned her attention back to the path in front of her.

"So you've been traveling with him?" Nessa asked. Curiosity burned in the younger woman's eyes.

"Part of the deal I struck with the King-Emperor. And it's been a bit of a chore, to be honest."

A confusing, disappointing, infuriating chore.

Nessa glanced back toward that gate herself, but she didn't pressure Cas to elaborate. "Before you ask," she said instead, "Rhea is with Asra. We should go see them."

"I will. But I..." Cas searched for an excuse. "I want to get cleaned up first."

"Yeah, I wasn't going to say anything about the smell, but..." Zev began, and then ducked as Nessa turned and swiped toward his face.

"At least she has an excuse for the way she smells, unlike you," Nessa hissed.

He put a hand to his heart, feigning hurt. "When did you get so mean?"

"I bottle up all of my meanness and save it for *you*, because you're usually the one who most deserves it."

"Ouch," said Zev, while Cas and Laurent both stifled laughter.

The teasing, the laughter...it was almost as if the past week hadn't happened. As if Cas hadn't spent it away from her friends, caught up in a strange new existence and wondering if she was ever going to find her way back to *this*. She smiled a wry smile, grateful for the normalcy of this moment, as Nessa returned to her side.

"Asra was awake and alert when I checked on her earlier," Nessa said. "I'm not entirely sure what the royal doctors did for her, but it seems to have alleviated her symptoms somewhat, at least. You sure you don't want to go now?"

Cas nodded. It pained her to wait, but she wanted to make sense of the past days before she tried to hold a conversation with Asra about them. She *wanted* to see her —and she would, before the day was out—but for now, it was enough to know that she was safe and comfortable, and that Rhea was keeping her company.

Cas parted ways with her friends—at least for the time being—once they reached the hallway that her guest room was located on.

"Keep them out of trouble," she said with a nod toward Zev and Laurent, whose argument from earlier had already resumed.

"Maybe a lost cause, but I'll try," Nessa said as she gave her one last squeeze. "See you in a bit."

Cas went into her room, closing the door behind her and leaning against it with a deep sigh.

Anneka was rapping upon that door a minute later. She had apparently gotten wind of the fact that Cas needed to clean herself up, and despite Cas's initial protests, the servant woman insisted on barging in and assisting with these matters.

She drew a bath, procured a tray of fruits and pastries,

and made certain that fresh clothes were laid out upon the bed.

But after that she left, thankfully.

Cas wasted no time stripping off her filthy garments and stepping into the tub. Anneka had opened the curtains so that sunlight filtered in through the wavy glass windows, reflecting so brightly off the mostly white surfaces around her that it was blinding, and Cas paused for a moment to soak in the bright warmth of it all.

As she climbed into the tub, more and more images of the past few days flooded over her. She kept coming back to the memory of the light that had briefly blinded her in Amon's house.

Of his daughter opening her eyes...

She hoped that girl would make a full recovery. But the thought of that was oddly painful as well, because it made Cas think, again, of all the people who *hadn't* made a full recovery. Had she had the power to save people all along? And was it too late for her to harness whatever power she had to save the person she cared about most?

She lifted her hands in front of her, turning them over and over, as if she might spot a divine mark that she had somehow missed for the past twenty-two years.

There was nothing there, of course.

But the longer she held those hands in the light, the heavier they seemed to become. The weight was starting to become unbearable, when suddenly she felt a faint, familiar twitching across her palms.

She clenched her hands into fists and plunged them

back underneath the water, panicking at the thought of creating another blast of magical light. Whatever she'd done before had been powerful enough to drive away that monstrous wolf in the woods. What would happen if she unleashed something similar within the confines of this room?

There was no telling.

Her chest rose and fell with deep, determined breaths. She kept her hands tucked beneath her. She was trying to remain calm. Optimistic.

What was *happening* to her?

She had come back with more questions than answers. She was no closer to figuring anything out, and the burden of it all made her body sink a little lower into the tub. She clenched her hands more tightly as her hair fanned out around her. Her nostrils burned and her throat itched from the pungent, floral scent of the water... Anneka had overdone it with the bath salts. Not that Cas would complain about it; in spite of the smell, and even the anxiety thrumming through her, this still felt heavenly after nearly a week's worth of exhausting battles and hard riding.

Her eyes closed, and she was drifting toward a trance-like state when she heard footsteps in the adjacent bedroom. She sat up abruptly, sloshing water over the edge of the tub as she did. Her gaze fixed on the heavy wooden door, on the curled body of the tiger that was engraved in the oak.

Probably just Anneka dropping something off.

She kept her breaths calm and her body still so that she could listen. The servant woman had a tendency to hum as she worked, and the swish of the long, lace-trimmed dresses she usually wore was distinct. Several minutes passed, and Cas heard neither humming nor swishing. She also didn't hear any door open or close.

Someone remained in her room.

Her clothes were still on the bed, but at least there was a thick robe hanging from one of several hooks in this washroom. Cas squeezed the water from her hair, toweled off, and wrapped that robe around herself. Her hands still twitched and her breathing remained raspy. Uneven.

Those breaths didn't even out when she walked into her room.

Because Elander was reclining on her bed, his hands tucked behind his head, his eyes lost in thought as he stared at the stamped tin ceiling. He'd kicked off his boots and tossed his coat onto the nearby chair next to the pile of her own clothes, which he'd apparently moved to avoid laying on. He was the picture of comfort. And her thoughts briefly drifted to how comfortable she had been the other night while falling asleep in his arms.

She snapped back to reality just as quickly.

"You popping up everywhere like this is getting a bit ridiculous," she said, flatly.

"I knocked," he said with a nod toward the door. "You didn't answer."

"In most cultures, that means *don't come in.*"

"I know that." He rocked up into a sitting position and reached for his boots. "But I was just hanging around to make sure you weren't drowning yourself in the bath."

"Why would you think I was trying to drown myself in the bath?"

He shrugged. "You've been in a terrible mood these past days, so maybe I felt the need to check on you."

She snapped her mouth shut, swallowing the retort that had been building inside of her.

Even after two days of her treating him as coldly as she could, he had still felt the need to *check on* her?

It means nothing. It was just more of his *putting up with her* and following Varen's orders.

"This is a complete invasion of privacy," she growled at him.

"Sorry. But I also felt like I needed to talk to you again, in *private*, before you saw the King-Emperor." He stood and started to move closer to her, but reconsidered— perhaps because she was half-naked—and he moved instead to the dresser closest to the bed. He picked up an ornate, silver mirror and he twisted it around in his hand, studying his own reflection as he spoke. "I'm not sure what I said or did to upset you this time, but it doesn't matter."

"No, it doesn't," she quickly agreed.

A corner of his mouth quirked at her sullen tone. "Varen will be calling for you shortly, I'm sure. I just wanted to remind you to keep quiet about what happened with that girl in Belwind. And about that light

347

you summoned in the woods, *and* about that encounter with the lesser-spirit, Kiri."

"That doesn't leave much for me to tell him, does it? So what am I supposed to do, lie to him?"

"I didn't say *lie.* I just want you to be careful of what you reveal for the moment. I've worked hard to make certain the rest of the ones who were traveling with us remain silent on these...*sensitive* matters, so—"

"By which you mean you've been making death threats and maiming people who don't comply?"

"I haven't maimed anybody. Yet. But I did what I needed to do, and I'm only asking you to do the same." His tone was bleak, oddly hushed, and he looked as if he was considering explaining more about what he'd *needed to do*, but a sudden knock interrupted them.

"Promise me you'll be careful," he urged.

Another pound against the door.

Cas didn't reply to Elander. She only tightened the sash around her robe and then stormed around him to yank open the door and stop that insistent knocking. Nessa and Zev stood on the other side. They barged in immediately, and Cas briefly wondered if there was a damn sign on the other side of that door that invited people to do this.

Her friends both stopped abruptly at the scene before them. She understood why—because here she was in nothing but a robe, while Elander had tossed his coat aside and made himself comfortable...

Nessa remained behind Zev, eyes downcast and

cheeks flushed, while Zev coughed pointedly and said, "Sorry if we interrupted the beginning of something here."

"You absolutely did *not*," Cas hissed.

His eyebrows lifted.

"He wasn't invited in," she muttered.

Zev gave her a curious look. And her exasperation must have been evident all over her face, because his smile quickly fell. "Then maybe he should leave?"

She wasn't sure how to reply.

"I'll leave as soon as she agrees to what I said," Elander said.

She lifted her glare to meet the one he was giving her, but she still didn't agree to anything.

"No. I believe you'll leave *now*," Zev informed him, stepping toward him.

"Or else?"

"Or else I will set you on fire and dance on your fucking ashes."

Elander bared his teeth in a wolfish impersonation of a smile. "Why don't you try that and see what happens?"

Zev laughed at the challenge and lifted his hand. Smoke appeared in his palm, weaving in and out of his fingers like a snake. In a blink, it could all turn to fire—so Cas moved quickly to grab his arm and prevent that from happening.

"*Don't* try it," she said to Zev, with a cross look over her shoulder at Elander. "Neither of you try anything."

Nessa moved to help, putting a hand against Zev's chest while Cas moved back to the door and held it open.

"Just go away, please," Cas said, her eyes locking on Elander's as she jerked her head toward the hallway. "I agree to what you were talking about before, okay?"

He studied her for a moment, clearly searching for any sign she might have been lying. But then he nodded. He calmly grabbed his jacket, draped it over his arm, and left without another word.

Cas exhaled slowly.

The feather-shaped mark on Nessa's skin was glowing. She'd filled the space with her warm, calming magical energy, but smoke still continued to twist around Zev's hand. His voice was tight with suppressed irritation as he looked to Cas. "What exactly did you just agree to?"

Cas bit her lip, hesitating. "There are some things that happened on our mission that he—no, *we*—think would be better to keep to ourselves."

Fresh anger flashed in Zev's eyes. "What kind of things?"

"Nothing like *that*," Cas said, quickly. "Just...things with, um, with my..." She tried to think of a less-alarming word than *magic*. But this was the only explanation she had come up with, and to try and pretend it was anything else felt like lying to her friends. "With my magic," she finished, quietly.

They stared at her.

"You don't have magic," Nessa said with a confused little smile.

350

Cas closed the door to her room once more. She made certain it was locked this time, and then she took a deep breath and turned to her expectant friends.

Varen had already informed them of the agreement she had made with him, it turned out, and he'd briefed them on the mission she and Elander had been sent on— so she skipped most of the details of that mission and went straight to the moment when she had seemingly made that nearly dead girl open her eyes.

They were all quiet for a long time after she'd finished.

Finally, realization dawned over Nessa's face, and she said, "Oh. *Oh*—that same strangeness happened outside of Darkhand's that day, didn't it? You *did* do something that countered the captain's magic. Something that protected us both. But what did you do, exactly?"

"I'm not sure."

Nessa mirrored her frown and then fell silent again, her eyes glazing over in thought.

"So how tolerant do we think our young King-Emperor is going to be of not one, not two, but *three* unfamiliar magic users under his roof?" Zev asked, pointing at each one of them in turn. "Particularly when one of those magic users has no idea how to actually use—or control —her magic?"

"That's part of the reason I agreed not to tell him about it yet," Cas sighed.

Zev nodded, begrudgingly. "Maybe what's-his-face had a point."

"His name is Elander," Nessa offered.

"I'm going to stick with *what's-his-face*," Zev said, helping himself to the tray of food that Anneka had left.

"Speaking of the King-Emperor," Nessa said after a moment, clearly trying to redirect the conversation toward safer topics, "that's why we came up here in the first place. He's had a luncheon prepared for all of us—including you." She smacked Zev's hand away from that tray as he reached for a second pastry. "We should get going; it would be rude not to attend."

Cas agreed, and she dressed quickly and twisted her damp hair into a bun before rejoining the two of them outside of her room.

They descended the many winding stairs of the palace together, the air between them quiet but thoughtful after their conversation about secrets and magic. As they approached the same parlor that Cas had first met with Varen in—where their arranged lunch was apparently being served—they spotted Rhea walking toward them with Silverfoot perched on her shoulder.

At the sight of them, the fox jumped to the floor, bounded ahead of his master, and made a flying leap into Cas's arms. His rough tongue kissed her chin several times, and then he cocked his head back and let his gaze travel over her. His eyes lit up with that shimmering green color of his magic.

"You're really safe," Rhea said as Silverfoot's images of a whole, healthy Cas apparently passed into her mind. "Thank the gods."

They embraced. Rhea smelled like coffee and forest

and *home*, and Cas found herself not wanting to completely let go when they pulled away, so she kept her hand in Rhea's as they walked.

As a pair of servants pulled open the glass doors of the sun parlor, she finally dredged up the courage to clear her throat and ask, "How is Asra?"

"Resting peacefully."

Cas felt as if her chest had just been relieved of a massive stone—but mostly because if Asra was asleep, that meant there was no rush to go visit her.

But *why* was that such a relief?

Why was she still so afraid to see her? To admit to her mentor that she still hadn't found a way to reverse her sickness, as she had so desperately wanted to do?

Because you're a coward, whispered a nasty, anxious voice in the back of her mind.

She ignored that voice as best she could, and she forced a polite smile to the servants as she stepped into the parlor. Laurent was already waiting for them inside. His eyes were fixed on a book that he must have borrowed from one of the King-Emperor's libraries. He lifted his gaze and greeted Cas as she came closer. The fact that he had pulled his attention away from his studying was equivalent to an embrace from him.

The servants finished delivering their lunch—countless wines and sparkling waters and tray after tray of breads, steamed shellfish, and bright, perfectly ripened fruits—and then they all left with a bow and a promise to return soon to check on them.

Varen himself did not join their group. One of the maids apologized on his behalf and explained that the King-Emperor had gotten caught up in a meeting with some foreign diplomat from the southern empire, so Cas and her friends were able to privately dine and catch up on the past week's events.

It was wonderful to have her all her friends with her once more—but also a bit bizarre, thanks to the opulent decor and royal pomp and circumstance that surrounded them. And though none of them mentioned it out loud, Cas suspected they were all thinking the same thought: That this was perhaps the strangest adventure they had found themselves on yet, even in their long, colorful history of strange adventures together.

Zev grew more restless, more quickly, than the rest of them; his fingers tapped and trailed toward the gold-plated tableware laid out before him. "Lots of temptation in this palace," he commented, lifting a golden fork and sizing it up, clearly considering dropping it into the pocket of his coat.

"Don't," Laurent warned.

"Like they're really going to miss a few pieces of silverware."

"We're above petty theft," Rhea reminded him.

"I've never actually agreed to that rule."

"Well, we're above stealing from our *employers,* at least," Laurent insisted.

"Just trying to make the most of this golden opportunity," Zev said with a yawn.

"If we can manage to help the King-Emperor as he's asked, then I have a feeling we're going to be rich enough that we'll never have to make use of any more dubious *opportunities*," Nessa said, her tone a bit dreamy.

Zev placed the fork back onto the table. "You did get that reward agreement in writing, I hope?" he asked Cas.

"I...well, not exactly."

"We've talked about this." He frowned. "Tangible contracts are our friends."

"You have to stop taking people at their word," Rhea added, her tone lovingly stern.

"But he's obviously been generous to us thus far," Nessa offered, coming to Cas's defense in spite of the doubt now etching its way across her own face. "So maybe we *should* trust Varen to keep his word?"

The others remained unconvinced.

"I'm drawing up an official contract this evening," Laurent said flatly.

Cas hugged her arms to herself and leaned back against the wall. "This all feels like it's gotten bigger than missions and contracts."

There was a long, uncomfortable silence—as if they all thought she might have been joking.

"What do you mean?" asked Rhea.

"Varen believes that the Fading Sickness is divine in origin," Cas said. "And I think he's right. And it's more than just our reward at stake, or even just Asra's life, it's..." She trailed off, her voice growing thick with emotion as she thought about all the black curtains blowing in the breeze back in Belwind. About the Rook God's monsters and all the people they'd killed, and about her magic that had seemingly *summoned* those monsters...

Gods, this is all a giant mess.

Her friends exchanged more uneasy looks, clearly unsure of how to respond.

Finally, Zev cleared his throat. "If we end up having to battle the gods, I vote we charge *at least* triple our normal service rate."

"I'll add that to the aforementioned contract," Laurent said with a humorless chuckle.

Nessa sighed. "You two are ridiculous."

While her friends continued to discuss the details of this contractual agreement, Cas let her eyes wander towards what she could see of the courtyard through the glass walls around them.

Something just out of sight appeared to be causing a commotion—several people were rushing to the north end of that courtyard, and after a moment she heard an odd, distant roaring sound, like a rumble of thunder muted by thick cloud cover.

"You think that magic you used is divine in origin, too?" Zev suddenly asked, sounding marginally more serious now. "Even though there hasn't been any sign of any sort of mark on your hand or elsewhere?"

"Magic?" Laurent and Rhea echoed in unison.

Cas tore her gaze away from whatever was happening outside, and she quickly gave the rest of her friends the same explanation she had given to Nessa and Zev in her room.

"I don't know if it's divine in origin," she concluded. "But I don't know enough about any other types of magic to even *guess* at what else it might be."

The five of them thought it over for a long moment, and then Nessa glanced in Laurent's direction. "There are some elven-kind that have magic, right?"

He shrugged, looking a touch uncomfortable, as he usually did whenever this part of his bloodline was alluded to. "I'm not exactly an authority on the race," he said. "But they say the elves of the Moreth Realm keep that area along the north of the desert fertile and flourishing by way of their innate magic. And that the labyrinths and protective walls they've built around it all are clearly not the result of any ordinary labors. Neither of these things sound like the same kind of magic that Cas described, though. And, technically, elf magic has its origins in the divine as well. It's just more...complicated."

"And I'm definitely not elf-kind anyway," Cas insisted.

"You don't *look* elvish," Rhea agreed, "but you also don't know who your true parents were, right? The Lord and Lady of House Tessur took you in, but before that...."

Before that was a blur.

Everyone present was aware of this facet of her history. Cas couldn't think of a logical refute to Rhea's point; her gut told her it wasn't true—her magic was not elvish—but she couldn't explain that feeling. So she simply kept silent.

"Maybe Asra could offer some sort of insight?" Rhea suggested. "She's known you longer than anybody, so if anybody would know whether or not this magic was a *new* thing, it would be her."

Cas didn't reply right away, because at that moment she noticed one of the servants lingering just outside the doorway. His hand was braced against the frame and his body was tilted in such a way that made it clear he was trying to remain unseen. She stepped toward him and stared harder, and he abruptly moved away.

Had he been hovering at that door, just out of sight, this entire time?

They had all been speaking in appropriately hushed voices. Still, an uncomfortable feeling crept up her spine.

Had Varen instructed his servants to spy on them?

He probably assumed she would be more forthcoming with her friends than she would have been with him. Which was true enough—but it still annoyed Cas to think that he would try to glean information from her in this way.

It was fast becoming exhausting, trying to make sense of the motives and plans of everyone who lived in this damn palace, and not being able to trust any of them.

"We're being monitored," Cas said, just loudly enough for her friends to hear.

Their conversation trickled to a stop. They silently turned their attention back to the food that had been prepared for them, and soon each of them was lost in a world of their own thoughts.

Cas couldn't bring herself to eat; her stomach twisting too tightly with frustration and doubt. Instead, she paced along the wall of windows and went back to staring out at the courtyard beyond it.

Her gaze soon found something interesting to lock on to. A woman with waves upon waves of bright auburn hair was walking across the grass, her eyes scanning the skies. No, not walking—*storming*. Her oddly scarred face was pinched into an expression that only added to her violent demeanor, and as Cas watched, the woman lifted her hand and gave a shout that was muffled by that thick glass between them.

A moment later, the source of that low roar from earlier twisted into view: *a dragon*.

It rocketed toward the red-haired woman, arched its serpentine body up at the last moment, flared its wings, and landed with delicate precision before her.

The woman proceeded to stride fearlessly toward it.

The dragon lowered its head and allowed her to grab one of its curved horns and swing herself up onto its back. Then it lifted into the air with a few mighty flaps, its pearl and amethyst scales sparkling like a thousand jeweled daggers in the sun. As it circled the yard and let its rider adjust her position, the beast swooped close enough to the window that Cas had to make a concentrated effort to not draw back in alarm.

A trio of servants had entered the room while she was busy staring, and one of them offered an explanation. "A messenger sent by the High King and Queen of Sundolia."

"That must have been who Varen was meeting with?" Cas guessed.

"Yes." The servant's voice was heavy with something. Was it concern?

Cas watched the dragon and its rider until they became nothing more than a silhouette against the mid-afternoon sun. The woman's scarred face stayed in her mind.

She had looked *furious*.

What had she and Varen been meeting about?

"I'd like to speak with the King-Emperor," she said, turning back to the servant. "Where is he?"

The servant looked taken aback at the sudden demand. He started to mumble out something that sounded like an excuse, but Cas cut him off.

"I will see him *now*."

Because it felt as if strange magic and monsters—and the very gods themselves—were pressing in from all sides now, and so she could not afford to stand still.

CHAPTER 21

THE SERVANT LED CAS OUTSIDE TO A HILL THAT OVERLOOKED A section of the palace yard that was dotted with rose bushes and vine-wrapped trellises. Once there, he stopped and pointed to a small grouping of benches flanked by two statues carved into the same tiger that featured on the Solasen family crest; Varen was seated there, his elbows resting on his knees and his head bowed in thought. The servant didn't seem eager to interrupt that thinking, so Cas left him and walked to Varen alone.

A sword rested on the bench beside the King-Emperor, as though he had withdrawn it and intended to use the tigers around him for target practice—the wooden statues looked like they might have taken the brunt of the ruler's frustrations more than once in the past.

But the blade remained clean and sharp today, and

Varen's hand was nowhere near its sapphire-embedded grip.

"You seem troubled, Your Majesty," she said as she approached him.

"Oh—hello Casia dear." He lifted his head toward her, frowning slightly. "My servants explained that I was regrettably caught up in a meeting until just recently, I hope?"

"Yes; I saw the messenger leaving."

"...Not just a simple messenger," Varen informed her. "Lady Sade Ellison. She is outranked only by the High Queen and King of Sundolia themselves. We've graduated from simple messages to more *personal* visits, I'm afraid."

"What exactly was the meeting about?"

He picked up his sword, sheathed it, and then he nodded toward a path that wound its way deeper into the gardens. "Walk with me?" he suggested.

She agreed, and they strolled for several minutes before Varen managed to decide on the best place to start.

"The Fade has not yet crossed over the Wild In-Between that separates our empires," he said. "But the increasing number of cases on those border cities near The Between is...*concerning* to the rulers of that southern empire." He paused, briefly studying a rosebush overtaking their path and frowning at the number of holes that some sort of insect had eaten into its leaves. He broke a few of the dead blooms off and tossed them aside before continuing.

"Over five years have passed since the former Sundolian high king was overthrown by his son. The previous high king did not care nearly as much about this sickness, because the Fade—as you and I discussed before—disproportionately attacks the ones who carry no divine mark, and he cared little for the ones who were unmarked. But his son is different. As is his queen. And they are both very adamant about us—or *me*, specifically—getting this under control so that they can protect *all* of their people, marked or not."

"But that's how it should be, isn't it?"

"Yes, of course, it's just..."

Her voice softened. "A lot of pressure from a very powerful neighboring empire?"

His smile was tired. And a bit grateful, perhaps, at that understanding tone of her voice. "Yes," he said.

They strolled on in silence, winding their way along a small stream until they came to a spot edged by trees covered in white blossoms. He came to a sudden stop between the flowering trees, and he looked up. High above was a balcony not unlike the one attached to Cas's own room. Curtains were drawn over the windows on either side of it, and Varen stared at it all for a moment, lost in thought again. Cas started to ask who this room belonged to, but he spoke before she could.

"I used to dream about her coming back," he said, very quietly.

Cas tilted her head toward him, curious.

"My sister, I mean." He nodded to that room above, which had presumably once been hers. "The one who *should* have been ruling this empire. After my father died, I used to dream about her coming back and taking this cursed crown from me. Or at least coming back to help carry its weight."

As guarded as she was attempting to stay around this man, she couldn't fend off the raw stab of sadness she felt on his behalf.

"But It's been a long time since I had that dream," he said.

Cas wasn't sure how to reply.

"I'm alone in this rule," he continued, as much to himself as her. "I've accepted that—though loneliness does do strange things to a mind, Casia." He still had one of those dead rose blooms in his hand. He was absently plucking one petal from it at a time and letting it flutter down into the carpet of white blossoms already littering the ground.

"It does," she agreed, thinking of how lonely she had felt just in the few days she'd spent traveling back from Belwind.

What was it like for him to live in such a massive palace without any sort of family by his side?

"But enough about me and my lonely rule," Varen said. "I'm hoping you have some good news for me. I haven't had a chance to speak with Captain Elander, thanks to that meeting with that wretched Sundolian woman. Do fill me in on what the two of you encountered while you were away?"

She hesitated only a moment. She had been

rehearsing safe things to say ever since that encounter with Elander in her room; she was prepared for this.

So she told him about the rows and rows of black curtains they'd seen in Belwind. About the girl, Brynna —but not what had become of her. And she told him about both monsters she had crossed paths with—but not about how she had driven one of them away, about the nightmares she'd personally had of that wolf monster, *or* about how she might have been responsible for summoning both of those monsters to this mortal world.

He seemed to be taking all of this new information in stride. He considered her words carefully, only inter- rupting her to mutter an occasional, captivated comment about how fascinating he found it all.

Finally, silence stretched between them for several moments, and he asked, "Anything else to report?"

The question sounded innocent—she had no reason to suspect that he knew she was keeping details from him. But it still seemed as if he had taken hold of her heart, like he was wringing it and trying to squeeze a confession out of her. It hurt. It felt almost...*cruel* to keep secrets from this man. He had shown her and her friends plenty of kindness, hadn't he? Elander was wrong about him. He *had* to be wrong.

And yet something still made her lie.

"No," she told Varen. "There's nothing else that I can think of."

He accepted the lie with an easy smile. "Well, this is

an excellent bit of information to start with, anyway. Now we just need to make some sense of it."

Cas numbly agreed.

He led her to a small side door of the palace, through a hallway lined with busts of long-dead Solasen family members, and from there they took several staircases up to the same library they'd met in previously.

After a few minutes of searching the shelves, he found the book he was looking for. He rapidly flipped through the pages as he made his way back to her side, and then he plopped the leather-bound tome onto the table before her.

"Is *this* the wolf you saw?" he asked.

Cas peered into the book, her fingers gently smoothing the yellowed pages. Her eyes widened a bit and her heart fluttered as she took in the image. Curved and pointed ears. Body surrounded in shadows. Eyes like empty stars.

"Yes," she whispered. "Or, I mean, it looks very simi-lar, at least." There was a symbol shaped like a black bird in the margin—the Rook God's symbol. "Elander told me that this wolf was a servant of the upper-god, Anga, as was that other monster we fought."

"He's right. There's more to it than that, however—at least where this wolf beast is concerned."

"More?"

"Mm." He flipped a page, and suddenly Cas was staring at a beautiful man with the same shining, whitish-blue eyes as that wolf. His ears were slightly pointed like that wolf's as well, and his body surrounded by those same shadows that seemed to be an extension of his muscular body. But his hair was long and silver, not black like the fur of the beast—though there was a crown of black spires perched upon his head. He carried a sword with a white stone in the center of its grip, and its blade glowed with swirls of dark purples and blues.

"The middle-god, Kerse," Varen explained. "The wolf is the form that Kerse often took whenever he walked this mortal world. Almost all of the more powerful gods and spirits of our world were known shapeshifters. They could appear as humans, but also as whatever beast form they happened to favor at whatever given time. And most of them had regular forms that they took—back when their walking among this world was a more common thing."

Another flipped page, and this time Cas's eyes fell over the same symbol that Zev carried on the palm of his hand.

"*Moto*, the middle-god who gives power to the Fire-kind," Varen recited. "Here he is in his god form." He pointed to the being beneath that symbol—a dark-haired man with curved horns and unsettling red eyes. "And here he is as a great eagle with fire-tipped wings... My cousin once told me he'd seen that very eagle soaring above the Glashtyn Sea, along the coast of the Windhaven Realm. Though the validity of that is debatable, of course."

Cas kept flipping the pages, mesmerized by each new

image. None of her books at home explored this aspect of their world's myths and magic; she doubted there *were* many books like this in existence—at least in this empire. Varen's father had done so much to erase everything to do with these gods and goddesses and the magic they'd given...So much had been lost, and Cas felt as if she couldn't turn the pages fast enough to find these lost things.

There was *Intaba,* another of the Marr—the middle-god of Strength and Turmoil, whose symbol was the mountain and whose favored form was that of a great hulking bear.

Santi, the Sand deity, the middle-goddess of Time and Space, who often took on the form of a winged lioness.

Inya, the middle-goddess of the Moon, who preferred to roam the mortal world as an elegant white stag, or occasionally a lean white dog...

All of their beast forms were accompanied by their god forms, and like that hauntingly beautiful image of the middle-god of Death, Cas felt as if she was sinking into the pictures the longer she stared at them. As if she couldn't leave the story those pictures told, now that she had looked upon them.

Finally, she turned back to the image of Kerse's wolf form and managed a clear thought. "So you believe that was Kerse we encountered outside of Belwind?"

Varen considered this for a moment before committing to a nod. "It seems impossible, doesn't it? It's been so long since any of these divine beings have been spotted in our empire. But then again, if it's true...then you two may have found the source of the Fade."

"Not so much *found* as lured him out," she mumbled.

He slowly closed the book he'd been holding. "What do you mean?"

Panic flickered through her as she realized what she'd just said. She hadn't told Varen of the theory she and Elander had discussed—that her strange magic had been what triggered those monsters into appearing. She wouldn't tell him.

Even though she so desperately *wanted* to.

She wanted his help in making sense of her; she wanted to tell him all about that apparent magic she'd used, and then she wanted to just stand there and wait while he excitedly ran back to his shelves and plucked out another book that contained a full explanation for her strangeness.

But she had made a promise to Elander. And for reasons she did not fully understand, she still wanted to keep that promise.

At least for now.

"I just..." She fumbled for a convincing lie. "I meant because of my Fade-marked qualities—I'm sure that Kerse would be able to sense me, if he was roaming around. If he's killing people off, then I'm sort of an unfinished job as far as he would be concerned, right?"

"Yes, that's a good point," Varen said.

But he looked suspicious.

Cas focused her efforts on breathing normally, and

then on resuming her flipping through the book on the table in front of her. It wasn't difficult to become reabsorbed in that tome, at least, which made it easier to avoid looking back into Varen's questioning gaze.

"Let's just keep an eye out for this monster," Varen said after a pause, his tone difficult to read. "Perhaps we'll lure him our way again somehow."

She lifted her gaze toward the King-Emperor. "And if we do encounter him again?"

"Then we will have to find a way to stop him, won't we?"

The words sent an odd tingle over her skin. She thought of Zev's comment from earlier, and she found herself silently rebelling against the very idea of it all. She had not signed up to go to battle against a damn *god* —even if she was being paid three times her normal rate for it.

But then again...it was not simply about contracts and coins anymore. And as terrifying as it was to think that she was a part of something bigger than that, it was also hard to believe that she had stumbled into this all by coincidence.

Because she had been dreaming of that god for years.

"I'll need to do some more research on this development," Varen said, his soft voice hardly penetrating her racing thoughts. "It seems I should have been focusing my efforts on monster sightings as well, rather than just on the clusters of the Fading Sickness that have sprung up as of late. I wonder what other forms Kerse has taken in the past..."

He kept talking, but suddenly she couldn't hear him. She could focus on nothing except the page she had just reached in the book—because she had just stumbled upon another familiar character from her dreams. Not the wolf, but the woman—the winged woman clothed in gold and white who never helped Cas whenever that black wolf descended with all of its shadows and teeth. And according to this book in her hands, this stoic woman was not a woman at all. She was *Solatis*, the Sun Goddess...and one of the three Moraki who had created the worlds.

So here was another glaring, disturbing sign that Cas was not here by accident.

"Casia?"

She gave her head a little shake. "Yes?"

"I asked if you would like to accompany me while I go speak with Captain Elander?"

She should have said yes. A large part of her *wanted* to say yes, because she wanted to speak with Elander herself. She wanted to return to a moment like the one by the camp fire, or beside him on the bed, when they were able to freely talk and try to make sense of things together. As annoying as he was sometimes, she had to admit that talking to him had proven oddly comforting.

But Varen being there as well complicated things. The thought of having to keep her more dangerous questions

371

and discoveries inside of her while also being subjected to Elander's glare was...well, *unappealing*.

And she had other people she needed to talk to first, anyway.

Maybe she and Elander could find a way to speak in private later.

"I'm very tired," she lied.

Varen's smile was easy once more, betraying no more of the suspicion he was almost certainly still feeling. "Understood. It was a long trip for you, wasn't it? I should have been more considerate of that before making my suggestion."

"It's fine." She closed the book of gods and goddesses and hugged it to her chest. "May I take this with me to study later?"

"Of course."

Cas thanked him, then turned and hurried off without a backwards glance. Racing away like this likely looked even more suspicious, she knew, but she couldn't slow down.

She had to get out of that room before she said something that she truly could not take back.

INSTEAD OF RETIRING to her own guest room for the afternoon, Cas found her way to the room Asra was staying in. The second Asra spotted her, she smiled, and Cas suddenly felt like she was walking into her own house after a very long time away.

Asra sat up on the settee she'd been curled up on, and she stretched her arms out wide.

Cas placed the book she'd borrowed on a nearby dresser and hurried to embrace her.

Asra squeezed her the way she always did—a series of quick little clutches followed by one long hug that felt like it might never end. So much weaker than her hugs used to be, but Cas could tell her mentor was giving it all the strength she had, and that was enough for now.

"I'm so glad you're awake," Cas told her, her words muffled against Asra's bony shoulder. And it was the truth; she wasn't sure why she had been afraid to come in here before. It was true that she still had more questions than answers for Asra—but they had faced plenty of questionable situations together in the past, hadn't they?

Cas pulled away from her boney embrace, but she stayed close, perched in the corner of the settee with her hand gently clasped over Asra's thin arm.

A servant brought them tea, almost as if on cue, even though Cas hadn't told anyone she was coming here. The number of servants in this palace—and the way they seemed to be aware of everything she did—was becoming more and more unsettling.

Or perhaps Cas was just paranoid. But she couldn't stop thinking about the suspicious look Varen had given her, or about the possibility that he had instructed his servants to listen to her conversation with her friends earlier...

"They've been taking good care of me," Asra

remarked, lifting a priceless-looking teacup from its equally priceless-looking saucer and studying it. Her brow furrowed, as if she thought it was almost too expensive to actually drink from.

"I'm glad," Cas said.

"What did you do to warrant such lavish treatment, anyway? Nothing devious, I hope."

"When have I ever done anything of the sort?" Cas asked with a perfectly devious smile.

Asra gave her a stern look that quickly dissolved into a grin.

"I'm helping the King-Emperor because I believe in his mission. I wasn't coerced, really," Cas told her. And *that* was the truth as well.

Wasn't it?

"Good," Asra said. "Not that I really believed you *could* be talked into anything you didn't want to do. You've always been the most stubborn member of my little collected family, haven't you?"

"Yes," Cas agreed, distractedly. She sipped at the bitter, too-hot tea for a moment, thinking.

"You seem troubled. What is it, my little restless heart?"

Cas froze with the teacup inches from her lips. "Can I ask you something, Mama?"

"I've never been able to stop all your questioning before, have I?"

Cas smiled, though she didn't really know where to start this time. She dropped another lump of sugar into her tea and swirled it around for a few seconds before she found the courage to continue."Have I ever shown any signs of possessing magic?"

"You?" Asra looked confused. "You have no mark."

"I know, I just..."

"Although...you used to *pretend* you did, particularly after Rhea and Zev came to live with us."

"Because of the Fire-kind mark on Zev's hand?"

"Mm-hm. You were so jealous of his magic."

"Was I?"

"Yes. But then, he always used to tease you about your lack of it."

"Of course he did," Cas said, her smile turning wistful.

"I distinctly remember one incident where Zev was showing off with his magic, setting fire to a group of straw targets he'd set up. You shouted that you had just discovered you were Ocean-kind...and then you proceeded to douse both the targets and him with several buckets of water that you'd drawn up from the well that morning." Asra laughed a quiet, weak little laugh. "But no, Casia, my heart, despite his teasing, you did not manage to perform any obvious feats of *real* magic. Not against him or otherwise. At least not while I was watching. And that's probably for the best; I barely managed to keep up with the two of you as it was, even with Rhea's help." The laughter in her eyes faded quickly, and her brows pinched together in a way that made Cas think she had more to say.

"There was no other instance where I even *tried*?" Cas

pressed. "Or perhaps some weird, unexplainable things that happened around me?"

Asra frowned. She was quiet for a long moment. Then she hung her head, almost as if she was ashamed of whatever it was she was holding back.

"What is it?"

"I've never told you this—because I don't know that it's true. I can't say for certain that *you* are the reason it happened." She placed her teacup back onto its saucer. Her hands shook, causing the ceramic dishes to *ting ting ting* against one another. "I've always told you that I feel stronger after sitting with you, though, haven't I? I don't know if it's *magic*. I always told myself it wasn't, because it's not like any obvious sort of magic that I've ever encountered, or that I could easily define or name. But..."

"But?"

"But soon after I plucked you out of the street that day...that was when the Fading Sickness I carried seemed to...*stop*. Or slow considerably, at least. Before that, it had been progressing so rapidly that I had already started to make my last wishes known to my partners at the time. The night before I found you was actually the night my eyes lost their true color and, as you know, it's usually not long after that before the madness takes hold on a Fade-sickened mind."

Cas stared at her, lips parted slightly, unsure of what to say.

"That day I first picked you up and held you against me, for a moment I felt a warmth, a lightness unlike anything I'd ever experienced. And yes...I suppose it *did* feel like magic. But I never mentioned it because I thought I'd imagined it. Or maybe I didn't want to believe it. You were so young, so fragile; I think I was trying to protect you. I didn't want you to think you were responsible for keeping me alive. It should have been the other way around. I *wanted* it to be the other way around—especially after I learned what you had already been through." This time, her laughter was as bitter as that tea they'd been sipping. "But now here we are, and it seems I ended up depending on you anyway, hm? Funny how life goes in circles like this."

Cas placed her cup back on the tray between them and stood up, overcome by a sudden need to move. To pace. To shake off the panic that was sliding over her like an unwanted caress and making her hair stand on end.

"Forgive me. I should have said something before now."

Cas shook her head. "There's nothing to forgive."

Asra watched her pace for a moment, and then she attempted a smile that never fully materialized. "Well, *this* was a rather exhausting conversation, wasn't it?"

Cas stopped walking. "I'm sorry, I—"

"There's nothing to forgive," Asra said, her voice soft and suddenly faraway. "But I would like to rest, just for a moment. Can you hand me that blanket over there?"

Cas hesitated, trying to think of something to say that might invigorate her once more, but Asra still insisted that nothing *needed* to be said. In the end, Cas retrieved the blanket and covered her up without another word about the matter.

Asra's *just for a moment* soon became several moments. And then it stretched into an hour, during which Cas sat with her back against the settee and her forehead resting against her drawn-up knees, listening to Asra's rattling breaths as she fought to keep her own breaths steady. Her fingers tapped against her legs, counting, while outside grey clouds were moving over the afternoon sun, darkening the room until it began to feel entirely too much like a crypt.

Cas finally turned to face Asra again. "Open your eyes," she whispered—even though she knew it was likely pointless. "Please?"

No response. Cas laid her head on the settee and grasped Asra's frail hand. *Think. You have magic. You just have to figure out how to use it.*

She closed her eyes. They stayed closed for several minutes, until she felt a sudden burst of warmth against her cheek, and she blinked her eyes open and sought the source—the window. The sun had momentarily peeked its way out from behind the gathering storm clouds. A light in the darkness, just like she'd seen in the forest outside of Belwind.

And just as before, a quiet surge of confidence came with it.

She had redirected the light before, made it swallow up a beast that might have been the God of Death himself.

She had redirected sickness and death away from that little girl in Belwind.

And apparently she had protected Asra for *years*, at least in some small way.

She didn't know precisely what she was capable of, not yet, but she was capable of *something*. Her entire body was shaking with that feeling of possibility. Her hand twitched—that same painful, powerful precursor to magic she'd felt several times now.

"Whatever sickness is in her, let it find another host..." She mumbled the words under her breath, like a prayer to a deity she didn't fully believe in. Her hand spasmed more furiously. Her eyes darted around the room, searching for a place where she could send those foul energies inside of Asra. There were no plants in here. No other living things. No visible monsters. But maybe...

Let that sick, evil energy come to me, then.

Her body shook harder. She realized in an instant what a foolish experiment this was—but it was too late. The light was already swelling around her. The world was swaying, a terrible popping sound vibrated in her ears, and her skin...her skin felt as if it was cracking from the pressure of whatever power was attempting to escape her. Her body convulsed violently.

Her head slammed back against the floor, and darkness swallowed her up.

CHAPTER 22

CAS OPENED HER EYES TO A SPINNING CEILING.

The sunlight was no longer beaming in through the window; it had been fully engulfed by those storm clouds. She was on her back, white dots dancing in her vision. She reached up, as though she could swat those dots away.

Someone caught her arm and held it still.

Then that same someone was picking her up, cradling her against a broad, firm chest. She recognized Elander's earth and spice scent before she heard his voice, before she felt the vibrations of that low voice against her cheek.

"What did you just do?" he demanded.

Her words slurred out. "Why do you always assume I did something?"

"Because it's *always* you when something strange happens here lately."

"That isn't—"

"And because I felt it, and I'm guessing that every

380

other magically-inclined person within a fifty-mile radius did too."

She tilted her head and stared at him, her chest heaving and lungs feeling entirely too small. Everything about her body suddenly felt too small for what was happening—for this power that was apparently dwelling inside of her.

"Also..." His gaze fell to her hands.

She lifted them in front of her, away from the grip they'd automatically clenched into his shirt.

They were glowing.

Footsteps sounded from the hallway.

"Can you walk?" Elander asked.

"Of course I can *walk*," she snapped, hopping out of his embrace. Her feet hit the ground, and her legs promptly buckled under her weight.

"Of course," Elander deadpanned, catching her by the arm just in time to save her from slamming into the corner of a dresser. He steadied her and started to pull her across the room, but Cas dug in her heels.

"Where are we going?"

"We're hiding someplace until *that* stops," he said, jerking his head toward her hands.

Her gaze darted, not toward her hands, but toward Asra. The older woman's breathing seemed more peaceful now, perhaps...but she still hadn't opened her eyes.

"She's fine for the moment," Elander insisted. "She's going to have bigger problems—*all* of your friends are—if Varen starts asking questions about your magic."

She couldn't think of a good argument to that. Not at the moment, anyway. Her head was still spinning too quickly. The footsteps in the hallway were pounding closer, so she allowed Elander to lead her through the adjoining washroom, into an unused guest room attached to the other side, and then out into an empty hallway. From there, they crept along that dimly lit hallway, quietly testing doors until they found one that was unlocked.

This door led to a small sitting room that was being used mainly for storage. Once inside, Cas adjusted a small lantern next to a shelf piled high with neatly folded linens. As it flickered to life—a soft, barely-there brightness—she leaned back against the side of the shelf and tucked her glowing hands under her arms and out of sight.

Elander kept the door slightly cracked and stayed next to it, listening and watching. "You're lucky I was close by," he said. "I got to you as soon as I could, but I saw a servant walking in the opposite direction before I came into that room—there's a chance they saw more than they should have." He looked more worried than furious, and a tiny bit of guilt twisted through Cas.

"I'm sorry," she said. "I wasn't trying to cause more trouble, I was just trying to..."

"I know what you were trying to do. And I should have known you were going to try and do it."

His tone had not been entirely unkind, but she still couldn't keep the bite out of her own. "I'm frustrated."

"I know."

"I feel like I'm simmering with this magic that could be useful to people—that could save lives—but I don't know how to use it, or even what *it* is."

Silence. He kept watching the door. Was he even really listening to her?

"And Varen might be able to *help* me figure these things out, you know. He has countless books and advisors and—"

"He is not a helper."

Her face grew hot. "You want me to be careful around Varen, but what about being careful around *you*?" she hissed.

He finally took his eyes away from that crack in the door. His stare was cold. Calculating. Intimidating.

But she steadied herself and kept talking. "Because I overheard you talking with Caden and Tara the other morning, you know."

She expected him to deny that he'd said anything wrong. Instead, he asked, "What did you hear, precisely?"

"That...that you think I'm a burden and you're only putting up with me for the sake of staying on Varen's good side, for starters."

Something flickered in his icy eyes—something that made his glare soften briefly around the edges. It looked like regret. Maybe. But he didn't take back anything he'd said. "And what else?" he asked.

She swallowed hard. "And you were talking about being close to...something. To finishing some sort of plan other than the one you and I were supposed to be working on."

"And you want to know what that plan is."

"Yes."

"Fine."

"...Fine?"

Her pulse skipped wildly as he closed the door completely. Locked it. And then he stepped toward her, lowered his voice, and said, "There are rumors that the King-Emperor—or his ancestors, rather—might be responsible for the Fading Sickness. You've heard them, I'm guessing?"

"I...yes," she admitted.

"Our so-called *secret* plan is related to that—although it's not really a secret if you've been paying attention. I told you I don't trust Varen."

He *had* told her that. Several times.

"But the ones I've trusted to help me with this plan—Caden, Tara, and a handful of others—they don't trust *you*. And, well...should they?"

She found it difficult to meet his piercing gaze, suddenly. "Why shouldn't they?"

"You've warmed up to the King-Emperor awfully quickly. So it's hard to say which side you're on."

"I wouldn't say Varen and I are best friends." She unfolded her arms and stared at her hands. Her palms still tingled and occasionally twitched, but they were no longer glowing. "And I haven't told him about my magic. I didn't tell him about my dreams, either—or about anything else you asked me not to talk about. I *could* have. But I didn't."

"Yes, but you feel guilty about not telling him."

"It's not fair to make me choose sides."

"Life is not fair, Thorn."

She glowered at him. "Well, I don't know what you want me to say."

"You don't? Have I honestly not made my position on this clear enough for you?"

"He's given me far more information than *you* have. He talks to me like I'm intelligent, and like I'm an ally—not like some child that he got burdened with. And he's been almost nothing but friendly to me since I arrived here, so how do I know he doesn't really want to be allies? How can I be—"

She swallowed a gasp as Elander stormed closer to her, cutting her off. "He. Is. Not. Your. *Friend*."

"He's much friendlier than *you*, is all I'm saying," she shot back.

His smile was fierce. "Varen de Solasen would cut out your heart tomorrow if he thought it would help protect him from his many enemies."

He didn't move away from her. His closeness was making it difficult to form rational sentences, so she just went back to glaring at her hands. Her stupid hands and the lingering twitches of that *stupid* magic that she couldn't make sense of.

"And maybe it *would* protect him," Elander mused. "Maybe he could use you and that magic of yours in some way. I don't know. But what I do know for certain is that if Varen decides he *can't* use you anymore, then he will dispose of you like he disposes of everything else that isn't useful to him. I have seen him do it. The pardon he's granted you and your friends is not indefinite. Trust me."

She started to fire back with several arguments, only to swallow them. "I just want to understand what's going on with me."

He studied her for a beat, and then the harsh lines of his face softened a bit. "We'll figure it out."

He'd said that once before, and so far they had done nothing of the sort. And yet... Something in his voice made her believe it could still be true.

She exhaled a sigh—a quiet surrender. A brief truce. The world outside of their hiding place grew silent and still. She could have insisted on leaving at that point.

But she didn't.

They stayed together in that tiny room for what felt like an hour at least. Elander leaned against the wall next to her and closed his eyes in thought. The dim glow of the lantern only just managed to outline his shape in the darkness, and Cas was reminded of the night she had met him, of the way his powerful frame had stood out against the fireplace he'd sat in front of.

And, just like she had that night, she ended up staring longer than she meant to.

"I don't want him to hurt you," Elander said, very suddenly and very quietly, and without opening his eyes.

"Why?"

The challenge in her voice seemed to catch him off guard. It took him a long time to answer, and even then, all he said was, "I'm not sure."

"Not sure?"

"I just know that I don't want you to be my enemy, Thorn. And I—" He cut himself off. Knocked his head lightly back against the wall a few times, and then finally opened his eyes. He turned to face her, and she realized precisely how close their bodies were. Close enough that she could have easily pressed against him after only a few small steps.

He didn't close the space between them. He didn't speak, either—he just stared at her with those inhumanly beautiful blue eyes. The stare felt as intimate as any touch, and a warm thrill spiked through her blood.

What had he almost said a moment ago?

Why was he looking at her like he still wanted to say it?

"You what?" she pressed. She took a step closer to him. And then one more. He watched her moving as though she was a target—not prey, but another predator moving into territory that he had not intended to share.

"I want to keep you safe." It came out as a near-growl. A frustrated growl that suggested she was pushing him close to an edge that would be dangerous to tumble over.

"Safe," she repeated on a breath.

He started to reply but paused, as if giving her a chance to step away from that edge.

She didn't move.

"What are you doing?" he muttered.

She repeated his own line back to him. "I'm not sure."

He reached a hand forward and cupped her cheek. His thumb trailed across her lips. Parted them. "I wish you hadn't come along and complicated things," he said, his face angling toward hers as his other hand slipped beneath the hem of her shirt and found skin. "But now I just want you to be safe. That's all."

That wasn't all.

She could tell by the torn look in his eyes that he was *still* keeping things from her.

Always, *always* keeping things from her.

But the closer his mouth came to hers, the less she cared about what those things might have been. She was a fool to not care, and she knew it, but *gods* he was beautiful and his fingers moved over her skin with an intoxicating boldness—like they didn't intend to stop until they had explored every inch of her—and suddenly her eyes were closing, surrendering to the feel of his lips finally brushing over hers.

Soft.

She hadn't expected such softness. And she hadn't expected to feel so devastated when that soft kiss ended almost as quickly as it had started and he pulled away from her, shaking his head.

"I shouldn't have done that." His voice was a rasp.

"No. You probably shouldn't have." Her words were just as hoarse as his had been. "But maybe you should do it again."

His fingers threaded their way through her hair, taking a commanding grip and using it to tilt her face up. His gaze burned down into hers, a lustful combination of vexation and desire that made his eyes seem darker, like the depths of the sea that were just out of reach of the sunlight. "And what if I want more than just another kiss?"

The question made her stomach clench with more of that foolish desire. "Then you shouldn't stop at just another kiss," she whispered.

He sucked in a breath. "Don't tempt me, Thorn."

"Why not?"

"Because." His grip in her hair grew tighter, as if he were trying to hold on to something—anything—to keep himself from sinking deeper into that temptation. "This isn't a good idea."

"I promise you it's not the worst one I've ever had."

"I don't doubt that." His laughter was a bit quiet. A bit... *wicked.* "And I promise *you* that there is currently nothing I would like more than to carry you up to my bedroom and pleasure you until you couldn't think straight. Or walk straight, for that matter."

She couldn't think of a proper response.

"But it's more complicated than that, I'm afraid," he said. "And if I did what I wanted with you, it...well, it wouldn't be a very effective way of keeping you safe."

The heat flaring inside of her was from more than just desire, suddenly. "Did you ever think that maybe I don't *need* someone to keep me safe?"

"I have thought that, actually."

"But apparently you don't believe it."

"I believe it's complicated," he repeated.

She wanted to understand exactly what he meant by *complicated*. But she was tired of talking in frustrating circles. And more than anything—at least in that moment—she wanted his lips against hers again, even if it was only one last time.

"Just one more kiss, then," she proposed, softer.

For a brief, almost painful instant, she thought he would deny her. His gaze darted toward the door. *Searching for an exit?* She started to turn away herself, embarrassed by the rejection—

He caught her and pulled her lips against his. Gentle at first, just as before. He held her face in his hands and he kissed her slowly, and her eyes fluttered shut as she lost herself in the easy, confident way his mouth moved over hers. Her fingers trailed along his arms. His chest. His stomach. She could feel the ridges of muscle underneath his shirt, but it wasn't enough. She wanted skin beneath her fingertips. Wanted to feel the pulse and throb of those muscles, the way they would respond to her touch...

As his lips moved to her neck, her fingers slipped under his shirt. A low snarl of sound escaped him, and he snatched her hands, interlacing her fingers with his to stop their roaming.

If her hands had been able to move freely over him, something told her he wouldn't have been able to stop at *just one more kiss*. The thought was thrilling. But then, so was the way he held so tightly to her hands and pushed them back against the wall. She teasingly tried to resist his hold. He only pinned her more firmly against the wall, slipping his fingers from hers and wrapping his hands tightly around her wrists instead. His mouth came down against hers again, more viciously this time. He took her bottom lip between his teeth, and she squirmed. His hips pressed into hers. She gasped into his kiss as she felt the considerable length of him brush against her. His tongue pushed into her mouth, and her gasp became a soft whimper of pleasure. A shudder ripped through him at the noise. She sensed it, and then she felt his muscles tensing against her as he forced himself to go still. To hold himself back.

Just one more kiss.

That was all they had agreed on.

What a stupid agreement.

His mouth remained against hers for only a moment longer. He planted one last chaste kiss against her lips, and a trail of them along her jawline, before finally pulling away. He took a deep breath. He seemed dizzy.

Or maybe that was her.

"No more of that." The still-rough tone of his voice made her dizziness worse.

She tried to nod, to agree, but she couldn't move. She had never been kissed like that before. Every nerve in her body still felt deliciously tingly. It made her wonder what else he was capable of making her feel, but...

No more.

The thought slammed down like an iron gate, closing off her heart.

Because she knew he was right. *More* would only lead to more complications. He was the right-hand to a king that was already suspicious of them both. His friends didn't trust her. Her friends didn't trust *him*. And they all had much bigger things to worry about.

The sound of voices outside reminded her that they were in a palace full of people, and that at least some of those people were going to start wondering where she and Elander had disappeared to. She forced herself to take a step away from him.

"Back to more important matters," Elander said.

She nodded, even as that iron gate around her heart rattled a bit in protest. "But where to start?"

"I need to make sure that nobody important realized that the magical energy from earlier came from you. And then we need to figure out how to better channel that magic of yours. To safely release it somehow, before you end up blowing up part of the palace by accident."

"You have magic—and control over it. Can help me?" The words came out before she could stop them. She still wasn't certain that being so vulnerable with him was a good idea, but she couldn't seem to help herself.

His eyes slid over her, pausing for a moment on her lips. It was obvious he was still thinking about a different sort of private lesson. One that had nothing to do with her magic.

She cleared her throat. "Focus, Captain."

His smile was sly. "Yes," he replied, "I'll do what I can to help, of course." He reached and tucked a strand of hair behind her ear.

She shivered.

"But it will have to wait a day or two because the King-Emperor has requested that I go to Edgekeep on his behalf. I need to speak to the Lord of the Bywilds Realm about the alarming number of Sundolian soldiers stationing themselves along the empire's border. Our *friends* to the south are starting to concern him."

Cas thought of the fierce woman and her dragon from earlier, and she nodded solemnly.

Elander drew his hand away from her and straightened his shirt, rolling up and readjusting the sleeves that her hands had unraveled. "Just try not to do anything to aggravate that magic of yours while I'm gone. Can you manage that, you think?"

"I'm not sure."

He gave her a rueful glance as he moved toward the door. "At least you're honest."

She shrugged.

"Come on. I'll walk you to your room."

She suspected the offer was less about chivalry and more about making sure she didn't do anything foolish between here and there, but she didn't protest.

And—the Moraki and Marr both help her—she actually *enjoyed* strolling through the halls at his side. Something about it felt almost natural. As if they had done it a thousand times before. Her heart was still beating a bit unsteadily from their kiss, her skin still humming with electricity that she didn't necessarily want to lose...

A sudden commotion behind them snapped her back down to earth.

Several servants rushed past them a moment later, and Cas caught the scent of lavender and alcohol. The nauseating smell stirred an equally nauseating memory —one of the dead woman she'd seen when she first arrived at the palace.

"Another dead," Elander muttered. "I thought I sensed something a few moments ago."

Cas's entire body tensed. "Varen is going to be calling for both of us."

He nodded, concern furrowing his brow. His eyes fell to her hands. They were both likely picturing the same thing—a repeat of the scene she'd created at that house in Belwind, or another like the one she'd just caused at Asra's bedside. Only this time, with the King-Emperor as a potential witness.

"I'll deal with it," Elander said, decisively. "You should continue on to your room."

"But Varen..."

"I'll tell him you weren't feeling well."

She stepped out of the path of another servant, and then she stood still for a moment, hesitating.

"Go on," Elander urged.

It was the smart thing to do. Or the cowardly thing. She wasn't sure which. But either way, it meant she would live to fight another day, as would her friends. So she nodded and turned toward her room.

"Casia."

She glanced back to him, curious. She couldn't remember the last time—or *any* time, really—that he had used her own, chosen alias and not the silly nickname he'd unceremoniously bestowed on her.

"If I don't see you before I leave tomorrow," he said, "then until I get back, just...be safe."

She only nodded again. She didn't trust herself to speak. The concern in his tone had caused a strange sensation in her stomach. She wasn't sure what it was; she couldn't—wouldn't—put a name to that fluttering feeling. It might not even be *worth* naming. It might be gone before the morning.

Gods, she *hoped* it would be gone.

Because somehow it felt more dangerous than any of the monsters they'd faced together thus far.

CHAPTER 23

ELANDER WAS GONE FOR FIVE DAYS.

Cas spent most of that time by Asra's side. When she wasn't there, she was generally by herself, meditating and pacing and trying—desperately trying—to keep her anxiety from running away with her.

On the third day, two more deaths occurred within the palace walls. And from that third day onward, Cas suspected that Varen did not sleep any longer than a few minutes at a time. He sent for her at all hours of the day and night, summoning her every time he came up with a new theory or encountered something even the slightest bit interesting in one of his books.

He was going mad with his need to make sense of things, to find a way to control those things, and it was exhausting—mostly because Cas had to tread so carefully around that madness. Trying to keep her magic a secret from him was like trying to walk across a field littered with hidden holes. One wrong step, and she knew she might very well end up tumbling down into a bottomless pit with no hope of catching herself.

The dawn of the fifth day found her in the sun parlor that had become a favorite haunt of both her and her friends. Rhea and Silverfoot lounged in a patch of sunlight; Zev was attempting to eat his weight in bread and butter; Nessa sat with her back against Laurent, flipping idly through a book. It all looked oddly normal in the face of everything happening in the empire outside. Like a calm center in the middle of a building storm.

But Cas could not keep still. Her gaze kept drifting to the courtyard outside, until she finally caught sight of a company of soldiers riding through it. She didn't see Elander, but she did spot Tara and Caden—and she assumed that their captain could not have been far behind them.

She started for the door.

"Going somewhere?" Laurent asked.

"I was, um...yes. I'm just restless, is all, so I thought I might go for a walk."

Rhea cupped her chin in her palm and cocked her head to the side. "Elander was supposed to be back this afternoon, wasn't he?"

Cas blushed at her knowing tone.

"I think you're right," Nessa said, hopping to her feet and going to the window to look for herself.

"We're being dumped for that pretty boy captain, aren't we?" Zev lamented.

"I am not dumping anyone." Cas tossed a furtive glance at the doorway, searching for any servants who might have been eavesdropping on their conversation. She saw no one, but she still lowered her voice before adding, "He just...he promised to help me practice my magic when he came back."

There was a brief, uncomfortable silence as her friends exchanged worried looks and clearly tried to come up with an argument against her plans. But no one present could deny the fact that she needed that practice.

As per usual, it was Zev who eventually shattered the quiet: "You could have asked me for help."

Cas made a face. "You don't even like using your own magic. I assumed you wouldn't want to help."

She also doubted he was skilled enough to help her, though she didn't say this out loud.

Zev shrugged. "I don't actually care one way or the other, for the record. I was just making a point."

Cas frowned. She knew that he wouldn't have admitted it even if he *did* care.

"Just be careful," he continued. "Because if he hurts you, you know I'm obligated to murder him, right?"

"And I'm obligated to help," added Laurent.

Nessa gave them both a withering look before turning back to Cas with a slight grin. "Because nothing says friendship like being willing to murder on your behalf, right?"

"She's right, you know," Zev insisted.

"And I'm really not in the mood for murder today," said Laurent with a yawn. "So yes, do be careful."

"You're all mental," Cas said, reaching for her coat.

"They really are," Rhea agreed, and Silverfoot barked his agreement as well. Rhea gave a quick clap, and obediently the fox jumped into her arms. "Go if you must," she said to Cas, carrying Silverfoot over to her. "But at least take him so we can keep an eye on you."

Cas shrugged into her coat. "You all worry too much."

"In our defense," Laurent said, "the last time we let you out of our sight, you went and made a deal with the King-Emperor that has effectively pulled us all into a war that might end up pitting us against the gods themselves."

"And without so much as a tangible contract for our services," said Nessa with a wistful sigh.

"You make questionable decisions when left to your own devices," Zev added. "That's what we're saying, if you didn't get our point yet." The teasing comment earned him a smack to the back of his head, courtesy of his sister. Her aim was impressive, given her lack of sight. Perhaps because she'd done it so many times at this point that it required no more effort or focus than breathing.

Cas relented with a sigh, and she held out her arms and let Silverfoot jump into them. "Fine. I'll take the fox. And I'll try not to make any more *questionable* decisions."

Such as hiding in storage rooms and kissing questionable men.

She hurried from the room before her friends could see the blush this memory caused her.

Once outside, she met Caden and Tara at the head of the path that led down to the stables. Caden barely spared her a glance as he loosened his horse's tack.

"What do you want, Fade-marked?" he asked.

Tara gave her a sympathetic look, clearly ruffled by her companion's rudeness.

But Cas didn't need sympathy; she only needed information. She glared at Caden. "Where is Elander?"

Caden's jaw tightened at her demanding tone—and at the low growl rumbling in Silverfoot's throat. He stared them both down for a moment, until it became clear that Cas didn't intend to back away. He averted his eyes once more. "Dealing with a bit of unrest we encountered on our way into the city. He'll be along shortly, I suspect."

The group of them stood together on that path for several more minutes, talking. Tara nervously tried to keep the peace, while Caden stubbornly refused to leave Cas's side, clearly against the idea of her being alone with Elander—whenever that captain decided to make his appearance.

Finally, another small cluster of soldiers trotted through the distant gate, with Elander following closely behind them. Five days of traveling had taken its toll on him—his skin was glistening with sweat, his long hair was disheveled, both he and his horse were coated in a thin layer of dust—but he still managed to look more handsome than he had any right to after almost a week of travel on horseback.

A nervous wave twisted through Cas at the sight of him. She quickly dismissed it as more anxiety caused by the unpredictable magic they would soon be practicing together, but she couldn't dismiss the thought that was suddenly roaring loudly between her ears...

She had missed him.

And he had missed *her*, judging by the way his tired eyes brightened at the sight of her.

"I expected you sooner, Captain," she informed him.

He flashed her a crooked grin. "Sorry I'm late."

"We have a standing appointment, if you'll recall."

"I haven't forgotten." He hardly took his eyes off her as he dismounted, even as he handed Caden his reins and said, "See to my horse."

It was not so much a request as a demand, and Caden bristled at it. "Captain, shouldn't you go give the King-Emperor our report in person?"

"It's half-past noon," Elander said as he removed his riding gloves and tucked them into the pocket of his coat, "and if I know Varen, he's likely napping at the moment."

Cas doubted that—she was still convinced that the King-Emperor had given up sleep entirely in favor of research—but she didn't say so.

"Then his other advisors will want to speak with you," Caden insisted.

"Just see to my damn horse," Elander growled.

Caden shot one last fiery glance in Cas's direction

before snatching the reins and giving a slight bow. "Yes, sir."

Tara grabbed him by the sleeve and pulled him into motion. Elander stood for several more minutes glaring in their direction, as if daring them to turn around and protest his orders again.

They didn't.

Once they were out of sight, he started to walk in the opposite direction. "Come on, then. Let's find someplace more private to chat about things."

Cas hurried to catch up with his long-legged strides, but she couldn't help casting one last glance in the direction Caden and Tara had disappeared. "Are you sure they aren't going to cause trouble?"

"I command them, not the other way around." The still-dark tone of his voice did not invite an argument. She might have started one, anyway, if not for her eagerness to stay in his good graces—at least long enough for him to help her as he'd promised.

"Speaking of causing trouble..." he said after a moment, tossing a wary look at the fox cradled in her arms.

"Don't worry. I won't let him attack you this time, as long as you behave."

He snorted. "I'll try."

They walked side-by-side, seeking out a less crowded spot. The tension soon slipped from his shoulders, the edge softened from his voice, and it turned into a pleasant stroll through the vast, rolling grounds of the palace—even in spite of the nervous wave still tumbling through Cas. Because she felt it again, same as she had the other night—that odd sensation that they had walked together like this countless times before, which made it feel safer and more comfortable than it should have.

After a few minutes, she stirred up the courage to ask, "How was Edgekeep?"

"Bit of a war zone, honestly."

She stared, willing him to elaborate.

"The people are scared." He kept his eyes straight ahead as he spoke. "And they should be."

He didn't seem eager to talk about it, and she didn't pressure him any further. But she had a sudden, fierce desire to help those frightened people. It was yet another reason to embrace her magic.

"Things have been relatively calm here," she informed him. "Two more deaths. But I didn't blow anything up while you were gone."

He cut her a sideways glance. "And I am extremely impressed by that last part."

"Well, you know I did it solely to impress you."

"I assumed," he replied, matching the sarcastic tone of her voice.

"And I can be more impressive with a little more magical training, I suspect," she said, after quickly glancing around to make certain no one was close enough to overhear her.

"You're going to be relentless about this, aren't you?"

"I like to think my *relentlessness* is one of my better qualities."

"When it isn't getting you into trouble, I suppose."

They walked a short distance more, eventually reaching an ill-kept edge of the palace grounds. The outer defensive wall loomed in front of them, covered in vines. There was a narrow stairwell carved into the stone—one that Cas would likely have overlooked if Silverfoot hadn't leapt from her embrace and gone over to sniff through the withered foliage that covered it. He rooted out a path, climbed to the top of the wall, and then proceeded to patrol along its top, searching for threats on both sides.

"His eyes are glowing," Elander commented.

"Air-kind magic," she informed him. "He and Rhea share a connection that allows her to see whatever he sees."

"Fascinating." He cocked his head back toward her. "But also a little disturbing to know we're being spied on."

She arched a brow. "You were planning on behaving anyway, right?"

"I said I'd *try* to behave," he corrected.

"You'll just have to try harder, I guess."

"No promises." One side of his mouth tipped up. "It's been a long five days since that moment in that storage room."

She tucked a strand of hair behind her ear. Untucked it, only to tuck it back in again. "I don't know what you mean."

"I can elaborate."

"Don't," she warned.

His smile widened.

"Focus, Captain."

"Yes ma'am."

She turned away to hide her blush. They hadn't passed another person in several minutes, and Silverfoot had already curled up on top of that wall, apparently satisfied that they were safe for the moment. But Cas still did some more scouting of her own before turning expectantly back to Elander.

"Do you think we're safe here?"

"It's probably the most secluded spot on the palace grounds." He shrugged. "Also, you're with me."

"Right. My hero."

He chuckled at her tone. "I only meant that the people of this palace are used to *me* having magic—and most of them tend to steer clear when I start practicing it. From a distance, they'll assume anything strange they see or feel is me, not you."

"Good point," she conceded. "So, where do we start?"

"I've been doing a lot of thinking about that while I was away, actually."

"And?"

"And your magic thus far has done a few things that we clearly agree on, yes? It has seemingly reflected everything from sunlight, to my magic, to the Fade's effects, and it's protected you from sickness and poison...So I've considered two possibilities: Moon-kind magic, which, among other things, sometimes allows a bearer to reflect or amplify other kinds of energy. Or Sky-kind magic, which usually manifests as an ability to create shields and other forms of defense."

Cas lifted a hand to that moon-shaped scar along her jawline. "But which one is it?"

"Hard to say. But the magic of the divinely marked doesn't always follow clear lines. Every magic user is different, and occasionally there's some overlap in abilities—even amongst people who carry different marks. And in this case, both the middle-goddesses of the Moon and the Sky derive their power from the upper-goddess of the Sun, Solatis, so it could be that—"

"I've dreamt about her." The words exploded from her mouth. She had been holding back so much information over these past days during her countless conversations with the King-Emperor that she couldn't help herself.

Elander stared at her, his lips parted slightly in shock. It was almost identical to the look he'd regarded her with when she'd told him of her nightmares about that shadowy wolf.

"Varen, um, showed me her picture in one of his books the other day," she explained. "But I didn't tell him that I'd seen her before, of course."

He was frowning, suddenly.

"I take it that my visions of her are a bad thing, for some reason?"

"I just don't know how much help I'll be in guiding your magic," he said, "if it's truly connected to Solatis."

"Why do you say that?"

"Because my magic ultimately comes from Anga, the Rook God, not Solatis. They're two very different supreme deities. Two deities that eventually became *enemies* according to most legends."

"Enemies?"

"Yes. Although that's another story for another day."

"It's all divine magic though, right? How different can the process of summoning it be?"

"We'll see." He considered the question for another moment, and added, "But remember that we're only assuming that your magic is, in fact, divine."

Cas nodded.

"Either way," Elander continued, "let's try something shall we? I want to see if you can stop my magic again, as you did that day at Darkhand's. But on purpose this time."

She took a deep breath, trying not to let her fear show.

He saw it anyway. "Don't worry," he said. "I'll be gentle."

Her eyes narrowed. "Be as rough as you want."

There it was again—that hint of a mischievous smile flirting with his lips.

"You know what I meant," she hissed. "Also? I'm glad you're taking this seriously."

"Sorry," he laughed. "Sorry. Okay, are you ready?"

"Yes," she lied.

He hesitated only a moment before lifting his hand between them. His fingers beckoned. As easy as that, his power came to him, as though summoned from the air itself. That air grew heavier. Darker. Cas felt his magic brushing over her an instant later, same as she had that day he'd arrested her, like a cold wind that permeated her skin and dove straight into her bones. It was terrible and painful and all-consuming, and she wanted to curl into herself, to disappear into the darkness and never reemerge from it.

Somewhere far behind her, Silverfoot whimpered uncertainly. The sound made her think of her friends. They were watching over her. Worried about her. And she didn't want them to be afraid on her behalf. She could picture it now—if she fell to this dark magic, they would be storming this way in an instant with their weapons drawn and murder in their eyes.

She couldn't fall to this darkness.

The instant she thought that, her palm twitched. Light flared between her and Elander, and she imagined it wrapping around her, pushing the cold from her bones and her lungs and filling those spaces with protective warmth. Her eyes briefly closed, and when she opened them again, both the overwhelming light and darkness were gone. The air was back to normal.

Elander was watching her carefully as she caught her breath.

And she hadn't blown anything up.

"Good." He gave his marked wrist a shake, as if to rid it of a cramp. "Now, this time I'll actually put some effort behind it."

She braced herself as he stepped back to her. There was no real warning this time—just a flurry of movement, and then darkness flashed in her vision. In between those flashes of dark, she saw a horrifying image of herself lying on a barren scrap of land, her body motionless and drained of all color.

The cold came back, paralyzing her more completely this time. She tried to lift her hand to ward it off.

She failed.

She tried to raise her eyes to the sunlight that she knew was somewhere high above.

But she couldn't.

Why couldn't she look up?

The darkness around her was complete and awful, and she was going to die right there, just like this.

"Tell me to stop if you want me to stop." Elander's words were a distant buzzing in the back of her mind.

Somehow, she managed to shake her head and mumble out something that sounded like, "Don't."

"Then fight back."

She tried, but it felt like parts of her were caving in with every attempt at movement—her heart, her lungs, her entire body...all of it was *collapsing*.

"Fight me," he said, more urgently, "or this experiment is over."

"I'm trying." Her voice was tight with frustration. With fear. With irritation. She closed her eyes and tucked her head toward her chest, staving off a sudden urge to scream. Her right hand lifted on its own accord, and she felt something more powerful than that tingling warmth she'd summoned before. Something that burned its way up the veins of her arm and made her feel as if actual fire were only seconds away from igniting in her palm.

"There it is," Elander murmured, approvingly. "Now focus it."

"I can't."

"Relax."

She bared her teeth at the word. "It's not that simple. I can't—"

"*Relax*," he said again, taking her left hand and squeezing it. He released his grip just as quickly, but his fingers stayed close, tapping occasionally against her palm.

She could hardly breathe.

She couldn't hear.

She felt as if she had fallen out of existence and time...

But she could feel each of those taps against her palm, like tiny little affirmations—proof that she was still there. *Tap, tap, tap*. He was trying to help her *stay* there. He'd been paying attention that night at the inn, when she had explained her method of anchoring.

Tap, tap, tap.

She counted them. All the way up to ten, and then back down again—

And then she surfaced from the darkness.

Just briefly. Just long enough to lift her head to the sky and remind herself of what the sunlight looked like. That was all she needed. She gasped as a burst of electricity—

not warmth, not light, not fire, but powerful and raw *electricity*—flew to her fingertips. At the last instant she managed to wrestle control over it and aim it somewhere other than at Elander's chest. It shot past him and struck a tree in the distance, causing a small explosion of wood chips and dust and smoke.

She stared at that smoking tree, speechless.

That power had felt like a solid extension of herself—a tangible whip of electricity. It hadn't been perfect, but it had been more controlled than anything she'd managed thus far.

And yet, when she excitedly looked back to Elander, she found his face contorted with concern.

"That didn't look like either of the two magics we discussed earlier," he said, very quietly. "It looked like Storm-kind magic."

"Is that a bad thing?"

"It's just...a new thing. Another new thing. You're full of endless surprises, aren't you?" He tried to smile. But the expression never reached his eyes, which soon glazed over in thought. Cas knew him well enough at this point to recognize that look; it meant he was keeping things from her.

Of course.

She rubbed at her palms, which still burned with occasional pulses of stormy energy. "Right. I was supposed to be trying to reflect your magic, wasn't I?"

The question hung in the air while he stared at the

smoking tree trunk. Finally, he shifted his gaze back to her and started to speak—

Only to be cut off by an arrow soaring over their heads.

It stabbed into the ground a few feet away from them. Elander took a step closer, studying the black and strangely twisted shaft of the projectile...and then quickly took a step back.

"Fuck," he muttered.

A second later, the ground surrounding that impaled arrow...*died*. The grass turned black and withered before their eyes, and then that grass was gone in a *puff* that left behind only scorched, cracked earth.

Elander raced for the wall. He scaled its steps and leaned out over the top of it, scanning the distant city.

Cas followed just behind him, and what she saw on the other side made her forget how to breathe for a moment.

Dozens upon dozens of black-winged creatures marched through the streets, all of them filing toward the palace.

At a glance they appeared human-like—aside from those skeletal wings. But a closer examination of their faces revealed that they were missing...*everything*. They had heads—narrow, diamond-shaped heads—but they had no faces. There was only a smooth canvas of white skin, devoid of even a simple mouth. The pale smoothness was a stark contrast to the rest of their lithe bodies, which were wrapped in black strips of cloth that fluttered in the slight breeze. Each of them carried an identical longbow that appeared to be made of the same twisted, dark material as the arrow they'd shot.

"What are those things?" she asked in a horrified whisper.

"The *namtar*—or *void archers*, as they're more commonly called. I took care of one earlier when we first came back to the city; apparently he wasn't alone."

"Let me guess...more servants of our friend the Rook God?"

"Yes."

"Do you think my magic drew the rest of them out?"

His jaw clenched, but he didn't reply. Instead, he hurried back down the wall and stormed toward the palace. Soon she heard him bellowing out orders, directing the guards in the yard to summon more help and prepare to fight.

Cas braced her arms against the stone and turned her eyes back to the city. People were running into their houses, screaming as they went. The archers marched on by them, indifferent to the noise, seemingly focused on reaching the palace and nothing else.

Or on reaching *her*.

Silverfoot scampered over, his fur bristling and ears twitching. Cas wrapped an arm around the tiny fox and pulled him close. He sank against her chest as a screech rose from one of the archers, answered by three more awful, shrill cries.

When Elander finally returned, he had his Ice-kind

sword—the one he'd wielded on the first day they'd met —sheathed at his side. He also had a finely made bow and quiver, which he offered to her as soon as she hopped down from the wall.

"I'm still not convinced you can manage your magic without blowing something up," he said, beckoning her to follow as he started to walk toward the front gate, "but I know you can handle a blade, at least. Are you any good with a bow?"

"Better than I am with a blade," she said, snatching the weapon from him.

"Good. Aim for their head—their skin is tough, but you should be able to penetrate the back side of their skulls."

She nodded, somewhat numbly. Her hand closed more tightly around the curve of the bow, just as a horrible sound reached them— a scream of pure terror, cut off midway by the *thwap* of an arrow striking its target, and then a gurgling, bloody wheezing for breath.

Then silence.

The first of the guards at the main gate was dead.

Elander withdrew his sword. "Brace yourself, Thorn. I have a feeling this is going to get ugly."

CHAPTER 24

THE POOL OF BLOOD AROUND THE FALLEN GUARD SPARKLED IN the late afternoon sun.

The void archer responsible for his death had met his demise by the time Cas and Elander reached the gate. Its body was being hacked to pieces by the guards who remained, and its wings had been torn from its back and cast aside. Blackish-red liquid oozed over its white, featureless face.

While the gate was being further secured, Elander ordered the fallen archer's head to be severed from the being's unnaturally long neck, and then for it to be carried up to the top of the wall and launched back into the approaching archers on the other side—a morbid gift that led to a deafening protest of screeches.

Cas had yet to spot any sort of mouth on any of the archers, but still, those shrill cries continued. It felt as if they were injecting those screams directly into her head;

she clapped her hands over her ears and moved away from the gate, nearly backing into Zev, Laurent, and Nessa as they approached from the direction of the palace.

The men carried swords, and Nessa's arms were wrapped around a bow, her eyes wide and her lips set in a grim, but determined, line.

A small army's worth of royal soldiers were not far behind them. The ground shook with their footsteps, and the air filled with the tremor of their voices and the metallic thunking and clinking of helmets and chainmail hastily being pulled on.

Elander went to organize the newly arrived soldiers just as another chorus of shrieks rose from outside of the wall.

The secured gate rattled as two of the void archers slammed against it. They attempted to snake their long arms through the bars, but a trio of swords fell quickly, cutting them off. The archers fell backwards, blood streaming from their stumpy arms. Their screeches grew louder even as they retreated—at least until they were out of sight. Then...

More silence.

Everyone present tensed, waiting for the next group of enemies to rush the gate.

But none came.

One of the gate guards crept closer to the bars and peered out—

He scrambled back and promptly lost his balance, falling on his rear, as one of those black, twisted arrows struck the ground just before the bottom of the gate. The ground around the arrow turned black, and Cas held her breath as that blackness swiftly reached higher, wrapping a shadowy pattern around the bars. The shadows soon evaporated with a hiss. The gate was still intact, but now it looked as if a giant beast had bitten into the bottom bars, leaving them jagged and compromised.

A line of soldiers rushed to the top of the gatehouse, readying their bows and taking aim at anything moving toward them.

Cas gripped her own bow more tightly. Silverfoot weaved in and around her ankles, his eyes shining and an occasional unsettled yip escaping him.

Zev cut his gaze toward Cas. "I had a feeling it wouldn't take long for chaos to erupt once we let you outside."

He was only teasing her, and she attempted a rueful smile—but she couldn't stop thinking about the beast she had drawn into the city of Belwind. About the bodies it had tossed from one end of the square to the other. The terrible *thumps* those bodies had made...

"I thought Rhea might have been mistaken about what Silver saw," Laurent muttered. "But no, those bastards really are as ugly as she described them, aren't they?"

The fox stopped his nervous weaving and snorted indignantly at this comment, as if Laurent was a fool to think the images he'd sent to Rhea weren't clear and concise.

Elander returned suddenly, eying the compromised gate. His gaze then turned to a soldier yanking on a helmet, and he frowned. "Armor won't hold up much better than those gate bars did; I've never seen any kind of armor that can withstand the energy they're firing. We're better off going for stealth as opposed to trying to attack outright. The void archers find their targets by sensing movement—even the tiniest of vibrations in the air. And if they sense you...just try to avoid their arrows."

"Don't get shot with the arrows," muttered Zev. "Solid advice."

"You're also welcome to run back inside and hide if that's more your style," Elander informed him, which elicited a gruff laugh from Laurent and a small, nervous giggle from Nessa.

After that, everything began to move very quickly. The group of soldiers at the gate volleyed line after line of arrows to create a diversion, drawing more and more of the archers toward them while Elander led Cas, her friends, and the rest of the king's soldiers down the wall and to various strategic, smaller openings that they crept out of in groups of three and four.

Soon, all of the soldiers had dispersed, leaving only Cas and her friends. Elander kept up a swift pace until they came to a bend in the wall. There was another gate-house here, and the roof of it was already dotted with bow-wielding soldiers who were taking aim between the openings along its edge. Nessa climbed up and found an empty spot along this parapet, Silverfoot trailing at her heels.

Elander paused next to the passage that led under the gatehouse and out of the palace grounds. "You could go with them," he suggested to Cas, glancing up at Nessa and Silverfoot. "It would be safer."

She made a face. "This bow is better suited for short-range firing," she informed him. "And also? I'm not hiding on top of that wall while you go out into the city and do all the dirty work."

He exhaled a slow, weary breath, but he didn't argue; she could tell by the almost-smile on his lips that this was more or less what he'd expected her to say. He disappeared through the passage, his sword ready and lifted at his side.

Cas readjusted the quiver against her back. She didn't intend to distance herself from these void monsters any more than she had distanced herself from the monsters in Belwind. If they were truly here because of her, then she would meet them head-on, and she would make each of her arrows feel as personal as possible as they impaled those frighteningly blank heads.

She was through the passage an instant later, Laurent and Zev following close behind.

"Just another routine hunting expedition, right?" whispered Zev as they stalked through the streets, following the sounds of screams and shrieks.

"Yes, except this time you're actually going to have to

be *quiet* once we get close to our prey," Laurent replied. "No screwing around like you usually do."

Zev started to protest, but Cas shushed them both and beckoned them to follow her down a narrow street. She had just heard the disturbing sound of human screams—clearly *young* human screams—amongst the monstrous shrieks and bellowing voices of distant soldiers.

They reached the end of the narrow street, slammed to a stop just before emerging onto a wider road, and they watched as a trio of young girls stumbled across that sun-drenched road. The girls' faces were red and twisted with horror, their steps tired, wobbly, and weak. One of them tripped. The smallest of them kept running, but another stopped to help the fallen girl; she tried desperately to pull her back to her feet, but the girl who had tripped could only sob and crumple uselessly back to the road, over and over again.

Cas saw the archer hunting them just as it took aim and fired.

An arrow sailed toward the girls, black shadows streaming out behind it like the flags of a ship caught in a violent storm.

But Zev was more violent. And he was faster. Cas had just taken a step toward the girls when a flash of fire streaked through the air and collided with that dark arrow. It wrapped around the darkness and held it in; it was all oddly suspended in mid-air for several seconds, still at least a dozen feet away from its targets.

Then it exploded.

The explosion was small, but it scattered fire and darkness over most of the road. It was distracting, disorienting, and loud enough that Cas chanced a sprint toward the archer's back as it was all settling. Laurent followed her lead.

As the falling embers of fire flickered out and the darkness evaporated, everything became eerily silent and bright.

The girls had managed to sneak to some place out of sight.

The archer stood on the edge of the road. His head twisted from side to side, as if shaking off his confusion. He quickly sensed Zev and took aim once more—but by this point, Cas and Laurent had both managed to circle wide and slip behind the monster. Cas had a clear shot at the back of his head.

She took it.

Her aim was true and her arrow sank deeply into the archer's long neck. It started to convulse wildly, but she was taking no chances; she followed up with a second shot that pierced the back of its skull. It screeched as it crumpled to the ground. And then it folded out of existence before their eyes, crumpling more and more tightly until it was nothing but a dark blight against the road— as if it had caught fire and burned so thoroughly that nothing was left to mark its once-existence except a scorch mark.

Cas stared at that black spot, trying to make sense of what she'd seen. But its death screech had attracted attention, and an instant later, she had to move again. Seven more archers were racing up a side street to her left, hurtling toward her and Laurent.

Two of them gained a commanding lead on the others.

Laurent rushed to confront them, elegantly twisting and darting from side to side to avoid the arrows being fired at him. Those arrows did not come in rapid succession, Cas noticed; the archers seemed to create them out of thin air, but the process of summoning the magic for them took time. And the bows they shot them with were strange, almost as if...

Before she could look closer at the weapons, she noticed another archer that had separated itself from the group that was charging toward her; it had fallen behind the rest.

She moved swiftly to pick it off.

She managed to pierce its throat with an arrow. It wasn't as effective as shooting it in the back of the head— it merely stumbled a few steps, jerked out that arrow, and continued to run. But Zev had worked his way around behind this approaching group, and the stumble of that straggler had given him a chance to catch up to it. In a flash of steel and fury, his blade was stabbing toward the back of this straggler's head.

Cas caught a glimpse of an arrow streaming toward her. She sprinted as far and as fast as she could to avoid the entire circle of destruction that arrow would leave, and then she disappeared back into the narrow street they'd taken earlier, weaving her way through ramshackle porches, piles of boxes, and a few covered vendor displays. She crouched down next to a porch that was littered with stone vestibules overrun with flowering plants.

Laurent and Zev found her a few moments later. The three of them knelt together and regrouped, watching the entrance to the shady street while the heady and sweet fragrance of those flowering plants tickled their noses.

Laurent had successfully killed the two he'd charged earlier, but four of the archers still remained, standing back-to-back as they moved as a synchronized unit down the smaller street, seemingly smart enough to have realized that Cas and her companions knew their weak spot.

"Let's finish dividing them," Laurent whispered as they came closer.

Cas and Zev both nodded.

Of the three of them, Laurent was the fastest, so he sprinted out of their hiding place first. He ran right at the archers, moving too quickly for them to lift their weapons and properly aim at him before he sped past.

Two of the archers peeled away from their group and gave chase.

As they disappeared from sight, Cas and Zev backed further down the side street, drawing the remaining two archers after them. They divided, went to separate hiding places, and kept completely motionless for a moment— just long enough that the archers lost track of them.

And then they both exploded into a run, moving in

opposite directions to confuse the archers and their motion-centric senses.

After a minute of this tactic, the two archers were forced to focus on only one target each, which allowed Cas and Zev to pull them completely apart. With a series of disorienting stops and starts, Cas led hers toward the more wide-open street that Laurent had disappeared onto—she'd need the space if she was going to get around behind it.

The archer followed her at a distance, its long strides silent and its body rippling with tension.

Cas paused at the intersection of the two streets, and held her breath. She was perfectly still, despite the urge to turn and search for Laurent and make certain he was okay. The sun beat down upon her back, and a bead of sweat formed on her forehead. The bead dripped down along the curve of her nose. Then came another.

She reached to dab them away.

The archer sensed that movement and charged.

Cas danced from left to right, preparing to sidestep and outrun its arrow. but it didn't fire anything at her. It only ran past her...and then it kept going. She stumbled to a stop and watched it go. And go. And go.

It was really running away from her.

No. It was trying to confuse her, just as they had been trying to confuse *it.*

And it worked.

It disappeared completely. Her guard lowered while she puzzled over its actions—just for an instant. But it was enough. An arrow she hadn't seen coming struck the quiver slung over her shoulder, and that quiver immediately turned the same dead shade of black as the scorched bit of road from earlier. Cas flung it away from her body before the dark energy could touch her skin, instinctively darting toward a new hiding place behind a section of iron fence, and she froze.

She let out a curse. Her eyes rapidly scanned the streets, searching for her attacker. She saw nothing. No movement. No shadows. No sign of Zev or *either* archer.

After a minute of holding her breath and listening, she crept forward and started to kick through the ashes of her quiver, searching for any arrows that might have survived that destructive magic.

A hand closed around her arm. "*Leave it.*"

It was Zev. Without another word, he pulled her back behind the fence. She started to open her mouth to reply, but his head jerked to the left, cutting her off. Her eyes followed his movement, and she finally saw the archer who had fired that shot at her.

It was alone.

Where had the other one gone?

"You can have my sword," Zev offered. "I can use magic if I have to."

Cas knelt down and carefully and quietly placed her bow aside and took that blade from him. After their exchange, they kept perfectly still and watched the one remaining archer stalk its way up and down the street. It seemed to be trying to startle them into movement; each of its steps was calculated, its pauses strategic, and after every few feet, it would stop and violently knock over anything that wasn't fastened to the ground in some way.

The slow, methodical method of this hunt was far worse than the way it had charged her earlier.

It gave Cas's mind time to think. To panic. Her breathing quickened and her fingers twitched, desperate to dig into the dirt or to tap against the iron post her hand was clenched around. She fought off that urge for a minute, two minutes...until the archer came close enough that she swore she could smell the stench of death roiling off of it.

Her hand slid from the fence and hit the dirt.

The archer's head snapped toward her.

Cas didn't think it was possible to become any more still than she already was. She tried anyway. She didn't breathe. She lost herself in the silence, the stillness. Tried to picture herself someplace safer. Closed her eyes. Opened them again.

The archer was still there.

Another breathless moment passed before it finally twisted its head away.

Cas watched it as it moved on from where she and Zev crouched, and the bow it carried struck her as strange once more. Now that she had a chance to look more closely at it, she could see that it was actually a part of its body. Like another appendage—one that it could shift and change at will, apparently, because as she stared, it began to morph. To dissolve into a cloud of darkness.

There was nothing except that darkness for several seconds—the same silvery black darkness that had been over Oblivion, and the same kind that the garmora had breathed out—and then the formless mass became solid. Longer. Sharper.

A sword.

The void beast walked back toward them, swinging the newly-emerged sword and sweeping that decaying darkness over everything it sliced into.

"I don't think I can get behind it on this narrow street," Cas whispered. "But if we can cut off that appendage that it's using as a weapon, then it's essentially defenseless, right? It doesn't seem like they're very strong, physically speaking."

"I'll distract it if you want to get close enough to cut it," Zev suggested, lifting his hand and pressing his fingertips together. Flames sparked from the gathered point of them.

Cas's eyes were momentarily drawn to the small fire —she couldn't help staring at it. She *was* jealous, even now, and just as Asra had said. He didn't even regularly use his magic, and yet he made it look so effortless...

She gritted her teeth, annoyed at herself for letting such thoughts distract her. She didn't have control over her own magic, no. Not yet. But what she *did* have was a sword in her hand, and she knew perfectly well how to use that.

"Okay," she agreed. "Ready?"

"Born that way," Zev replied, already darting

forward. The second he stepped onto the same path as that creature, it sensed him. Its neck arched like a snake preparing to spit, its sword-arm lifting and twisting through the air as though it was balancing the weight of the weapon.

Cas sprinted directly at it, just as Laurent had done earlier.

Her boldness, coupled with the fireball Zev was forming to launch, left their target confused and briefly hesitant.

She didn't give it time to make up its mind about its next move. With a burst of speed, she was upon it, sword swiping up, cutting through hard flesh and muscle. The strike didn't sever the appendage completely, but it cut deeply enough to leave its weapon-arm hanging limply at its side. Blood oozed out. It smelled oddly of mold and dust.

Cas danced back and away as it rushed her. It somehow found the strength to lift that bleeding arm and attempt to swing it at her. Blood splattered her face as she brought her sword up and parried it.

Disgusting.

She wanted to stop and wipe the blood away, but she didn't dare. Not while black cracks of energy were spider-webbing their way through her blade—blossoming out from the places where that blade had come in contact with the foul creature before her. Her instincts told her to cast her weapon aside before those shadows started weaving up her arm.

Instead, she clutched her sword more tightly and desperately thought of light.

The blade flashed and the darkness fled from it.

She inhaled sharply.

Had she really just managed to do that?

She lunged to the right and swept completely around the creature, dragging her foot across one of its ankles as she went. Once it tripped forward, the back of its head was within easy striking distance. She bounced back and jammed her blade into the soft place where its neck met its skull.

It fell face-first onto the street, twitching violently. Heart pounding and arms aching, Cas put a boot between its shoulder blades, yanked her weapon free, and then staggered back.

As soon as she managed to extract her blade from its neck, the void monster crumpled out of existence just like the last one, leaving nothing more than a black stain behind.

"Next," said Zev, turning her around and shoving her into motion before she even had a chance to catch her breath. It was better that way. *Keep moving.* She needed to keep moving, and he knew it—because if she had paused to fully take in the sight of what they were rushing toward, panic would have overwhelmed her and brought her to a stop.

Framed by houses on either side, the larger of the two roads loomed ahead, and Cas counted three archers along its distant edge. As she ran closer, she saw Laurent to the right of those monsters—and to *his* right were three more archers.

He was surrounded.

And every single one of those void beasts had an arrow formed and pointed at him.

CHAPTER 25

SHE WASN'T GOING TO REACH HIM IN TIME.

Zev cursed and drew to a stop, apparently realizing this same thing. Fire-kind words raced from his lips. He raised his hand and took aim.

Cas's mind threatened to haze over even as she kept running, but one thought managed to emerge through the fog: *A single Fire-kind spell won't be enough.*

She stopped as well, and she threw her hand forward, thinking only of trying to help Zev. She knew no spells to use. No words that would call any magic fully into her control. She still didn't know where her power even *came* from. But she had summoned light a moment ago. She had felt that power enough times that she believed in it, and now she was desperate and determined to use it all for something *good*.

Electricity exploded from her palm at the thought.

It sparked through the air, and more seemed to

converge from the sky itself. Too much more; her body convulsed as the electricity all converged into a single, swirling point high above her. The weight of the entire mass of it settled over her. She felt her knees buckling, but she forced herself to stay upright. To *aim*.

Her body was on fire with the effort of trying to control it, every one of her muscles protesting what she was attempting to do. She lifted her hands. Braced her stance—

And then she twisted her arms toward the closest line of archers.

The energy left her control so suddenly that it felt as if she had pitched over the side of a cliff—she was free falling, lost without that energy's weight.

She dropped to her knees and then slumped forward. Her face hit the road. She rolled onto her side and managed to look up in time to see a twisting rope of lightning encircling three of the void archers.

One, two, *three* explosions of shadows that sparked with electricity.

Three harrowing, otherworldly screams as those beings caved out of existence.

Cas's cheek fell back to the gritty road. Rocks stabbed into her skin. She was dazed, and her eyes watered from the stinging pain spasming through her muscles, but she blinked enough tears away to watch Zev's magic and Laurent's blade finish off the rest of the archers.

Once it appeared they had things under control, she finally let her eyes close completely.

She woke up minutes later to find Laurent kneeling beside her, helping her back to her feet. "That was a neat new trick," he said, his mouth set in an even line and his gaze uncertain.

Zev just stared at her, speechless for perhaps the first time in his life.

Cas managed a nod. It had been impressive magic by any standard—but she had only *just* managed to control it. Elation and terror twirled a strange dance in her stomach. "We can talk about it later," she told them.

Before they could press her further about the matter, a series of shouts caught their attention.

They ran toward the noise.

Following it took them to a section of the city filled with old houses and shops that looked mostly abandoned; the ramshackle buildings had been built practically on top of one another, and the sagging roofs and crumbling walls hastily patched with tattered cloths made it difficult to tell where one place ended and another began. There were also too many broken windows and cracked doors and chunks of debris to count —some of which appeared to have been caused recently, judging by the tell-tale black death marks that blighted them.

A battle had clearly just taken place here.

But now the space was empty and silent.

They crept through the quiet wreckage, and soon the air grew cold. *Unnaturally* cold. All three of them felt it. They slowed and shivered almost simultaneously, and

Zev glanced at her. "Is that your captain and his weird magic at work?"

Cas hesitated. She knew Elander's magic at this point. It *was* him, she suspected, but it didn't feel like his innate power.

"I think it's Ice-kind magic," she told Zev. "He has a sword that—"

The silence was shattered by a sudden commotion coming from inside one of the dilapidated buildings. Glass shattered. Wood cracked and splintered...and then Elander emerged from that building, knocking out a door that had been hanging on one hinge as he came.

Two void archers followed him, one wielding the typical bow, while the other had shifted his weapon into a black sword.

Elander moved with deadly grace and precision, drawing those archers after him, his own sword aglow with the blue tint of its wintry magic. He swung his weapon in a fluid arc, mouthing a spell as he did. The air between him and the archers sparkled with tiny crystals of ice.

One of the archers made the mistake of stepping into that sparkling air. His body instantly glazed over with a layer of frost that became thicker and thicker as the seconds passed.

Cas didn't think beyond her need to keep moving. She rushed to the frozen archer and relieved him of his head with a mighty swing of her sword.

Elander finished off the second archer before glancing

in her direction. "I was wondering where you'd run off to."

"You know me," she huffed, wiping the latest flecks of blood from her face. "I've just been taking a leisurely stroll through the city."

"Typical."

"And we've killed no less than a dozen of these bastards during that stroll."

He looked momentarily disturbed by this number —*had he sensed her using her magic a few minutes ago?*—but all he said was, "Excellent. New plan, however: We need to fall back toward the main gate." He turned and shouted this same order at Laurent and Zev before pulling Cas in the direction of that gate. "They're still trying to break their way into the palace," he said to her. "The majority appears to have gathered there now, and I think we can surround them and finish them off easily enough if we're smart about it."

Cas nodded determinedly, though she felt a little sick at his use of the word *majority*. They had already killed so many; how many could possibly be at that gate?

"Are you all right, by the way?" He tossed the question at her casually, but it felt like catching an explosive Fire-kind crystal that was only seconds away from igniting. Because she could tell by his frown, and by the way his eyes lingered on her as he asked it...he *did* know she had used magic earlier.

Of course he knew.

If nothing else, her exhaustion from the magic was likely evident to anyone paying attention.

All the same, she was preparing to deny any lingering after-effects of her power—but her reply was cut off by a gasp as an arrow struck the ground just in front of them. They leapt away from the darkening, cracking ground just as Laurent called out to them, warning them of the archer's position.

A quick search found that archer perched in the balcony of a nearby house.

"Annoying bastards," Elander grumbled—and then he was off, scaling the partially collapsed roof of that house, swinging his way onto the balcony and flying recklessly toward that archer. He somehow avoided the arrow it fired at him. His sword was unsheathed in the next breath, and for a moment, Cas couldn't keep track of him amongst the swirling tangle of Ice-kind magic and the black energy given off by the dying archer.

He didn't see the second arrow flying toward him.

This arrow didn't pierce him either—but it did strike the balcony he stood on. The resulting dark shockwave shook that balcony free of its bracings, and it collapsed down along the front of the house, causing the entire front wall to cave inward and swallow Elander up as it went.

Zev and Laurent set off to find the one responsible for this latest arrow, while Cas started to race for the destroyed house.

As she approached, Elander emerged from the rubble.

Covered in dust, coughing violently, and wiping blood from his face...but alive and relatively unscathed.

Thank the gods.

"You reckless, foolish, *absolute*—" His head tilted toward her, a trace of a smirk on his face, and Cas caught herself. Swallowed her concern. He didn't need to know that she had almost panicked over the thought of him getting injured; his arrogance was already unbearable enough as it was.

She took several deep, calming breaths. "Negotiating with death again, I see."

He coughed a few more times, and then his smile became more blatant. "I get better at it every day."

"Idiot," she growled.

"Watch yourself," he replied, grabbing her arm and pulling her out of the path of yet another arrow. They huddled together for a moment, watching as Laurent finally managed to dispose of the one who had fired it, and then Cas jerked an elbow into Elander's ribs so she could slip out of his hold.

"Back to the gate," she reminded him, "and no more showing off or *negotiating* along the way, please."

He stood, rubbing the spot where she'd elbowed him, that smirk still lingering on his face.

Cas turned away before he could see the second sigh of relief escaping her.

Together, the four of them raced through the streets, picking off a few more archers as they went, but at some point, Cas and Elander got separated from her friends.

She thought nothing of it at first; it had happened often enough during their missions together—particularly chaotic ones like this—and they always found their way back to each other in the end.

She told herself they would be waiting for her at the gate.

They weren't.

Still, Cas tried to focus on the battle that *was* awaiting them at that gate, and the instructions Elander gave her. He brought her to a small hill that gave her a distant but clear view of the palace, told her to wait for his signal, and then he crept away to make sure the rest of their soldiers were in their proper positions.

Minutes passed. Zev and Laurent still hadn't caught up with her. The wind hissed through the trees. The sun seemed to be setting at an unnatural pace, and her scalp itched as a terrible, foreboding feeling swept over her.

More screams in the distance.

She closed her eyes against the sound and waited for it to stop.

The screams grew louder.

She had no way of knowing if her friends were involved with those screams. Nothing was clear except that terrible, itching feeling inside of her. It wouldn't go away. She tried, once again, to focus through it.

She couldn't.

And then, for what felt like the hundredth time that night, Cas found herself racing toward the distant sounds of terror.

She followed a well-worn road toward the outer edge of the city, and eventually she came upon a large yard that sloped down to a small house.

A house that was surrounded by archers.

A few dozen soldiers and townspeople surrounded those archers, their weapons raised and aimed. Laurent and Zev were there as well. They had clearly stopped to help; Laurent was holding a woman, preventing her from running toward that house, while the fire around Zev's hands glowed brighter and brighter.

Even from a distance, the tension of the standoff was palpable. Cas hesitated at the edge of the yard, watching for a moment, trying to decide on the best way to help.

Suddenly, the woman Laurent had been holding back broke free and sprinted for the house.

Cas didn't even see the arrow flying toward that woman—not until it struck her chest.

The woman fell to the ground. Within seconds, her body was nothing more than a charred husk. The air filled with the pungent scent of her flesh sizzling against grass.

Zev stormed toward the archer responsible for the shot, and Cas felt as if her own chest had been struck. As if her heart had actually *stopped*.

Because even as Laurent joined Zev, they were still terribly outnumbered. None of the townspeople moved to help—most of them were still staring at that smoldering pile of ash the woman had been reduced to. A few soldiers started to take action, but it wasn't enough. There were too many of those monsters, and they seemed viciously determined to keep the house surrounded—to hold whoever was inside of it hostage.

Cas's feet were suddenly moving without her say-so, carrying her into a mad dash toward her friends. She didn't think she could manage another blast of that electricity she had used earlier, but she had to do something. *Anything.*

As she reached the bottom of the hill, her gaze happened to glimpse a pale sliver of moon hanging in the early evening sky. Thoughts of her earlier conversation with Elander filed rapidly through her head.

The Moon-kind. The magic they possess. Magic that can reflect things, amplify things...

And then one last thought: *This is foolish.*

This final thought was the loudest one in her mind. Because she was again playing with dangerous things she did not understand, and she knew it.

She stepped forward anyway, her eyes on that faint sliver of moon, her hand shaking as she lifted it in front of her. She breathed in deep. The world seemed to slow and shrink, all of it gathering a little closer toward her with every deep inhale. Her gaze flickered from the moon to the fire glowing from Zev's hand, and she had only one thought from that point on—

Let it be enough.

The blast that left her was far, far more powerful than she had intended for it to be—such an enormous amount of power that she was thrown back against the grassy hill. Still, she somehow managed to keep her eyes

440

open, to shield them from the intense wave of energy that ricocheted back toward her, so she saw that power she'd unleashed as it tangled itself up with Zev's magic. As it made it brighter. Bolder. As it *amplified* it. It created an entire wall of fire that stretched from one end of the yard to the other—long enough that not a single archer was spared as that wall pushed forward. It incinerated them as if their bodies had been made of dry straw.

But the fire did not stop there.

Cas *tried* to stop it, but it was far beyond her control at this point.

The small house those archers had been surrounding was engulfed in seconds.

Screams. Windows popping. A *whoosh* of wind and exploding flame. A pause, a moment of stunned silence, save for the crackling of wood and the howl of swirling fire. And then more screams, *so many screams...*

Cas pushed herself to her feet and ran towards the inferno.

Somebody shouted for her to stop. She didn't know who, she could barely hear them over the pounding words in her head, words that were chasing her as she raced across the yard: *What have I done? What have I done, what have I done...*

She felt as if she had left her body behind in the grass —but somehow she was still running. Somehow she reached the house. Somehow she found a window that had been blown out, and she hurtled through it, and once she found her balance, she began to search and shout for anyone who might have been inside.

An eternity seemed to pass before she heard a response. A small voice. *A child's voice.* She dropped low to the ground, beneath the worst of the smoke, and she crept as fast as she could through the burning house. Walls were peeling away, revealing the support beams underneath. Several of those beams were catching fire. They shifted and *popped* around her, every one of those pops showering her with bits of ash and ember.

After a minute of searching, her eyes were drawn to a large doorway, to the frame that was wrapped in flames. Through the opening that was quickly filling with black smoke, she thought she saw movement. She staggered closer, and she saw him—a young boy cowered in the room on the other side, his eyes on the door that he was clearly trying to work up the courage to walk through.

Cas managed a few more steps toward him before the top of the door frame collapsed.

She threw her arms up to protect herself, and then lowered them just in time to see the boy's face being lost in a swirl of flame and smoke.

She felt a scream rising in her throat. It never came out. Her throat was far too dry—so dry that it was becoming difficult to swallow or even breathe, much less make any sort of sound. She had to keep going. To keep crawling. To make it into that room.

Her skin was tingling—or blistering and melting off, perhaps. The heat made it impossible to tell what was truly happening to her, and that same heat made her delirious enough to believe that the tingling might have been her magic, and that it could still protect her and that boy somehow...if she could just *reach him.*

This mad belief was enough to send her leaping over that fallen door frame and all of the beams it had pulled down with it. The flames licking up from it all somehow did not catch on her pants or boots. She landed awkwardly on the other side, but kept her balance.

And there was the boy, curled up, unconscious, on the floor.

She gathered him up in her arms and kept moving.

She didn't know where she was going. The smoke roiled more thickly than ever, but it seemed to be funneling towards something to their right. Her dazed mind decided to follow this movement, and soon she caught a glimpse of dark blue—of *sky*—through what she assumed was a distant window. Her eyes were as dry as her throat, and she desperately wanted to close them.

But she would not lose sight of that patch of blue.

She followed it like it was the last drop of water in a desert.

And then, before she even realized what she was doing, she was leaping through a low opening and tumbling out of the inferno as recklessly as she'd raced into it.

She stumbled to her feet and made it a few dozen steps or so before exhaustion overwhelmed her and she lost her footing again. She rolled to the ground, still cradling the child tightly to her, attempting to break his fall. Once they were resting on spiny grass, she wrapped herself around him and continued to try and block him from the smoke that rolled over them in waves. Embers were being whipped about by the wind, and little fires were spreading across the yard, blazing paths that came dangerously close to the spot where Cas was huddled up.

She knew she needed to get up, to get to a safer place.

But she couldn't move.

She was trying to force a cry for help from her parched throat when the largest of those fires surrounding them suddenly parted. The movement was unnatural, so she wasn't surprised to see Zev walking through those parted flames a moment later. He took the boy from her while she struggled to her hands and knees. Laurent was at her side a second after that, wrapping her up in his arms and hauling her away from the burning house.

They left her and the boy at the top of a distant hill, and then they returned to help put out the fire.

That burning house seemed very far away, now.

All of the chaos in the city did.

The crickets chirped as though nothing had happened. The wind was refreshingly cool against Cas's cheek. The moon grew bolder against the darkening sky, and she stared at it until she could no longer keep her eyes open, and then she drifted out of consciousness, chased into the darkness by visions of dancing flames.

CHAPTER 26

It had been four days since the fire incident, and Cas had spent most of that time locked in her room after claiming she needed to be left alone to fully recover.

This claim was only partly true.

She *should* have needed days to recover. A normal person would have needed days to recover.

But she was slowly accepting the fact that she was not in any way *normal*.

She barely noticed the lingering effects of the smoke she'd inhaled. She didn't have the normal burns that she should have suffered after walking through flames, either. Her skin remained smooth and free of blisters, thanks to that otherworldly protection she seemed to possess.

The boy she'd pulled from that burning house had had no such shield.

His face and neck would forever carry the marks of

that night, and the image of his red and peeling skin would forever be imprinted in Cas's mind. She had only glimpsed it before she was whisked back to the palace, but it had made her think of the burns that marked Darkhand's face. Of the fires he'd survived and of all the destruction he had caused in the years since suffering them.

She didn't understand why she had protection against such things.

She didn't understand why she had magic that could set entire houses ablaze.

All she knew was that she felt like a walking disaster waiting to happen—which was why she was better off staying locked in her room.

No one had told Varen about the latest disaster she'd caused, as far as she knew. Or—more likely—no one had managed to positively identify Cas as the one who had set fire to that house. The scene had been violently chaotic. For better or worse, the details of what exactly had happened seemed to have been lost. And even if they hadn't been, the King-Emperor, for his part, didn't seem concerned with her; he was more concerned with the substantial number of soldiers he'd lost to those void archers.

Thus she passed entire days in her room, unnoticed. While within the relatively safety of that room's walls, she had drifted in and out of a dazed state, never quite falling asleep. But in the moments when she inched closest to sleep, her visions of Solatis returned.

There was no wolf to face off against the upper-goddess this time.

No shadows.

Only that golden Goddess of the Sun watching her, expectantly and without speaking.

Cas was on the verge of slipping into another of these light-drenched daydreams when she heard a knock at the door. Reluctantly, she crawled off her bed and crossed the room.

"Who is it?" she called.

No reply.

Biting her lip, she pulled the door open.

In a flash of grey and white, Silverfoot slipped inside and proceeded to make himself cozy on the satin-trimmed ottoman. Cas sighed in his direction before turning back to the two who had arrived with him—Rhea and Nessa.

"I was still resting," she informed them.

"Liar," Rhea said.

Nessa offered a sheepish smile. The air was warmer, suddenly, and Cas recognized her Feather-kind magic at work. She tried not to fall under the spell of it, but it was difficult not to; it felt like stepping outside on a summer evening, into the sort of balmy air that made one momentarily forget their troubles.

"You have to come out of this room eventually," Rhea continued. "And we all know that you're fine. You're just hiding from us."

"I set a house on fire and nearly burned several people alive," Cas said, flatly. "I am not *fine*."

"I meant physically," said Rhea, frowning. "And the rest isn't going to be fixed by lying in bed all day."

"Are you sure about that? It's a very comfortable bed," said Cas with a shrug.

Rhea pursed her lips.

"You made a mistake, that's all," Nessa said, softly.

"It was in the heat of battle," Rhea added, "and your magic got away from you. It happens even to people who have been wielding magic for years. Do you know how many times Zev has accidentally set something on fire? When we were children, there were countless times when we had to sleep without blankets because that idiot had set fire to them in his sleep the night before."

"And you saved far more than you hurt," Nessa insisted.

Cas didn't argue. Partly because it was pointless—they were at least as stubborn as she was, and she was outnumbered—but also because the Feather-kind magic was still swirling in the air between them and making her feel sleepy and stupid.

"If I agree to join you all for dinner shortly, will you leave me alone for now?" she asked.

Nessa and Rhea considered for a moment before nodding.

"One hour?" Nessa suggested. "We can meet in the banquet hall closest to the throne room."

Cas agreed, and she shooed Silverfoot from the room, waving goodbye and swiftly closing the door behind them.

She had no intentions of eating dinner.

But she couldn't stay in this room; she suspected they would be back to get her when she didn't show up—and they would likely come with reinforcements. Rather than facing that, she grabbed her coat and set a path for outside.

Fresh air didn't seem like the *worst* idea at the moment, anyway.

She kept her eyes downcast until she had made her way through the palace, out a small side door, and to a section of the yard that seemed relatively empty. The flowers and bushes here were maintained, but only just so; the pathways were all only one missed pruning away from being overrun. It made the space feel more intimate, even when her thoughts were interrupted by occasional footsteps or voices.

She had been walking for several minutes before she heard a voice she recognized—Elander's. She spotted him in the distance once she rounded a curve along her path; his tall frame was easy to spot amongst the group he was standing with.

He hadn't seen her yet. She could have turned and gone the other direction, and he never would have known she'd been there.

Instead, she stepped over to a bench that was covered

in dead leaves and some sort of dried red fruit that had fallen from a nearby tree. She brushed it all off and sat down, gripped the rough stone edge of the seat, and lifted her eyes skyward.

That sky was splashed with golden orange light, the last show of a sun that was slipping behind the distant mountains. It made her think of her light-splashed daydreams. She didn't want to see the Sun Goddess—or feel her frustrating silence—again, so she made certain not to drift off. Her fingers tapped the stone and her eyes darted constantly about, seeking tangible things. Trees. Stone statues with sapphire jewels. Flowers. Birds. Rocks. Elander, who had his back to her.

He *still* could have walked away and never seen her.

Fate eventually turned him in her direction instead.

He spotted her, and a minute later, he was walking over and sitting down on the bench.

They didn't speak at first. They hadn't spoken at all since that chaotic, fiery night; she assumed he was furious with her for her reckless use of magic, and for running off when he'd given her a clear role to play in that battle for the front gate. She didn't know the total number of soldiers killed at that gate, but more than once, she had found herself questioning if that number might have been lower if she had only stayed and done what he'd asked of her.

Instead, she had dashed off and burned down some innocent family's house.

He had every reason to be furious with her, really—

though his fury could not possibly match what she currently felt toward *herself*.

But he didn't seem angry at all. He only glanced at her fingers as they tapped the stone, and then he offered her his arm. "Need an anchor?"

The question caused a small smile—the first genuine one she'd managed in days—to curve her lips.

"Maybe," she admitted, hesitating a moment before taking his arm.

He helped her to her feet, and they strolled for several minutes before she spoke again. "You know, I actually came out here because I was running away from everybody," she said, staring at that grip she'd placed on his arm. She hardly remembered putting it there. The movement had simply felt...*natural*.

"Trying to escape the servants barging in and out of your room?" he guessed.

"And my friends." She pressed her lips together, but it was too late; the words had escaped her without thought, and now he was watching her even more curiously than before. "They mean well," she said with a shrug. "But they're a bit exhausting at times."

"Ah. Understood."

"They want to talk. But I'm not sure how they would react to the thoughts that have been going through my head these past four days."

He considered this for a moment. "And how do you think *I* would react?" he asked.

She cut her eyes sideways, studying that curious

expression of his before turning her gaze straight ahead once more. "With a lecture," she concluded.

He laughed. "Try me."

She chewed on her bottom lip, hesitating again. He didn't pressure her. He just waited. Finally, she rolled away the tension in her shoulders and said, "Last week, when I tried to help Asra...when my magic caused that weird light and energy... less than an hour later, someone else in the palace was dead." She pulled away from Elander and started to pace. "Was it me that killed them? Did I redirect what should have been Asra's death, somehow?"

He wasn't the type to lie in order to spare her feelings. And so he didn't.

"It's possible," he told her.

"Possible." The word felt heavy and sharp in her throat.

"It's also possible the two things weren't related. There were plenty of deaths in the palace before you came to it."

Cas drew to a stop, shaking her head. "I *saved* that girl in Belwind—that's what I've been telling myself—but where did that death, that sickness, that was intended for her actually *go*? Those plants died, but they likely didn't contain all of that sickness I pushed away from her, did they?"

"Probably not."

"Have there been others?" She started to pace again. "Asra told me that her Fading Sickness stopped advancing once she found me. But if I was, I don't know, *reflecting* it elsewhere, then I might have been unknowingly making *other* people sick to protect her. I might have been leaving a trail of bodies in my wake for my entire life without even realizing it, right?"

His brow furrowed. "I don't know."

She felt like she was going to vomit, but she had started to talk, and now she couldn't stop. "And then, of course, there was the other night, when I was trying to help, and I ended up reflecting that fire so recklessly that, well..."

"That was different."

"But still destructive."

"All magic has a dark side," he informed her. "A dark, not always controllable side."

The words sent a shiver down her back. "I don't want dark and uncontrollable magic. I'd rather have no magic at all."

He didn't respond to that. His gaze was sympathetic—but also curious again, as though he didn't quite understand how someone could give up magic, regardless of how dangerous it could be.

And before she could try to make him understand what she was saying, they were interrupted by the sight of Caden and Tara hurrying toward them.

Tara's gaze was fixed on the ground ahead of her, and she mumbled silently to herself—perhaps trying to gather the courage to deliver whatever message she had.

Caden's eyes were fixed on Cas. He looked furious,

and she didn't miss the way Elander subtly moved to block her from his view as he approached.

"What is it?" Elander asked.

Tara hesitated under his glare for a moment before she managed to swallow hard and say, "He knows." Her eyes flitted over Cas for an instant before she continued, "Someone told Varen what the Fade-marked and her magic did the other night. And he—"

"More than one person," Caden interjected. "An entire group of townspeople went to him this afternoon with their grievances and concerns." He jerked his head toward Cas. "Concerns about her."

Cas felt like she had plunged into an icy river.

"They don't have proof of anything," Elander insisted, calmly. "Nothing more than what they claim to have seen, and there was a lot of strangeness to be seen that night."

Caden gave him a withering look. "You think Varen won't find proof, somehow? Especially now that he has cause to look for it?"

They were quiet for a long, tense moment.

"You can't honestly have believed it was going to work out with no consequences. And even if someone else didn't tell Varen the truth, she would have let it out eventually." Caden's gaze slid toward Cas, and she would have sworn his eyes flashed to the color of blood. "Her mind is weak."

It happened in an instant—a pressure against her skull, as if he had reached out and dug his fingernails into it and started to squeeze.

She quickly realized what was happening—*he was trying to pry into her mind with magic*—but before she could move to protest, Elander spoke.

All he said, in a voice as cold as his magic, was a single word. "Stop."

Caden did not stop.

The claws of magic tightened around Cas's mind, and a pained gasp escaped her.

An instant later Elander had Caden by the throat. He lifted him several inches off the ground, and his voice somehow reached an even more terrifying level of cold as he gave a second command. "Keep your fucking magic *away from her.*"

Caden coughed and sputtered for breath. His face turned an alarming shade of red, while everything else around them seemed to be losing its color, all of it darkening and withering within the circle of Elander's building magic.

The magic squeezing her mind subsided, and Cas rushed forward to put a stop to things before they ended up with a second out-of-control-magic incident to explain.

But Elander threw Caden away before she could reach him.

Caden stumbled a few steps and then caught himself against a bench. He pushed off that bench and spun back to Elander in a rage, the betrayal he felt obvious on his face. "Why the hell are you so protective of her?"

Cas froze in place, heart pounding, suddenly desperately curious to know the answer to this as well.

Elander didn't reply.

Tara's voice was uncharacteristically bold as she intervened. "You know this could ruin everything we've been working toward, right? If Varen finds out you—no, *we*—knew about her magic..."

"I'll deal with it," Elander growled.

She and Caden both stared at him. Caden rubbed his neck, still looking furious. Tara's bottom lip quivered slightly, but she still did not look away.

Finally, Elander acquiesced with a soft sigh and added, "But ready the others, just in case."

The tension held, but the answer seemed to satisfy them enough for the moment. Tara bowed her head slightly. Caden gave one last seething look, and then the two of them headed off in the direction of the stables.

"Ready them for what?" Cas asked once they were out of sight.

Elander only shook his head, his eyes glazed over in thought.

She scowled. "More secrets? Really?"

"I'll explain later," he promised. "If it comes to that. But for now, let's focus on what *you* are going to do."

"It's obvious, isn't it? I have to go talk to Varen."

He looked as if he was holding in another sigh.

"I'm not going to run away, if that's what you were hoping for. Have you learned *nothing* about me? You

456

should know better than to have even thought I would run."

"True," he conceded. "You do have a very strong history of racing *towards* things that could get you killed."

She ignored the quip. "Maybe I can just come clean? I could talk to him and make him understand."

He shrugged. "Or maybe you can just set him on fire and be done with it."

Cas made a face. "That's helpful, thank you."

"I was joking. Mostly." His grin was genuine, though his eyes still betrayed the wariness he was feeling.

She had expected this wariness, so she wasn't deterred. "Come with me?"

A muscle in his jaw clenched. Likely from the effort of holding back all of his objections. Still, after a moment he nodded, and they headed inside.

Cas glanced over her shoulder several times, making certain neither Tara nor Caden had followed them before she said: "By the way, I don't need you to choke anyone else on my behalf...just so you know."

He shrugged. "I was looking for an excuse to choke him. He's been getting on my nerves lately."

"I'd gotten the impression the two of you were close."

"We were."

"What happened? Is it just about me? Or is there something else?"

"It's complicated."

"Everything is complicated with you, I've noticed."

"We have that in common," he said, flashing her that particularly roguish version of his smile—the one that always seemed to wither her resolve at an alarming rate.

She shook her head at him, but they made their way deeper into the palace without another word on the matter, seeking out servants and inquiring about the King-Emperor's whereabouts.

But in the end, Varen would not see either of them.

He was in his throne room, as the servants had told them; Cas could *hear* him on the other side of the door to that room, having a conversation with several people. But one of the guards at that door informed her that Varen did not wish to see her tonight. Whatever she needed to talk to him about, it would have to wait until morning.

It was not a good sign.

He had never made her wait so long to speak. He had held meetings with her at all hours of the night, and he had frequently interrupted his meetings with his own senior advisors in favor of meeting with her.

Something had clearly changed.

She backed out of hearing range of those guards, but she couldn't take her eyes off the throne room door. She was desperately hoping Varen might change his mind, throw it open, beckon her inside, and apologize for making her wait.

He did no such thing.

"I wish we could just get this over with. The waiting is worse."

"I imagine that's precisely why the bastard is making you wait," Elander said.

"To torture me?"

"Yes. Well, that, and he's probably busy gathering more evidence against you. He's never been one to act rashly—he's very unlike his father in that regard, at least. He always talks about *knowledge* being a sharper and more deadly weapon than any blade. The problem is that once his studies have convinced him of something, it's very difficult to get him to change his mind...even if he's studied incorrect facts."

Cas thought of the first meeting she'd had with him, of how Varen had come prepared with so many of her previous aliases memorized. He had read her criminal record. Studied it. And the vast amount of knowledge he'd seemed to possess about her—and about so many other things—had made her feel foolish and small and desperate to prove herself to him. It hadn't occurred to her that he might have been trying to intimidate her on purpose, to wield his knowledge as a weapon. But now...

"I don't like any of this," Elander muttered, turning and starting to walk away.

She followed, and they headed toward her room in silence.

They had a brief encounter with Laurent along the way; her failure to show up at dinner hadn't gone unnoticed, as she'd predicted.

She said a small prayer of thanks that it was Laurent who had come to find her, and not one of her other friends, because he wasn't the type to pry. And he *was* the type to go back to those others and inform them that she wanted to be left alone, and to insist that they listen to her request this time. She also told him that there was a chance Varen was unhappy with her—that they should be on their guard, just in case—and he agreed that this was more important than worrying or arguing about why she wanted to be alone.

And yet, as she watched Laurent walk away, she realized she wasn't sure she *did* want to be entirely alone.

It must have been obvious on her face, because as soon as they reached her room, Elander turned to her and said, "I'm not leaving you by yourself tonight."

He opened the door and stepped into her room first, his eyes scanning from one corner to the next, as though he expected Varen might have prepared an ambush for them.

"I can manage," she said. "I don't need a guard."

"I know," he said, distractedly, as he continued his scanning. "But I was hoping you could protect *me*."

Cas started to roll her eyes, mostly out of habit, but she held her tongue. She was too tired, too distracted by too many other things to argue the matter. She was also dangerously close to drifting away into that disconnected state where the Sun Goddess always seemed to find her. Elander provided a constant, tangible presence that helped keep her awake and aware—and away from that confusingly bright dream.

So he stayed. He didn't ask her to talk. Or eat. Or

sleep. Or calm down. They simply existed in the same space for a while; she was a ship drifting aimlessly about, and he was the lighthouse that she occasionally found herself looking for when she needed to see something real. Something solid.

An anchor.

Eventually, her drifting led her out onto the balcony.

Minutes later, he followed.

It had started to rain. The balcony was covered, but the wind blew the drops sideways with enough force that Cas was soaked within minutes. She let those drops hit her. She wanted them to sting her skin, to make her cold, to make her feel miserable.

To make her feel *something* other than numb.

It worked, at least partially; she was more aware of her body than ever. But her hands still felt foreign when she held them in front of her—and even more so when a bolt of lightning cracked through the distant sky.

She felt panic surging through her. At first it was only that old, familiar panic that storms had caused her ever since her parents' deaths. A panic that soon felt almost reassuring, because at least it was a demon she had experience with. One she knew how to fight.

But when she reached for the railing to steady herself and tap her fingers against it, her anxiety exploded into new, dangerous territory—because electricity leapt from her touch and wrapped around the balcony railing.

She staggered away from that railing, colliding with Elander as she did.

"Remember when you said we would figure this out?" she asked him after catching her breath. She clenched her still-sparking hand into a fist and pulled it against herself, desperately willing the magic to stop.

"Yes," he said, steadying her against him. "But in my defense, you have proven extraordinarily difficult to figure out."

Her hands finally stopped crackling with electricity. She shoved them under her arms and lowered her gaze to her boots. "Well, some things are becoming clearer, at least."

"Like what?"

She hesitated. "I thought I could help the empire by working with Varen." Her words came out in a whisper; she wasn't even certain he could hear her over the rain, but she couldn't seem to make herself louder. "I...I was going to save so many people. Instead, it looks as though I might be more of a villain than a savior."

He was in front of her, suddenly, his hand hooking underneath her chin and lifting her eyes to his. "You are not a villain, Thorn. I believe I have *that* much figured out, at least."

"Not a villain, maybe, but a danger, at least. So can I really blame Varen if he wants to cast me out or..."

Frustration bubbled up and stole her words. More sparks flew from her fingertips—perhaps because of that frustration—and the sight only made her more furious. Which led to *more* sparks. It was on its way to becoming a dangerous, never-ending cycle when Elander finally grabbed her hand, sparks and all, and wrapped it up in his much larger one.

"Enough," he said, pulling her tightly against his chest. He kept his hand wrapped around hers, even though those hot flickers of electricity had to have been causing him pain. They were certainly causing *her* pain. But the pressure of his powerful grip also seemed to help her keep that magic in check, so she didn't try to pull free.

Eventually, she even maneuvered her fingers into his and squeezed back.

Another minute passed, and then she was breathing calmly again, her magic settling into a soft buzzing beneath her skin.

He still didn't let her go.

"Aren't you afraid that I'm going to accidentally set you on fire or make you explode if you keep holding me like this?" she asked, drily.

"Terrified."

She knocked her head against him in frustration, and his body vibrated with quiet laughter.

When he finally stopped laughing at her dramatics, she drew back, going just far enough to properly see his face. His arm hooked around her, preventing her from going any farther. The pressure against her felt possessive suddenly, and her entire body flushed with warmth as she met his eyes. Raindrops clung to his lashes, and the blue gaze beneath them seemed even more mesmerizing than usual. He was soaking wet, just as she was.

But he hadn't once complained about standing in the rain with her.

"I'm absolutely terrified," he repeated as he reached and pushed aside a strand of her hair that had plastered itself to her forehead. Then he wrapped his other arm around her and pulled her closer. "And yet, the thought of missing my chance to hold you like this is somehow *more* terrifying."

She sighed. "You're a fool."

"Yes. But we already established that the other night, I believe—when I kissed you in that room. I assume you remember that foolish kiss?"

"Vividly." Her body shuddered pleasantly—involuntarily—at the memory.

He seemed to be aware of the effect his words had had on her. *Very* aware of it, judging by the fiery desire that suddenly darkened his own gaze. "Good. I'm glad it left an impression."

That dark look sent another tremble over her skin. She tried to focus on that pleasant sensation, on the feel of his strong arms wrapped around her, and not on the panic and confusion that still hovered just beyond the edges of them like an avalanche waiting to be triggered.

That avalanche felt inevitable.

But so did they, all of a sudden.

Inevitable that they would find themselves standing together like this. Again. And she again had that feeling, like she so often had with him, that she had been in this place with him a thousand times before. That it was a warm, safe, *familiar* place that they had only been walking each other toward since that fateful night when she'd decided to rob him.

She kept her eyes on his, and she spoke just loudly enough to be heard over the wind and the rain. "If you were truly a fool, then you wouldn't miss this chance to leave another foolish impression."

CHAPTER 27

HIS LIPS WERE AGAINST THE HOLLOW OF HER THROAT IN THE next breath.

From there, he moved up along the curve of her neck, to the sensitive spot where her pulse throbbed noticeably against her skin. That pulse raced at the mere closeness of him, and when his tongue flicked teasingly against it, its pounding became so rapid and erratic that Cas briefly thought she might faint. His tongue teased just long enough to cause her that light-headedness, and then he moved and crushed his lips against hers.

The heat of her need tangled with the cool taste of raindrops. The combination was staggeringly good. So good that she wanted to cry out in protest when he slowly pulled his mouth from hers.

She braced herself for an ending similar to last time, where he would shake his head and insist they couldn't be fools any longer, and that he regretted leading her to believe otherwise.

But the mischievous curve of his mouth said he didn't regret what he'd just done at all.

"So what happened to *it's complicated*?" she asked.

"It's still complicated. More complicated than ever." His eyes fell to her lips, and he stole another soft, slow kiss before leaning back and adding, "But something about tonight is making me feel even more foolish than I did the last time we were alone like this. I blame the rain."

"You prefer rainy days," she recalled from their conversation back at the inn in Belwind.

"Yes. Although tonight it's more about the way you look in that rain than anything else."

"Which is like a half-drowned rat dredged up from the river, I suspect."

"The most stunning half-drowned rat I've ever seen."

"You're just trying to make me feel better after this terrible day."

He gave a noncommittal shrug, a grin still tugging at the corners of his lips. "Yes and no."

For the second time that evening, she couldn't help smiling at him.

"But I think you should get out of the rain before you freeze to death," he said, "regardless of how stunning you might look while doing it."

"I'm not cold."

"Your shivering suggests otherwise."

His mentioning it somehow made that cold worse; a

violent shudder rocked through her, nearly taking away her breath. He gave her an expectant look, and she admitted defeat and followed him inside.

"This has to be one of the first arguments with you that I've actually *won*," he commented as they stepped into the bedroom. He squeezed the rain from the waves of his hair and gave his head a shake, slinging water droplets against the wall as he did. The movement made her think of a dog. A very handsome dog—but a dog nonetheless.

"Don't get used to it," she said as she disappeared into the washroom to change.

He stayed on the other side of that room's door while she slipped out of her wet clothes. There was something very...*arousing* about the fact that nothing more than a single door separated him from her nakedness. A door she'd absently left cracked open, at that. He could have seen her—all of her—if he'd bothered to look. He didn't come anywhere near that cracked door, but the possibility that he could have was almost as thrilling.

She dressed slowly, stepping into one of the countless night gowns that now filled the spacious closet within the washroom. It seemed like the collection of those gowns had doubled every night that she'd stayed in the palace. The green one she'd chosen was among the simplest. It was a modest length, and it revealed nothing but the faintest hint of her curves and the peaks of her breasts—peaks that were still stiff from a combination of the cold and his kiss—but the silky material of that gown rose and fell with her movements in a way that made her feel undeniably beautiful. Alluring, even.

And Elander's thoughts were not far off from her own, judging by the way he watched her as she stepped back into the room.

She settled down on the edge of her bed. He looked as if he was considering crawling in beside her, but she stopped him with a look. "You know," she said, "I'm not convinced that you refusing to leave me alone tonight isn't all just a ploy to get into bed with me."

"Even if it is, are you really complaining?"

She wasn't.

"I'll sleep on the floor if you want me to."

She didn't.

And he could tell she didn't, if the faint smirk that crossed his face was any indication.

"Well, you aren't getting into my bed with those wet clothes on," she informed him.

"Then I'll take them off."

She exhaled a slow breath. She probably should have seen that response coming. "Or you could go to your own room and change."

"What part of *I'm not leaving you alone tonight* did you not understand?"

She tucked a strand of hair behind her ear. "Fine. Stay."

So he did. He set about creating a small blaze in one of the room's two fireplaces, and then he proceeded to take off both his coat and his shirt, carefully arranging them on the hearth to dry. He showed a small bit of mercy, at least, and kept his pants in place—though he stripped off the belt that was holding them around his lean waist, which allowed them to slip low enough to reveal the hard lines of his lower abdomen. Lines that drew her gaze and made her mind wander toward dangerous places, because there it was again—the *possibility* that was somehow almost as devastatingly sexual as seeing the actual thing.

He turned his back to her for a moment, poking at the newly-ignited flames, so she stared without restraint. The lingering bit of dampness on his skin made his muscles glisten in the firelight, highlighting every powerful edge of him.

Gods.

She finally made herself look away, only to hear him stepping toward her a minute later.

"Are you okay?" he asked.

She gripped the edge of the bed and nodded, even though she wasn't, not in any way—how could she be okay? She had just realized an awful, undeniable truth.

She *wanted* him.

All of him and his annoying, beautiful self. She wasn't too proud to admit that—at least to herself. At least in that moment. But she knew the complications that came with that wanting, as did he. And when he asked her if she was *okay*, it only reminded her of all of those complicated things. Of the trouble that was waiting for them outside of this room.

They were quiet for a few minutes.

He eventually turned back to the fire, but still tossed the occasional concerned, uncertain look in her direction, while she clenched and unclenched the bed's covers, thinking.

"I'm in trouble, aren't I?" she finally asked. "No matter how many times I rehearse the potential upcoming conversation with Varen, it always ends with me in very deep trouble."

"You could still leave," he offered.

"Then *you* would be in trouble, for letting me go."

"I'm not afraid of a little trouble."

"Neither am I," she said. "But this wouldn't end, even if I ran. And *that* is what I'm afraid of. If I don't answer for what I've done, then who will? Who would he attack in my place? My friends, or who knows who else..."

He crossed the room, a thoughtful expression on his face. "I had a feeling that's what you were over here worrying about."

"You have me all figured out, don't you?"

"I do." He sat down beside her. Hesitated. And then he quietly added, "Maybe because I sometimes feel like I've known you for a very long time."

She stared at him, heart thudding clumsily in her chest, wondering if she should tell him about all of the times she had thought that exact thing.

"Sorry," he said. "Did that sound strange?"

She only managed to shake her head and say, "No. No, I feel that way too."

They stared at each other, hardly managing a breath

between them. Her face warmed. Her hands desperately wanted to tap and fidget, but she didn't move. Didn't look away.

"I still feel like we could know each other better," she whispered.

"What did you have in mind, precisely?"

"Do I really need to elaborate?"

"No. I just wanted to hear you say it out loud."

Her blush deepened, and she started to look away, but he cupped her cheek and held her gaze to his.

"What did you have in mind, Thorn?" The question sounded more like a command.

He kept his eyes on hers, but his fingers slid to her throat and then down to the narrow valley between her breasts. The touch made her feel more brave and more foolish, so she lifted her chin and said, "The other night...I still don't think you should have stopped at just another kiss."

"I see." His hand cupped her breast, and his fingertips brushed over the hardened peak at its center.

"You told me I wouldn't be able to think straight—or walk straight—when you were finished with me, as I recall." His fingers pinched that hard nipple, and her next words came out accompanied by a gasp, "So I want you to prove it."

He brought his face closer to hers. Their noses brushed. "I feel like this is just you searching for a distraction from what's to come," he murmured.

"Even if it is, are you really complaining?"

He wasn't.

"You can still leave," she added with a shrug.

His eyes danced with amusement at the echo of his own words.

And then he was leaning into her, pinning her between his hard body and the bed, his mouth capturing hers with rough, barely-restrained movements.

She wrapped her arms around his neck. He grabbed her by her hips and lifted her easily into the air, pulling her tight against him for a moment while his tongue continued to explore her mouth. Little fires ignited everywhere her body pressed against his bare skin. His grip on her shifted, one of his hands moving to cup her and hold her between her legs, and she moaned into his mouth and took his bottom lip between her teeth.

She was on her back in the next instant, her head sinking into the pillows. His hands ran the length of her body—tracing it, worshipping it—before moving to push the bottom of her night gown up and out of his way.

He trailed kisses along the soft skin of her inner thighs. Her back arched, and his kisses moved higher, briefly pausing and teasing against the needy ache at the apex of those thighs before following the lines of her hips up to her navel, her breasts, and then finally bringing his lips close to her ear so he could whisper, "Are you sure you want to do this?"

She nodded, breathless.

"And you're...protected?"

"Since the first time I mentioned a strange boy's name

to Asra," Cas said, cringing a bit at the memory. Asra had been adamant—and loud—about her lack of desire to be a grandmother.

Elander moved his lips from her ear, but he stayed balanced on his knees, straddling her on the bed. He arched an eyebrow. "Just out of curiosity, have there been a lot of strange boys since?"

"You're the strangest so far."

He huffed out a laugh. "You're my strangest as well."

"See? We're perfect for each other."

"I would tell you, *again*, how very wrong you are about that, if only you didn't look so damn attractive underneath me."

"Why don't you just kiss me again instead?"

He leaned closer once more, bracing a hand on either side of her, but stopped short of letting his mouth brush over hers.

She reached up and threaded her fingers through the still-damp waves of his hair. "I want this."

"So do I." He exhaled the words on a soft breath. The quick kiss he planted against her lips a moment later was equally soft and sweet, but the curve of his own lips was perfectly sinful when he drew them away.

He sat upright again, pulling her with him as he did, and he made quick work of taking off her gown and everything beneath it. The rest of his own clothes landed in a pile on top of hers shortly after, and then he laid her back against the mattress and admired her, his hands caressing every curve and dip of her body, every scar and imperfection laid bare for him to see.

His eyes found hers, and they burned so fiercely with need that it likely would have frightened her if her own need wasn't burning just as brightly.

He kissed her gently on the forehead, and then he stood and walked across the room to check the lock on the door, completely unashamed of his nakedness—not that he had any *reason* to be ashamed. He looked like a damn god strolling across his own personal domain.

She was nearly trembling with desire when he strolled back to her, took hold of her hips, and jerked her toward the edge of the bed. He leaned closer once more. But there was no clothing to separate them this time—nothing but a tiny sliver of heat and space between her ache and the hard length of him. The tip of that hardness teased her entrance as he brushed his hand across her jaw, and then across her lips. His fingers paused against those lips, patiently waiting until her mouth opened and she followed his unspoken command to take those fingers and suck them.

After a minute of this, he pulled them out, dragging them across her lips as he did, and while they were still warm and wet, he slipped them between her thighs and pushed one of them inside of her. And then another. And then a third one, stretching her and pushing against her walls until she thought she might collapse from the sheer pleasure of that intentional pressure that moved in expert circles within her.

His other hand soon pressed to her thigh, applying even more commanding pressure. "Spread your legs wider for me," he ordered.

She did, but not quickly enough—or wide enough—apparently, because *both* of his hands were on her thighs a moment later, pushing them farther apart. His knees nudged against hers, keeping her legs in that position, while one of his hands moved to stroke himself.

His fingers were back against her moments later, testing her wetness and adding his own to it before entering her with one powerful thrust.

The stretching his fingers had done was nothing compared to the delicious burn of that thrust. Or the one that followed it. It was briefly painful, but that pain was swiftly eclipsed by the pleasure that waited just on the other side.

She closed her eyes and lost herself in that pleasure, in wave after wave of it pounding against her until her entire body shuddered with her complete release. She started to cry out, but Elander's mouth closed over hers, silencing her as his own surrender shattered through him and spilled into her.

He stayed inside of her for several minutes after that, his body warm and safe and heavy against hers. Every aftershock—every twitch, every last throb—of his release sent another tiny curl of pleasure through her. And every one of those pleasurable shivers emptied her mind a little further. She was blissfully unaware of almost everything else.

She would have been a fool to think such bliss could last beyond that night.

But for once, she wasn't thinking beyond the moment she was in, and her thoughts were a thousand miles away from the troubles that the morning would bring.

A SHORT TIME LATER, they had managed to untangle themselves and clean up, only to fall back into her bed together. The morning felt like it was an entire lifetime away. They huddled under the blankets, still mostly naked, her back against his chest and his arm wrapped around her waist, holding her close. His hand moved over her occasionally, absently tracing patterns against her skin.

She thought he'd fallen asleep, but then his low voice whispered against the back of her neck: "That was more than just a distraction earlier, wasn't it?"

Her reply was equally soft. "It felt like more."

He drew her closer, burying his face into the curve of her neck, breathing her in slowly and then exhaling just as slowly.

"Did you mean what you said before we...well, you know?"

"Which part?" he mumbled against her shoulder.

She swallowed a few times, stalling while she waited for her courage to catch up to her thoughts. "The part where you said that sometimes it feels like you've known me for a very long time."

477

He kissed her shoulder, but then drew his mouth away so his reply was quiet but clear. "Yes."

"Why do you think that is?"

He considered for a moment. Yawned. And then he said, "Your mind never stops working, does it?"

"No. Asra has always referred to me as her *restless heart* for a reason." She rolled over so they were facing each other. "Although..."

He brushed a knuckle across her cheek. "Although?"

"My mind might have stopped earlier. Just for a few minutes."

He grinned a lazy, sleepy grin. "I could stop it again, if you'd like."

The sore spot between her legs pulsed willingly, but she shook her head. "One time was probably enough recklessness for one night."

"It was very reckless," he agreed. "Further proving my point that you tend to run toward dangerous things."

"Are you really suggesting that you're *dangerous* to me? Because I'm not sure I believe that."

"I am incredibly dangerous, you silly woman."

"You're grumpy and arrogant, and occasionally broody, and your magic is terrible—"

"So flattering."

"—but the dark and dangerous thing is actually an act, I'm beginning to think."

"Sorry to disappoint you, but it's not an act. I'm all dark and dangerous, all the way through. My heart is actually just a barely-functioning blob of blackness."

She arched a brow.

He shrugged, and his grin never faltered—but his eyes didn't quite meet hers for some reason. Instead, he yawned again and closed those eyes, apparently content to go to sleep without arguing the matter any further.

"It's a bit too late to try and warn me, either way," she informed him, sitting up. "Plus, I'm quite certain you were running toward me at least as fast as I was running toward you."

"I never said I didn't have my occasional moments of recklessness."

She tilted her head back toward him, a sudden curiosity taking hold of her. "Speaking of which...you asked me before how many strange boys I'd been with, but I never asked about *your* past relationships."

He popped one eye open. "Do you really want to have this conversation right now?"

"Yes." She cocked her head to the side. "Why wouldn't I? Do you have some wild, out-of-control erotic history that you haven't told me about?" She pretended to look scandalized. "Wait, were *you* actually the one preparing to service people that night at Madam Rosa's Inn?"

He chuckled. "No."

"How many other women, then?"

He didn't reply.

"Men?"

He snorted. "Just women. And just one, really."

"Only one?"

"Only one that mattered in the end."

"How did it end?"

"I tried negotiating with Death on her behalf." He sat up, scooted to the edge of the bed, and reached for his pants. "I failed."

"You...oh." She averted her eyes as he dressed. It seemed silly after what they'd done earlier, after all she had already seen. But there was something in his expression that she *hadn't* seen before—a flicker of vulnerability that felt wrong to stare at—so she kept her gaze on her own hands as she said, "I'm sorry."

"For what?" He crossed the room to check on the clothing he'd spread out to dry. Shook out his shirt, slipped it on, and rolled up its sleeves, all without looking at her. "People die. I've seen more death than most, given my position and my *terrible* magic. And you've seen your share of it too, haven't you? It's just another thing that has to be dealt with."

She frowned, her forehead creasing as she tried to think of an intelligent rebuttal to that—a logical one that his cool and calculated self might accept. But instead of a counterargument, she suddenly remembered what he'd told her about his position, and all of the duties that it entailed.

"Can you speak with her?" she blurted out. "I mean, in the same way you help Varen communicate with the kings and queens of the past?"

He folded his arms across his chest and fixed a hard stare on that nearly extinguished fire before him.

480

"You, um...you don't have to answer that. Sorry. I was just curious."

He didn't take his eyes off the glowing embers. "I've tried. I've never been able to reach her."

"You can't reach her?" The thought made her feel suddenly, desperately sad—like a cavernous pit had opened up in her stomach. "What does that mean?"

"I don't know. Mostly I try not to think about it."

So you should probably shut up about it, she told herself.

But she couldn't stop thinking of what it might mean. She searched for a way to redirect the conversation, but her curiosity about his magic would not settle. "Could I... see that magic?"

Finally, his gaze cut toward her. "See it?"

"As in, if there was someone in my past that I wanted to see..."

"Your parents?" he guessed.

"Not my real ones, but the ones who took me in when I was four. The Lady and Lord of House Tessur."

"Why do you want to see them?"

She didn't tell him the true reason. She couldn't bring herself to share what she'd thought of since their earlier conversation about the destructive side of her magic— that her adoptive parents might have been among those people her magic had accidentally killed. He would have disagreed with the very possibility of it, she was almost certain. And something told her he wouldn't agree to summon their ghosts so she could have a painful conversation about it all; he was too overprotective for that.

So instead, she shrugged and said, "I'm not sure. But my earliest memories are of them, so I just feel like...like maybe it would be comforting."

He looked doubtful, but after a minute he nodded. "We could try, I suppose."

A nervous fluttering started in her stomach, and it didn't cease as she dressed and then joined him out on the balcony once more.

The rain had stopped, but there was still a chill, damp breeze sweeping through the partially enclosed space, lifting the grey strands of her hair and battering them about. She shivered. Elander disappeared inside, returned a moment later with his coat that had been drying by the fire, and dropped it over her shoulders.

"Do we need to go somewhere more private?" she asked, peering down at the courtyards below. There were even more guards strolling about than usual. There was no chance that one of those guards wouldn't glance up at some point, she thought.

But Elander shook his head. "I'm not actually summoning anything solid into this realm. It's..." He paused, as if trying to find the right words. "It's more like I'm taking *you* to a place where those things can meet you. And only in a metaphysical sense. I'll be able to see whatever you're seeing, but no one else outside of the field of my magic will."

She hugged his coat more tightly around herself. It was still warm from the fire. Or perhaps it was the scent

that clung to it—earth and smoke and undeniably *him*—
that made her skin feel hotter.

"This will require a lot of focus from you," he warned.

"A lot of focus on what, precisely?"

"On who you want to see. On the feelings you have
toward those people. Clear memories of them, if you have
them, will make it easier to bring them to you."

Clear memories.

"I was never particularly close to Lady Tessur," she
thought aloud. "She was kind, but...distant. I remember my
father clearly, though. I remember his laugh. I remember
taking painting lessons with him, and I remember how he
used to make the most ridiculous faces whenever he told
me stories..." She smiled a bit at the thought of those faces.

"Focus on him first, then. And then on any image you
have of the two of them together."

She nodded, already sifting through those memories,
trying to decide on one that she felt she could sink fully
into.

"If we manage to bring them here," Elander continued, "you can *try* speaking to them if you want. But just so
you're aware, you probably won't be able to hear their
voices, and they probably won't be able to understand
yours either. Convening is one thing. It takes a lot of practice to be able to communicate across planes. You might
be able to glimpse them this time, but that's likely all
we'll be able to manage tonight."

Just a glimpse.

The thought was disappointing. She wouldn't be able to question them about any signs of magic she'd shown as a young child, or about any accidental spells she might have used.

But perhaps it was for the best. At least for tonight. Tonight, maybe she didn't need words or more confusing conversations; she just needed to see some part of her past as she remembered it, to see if that past might give her some sort of clue as to how all of her current chaos ended.

Either way, it felt like she was too far into this experiment to back away from it now.

"Ready?" Elander asked.

"Yes. I think."

"Good. Now, hold up your hand," he instructed, lifting his own. She mirrored him, and he pressed his palm flat against hers and closed his eyes. His lips moved with soundless words.

At first, nothing happened.

She tried harder to picture her father. The way his eyes would widen and light up when he came to the most harrowing part of a story, the deep rumble of his laugh, the paint splotches that had covered most of his clothing, the whiskers of his chin that would scratch her skin whenever he hugged her goodnight...

She felt a twinge of power spreading through her hand. It was different from the times she had summoned her own magic. Her hand didn't want to twitch with this power—her fingers felt too heavy to move at all. So incredibly *heavy*, as if she was balancing a giant boulder on the tips of them. After a moment, that weightiness began to sink through her entire body, making her bones feel so fat and useless that she was certain she was going to collapse, sink through the balcony and fall and fall and fall until she hit the ground below and sank through part of that, too.

But somehow, she managed to stay upright.

Elander seemed to be suffering beneath the weight of that magic, just as she was. His eyes fluttered open and shut as he fought for concentration. His breathing was slightly labored, and the muscles of his arm trembled from the effort of holding his hand still against hers.

She was about to ask if he was all right, when he finally pulled his hand away. He brushed the back of it across her cheek. Across her forehead. Let his fingers rest against her temple for a moment's worth of concentration, and then he took a step back. He nodded at something behind her.

She turned around, and for a long time, she could do nothing except stare.

The first woman she remembered calling *Mother* was staring back at her.

So was the only father she had ever known.

And they were not the storm and nightmare versions of them that had so often haunted her. They looked... warm. Healthy. Bright. *Solid*. Her mother stood in the doorway with her eyes lifted toward the sky, fidgeting— as she so often had—with the thick braid of her dark hair.

Her father stood beside her with his hands clasped behind his back, studying his surroundings with that familiar, scholarly glint in his eyes.

Cas lifted a fist to her mouth, stifling the overwhelmed little cry that tried to escape her. The air around her shimmered. A cloud of silvery blue collected at her feet. It was dotted with pulsing little lights, as if a handful of stars had fallen into it. It swirled up, weaved its way around her body, and then it twisted slowly toward her parents. It seemed as if it was beckoning her to follow it.

She did.

She walked along that trail of stardust until she was mere feet away from the apparitions of her parents.

Lady Tessur lowered her gaze away from the sky as Cas approached. Her eyes never quite found her daughter's, but the concentrated furrow of her brow suggested that she was aware of her. She looked to her husband, and her lips moved, but—as Elander had predicted—Cas could not her. But her father seemed to understand; his gaze turned in her direction. Searching for her.

Perhaps they couldn't see her yet. Perhaps they couldn't hear her. But Cas was almost certain they could *feel* her presence, and she could feel theirs.

And it felt as if they had never left this world at all.

"Elander, this is...incredible." As she breathed out the words, she glanced at him, wondering how much longer his spell could possibly last. She looked back to her parents just as quickly.

They were fading.

She had stopped concentrating, only for an *instant*, and now they were going to leave her again.

Frantically, she pressed her hands to her head and tried to think. She conjured up every warm feeling she could, every memory of home, of laughter, of smiles and stories and oh, if only she could remember their *voices*...

But she couldn't.

Her parents kept fading.

She was losing them. *Again*. Instantly, she felt like a child again, wandering the streets, looking for help. Starving. Aching. Searching. The memory of the King-Emperor's guards beating her senseless in the street surfaced above all others, and she closed her eyes and shook her head against the thought.

When next she opened them, the Lord and Lady of House Tessur were gone.

But the one who had taken their place—the one who had pulled her bloody self out of that street—was waiting for her. *Asra*. Relief flooded through Cas at the sight.

And then realization crawled up her spine and clawed cold, shiver-inducing fingers into her head.

"Asra?" she whispered. "Why are you here?" She pried her eyes away from the ghostly figure and turned slowly toward Elander, hoping he would tell her that he did not see what she did. That his magic had ended, and Asra was not part of it. She *couldn't* be a part of it, because that would mean...

No.

Elander was staring straight at that flickering figure. He looked confused for a moment, and then...horrified.

Cas's legs turned to mush. She braced a hand against the balcony railing. Squeezed it so tightly that it hurt. "Elander. Why is she here?"

He didn't reply. Not until Cas pushed away from the railing and started toward the door, and then the only word he managed to get out was: "*Wait.*"

She didn't wait.

She *couldn't* wait.

The walls felt as if they were closing in around her, and she broke into a run.

CHAPTER 28

SHE OUTRAN ELANDER.

His magic use had left him too slow to keep up with her, or he was intercepted by the palace guards that snapped to alarmed attention as she raced past them, or something else held him back—she didn't know. She didn't care.

All she cared about was getting to Asra.

She hurtled into that room where Asra was staying, and found that she was not alone. Four servants stood against the far wall with their heads bowed low.

"What is going on?" Cas demanded.

The servants kept their eyes on the ground and their hands fisted together in front of them.

Cas forgot about them for the moment as she rushed to Asra's side and checked her over. Cold skin. Closed eyes. Breaths that shifted no more air than a butterfly's wings, and a pulse that Cas could only feel if she pressed hard and kept perfectly still herself.

"*How long has she been like this?*"

Two of the women by the wall turned and fled. Cas stared at the doorway they'd disappeared through, horrified. Devastated. *Furious.* Earlier, she had wondered who Varen would attack as punishment for the dangerous secrets she'd kept from him.

Was this the answer to that question?

Had he ordered his servants to stop treating Asra because of her?

"Come back," Cas begged, turning to Asra and taking her hand. "This is my fault, but I'm going to fix it. Just come back, and *stay alive.* I'm going to talk to Varen, I'm going to get you your medicine and then I'm going to get you out of here and find a different solution to this, I swear I will. I just need to...to..."

She needed to fix this somehow. She *would* fix this somehow. Only...she couldn't move. She could have rushed to confront Varen—she wasn't afraid of confronting him. But she *was* afraid that Asra would be gone completely whenever she came back. The same thought pounded over and over in her head: *She can't leave me if I don't leave her.*

The thought made no sense. She knew it didn't. But she clung desperately to it all the same, and it kept her rooted in place. Seconds passed. It felt like much longer. Cas rested her forehead against the edge of the bed as she squeezed Asra's hand.

After several attempts, she received a soft squeeze in return. "It's not your fault, you know."

Cas lifted her head.

Asra was staring at something on the ceiling, the corners of her eyes crinkling as though—whatever it was—it was too bright to look directly at it. "It's just my time to go, is all."

"No, it isn't. Don't say things like that."

Asra kept her eyes on the ceiling, on whatever light she saw. "I didn't think I would be afraid in the end."

"*This is not the end.*"

"But I'm still afraid."

Cas heaved several deep breaths—in and out, in and out—trying to think of what to say. "So am I. I—" The words stabbed at her throat. It felt like her mouth, her throat, her lungs were all filling with blood, and now she couldn't *breathe*. Her speech came out in a whispered rush that Asra probably could not even understand. "I'm afraid all of the time, you know that. I am scattered and anxious and the fear doesn't really ever go away, so I just have to do things in spite of the fear. And so I *do*. I *can*. And that means you can too, so look at me—*look at me*—because we aren't finished, okay? The fear is not going to finish us, *this is not the end*, this is...this is..." She was out of breath. Out of words. Out of plans.

"Restless heart." Asra's hand squeezed hers one last time. "You have to stop fighting for me. There are bigger things that that heart is meant to beat for."

"No." Cas gripped her hand more tightly. Crushed it

so fiercely within her own that she was surprised when she didn't hear the sound of Asra's brittle bones breaking.

But she received nothing in response.

She no longer felt a pulse.

"*No.*"

She stood up. Took several slow steps away from the bed. Fury was the sole fuel of her movements now—the only thing that turned her head in search of answers. Her eyes fixed on one of the two remaining servants by the wall. A desperate madness surged through her. Her hand lifted before she could think, before she realized what she was truly about to do—

And then it was done.

Fiery pain burned through her veins. Power twisted through her body, weaved around her arms, concentrated at her fingertips. A flash of brilliant light blinded her, and when the white dots before her eyes faded away, the servant lay in the corner. Crumpled. Perfectly still. Her arms splayed out at awkward angles, like the wings of a bird that had slammed into a window.

Was she dead?

Cas didn't look closer to see.

Because Asra had returned to her. She still lived. Her eyes were still closed, but now she was taking deeper breaths, *louder* breaths, and she was surrounded by a soft light. By protective magic. Cas could protect her. She could keep pushing that sickness out of her.

It only required her to keep finding other places to put it.

Her eyes shifted toward the one remaining servant.

With a shriek, that servant pushed away from the wall and ran for the door.

Possessed by something she didn't understand, that she didn't *want* to understand, Cas moved after her.

A cough from Asra made Cas stumble. A split second of hesitation, and the servant was gone, and Cas had to make the decision to stay or to keep giving chase.

She quickly decided that she had to stay.

If I don't leave her, she can't leave me.

She wheeled around on unsteady feet, staggered back to the bedside, and dropped to her knees. She felt like she was reliving that first moment she had visited Asra in this room. And just as she had done that afternoon, her eyes darted frantically around in search of a place that she could redirect Asra's death toward. But again, there were no other living things to be seen. No plants, no people, no monsters.

Except for Cas herself.

Let that sick, evil energy come to me, then, she thought, just as before.

Light blinded her, just as before.

And she fell back, same as before.

But she did not lose consciousness this time. She felt every painful twitch and stab of her restless magic. She heard every sound, from the latest rain shower pattering the window, to her own breaths rattling in the collapsing cage of her chest, to her heart beating like mad, and then...

Footsteps.

Terror shot through her at this last sound, but she forced herself to keep breathing through it. Reminded herself that she had been here before. Lying on this same floor, staring at this same ceiling, trembling with these same aftershocks of magic. Elander had found her in this exact same place.

He would pick her up, same as he had that last time. They would escape this room. They would hide. They would keep trying to figure things out.

But it was not Elander's voice that reached her next. Not a lecture from him, but only two simple, breathless words from someone else, words that echoed like death knells through her skull—

"That *light*."

Cas lifted her head in the direction of that quiet voice, and she found herself staring at the King-Emperor and dozens of his heavily armed guards.

CHAPTER 29

CAS ROLLED OVER AND PUSHED HERSELF UP ONTO HER HANDS and knees. "I can explain," she coughed.

"I don't believe that will be necessary, Casia dear," Varen said, his voice chillingly calm as he moved into the room.

Elander shoved his way through the guards surrounding Varen a moment later. He took one look at Cas—at the waves of light rippling around Asra—and fear flickered briefly in his eyes before his face shifted into an unreadable wall.

"Captain." Varen kept his gaze on Cas, even as he addressed Elander. "You knew about this woman's magic, I've heard."

Cas held her breath.

Elander took a few more steps into the room. "Yes. I knew."

"You knew she was a threat to me—to my rule and my

empire—and yet you allowed her to continue to move freely about."

Silence.

Cas wanted to scream at Elander to say something. To blame her. To save himself. It seemed impossible that she would get away now, but there was no reason they *both* should suffer Varen's wrath over this.

The King-Emperor tilted his head toward Elander. "Prove me wrong. Use your magic to detain her and drag her down to the dungeons. Or is there some reason why you can't do this?"

Elander said nothing.

"Do it now," Varen said, "or you can consider yourself *dismissed* from my service—at which point I will consider it a risk to let you and your magic continue to exist in this empire. It's your move, Captain."

Elander still did not move.

Varen's gaze slid briefly back to Cas. "That's what I thought."

Cas stared at him, still hardly breathing, as he then turned toward the guards that were hovering outside of the room.

"Your sword, Seylas."

The mountain of a guard known as Seylas withdrew his blade at Varen's command, and he held it in front of him as he marched into the room, stopping at Varen's side.

The sight alarmed Elander enough that he finally moved, and he finally spoke. "This isn't necessary—"

"*Hold your tongue, Captain,*" Varen snarled. "You had your chance to prove your loyalty to me. You failed. So I will be handling this myself, and you will answer for your relationship with this woman shortly. Whatever conspiracy the two of you were forming against me, it ends now."

"There was no conspiracy!" Cas cried.

He spun toward her, eyes ablaze. "Do you think I'm a *fool*? Did you think I wouldn't eventually realize who you are? Or what you planned to do?"

"I don't know what you're talking about. I—"

"SILENCE!"

Shock made her comply. The entire room was momentarily shocked into that same tense silence. Nobody moved. Nobody spoke.

Asra's breaths sounded loud and clear in the silence, at least, and the sound of them kept Cas steady.

She's still alive. She's still alive, and I can still protect her.

Varen had created the quiet, and he was also the one that shattered it. "Seylas."

The man with the sword stepped closer to Cas. Her eyes followed his movements. They caught on the silver tiger curled around the hilt of his sword. On its sapphire eyes that were reflecting that light she had wrapped around Asra.

"I believe it *is* time we put her out of her misery, as we discussed earlier," Varen told Seylas.

Cas braced herself as the man moved closer to her. Her mind threatened to go numb, but she swallowed hard and

497

rose the rest of the way to her feet. She had to fight. To protect herself. That light she'd wrapped around Asra...she could wrap the same power around herself, if only she could find a way to focus. Her skin hummed at the thought. Little white lights fluttered around her, suddenly. Varen's eyes narrowed on them, as did the guard's as he continued forward.

But that guard stepped past her.

No—he *sprinted* past her.

Cas twisted and saw the glint of steel, the blade rising above the bed, and horrific realization skipped through her.

That protective light that had surrounded Asra had faded away. Cas had summoned her magic toward herself, not realizing she was taking it *away* from Asra in the same breath. She'd thought she was strong enough to protect them both.

She wasn't.

And now she didn't have time to reposition that shield of magic. She didn't have time to *think*. She lunged after the guard herself, ready to tackle him with her bare hands.

But she was too far away.

She was too slow.

The blade plunged into Asra's chest.

A cry rang out. It swiftly became a breathless gasp. A gurgle of blood. A choke into silence. Cas saw the drops of blood sprinkle the blankets and the floor, and everything else slipped out of focus. The light around her scattered.

And then she was screaming. She was screaming *so loudly*. Why was no sound coming out? Why was everything so *quiet*? She could think of only one explanation—that she had fallen through space and time and into the deepest hell where *nothing*, not even her own voice, made any sound or sense.

Somehow, Varen's voice floated all the way down to her hell. "Bind her."

She saw the men rushing toward her, but she couldn't make herself move.

Elander was quicker than those men descending on her. The first man met his fist, and that man fell back against the wall. The second man was stopped by magic; his face twisted in horror and agony as the space around him darkened and that deathly cold magic converged and caused him to crumple to the ground.

Then Cas thought she heard Varen's snarling voice again, rising above the commotion. *Take care of him first.*

They tried to. Guard after guard rushed toward Elander, blades swinging. And guard after guard hit the ground soon after they reached him. The room was drowning in blood and darkness and deadly, bone-shaking cold. But that frigid magic that had once terrified Cas now felt oddly comforting. She wanted to sink into the dark and the cold and never rise out of it again.

She just wanted to *stay*.

If I don't leave, Asra can't leave me.

More guards continued to pour into the room. Group

after group of them, until there were too many, even for Elander.

Again, Cas wanted to tell him to run. To leave her to her fate. She spotted a woman lifting a sword, preparing to strike, and she finally managed to force out sound— just Elander's name, shouted in warning.

He twisted, avoiding that woman and her blade. But a second guard was there to meet him, and this second guard was too quick with his knife. The knife plunged into Elander's side. Elander spun away from the strike, but his balance was off; he slammed into the wall and immediately clapped a hand to his side. It came away covered in blood.

Cas started toward him, but a fist caught her in the jaw and knocked her to her knees. She tasted metal and salt and spat out a glob of red.

So much blood. She was dizzy with the thought. Dizzy and surrounded by more guards than ever. She couldn't see Elander anymore, but she could hear him shouting at her.

"Casia, *get up!*"

She didn't want to get up.

"WAKE UP!"

She *was* awake. But Asra was not...she was not...she was *not....*

And she never would be again.

Cas felt hands roughly grabbing at her, pinning her arms behind her, dragging her upright.

Elander was still roaring at her, somewhere far in the

distance: "You can't go with them. *You can't*. FIGHT, DAMN IT!"

She didn't want to fight.

"Kill him," She heard Varen order. "And you three—" he pointed to Cas, to the ones holding her "—bring her along. I want to speak with her in private."

Cas tucked her chin toward her chest. Blood continued to trickle from her mouth. *She was not here.* She was someplace far away, where Varen and his soldiers could not, *would not*, be able to hurt her anymore. She felt herself being lifted. Her body dragging along the ground, because her legs refused to work for more than a few steps at a time.

The palace seemed distorted as she traveled through it, the walls and stairs and ceilings growing and shrinking as she passed them.

She closed her eyes.

When she finally opened them again, she lifted them without moving her chin away from her chest. Everything still seemed oddly misshapen, but she recognized enough to know she was in the throne room. She rested on her hands and knees. Varen sat before her on his throne. It was very quiet; they seemed to be alone.

"Casia." He spat out her name like a curse that echoed in that odd quiet.

She did not reply.

"Do not ignore me," Varen said, softer. "The rest of your friends still live. Unless you want that to change, I suggest you look at me when I am speaking to you."

Your friends still live.

She lifted her head and glared at him.

"That's better."

"Why don't you just kill me and get it over with?" she demanded, her voice raspy and thick with grief.

"Because I haven't decided, yet, whether you would be better off dead or alive. Make no mistake—I *want* you dead. But you may be too useful to kill."

"I won't be useful to you. I will *never* be useful to you again. I would rather *die*."

"Well, as I said, that's certainly a possibility."

She clenched her fists against the ground. Kept her chin lifted and her glare fixed on him.

"You made me look like a fool," he said. "I trusted you, and you took advantage of that trust, didn't you? You should thank your stars that I only killed one of your friends this night. That I am even *considering* letting the others live in return for your cooperation."

"You're insane."

"No. I am the King of Melech and the emperor of all of Kethra, and this is not a game. This empire is *mine*. It was thrown into my hands, and I was forced to embrace it— and I have. Alone. And I don't intend to let it go so easily now that I've worked so hard to secure my rule. *I* will be the one that keeps it from collapsing in spite of the gods and everything else. And if that means slaughtering the friends of those who would plot against me, then I will do exactly that. Continue to oppose me, and I will kill every single person that ever mattered to you. I will do it without flinching. My dear, I will kill *you* without flinching."

Just as he hadn't flinched that day in the marketplace while he'd watched the whips cut into her flesh and stain the street with her blood.

He had already shown her precisely who he was, and she should have believed it. She should have listened to the warnings Elander and everyone else had given her about this man.

She was a fool.

She had messed up. She was a fool and she had messed up so, so *badly*—so badly that she still wanted to curl into the floor and fade out of existence.

"Now," said Varen as he rose from his throne, "the time has come for you to make another choice, I believe."

But she couldn't fade out of existence, could she?

Your friends still live.

She had to keep going at least long enough to make sure they escaped.

There are other things that your heart is meant to beat for.

She would not end here.

She rose to her feet. There was a storm raging inside of her—a thousand storms just barely contained within skin. She only needed to harness one of them, and she could end this. She held tightly to that thought. Held it tightly enough that it became more than just a thought—it became a spark. A spark of electricity that became *more* sparks that swirled and danced within her control. She thought of that tree in the palace gardens, the way she had struck it with her controlled magic and turned it to splinters and dust.

"You won't kill anybody else." Her voice was a whisper. A threat.

Varen's gaze darted toward those sparks at her hands. His lips curved in a cold smile. "Still insisting on keeping up that *defiant* little attitude of yours, are we?"

"Yes."

"Don't be a fool."

"You won't kill my friends. And you won't kill *me*." She swung her hand forward, and the lightning leapt away from her hand and hurtled at the King-Emperor.

It struck the space directly below his heart.

And then it bounced harmlessly away from him.

And he *laughed*.

Her eyes widened as they followed the ricocheting magic. The ball of electricity streamed toward the ceiling, striking a chandelier. She ducked as bits of glass and metal showered them. And before she could even wonder about *how* he'd managed to block that magic, Varen was rushing toward her, whipping a dagger from beneath his coat.

She jumped back just in time to avoid being stabbed in the stomach. Her knees buckled slightly with the awkward movement. She toppled sideways, but caught herself on one hand and found the strength to shove herself back upright. She scrambled back until Varen was centered before her once more.

More lightning sprang to her fingertips, and without hesitating, she launched it.

And again it bounced right off of him.

"*How—*"

He rushed her again. His hand closed around her throat, and he slammed her head into the back of his throne and then continued to shove her, throwing his whole weight on top of her until she slid down over the arm of that throne, her body twisting painfully, awkwardly underneath his hold.

"Do you think you're the first person that's tried to kill me?" he growled. "And do you think that I am so *stupid* that I would have insisted on a meeting *alone* with you if I thought you would be able to do it?"

"How did you survive that?" The words slurred from her mouth.

He bared his teeth at her. "I was hoping you would stop playing the part of the fool and explain that to me as, ironically enough, I think I have *you* to thank for it."

The words confused her—but that may have been because of the lack of oxygen reaching her brain. His grip had only grown tighter, and she was almost completely upside down, her back digging painfully into the arm of the throne while the blood all rushed to the top of her head. The dagger remained in Varen's other hand, a glistening threat in the very corner of her spinning vision.

"Admit your true identity and your plans to me, *Casia Greythorne*, and perhaps I won't have you tortured for all of your countless deceptions."

She didn't reply.

She didn't know what he wanted her to say.

And even if she did, she would not say it. She would not yield to this monster of a man. He would not choke anything out of her—not her life or anything else. She didn't need magic to fight him. She didn't know *how* to use that magic to fight him—to break through whatever protection he apparently had—but it didn't matter.

Because she knew that she wanted to *live*.

She managed to summon one last burst of strength. Her knee rose up and struck his gut, and her head slammed against his an instant later. While he was dazed, she grabbed hold of his arm and slung him away from her.

The dagger in his hand went flying as he hit the floor, skittering across the marble and spinning to a stop a short distance away.

They both scrambled to their feet and dove for it simultaneously.

He got his hand on it first—so she twisted her reach and instead went for his face, slamming her palm up into his nose as he tried to lean away from her. Blood streamed from his nose, but he still managed to keep hold of the dagger and take several steps backward.

Dozens of guards were pouring into the room, summoned by the sounds of the violent battle.

She didn't take her eyes off Varen.

He continued to put space between them. His chest heaved. He didn't wipe any of the blood from his face, and his voice was still frighteningly calm as he looked to his guards and said, "Take her below. I want every guard we have to spare—*every single one*—surrounding her until we decide on the best way to properly deal with her."

A group of those guards stormed forward.

Her hands rose automatically, already bristling with magical energy. But she didn't attempt to summon magic against those guards, or against Varen. Instead, she turned and she looked to the windows against the far wall, to the sun that was just peaking over the distant hills. It was nothing more than a single point of hazy orange emerging against the foggy sky.

She focused on it.

And soon the entire room filled with light. Currents of electricity shot from her hands toward that hazy orange point, and the windows before her shattered.

The guards rushed to block off the shattered openings, but she was quicker. She darted around the few who managed to get in front of her. Varen screamed something as she raced past.

She ignored him, leapt through a broken window, and sprinted out into the breaking dawn.

CHAPTER 30

CAS DID NOT KNOW WHAT SHE WAS RUNNING TOWARD.

But with every pounding, splattering step she took against the damp ground, she became more and more afraid that she was not going to reach it.

She still kept running.

She made her way over the hills that rose and fell away from the palace. She frightened horses as she raced through pastures and leapt over fences. The edge of a forest awaited just ahead, and she told herself that she could lose the guards trailing her, if only she could reach the sanctuary of trees.

She caught flashes of those guards approaching in every direction, breaking through the fog, summiting the hills. Some on foot. Others on horseback. Too many to count. It seemed pointless to keep running, but she still did—

Until she saw the last obstacle standing between her

and the safety of the forest: a winding barrier that the fog had concealed until she came so close that she nearly toppled into it.

A river.

The Lotheran loomed before her, its waters far too swollen from the rain for her to swim through.

She skidded to a stop at the very edge of the churning water. Her lungs burned. She had lost all of the feeling in her feet. She thought of trying to use magic, but her body still ached from the last spells she'd used, and she feared that trying to repeat the powerful display she'd created in the throne room might shatter her completely.

She desperately turned her head back and forth, searching, but there was no bridge that she could see, and that river before her only appeared to stretch wider on both her left and her right.

There was no way out.

Dozens of guards on horseback were closing in.

She could not outrun them.

Despite that fear of shattering, she attempted magic one last time, but she could not seem to get her shaking hands to summon even a spark of light. So she did the only thing she could think to do—she clenched her hands into fists, and turned to face her pursuers. She would not let them see her fear.

Death came for her quickly, at least.

The rider in front reared to a stop. Drew an arrow. Released it.

That arrow struck her heart.

She stumbled back, slipping along the muddy bank, and she fell into the dark water.

CHAPTER 31

She was sinking. Twisting. Tumbling through dark, debris-filled water.

She was *dying*.

And then she wasn't.

A hand closed around her arm. Someone yanked her up out of the churning waves of the Lotheran. Pulled her through the mud and the rocks, and then left her on the banks of that river as they walked away.

Her fingers reached toward her heart. The arrow was still lodged in her chest, though part of it had broken off. She couldn't tell how much of the wetness around it was blood and how much of it was mud. She coughed and vomited up river water, heaving until she felt like she had nothing left inside of her, and then she twisted her head, searching for whoever had interfered with her death.

But there was no one there.

Why save me, only to walk away?

Guards had spotted her. They were marching toward her; the ground beneath her trembled with the pounding of hooves and the stomping of boots. She could feel it all —every frightening vibration of it—even over the droning of the river behind her.

She was still going to die.

They wanted me to suffer longer.

That was the only reason she could think of; the only purpose anyone could have had for pulling her from the river, only to leave her behind for the royal army to find.

She tried to roll back into that river. To her broken body and mind, it seemed like the better death, the kinder death, to just let the waters wash her away. But her body would not cooperate. Even her head suddenly felt too heavy to move. To hold up. So she laid it down in the soft mud, and she waited for death to finally, truly come.

But something else was coming for her first—something that was moving in those waters behind her with powerful, sloshing strides. She heard it rising out of the river. Plodding through the mud. Growling a low, menacing growl. A shadow overtook her, and a drop of water dripped down onto her face. And then another. Droplet after freezing cold droplet splattered her skin, dripping down from long, black fur.

Her eyes fluttered open and shut, trying to focus on the creature above her.

The wolf from her nightmares stood over her broken body, its head low and its teeth bared at the army approaching her.

Protecting her?

No; that didn't make sense.

Nothing made sense anymore.

But that army had stopped. Several members of it cowered away at the sight of the beast that had risen from the river. Others held their ground. A few brave souls stepped forward, drawing their bows.

The wolf did not seem to care about the arrows pointed at it.

With a growl still rumbling in its throat, it laid down beside Cas. It curled its massive body around her shaking form, and the movement swept shadows over her. Shadows that made her feel oddly warm and safe, that wrapped more and more tightly around her until she could think of nothing except that warmth and how badly she wanted it to carry her away from all of the pain and horror around her.

And that was precisely what it did.

———————

IT WAS SO, so cold.

A hand brushed Cas's cheek, and somehow she became even colder. She shook violently and whispered, "What happened?"

"I negotiated on your behalf."

She lifted a hand to her aching chest, expecting to feel warm, wet blood. She should have been dead.

Was she dead?

"Where am I?" she coughed.

A pause, and then, "Open your eyes."

She did as she was told. Her vision blinked slowly into focus, and she realized that she was lying on a balcony not unlike the one back at her room in the palace—except this one did not overlook a city. It overlooked a dark wasteland covered in silvery-black clouds. She pushed onto her hands and knees and crawled closer to the edge of the balcony, certain she was wrong about what she was seeing.

But she wasn't.

Her hands gripped the iron bars of the balcony's rail, and she stared out at the same place this disastrous journey had started: *Oblivion*.

Movement behind her.

She spun around, and her breath left her in a gasp.

The person standing behind her was not Elander. It had spoken in his voice, and yet it was not him. It was not a *person* at all. He was too beautiful to be a person. His eyes were silver and blue—every facet of those colors imaginable—and his hair looked as though it had been dyed with moonlight. His body towered over her, rippling with muscle and taller than any human she had ever seen. Shadowy markings swirled over his pale skin, and when he moved, more shadows rose and fell in his wake, following at his heels like dogs eager to do his bidding.

She realized, with another sharp intake of breath, that she had seen this being before. His picture had been in that book in Varen's library.

"Do you know where you are?" he asked, quietly.

"This is Oblivion."

He nodded.

"And before we came here, something pulled me from the river and I... I saw the wolf from my nightmares."

He slowed to a stop a few feet away from her. The air seemed to leave the room, fleeing from the power, from the magical energy that roiled around him like his own personal storm.

Cas forced herself to keep speaking. "You are the wolf."

"Yes."

That voice. That *voice*. The same one that had woken her up. The same one that had spent the past weeks talking with her, joking with her, arguing with her, comforting her and telling her she was *safe*. The same one that she had slowly been falling in love with. She knew that voice. But it shouldn't have been coming from this being standing before her. It wasn't fair. It wasn't *right*.

"You're..."

The incredible strength. The incredible magic. The fact that he had disappeared in those woods outside of Belwind, and then she had encountered that divine wolf beast...

Suddenly it all made too much sense.

"Go ahead and say it," commanded the...*creature* that had Elander's voice.

No.

Not the creature.

The god.

"Kerse." The word shuddered through her lips. "The middle-god of Death and Destruction."

He neither confirmed nor denied it; he simply stood there, head tilting as he stared at her with those inhuman, silver-blue eyes.

"The *fallen* middle-god," drawled another voice Cas recognized. Caden stepped into the room, but he didn't look like Caden. He had the same face, but his skin was a strange, ashen shade of grey, and his eyes had unsettling red rings around their irises. Tara followed closely behind him. Of the three of them, Tara was the least changed by the airs of Oblivion; her hair was still red—though it was considerably brighter. Her golden skin shimmered, and her eyes seemed brighter, as well—a bright shade of green that glowed oddly in the low lighting.

"Fallen?" Cas repeated.

"As are we," Tara said. "Well, not fallen *gods* in our case, but spirits. I am Eshma, the lesser-spirit of Shadows. Caden is actually Talos, the Blood spirit."

Caden gave a bored little wave at the proper introduction.

Cas stared at the three of them in turn.

Terror slammed through her chest.

And then fury.

She fought her way to a standing position. Her aching, broken body protested, but she managed to stay on her feet once she got there, and then to close some of the

516

distance between her and Elander. *"How could you keep something like this from me?"*

Instead of answering her, Elander turned to Caden and said, "We need to lock her away somewhere while I deal with...*them.*"

Caden nodded.

"Lock...Wait—no!" Cas darted forward, nearly tripping as pain spasmed through her legs and locked up one of her knees. She grabbed Elander's arm, partly to catch herself, and partly to jerk him around to face her.

Darkness exploded around them at her touch. It took only a glance from Elander, and suddenly Cas felt as if the entire world was collapsing toward her. Pressure closed in from all sides. She couldn't help but think of a grave—of cold dirt cascading down around her and burying her alive.

Fallen or not, he seemed more powerful than ever here in Oblivion, in this *godhaven* that he called home while within the mortal realm.

But he caught himself and reined in the powerful magic just as quickly.

The air settled, and Cas found her voice again. "How could you?" she demanded again. "I thought you were—"

He jerked his arm from her grasp. "You thought *what*, precisely?"

I thought you were my anchor.

The thought whispered through her head before she could stop it.

But she would die—utterly and completely this time

—before she said those words out loud. She stared at him, and he stared back, and the world reduced to just the two of them, to all the moments she had let her guard down around him.

How could she have been so damn *foolish*?

"Whatever you thought, you're better off forgetting all of it." Elander brushed his sleeve off with several quick swipes of his hand, as though he wished he could go back to a time before she'd touched him. "There are much bigger things to worry about now."

"You can't just lock me away from those things!"

"I can, and I will." He turned and started for the door with one last order to Tara and Caden. "Do what you must to keep her under control. You know she has a tendency to...cause trouble."

"You *bastard*." He paused but didn't look back, even when she stepped closer. "I trusted you. I didn't tell Varen the truth about my abilities because I *trusted you*. And now Asra is dead, and the most powerful man in Kethra is furious with me, and who knows what he's going to do to the rest of my friends *because of you and all your stupid lies*—" Her throat was too thick, too swollen with fury to keep choking the words out, which only made her *more* furious. She willed herself to calm down. Imagined herself as that rock in the middle of a storm-tossed sea, waiting out this latest attack. She didn't need him to be an anchor; she could wrap herself in a casing of stone and anchor herself.

"I am never going to forgive you for this," she said, her voice quiet—but calmer now.

He finally glanced back at her. For the briefest of moments, he looked as if he was thinking about apologizing, and the waves rising around her settled for an instant.

But he only turned and walked away without another word, leaving her at the mercy of his servants.

CAS WAS NOT certain how much time had passed. She assumed it had been an entire day at least—but really it was impossible to tell, because the sky in Oblivion always looked the same. Always grey. Always cloudy. Always starless.

But it didn't matter.

Because she *was* certain of one thing—she had already been here too long, and it was time to leave.

Caden and Tara had locked her in a room that contained nothing except a bed and a small, high window. At first, her body had been too weak to put up much of a fight. Her magic would not come to her, no matter how hard she tried to summon it. Her head pounded. Her mind kept threatening to disassociate from her surroundings, and it was tempting to let it carry her away to some place that at least *felt* safe.

Her chest ached worst of all, though the scar left by the arrow was minimal. It looked like a wound she had received years ago instead of hours ago; somehow, Elander—or one of his other minions— truly had *negotiated* away what should have been a fatal wound.

She didn't know why they had bothered to save her.

And she doubted they would have told her the truth if she'd asked. Telling the truth didn't seem to be their strong suit.

But whatever the reason for her being here and being alive, she was going to get the hell out of this place and away from all their lies, one way or another.

She slipped her coat and a pillowcase beneath two legs of the bed, making it easier to pull smoothly and quietly across the floor. Then she dragged that bed over beneath the window, stripped the blankets and sheets from it, and tied the linens together. With her makeshift rope slung over her shoulder, she hoisted herself up onto the window ledge and peered out.

It would still be a drop of ten feet or so once she came to the end of her rope, but she could survive that. She had fallen from worse heights; it was simply a matter of angling toward a proper landing. Easy enough.

She heaved the rope out and lowered it slowly, and she had just pulled herself more completely onto the narrow window ledge when she heard the door behind her open.

"Hey."

It was Tara.

Cas didn't look at her; she stayed balanced against the

ledge and continued trying to decide on the perfect angle at which to begin her descent.

"Going somewhere?"

"Yes," Cas snapped. "You can't keep me here. *He* can't keep me here. Whatever that arrogant bastard has planned for me, he can swallow down those plans and *choke* on them for all I care, because I'm leaving."

"The Fields of Oblivion stretch for hundreds of miles in every direction," said Tara, calmly.

Cas's stomach flipped at the number, but she gritted her teeth. "I don't care."

"You have no weapons."

"I don't care."

"You have no food or water, and you won't find either of those things within the fields."

"*I. Don't. Care.*"

Tara snorted.

Cas heard her stepping closer, but she still didn't look at her.

"Well, before you go," Tara said, "you should know that it wasn't all lies."

Cas still should have jumped.

She wasn't sure why she didn't.

"Or at least, I don't think it was. We didn't set out to trick you, and we certainly hadn't planned to bring you here. Elander's target was always Varen and the royal family, but...we didn't realize who you were until last night."

Her curiosity got the better of her, then; as much as

Cas wanted to escape, she also wanted answers. And of the three of her captors, Tara had always been the most forthcoming with her words. Cas still didn't trust her, but maybe...

With a sigh, she finally turned her gaze toward Tara. "I *still* don't understand who I am. And I still don't understand why Elander was targeting Varen."

Tara watched the door for a moment, anxiously tapping her knuckles against each other.

"You can talk to me," Cas said, quietly. "I won't tell Elander you told me anything."

Her gaze shifted to the death grip Cas had on that makeshift rope. "Maybe you should have a seat? You know, back *down here*."

Cas dangled from the window ledge for a moment, skepticism still making her hesitate. But then she secured her rope and dropped to the bed. She scooted to the edge, folded her arms across her chest, fixed her glare on Tara, and waited.

Tara threw one last furtive glance toward the door. "Let's start at the beginning, shall we?"

"Just hurry up."

"The beginning is important."

"*Then tell it.*"

"Right. Well, um, it started when Varen's father—the king who eventually became King-*Emperor* Anric de Solasen—made a deal with the Rook God, decades ago. This is how Anric became an emperor in the first place, how he toppled the other three kings and queens of

Kethra...*he* didn't topple them. The upper-god did it on his behalf.

"And in exchange, Anric swore that he would create an empire where divine magic flourished and helped restore the gods and their powers. Because it's the use of this magic, you see, that keeps the gods not only relevant, but capable of using their powers in any given realm. When this deal was struck, magic-users were already so thin amongst the Kethran Empire that most of the old gods and goddesses could no longer walk among the kingdoms of Kethra. And as his part of the deal with the Rook God, Anric was going to fix this."

"But Anric went against his word?" Cas guessed.

Tara nodded. "He believed he could eliminate the gods by doubling down on the practices that his father and grandfather had started—getting rid of even more of the divinely marked. It was foolish to believe that Anric would have done anything else, perhaps..." She paused, and her eyes darted away again—not toward the door this time, but toward the heavens, as if she was afraid that the Rook God himself might be listening. As if that upper-god might swoop down and punish her for referring to anything he'd done as *foolish*.

"But that god has a reputation for recklessness," she continued. "And the other Moraki let him make his deal, I assume, because they were worried and perhaps even a bit *desperate*. Because what if the erasure of magic in Kethra began to spread to the neighboring empires?"

Cas didn't reply, but she was listening intently now, her escape plans momentarily forgotten.

"If their magic disappears entirely from this world, then so too will those old gods," Tara went on, answering her own question. "Thus the Rook God made this deal—and part of it also guaranteed that he would keep the new King-Emperor safe. That Anric and any of his blood would have an unnaturally long life, a life that the gods themselves could not touch. But it granted no such protection for his people. And so when the deal soured, it was Anric's people—the unmarked ones, of course—who suffered on his behalf."

"The Fading Sickness," Cas breathed in realization.

So it *was* divine in origin.

More horribly divine than she could have guessed.

"The Rook God assumed that killing Anric's people would make that King-Emperor change his ways and repent." Tara frowned. "But the upper-god underestimated the stubbornness of man and the corruptness of Anric. No matter how many of his people died, Anric de Solasen still would not bow to the gods, and he did not stop his crusade to rid Kethra of magic. So the Rook God had to devise a new plan."

"But the gods could not touch Anric, because of that deal they made?"

"Right. So that upper-god made another deal, this time with his own fallen servant. He could not *personally* eliminate the Solasen bloodline—but he could send in someone else to do his dirty work. Not a true god, but the next closest thing to it."

A question she'd had earlier burned its way to the front of Cas's mind. "Why did Caden call Elander the *fallen* middle-god of Death? Why did he fall? *How* did he fall?"

Tara shook her head. "I...I don't think it's my place to tell you that."

The purse of Tara's lips made Cas doubt that she would be able to pry this particular truth out of her. So she tried another question instead. "What deal did the Rook God offer him?"

"It was simple. If he could successfully destroy the traitorous Kethran Empire—starting by eliminating the House of Solasen, among other things—then Elander's divine status, and all of his power and immortality and everything else that came with it, would be restored."

"Destroy the *empire*?"

"An empire that the Rook God has deemed too far gone to save at this point," Tara said solemnly. "The corruption in it will not spread, he has decided, because he will instead make an example out of its destruction. A warning for those neighboring empires to heed."

It took Cas a moment to catch her breath after these words. "So Anric didn't die of the Fade, like most believe."

"No. Elander killed him. He also orchestrated the death of the queen-empress years before that—and he *tried* to take care of the queen's children on that same fateful night."

Cas hugged her arms more tightly against herself, trying to fight off the chills that were lifting little bumps along her skin.

"He was instructed to eliminate the *entire* Solasen bloodline," Tara said softly.

"But he failed?"

"Yes. Because something protected the children that night. And that same something nearly killed him. It wrecked his power and forced him to flee the Solasen Court."

"He told me he spent some time in the southern empire, training. Was it after he fled?"

"Yes, that was true... to an extent. He went south until his powers were stable once more, and then he returned to try and finish the job he'd started. This return was when he managed to kill Anric. But Anric's daughter was long gone by this point."

"Gone?"

"Abandoned by her father, perhaps for her own protection. Or the protection of their bloodline, at least. And something still shielded Varen—something that made him immune to Elander's magic, and something that shielded him even from more...*mundane* methods of killing. Poisonings, stabbings, drownings.... Nothing seems to phase the young King-Emperor."

"I couldn't seem to harm him when we were fighting, either," Cas recalled.

Tara nodded. "Something protects Varen. And it isn't just the Rook God's magic, or the deal that god made with

Varen's father. Elander has spent years trying to determine *what* that other something is. He has been pretending to investigate the Fading Sickness incidents and anything else Varen instructed him to do, when in reality he was investigating *Varen*. It was only a chance meeting that led to him finally discovering the final pieces to the puzzle."

"A chance meeting?"

"With you."

"I don't..."

"Chance that he met you, and that you used your magic against him not once, but twice—and then a third time against those void archers. And last night, Varen himself clearly recognized you when he saw you use that magic."

The King-Emperor's words rang clearly in her mind all of a sudden: *Did you think I wouldn't eventually realize who you are?*

Cas gripped the edge of the bed more tightly.

"And when Varen recognized you," said Tara, "everything sort of...fell into place for us. We were fools to have not seen it before, really."

"I..."

"Don't you understand?" Tara asked. "Both of the Solasen children still live. One remains in his palace. The other—"

The door creaked open once more, making Tara jump. She stepped away from Cas and immediately bowed her head.

Elander's voice slid into their conversation a moment later, lifting fresh chills across Cas's skin as it came. "The other one is sitting right here."

She did not look toward him, because she could not move.

She should have jumped out of that window earlier.

Why hadn't she jumped?

"Your name is not Azalea," he continued, stepping inside. "It is not Thorn, or Casia Greythorne, or Silenna Tessur. It is Valori de Solasen, the true Queen of the Kingdom of Melech, and the Queen-Empress of the Kethran Empire."

Silence. Terrible silence. She didn't know what to say. And, perhaps because she didn't speak, a moment later she felt pressure against her skull—the fingers of magic reaching in, trying to extract her thoughts.

Blood-kind magic.

"She doesn't believe you," Caden informed him as he walked into the room.

"Well, she doesn't have to believe a thing for it to be true," Elander said.

Cas shook her head at those words—the same words she'd said to him weeks ago, on that first night they'd met. "You're wrong. I'm not her. I *can't* be her."

"But you *are* her. And you were there the night the former queen-empress—your true mother—died. And I believe you somehow protected yourself and your brother from the same fate."

"I don't remember *any* of that. Everything..."

Everything before her first adoptive home was a blur. Why?

Had that been her magic's doing as well?

"You were the light that saved Varen from me, and that somehow gave him lasting protection. The same light that managed to undo my magic—a feat that I had never encountered during all the years spent in this cursed, fallen form of mine."

She kept her gaze on the ground, watching his boots coming closer to her with heavy, deliberate steps.

"I don't know where that light comes from," he said. "I still don't know what you are, Thorn, or what you're truly capable of. But believe me when I say that I am going to figure it out."

He stopped directly in front of her.

"The Rook God wants the Solasen bloodline eliminated," she whispered.

"Yes."

"And you serve that god."

"Yes." He cupped her chin and lifted her downcast eyes to meet his. "Which means that you and I, unfortunately, have a very big problem."

AFTERWORD

Thank you for reading! If you enjoyed this book, please consider taking a moment to leave a review to help other readers find and enjoy it :) After you've done that, I hope you'll grab book two in the series, *A Twist of the Blade*!

Also, if you want to connect further, see behind-the-scenes stuff, get the first look at covers, teasers, character art etc... or just come yell at me for my cliffhanger endings, then you can do all that in my V.I.P. Reader's Group on Facebook!

S. M. Gaither is the author of multiple bestselling romantic epic fantasy books. And while she's happiest writing stories filled with magic and spice, she's also done everything from working on a chicken farm to running a small business, with a lot of really odd jobs in between. She currently makes her home in the beautiful foothills of North Carolina with her husband, their daughter and one very spoiled dog. You can visit her online at www.smgaitherbooks.com